A Darker Shade of Dead

A Darker Shade of Dead

BIANCA D'ARC

BRAVA

KENSINGTON PUBLISHING CORP.
www.kensingtonbooks.com

BRAVA BOOKS are published by

Kensington Publishing Corp.
119 West 40th Street
New York, NY 10018

All Kensington titles, imprints, and distributed lines are available at special quantity discounts for bulk purchases for sales promotion, premiums, fund-raising, and educational or institutional use.

Special book excerpts or customized printings can also be created to fit specific needs. For details, write or phone the office of the Kensington Special Sales Manager: Kensington Publishing Corp., 119 West 40th Street, New York, NY 10018; Attn. Special Sales Department. Phone: 1-800-221-2647.

Brava and the B logo are Reg. U.S. Pat. & TM Off.

ISBN-13: 978-0-7582-4731-5
ISBN-10: 0-7582-4731-1

First Kensington Trade Paperback Printing: November 2010

10 9 8 7 6 5 4 3 2 1

Printed in the United States of America

This book is dedicated with all my love to my mother, who passed away while this book was being written. She was an educator, researcher, law professor, and the inspiration for my own career aspirations. We went to law school together, took the bar exam together, and worked together briefly.

She was always my greatest adviser, and when I had a decision to make about whether to take a really good job or decline the offer and continue to write, she was the one who surprised me by saying, "Do what you love." She advised me to turn down the job opportunity and write. I have never regretted that decision, which allowed me to spend time with her and take care of her when she suddenly fell ill with cancer.

I miss her more than I can possibly explain. My life is as a shadow now, and I have no idea when or if it will ever become real to me again. I thank God for the time I had with my dear mom, and I thank her for always being such an inspiration. I love her with all my heart, and I know that love was returned unconditionally.

So I'd like to dedicate this work in memory of my mother, who left me too soon.

I love you, Mom.

With special thanks to Joy Roach, who helped me when I was in a pickle. Thanks also to Frances Bamford, who celebrated the sale of this novel, and the others in this series, with me over a scoop of ice cream.

Prologue

Quantico, Virginia—eight months ago

"This blows."

Dr. Sandra McCormick's voice echoed around the morgue. Well, it wasn't really a morgue. At least it hadn't been. The large room had been a perfectly good laboratory until the senior team members had decided to perform tests on cadavers. Now it was a morgue.

The temperature had been lowered to near freezing, and Sandra shivered in her lab coat. She'd donned her heaviest jacket under the lab coat she had borrowed from one of the men on the team who wore a much larger size, but it still wasn't enough. She was cold, dammit.

Cold, miserable, and all alone on night shift because she was low man on the totem pole. The science team had been together for a few months, working for the military on ways to improve combat performance. Specifically, they'd been trying to come up with substances that, when injected into people, would improve healing and endurance in living tissue. They were at the point now where they'd graduated from in vitro testing in Petri dishes to something a bit more exotic.

They weren't ready to try in vivo testing on living animals or people. Instead, the senior scientists had decided to take this grotesque step, administering the experimental regenerative serum to dead tissue contained in a whole, deceased organism. Personally, she would've preferred to start with a dead animal of some kind, but only human cadavers would work for this experiment since the genetic manipulation they were attempting was coded specifically for human tissue. They didn't want any cross-contamination with animals if they found a substance that actually worked.

As a result, she was stuck in a freezing cold lab in the middle of the night, watching a bunch of dead Marines. It was kind of sad, actually. Every one of these men had been cut down in their prime by either illness or injury. They had all been highly trained and honed specimens of manhood while they were alive. Some of them had been quite handsome, but their beauty had been lost to the pale coldness of death. They were here because they had no next of kin—only their beloved Corps—and their bodies had been donated to science.

The room was dimly lit. Sandra only needed the individual lights over each metal table on which the bodies rested to do her work. She'd holed up at a desk in the far corner of the giant lab space, entering the data she collected hourly for each body into a computer. Her fingers were already numb from the cold, and it had only been three hours. Five more to go before the day shift would release her from this icy prison.

She heard a rustling sound in the distance as she blew on her fingers to try to warm them. Her chair swiveled as she lifted her feet, placing them on the runners of the rolling office chair.

"That better not have been the sound of mice scampering around in here."

Contrary to most medical researchers, Sandra had never really been comfortable with mice. Little furry rodents still made her jump, and she shied away from any lab work that required her to deal with the critters.

The room was dimly lit. The only illumination came from the computer screen and desk light behind her and the single light over each table. The whole setup gave her the creeps.

Deciding to brave the walk to the bank of light switches on the far side of the room near the door, Sandra stood. If she had to sit here with a bunch of dead bodies all night, the least she could do was put on every light in the damned room. Why she'd ever thought the desk light would be enough, she didn't know.

She'd gone on shift at midnight and was slated to take readings every hour until 8 a.m. when her day shift counterpart would relieve her. Scientific work sometimes required a person to work odd hours. Experiments didn't know how to tell time. When the researchers were running something in the lab, she usually got tapped for the late night hours. Normally she didn't mind. The lab was usually a peaceful, comforting place.

But not now. Not when it had been turned into a morgue. Or maybe it was more like Dr. Frankenstein's dungeon, only without the bug-eyed servant named Igor. She'd definitely seen that old Mel Brooks movie one too many times in college. Thinking about some of the funnier lines from the comedy classic made her smile as she walked down the aisle of tables toward the door and the light switches.

"It's alive . . ." As she walked, chuckling to herself, she did a quiet imitation of Gene Wilder from the scene where he'd given life to his monster.

One either side of her were slabs on which the cadavers rested. A breeze ruffled one of the sheets that had been pulled over the body on her right.

It must've been a breeze. The sheet couldn't move on its own, right? She quickened her step, a creepy feeling shivering down her spine as the smile left her face.

A hand shot out of the dark and grabbed her wrist. She screamed. The fingers were cold. The flesh was gray. But the grip was strong. Too strong.

It pulled her in. Closer and closer to the body she'd checked only forty-five minutes before. He'd been dead at the time. Immobile. Now he was moving and—oh, God—his eyes were open and he was looking at her. His stare was lifeless as he drew her closer.

She did her best to break free, but the dead man was just too strong. She beat against his fingers with her other hand. When that didn't work, she tried pushing against his cold shoulder. Nothing seemed to help. She hit his face, his chest, anyplace she could reach, but he wouldn't let go.

He drew her closer until she was leaning across him, her arm over his head. Then he opened his mouth . . . and bit her. She gasped as his teeth broke through her skin. Blood welled as the icy teeth sank deep. Dull eyes looked through her as the dead man chewed on her forearm.

She went crazy, struggling to break free. She must've twisted in the right way because after a moment, she felt herself moving more easily. The next second, she was free.

He sat up, following her progress. She heard noises all around the lab now, echoing off the shadowed walls. She looked around in a panic. Other bodies were rising all around the makeshift morgue.

"How in God's name . . . ?" She gasped, clutching her bleeding arm to her chest as six tall bodies slid off the laboratory tables to stand in the dim, chilled room. She was so scared, she nearly wet her pants. The fear gave her a spike of clarity. She had to get out of there.

She ran for the door. Hands grabbed at her lab coat. She stumbled but caught herself before she could fall to the cold floor. She let her arms slip backward so the oversized lab coat came off, held in those strong hands that had come at her out of the darkness. She had no idea what had gone wrong with the experiment, but she wasn't about to stick around to ask questions. These guys were huge. Big Marines who were easily twice her size. And they didn't seem friendly.

If she could just get to the door. She ran, dodging and weaving around the tables and the reaching arms. They tried to grab the jacket she'd worn under the oversized lab coat, but they had a hard time getting hold of the slippery nylon fabric, thank goodness.

She crashed through the door, running for her life. She had to get help. She had to rouse the entire team. She had to get the

MPs, the Marines, and, hell, the National Guard if she could, to stop these guys.

She turned to look over her shoulder just once as she ran into the fringe of trees on the heavily wooded outskirts of the base. What she saw chilled her to the bone. In the dark of the night, she could see the dim, yellow, rectangular glow of the open doorway. Outlined there were the hulking shapes of dead men. The dead Marines were following her path outdoors at a slow, steady, lurching pace.

Chapter One

North Carolina—the present

"Idiot!"

Sandra swore as another driver zoomed up behind her car at what seemed like light speed. It was some kind of off-road vehicle or giant SUV because its headlights were at the perfect blinding height in her rearview mirror. The jerk had his brights on. She felt like she was under an interrogation lamp as he rode her bumper.

"Why don't you just pass me, you moron?" she muttered, annoyed to no end by the inconsiderate driver behind her.

It hadn't been a tough decision to decline the military's offer of transport by air. First, she would've had to leave Long Island days ago, allowing some faceless military personnel to do the job of packing her private things. No, thank you. She didn't like the idea of some stranger going through her personal stuff.

Second, Sandra wasn't good in airplanes. She avoided them, preferring to drive whenever she had to go anywhere, if at all possible. Her father had died in a plane crash. Since then, she had been unable to face the long tin tubes of death.

Third, her beloved car would've been left behind. The old Caddy was the only thing she had left of her father, the late Dr.

Henry McCormick. He had loved it almost more than he'd loved her, lavishing attention on it every weekend with long hours spent washing and waxing the thing by hand. She kept up the tradition in his honor, though she probably didn't spend quite as much time as he had on the old car.

This gas guzzler was also her last link to her dad. It was a land yacht, so long road trips really weren't that uncomfortable. She could sleep happily on the sumptuous padded leather of the seats and had room for almost anything she wanted to bring with her. They didn't make cars like this anymore, her father had often said. He'd loved the giant car and she did, too.

But the vehicle behind her could go straight to hell as far as she was concerned. What was the guy thinking? He'd zoomed up out of nowhere on the dark, deserted stretch of highway and instead of passing her, he'd been riding her tail pipe for the past ten minutes.

"Finally." She felt a stab of relief when the car pulled out from behind her to the passing lane. But he didn't pass. He crept up on her side, matching her speed and veering unsteadily into her lane.

"What is your problem?" she shouted even as she took evasive action. The giant SUV was going to hit her!

A panicked look out her window told her the SUV driver knew exactly what he was doing. She'd seen two male faces in the front of the giant vehicle. The driver and another man who was staring at her out the passenger side window. She knew him. She'd worked with him months ago.

Rodriguez. He may have a Ph.D. in molecular biology, but the man had always struck her as a pig. He thought he was some kind of smooth Latin lover. In reality, he was gross. A disgusting specimen of a man who thought he was super macho but was really a fool.

"What the hell is he doing?" she shouted aloud, talking to herself as the SUV came closer.

She chanced another look. It was definitely Rodriguez. He was pointing to the side of the road. He wanted her to pull over, and it looked like if she didn't comply willingly, his driver would be happy to force her off the highway.

It was the middle of the night on a deserted road. No way was she going to pull over like some lamb to the slaughter. She gunned the engine. The Caddy responded like an old tiger being let out of its cage. The big engine roared and she pulled ahead of the SUV.

But not for long. The giant black beast had quite a few horses under its hood as well. It kept pace with her around the next long turn of the highway and began to pull even with her again. She kept a panicked eye on it in her mirrors. She thought she saw the rear passenger window slide downward. A split-second later, she saw what looked like a handgun emerge from the blackened square of the backseat window.

The Caddy shuddered and jumped as the left rear tire blew. Sandra screamed. The steering wheel shook in her hands as she slammed on the brakes and tried to control the car. The bastard had shot her tire!

Her whole body shaking in fear, she moved the Caddy off to the shoulder. But first she hit a little button she'd had installed for just such emergencies. Thankfully, the SUV hung back as her call connected. She spoke aloud, confident the small microphone in the passenger compartment would pick up her words.

"My car has a flat tire. Could you please send help?"

She didn't want anyone to know she'd spoken with Rodriguez if she could help it. Chances are, this little middle-of-the-night meeting had been arranged because she'd ducked every attempt Rodriguez had made to contact her. She knew he was working for the enemy. Dr. Sellars had told her Rodriguez was part of the small group that had restarted their forbidden research. Sellars had tried to recruit her, and she had no doubt that Rodriguez wanted the same thing.

She gave her location to the operator as she rolled to a stop. There was little time. She had to disconnect the call or risk having Rodriguez know she'd already sent out an SOS. She didn't think he wanted her dead. Not yet, at least. She hadn't done anything to him personally. Heck, she hadn't even heard him out.

But he had to know she had been recruited by the military in the past few days. Otherwise, he never would have known to find her on this lonely stretch of highway that led ultimately to Fort Bragg, her new place of employment. She had crossed the border into North Carolina a little while ago. She still had quite a ways to travel, but Rodriguez's presence here confirmed her suspicions. He was most likely the person behind the sporadic zombie infestations at the base.

She rolled down her window but didn't get out of the car as she watched Rodriguez slam the passenger side door of the SUV now parked behind her. Its headlights glared over her car like twin spotlights giving everything a sharp black and white glow.

"You've been avoiding me, Dr. McCormick," Rodriguez accused as he walked up to her window. He gave her an oily smile—an expression she remembered with distaste from their previous time working together.

"I've been a little busy. And I told Sellars I wasn't interested in renewing the research."

"Then why are you here? A little birdy tells me you're working for the military again. I can't imagine what else they would want with you besides your knowledge of our last experiment. Now why would you throw in with the government goons when you could be working with me? I can definitely promise I'd pay better."

"It's not about the money. It never was, for me."

"Then you are a fool." Rodriguez looked away, cursing her under his breath. He seemed really angry and she grew even more afraid. She didn't think he would kill her. At least not yet. He'd try to woo her over to his side, if he possibly could. She expected he would give her a chance to decide in his favor before he took any truly drastic actions. He turned back to her, that oily grin back in full force. This couldn't be good.

"I know you let them out, Sandra." His voice dropped to a low, menacing tone. "You were the only one on duty. You ran away and left the door open. You let them rampage across the base in Virginia. You killed all those Marines. You, Sandra!" He badgered her, shaking his finger in her face, his eyes wild. The guy looked a little crazy, but his words were all too true.

Sandra's guilt was overwhelming. He wasn't saying anything she hadn't thought about over and over since it had happened. If only she'd closed the door behind her, locking the reanimated cadavers in the lab. But she'd been too scared. And because she was a coward, scores of innocent men had died, turned into those ravening creatures, prolonging the cycle of death.

"Stop it," she whispered. Rodriguez smiled evilly.

"I know something else I bet you wouldn't want getting out."

Dear God, what else? Sandra scrambled around in her mind, wondering what in the world this cretin could have on her. She'd never deliberately done anything bad in her life. Of course even the most casual of mistakes could be blown out of proportion and distorted to make her look very bad indeed.

"I know our late, unlamented colleague, Dr. Sellars, asked for your help with a certain formula. I also know that you solved his little scientific dilemma. You gave him the missing link to his equation. What do you think your military friends would think about that?"

She could say nothing to his threat. The commander wouldn't understand. He'd already read her the riot act about having continued her research to work on the serum she'd developed. That could be excused, he'd told her, because it saved lives. But he'd never understand why she'd helped Sellars. He'd never understand how Sellars had played on her vanity and her naïveté, coming to her with compliments and supposedly innocent questions.

She'd helped Sellars complete his chemical equations and solve the little scientific puzzles he'd posed to her. Only later did she piece together the conversations and realize he'd been using her. She had contributed to his new version of the contagion and she hadn't even known it at the time.

No way would Commander Sykes or his military superiors understand how stupid she'd been. They'd lock her up and throw away the key if they knew. And nobody would ever trust her again.

Sandra couldn't afford that. Not when she was finally working on a way to redeem her mistakes. She wanted the chance to solve the zombie problem once and for all. A scientific solution that would render the contagion obsolete. Her after-exposure serum was the first step. She only needed time and funding to perfect it. From there, she'd move on to a preventative that would stop the contagion in its tracks before it had a chance to infect anyone else.

"I can see I've given you something to think about."

"What do you want?" The words were dragged from her in a pained whisper. She could see her plans for the future—her plans for redemption—crumbling before her eyes.

"I want the same thing you gave Sellars. Your help. Your knowledge. Your expertise on the intricacies of our creation. I'm refining it, you know. Making it better. Making the creatures more intelligent. Not by much, I'll grant you, but enough so they're able to follow simple directions." He looked inordinately pleased by the horror he'd created. "They make a much better army when you can keep them under control." His obvious glee made her sick to her stomach. Only a fiend would find glory in the death, torture, and subjugation of others.

"You want me to work with you on the contagion?" Her voice was flat, dull. She felt her own horror growing at what he was trying to force her into. Worse yet, she didn't see that she had any alternative.

"Yes, Sandra. I want you on my team."

She heard a distant flushing sound. The sound of all her hopes and dreams going down the toilet.

"I just joined another team. You're too late." She had to try to salvage this situation.

"It's never too late." Rodriguez looked over his shoulder at something behind him on the road. "You think about what I've said. I'll give you a little time to come to your senses, but I won't wait long." He slammed his hand on the hood of her car, right over her head. It was a frustrated move, and she realized why he was retreating. Flashing lights shone in her rearview mirror, drawing closer.

Saved by the cavalry. At least for now.

Rodriguez flicked a business card at her. She caught it in a reflexive move and glanced at it. It wasn't printed. It was just a blank card with a handwritten number on it.

"Call me."

He climbed into his car and sped away before she could tell him it would be a cold day in hell before she called him. The highway patrol car pulled up behind her, and she was occupied with the concerned young officer for the next fifteen minutes while he verified her identity and waited with her for a tow truck. He either didn't notice or didn't comment on the way her tire had blown. It hadn't died of natural causes. It had been blown off by a bullet. One that was even now lodged in the old rim.

Luckily, car repair places weren't like hospitals. They weren't required by law to report gunshot wounds to their patients. With a well-placed *donation*, she ought to be able to get her car fixed with no questions asked. Either that or she could invent a sob story of some kind. It would depend on the nature of the mechanic who answered the summons for a tow truck.

As it turned out, Sandra hadn't needed to resort to either method. The guy who sold her a set of rear tires didn't bat an eyelash at the damage. He was more concerned about getting her to buy two tires instead of the one she needed to replace. She let him spin his tale about how the tires needed to be balanced properly and then quietly paid for two overpriced retreads. Anything to get back on the road.

She managed to pull into the base entrance only a couple of hours behind schedule. She stopped at the guard shack to identify herself and show the papers she'd been given, inviting her here. They searched her car and before they were through, Matt Sykes showed up, a concerned wrinkle between his brows.

"I heard you had some trouble on the road," he said as he walked up to her. "Glad to see you made it here all right." He shook her hand, and she could tell he was moderating his strength so he wouldn't crush her fingers.

That was considerate. She'd shared too many handshakes with men who didn't realize they were crunching her bones in their gorilla grips. It was nice to see the commander was thoughtful enough to consider such things.

"How'd you know about the flat tire?" She blurted out the question before she thought better of it.

"You're too important to this team to take chances with, Sandra." He tugged off his sunglasses, pinning her with his compelling, dark blue stare. "The minute that trooper ran your I.D., it sent up an alert that reached my desk a few minutes later. If you'll recall, I was against your driving here all by yourself. It would've made more sense to fly. We could've had you here in an hour."

"Yes, but I would have had to leave my car and all my possessions behind. Or worse, let them be sorted and packed by strangers." She made a face just thinking of such an invasion of her privacy.

"You let us pack up the rest of your stuff to put in storage. I don't see the difference." He truly didn't. She could see it in his expression. Typical of a man. He wouldn't think twice of letting a stranger handle his jockey shorts. She noticed he didn't comment on her car, he merely looked at it quizzically.

"Trust me. There is a huge difference. I brought the things with me that I didn't want to leave in storage. My clothes and other personal stuff."

He looked at the relatively empty backseat with one raised eyebrow. "You travel light."

She had to chuckle at his hopeful tone. "It's all in the trunk."

He wandered the few feet over to the back of the car where an MP was letting his dog sniff the contents of her open trunk. It was filled with boxes and a few garment bags that contained a portion of her wardrobe and personal items. The dog hopped down, having found nothing objectionable, and the

MP stepped away. The car had been cleared for entry to the base.

"Interesting choice of vehicle." Finally, Matt commented on the land yacht. It had taken longer than most, which was impressive. But in the end, everyone was curious about the giant old vehicle.

"It was my dad's," she said simply. The short answer seemed to satisfy him. He only nodded briefly and put his sunglasses back on, hiding his gorgeous denim-colored eyes.

"If you'll follow me, I'll lead you to your lab. You'll be quartered in the same building. I'll show you the best place to park and help get your stuff inside."

"That would be great. Thanks." Sandra was impressed at his offer of assistance. He really was making her feel welcome. It was more than she'd expected.

Too bad it was under false pretenses. At least on her part. The scene with Rodriguez had kept replaying in her mind as she'd driven the last miles to base. She didn't know what to do. She certainly didn't want to work for the bad guys. Rodriguez was a worm. No, he was lower than a worm. He was scum. She wouldn't throw her lot in with him no matter what.

But how could she avoid having him spill the beans about what she'd done? She was in deep trouble and couldn't see a feasible way out. Not yet at least. She'd try to play along for now and hope something changed before Rodriguez decided to force her hand.

Commander Sykes hopped back into the jeep he'd driven to the gate and led the way through the maze of buildings. She would need a map to find her way around until she got her bearings. After a lengthy drive through several outlying areas of the large base, he finally pulled into a spacious, mostly uninhabited lot and parked his jeep near a side door to one of the buildings it bordered.

Sandra parked the Caddy beside him and got out, stretching the kinks out of her back. It had been a long ride. She wasn't used to road trips—or being run off the road, for that matter. Things in her life had definitely taken a turn for the strange and frightening. She was doing things and dealing with people she never would have before. She didn't like it at all but had no idea how to go back to the way things used to be.

She and that first scientific team had let the genie out of the bottle. Now she had to do everything possible to cram it back in and make certain it could never escape again.

Sandra opened her trunk, noting three muscular, uniformed men rounding the corner of the building. She thought nothing of them until they veered in her direction. Matt greeted them and turned to face her; the imposing group ranged behind him.

"These are a few of the men you'll be working with," he informed her. "You probably remember Captain Beauvoir and Private Kauffman from the op on Long Island."

"How could I forget?" She shook hands with Beauvoir and Kauffman as they stepped forward. "How are you, Captain?"

"Very well, thank you, ma'am." He favored her with an intense smile. Xavier Beauvoir was one heck of a good-looking man. Shaggy blond-streaked brown hair, sparkling whiskey-colored eyes, and a physique that just wouldn't quit. He'd run the operation on Long Island. The man was sharp as a tack despite his lazy Cajun drawl. Still waters definitely ran deep with him.

Matt continued the introductions. "This is Simon Blackwell. He's a retired Navy SEAL, now working for us on a contractual basis. He's one of my men from Quantico."

She understood what that meant. No doubt this Blackwell fellow had been involved in the initial infestation. If he was still involved, he was more than likely naturally immune to the contagion.

"Good to meet you." She shook his hand as well, feeling guilty all over again about having released the first round of monsters. If not for her stupidity, this man would never have been exposed to the contagion. He'd probably lost friends to it, too. All because of her.

After the introductions, each of the guys picked a few boxes or bags out of her trunk and headed for the entrance to the building. She was surprised. She'd assumed that Matt had volunteered to help her carry her belongings. She should have realized he had volunteered his men to help her instead. Why would a navy commander waste precious time moving boxes and bags when he had a troop of men at his beck and call to do the work?

With the men doing the heavy lifting, it took only two trips back and forth to bring all of her belongings inside. Matt had gone in with her, showing her to a small dormitory-style room and giving her a key. He stayed inside, talking with her while the men schlepped her stuff up to her room.

"Your lab is fully equipped and waiting for you in the sub-basement of this building. You can access it from the flight of stairs down the hall, but you'll need your base I.D. and this key." He handed her another old-fashioned metal key on a small ring. "I'd like to take you over to get your base I.D. as soon as you're settled so you can have access to every area you need right away."

She looked at her watch. She was totally beat, but she understood his reasoning. Chances were she couldn't really go anywhere without base identification.

"I can go now, if that's convenient." She gave in to the inevitable even though she would rather have taken a few minutes to recuperate from her long drive.

Matt grinned. "Perfect."

Simon delivered the last of her belongings, and Matt dismissed the men. They waved good-bye to her and went on their way. She took a minute to look in the small mirror mounted on the wall above a chest of drawers and patted her hair back into place. They'd take a photo, she was sure. It couldn't be helped. She looked decent, but she'd never been very photogenic.

She followed Matt out to the parking lot. They took his vehicle, leaving hers parked where it was for now. It had a temporary pass on the dash that had been issued by the gate guard. That would keep it safe while she attended to more pressing matters.

"How is Lieutenant Archer doing?" she asked as Matt drove.

"Driving the nurses crazy." Matt's tone invited laughter. "He's at the hospital, in a secure wing, waiting for you as soon as you're ready to go over and check him out."

She hadn't liked the idea of leaving her patient, but Sam was in good hands. She'd been told there was another medical doctor on the team—a woman who'd dealt with an immune soldier before. Sandra had consulted with Dr. Mariana Daniels by phone before even considering leaving Sam in her care. The woman, while not a career researcher, had impressed Sandra with her understanding of the contagion and the way it affected the human body. She also had firsthand experience with immunity to it and understood what to look for in Sam's recovery.

"Could you drop me at the hospital after we get the I.D.?"

Matt seemed pleased by her request. "Definitely." He turned into another parking lot and found a space. "In fact, I'd like you to tell Sam to come see me as soon as he's fit for duty. I have new orders for him."

"I'll be sure to pass that along. If everything checks out, I'm going to release him today. Dr. Daniels sent me his test results electronically, and everything looks good."

"That's great news, doctor." He held the door for her as she entered the building. "We can use every man on this team that we can get."

The I.D. process was relatively painless. There was the dreaded photo, of course. And then a short wait for security to produce the card that contained a coded microchip. The chip would grant her access to specific areas of the base. With it, she would be able to come and go as she pleased in the areas she had been cleared to enter.

Matt drove her to the base hospital and stopped the car, but didn't park it. "I have to get back to work," he explained. "Call this number"—he gave her a slip of paper with a number scrawled on it—"when you're ready to leave. One of the guys will come over and drive you back to your quarters."

"Thanks for taking me around, Commander." She hopped down from the jeep.

"It was my pleasure, doctor." He looked like he wanted to say more but seemed to think better of the impulse. She shut the door and he tipped his fingers to her in a casual salute as he drove off.

Sandra turned toward the door and realized he'd placed her at the perfect entrance to the base hospital. The first thing she saw when she crossed the threshold was the personnel office. She'd have to check in with them before she could start roaming the halls and seeing her patient.

A few minutes later, with a shiny new sticker on her new I.D. card, she went to find Sam.

Across the base, another new member of the team was placing a difficult phone call.

"Hi, Dad. It's me, Sarah."

Sarah Petit, former Suffolk County police officer and newly hired military consultant, tried to break the news of her new job to her father. She hadn't been looking forward to this phone call. Her father was a retired NYPD detective who'd never understood why his little girl would want to be a cop.

"Sarah, honey, what's this I hear about you quitting the force?"

Crap. He'd already heard. "I was offered a really excellent opportunity with the government, Dad. I took it and I'm already on my way to start my first assignment."

The grim silence on the other end of the line didn't bode well. Finally, her father spoke.

"Does this have something to do with the *matter of national security* you stumbled into?" He emphasized the words letting her know he'd heard all about the cover story the military had fed to the local authorities about her involvement.

"How did you hear about that?" She realized as soon as the words were out of her mouth what a stupid question that was. Big John Petit was still connected, no matter how long he'd been retired from the force.

"Did you know your Chief O'Hara was an old acquaintance of mine?"

"Dad! Have you been spying on me the whole time I've been a county cop?" She thought she knew the answer to that one already, too.

"It wasn't spying, Sarah. O'Hara and I talked from time to time. It's only natural your name came up. He was really pleased with your work, sweetheart. I was so proud. But he called me last week saying you'd been in the hospital and now were working for the feds."

"Why didn't you ask me directly? I would've told you what I could."

"The phone works both ways, Sarah. Why didn't you even tell me you'd been in the hospital? You know I would've been right there with you if I'd known my only daughter had been hurt on the job. Attacked by two thugs in an abandoned building, and I had to hear it a week later from your chief!"

Okay, so she'd screwed up on that score. She should've called her dad, but she'd been afraid of just such a reaction. He'd have called her brothers, and they would have enveloped her in a layer of virtual bubble wrap for her own protection. Meaning they would have closed ranks around her, and all the work she'd done with Xavier—her new fiancé—would never have happened. They'd have made it impossible.

Speaking of Xavier, her family didn't know about him yet, either. Oh, boy.

She took a deep breath.

"Okay, Dad. I'm sorry. Things happened really fast after the incident, and I wasn't really hurt anyway."

"O'Hara told me you'd been hospitalized for nearly a week and he'd been ordered to silence by a bunch of Green Berets who stormed in and took over the morning after you were admitted. Exactly what the hell happened, Sarah?"

Oh, she knew that tone. Her dad wasn't only mad. He was hurt as well. She'd really screwed up.

"My head connected with a concrete floor, Dad. I was out of it for the first few days. And Chief O'Hara was complying with orders from a higher authority to keep it under wraps. I'm sorry you had to hear about this after the fact, but it really was, and still is, a matter of national security."

"Jeez, Sarah. What did you get involved in?"

"You wouldn't believe me, even if I could tell you." She had to chuckle at the bizarre truth of her statement. "Would it help you to know that Johnny is going to be working on the same team? I just found out this morning." Her brother was a CIA operative and former Marine. Maybe the news they'd be working together would help ease her father's fears.

"Johnny! Sarah, that's no comfort at all. Johnny's line of work isn't exactly safe. Now I'll have to worry about both of you. Where are you anyway? I went by your house after O'Hara called me, and it was locked up tight."

"On my way to my first assignment." She hedged, buying time. She'd have to spill the beans. That was what this belated phone call was all about. So much had happened in such a short time. She wasn't sure where to begin.

"Which is where?"

"North Carolina."

Her father breathed a gusty sigh she could hear over the phone. "Thank God for that. If Johnny's involved, you could've been headed for Timbuktu."

"No, Dad. We're strictly stateside." For now, she added silently. She didn't know where this new mission would lead and if the problem somehow spread overseas, she'd go where she had to in order to do her job. But her father didn't need to know that. "In fact, I'll be on a military base. I'm going to be living at Fort Bragg for a few weeks. My new job is as a consultant to the military."

She didn't specify which branch. He didn't need to know and the chain of command was convoluted. She reported to Commander Matt Sykes, U.S. Navy SEALS, but she was partnered with her new fiancé, Captain Xavier Beauvoir, a U.S. Army Green Beret. They both ultimately reported to the U.S. Special Operations Command (USSOCOM) commander—the admiral in charge of joint Special Forces operations—and they were authorized from the highest levels in both the military and civilian government power structures.

"Consultant? I don't like that word, Sarah. That's what they call mercenaries, you know." Her father's tone was suspicious.

She laughed outright. "You know as well as I do that I'm not a mercenary. Get real, Dad. The guys I'll be working with are soldiers, they don't know much about crime scene investigation. That's what I'm contributing to the team."

"And they don't have their own investigators? As I recall, each branch of the armed forces has an investigative service, and there's always the FBI. I can't believe a county cop would know more than the federal experts."

"Well, in this case, I do. I have firsthand knowledge that they need and I'm going to provide it. This really is a national security issue. If I could tell you what it's all about, you'd understand. Trust me."

"You saw something, or heard something, when you were attacked, didn't you? That's what makes you the go-to person."

"Yes, Dad."

She saw no reason not to confirm his suspicions on that at least. He'd been a police detective for far too long not to pick up on what she wasn't saying and piece together a plausible scenario. In fact, she was banking on it, because she really couldn't tell him much outright.

When her father didn't say anything further, she thought it was safe to continue. She had lots to tell him and little time to do it.

"There's more, Dad. I met someone. He's the soldier who came to see me when I was in the hospital. The guy who ordered everyone out and took care of me. O'Hara's met him, so I guess he told you about Xavier, right?"

"Captain Xavier Beauvoir," he confirmed. "O'Hara gave me his name and rank. I've tried to research him, but he's like a ghost. All I've been able to find out is that he's Special Forces and highly decorated."

"He's a Green Beret, and he's going to be your son-in-law."

"Good Lord, Sarah. Isn't this a bit sudden?" She heard the shocked outrage in her father's voice. She couldn't fault him for it. He had no idea what she and Xavier had been through together and she couldn't tell him. Not really.

"Dad, Xavier and I have been working together since he got me out of the hospital. He's saved my skin more than a few times. That kind of thing forms bonds quicker than usual . . ."

"You tell me not to worry, then you hint at the fact that this guy's saved your life not once but *a few times* already? Sarah, you're going to give me high blood pressure."

He was actually reacting better than she'd thought he would. "I know it's a lot to take in. And I can't bring him home to meet you just yet. We have something urgent we have to do in North Carolina. We're on the trail of some seriously bad guys, Dad. There's a team of us working on the case. I learned today that Johnny will be part of it, too. I thought that would be comforting to you. After all, not only will Johnny be there, mother-henning me to death, but a big, strong Green Beret will be devoting all his skill and strength to protecting me. Between the two of them, it'll be amazing if I can manage to do my job." Loving exasperation filled her voice. "I promise, I'll be safe. I can really contribute to this team and I want to be with Xavier. Johnny will meet him soon and he can give you a full report, okay? At least until we can get back up to New York so you can meet him in person."

"I guess it'll have to do. Dammit, Sarah, I'm not happy about any of this."

"I know, Dad. And I'm sorry. Things just happened. I've had very little control over anything since I got hit on the head and woke up to find Xavier at my bedside. But I wouldn't trade any of it. It's been scary and wonderful all at the same time."

"Love is that way, sweetheart." Her father's gentle tone touched her heart. "I want to hear from you more often, Sarah." The stern note was back. "I want a phone call every other day."

"I'll try, but we'll be on a night shift for a while. I promise to call at least once a week."

"Three days a week, Sarah. No less."

"Twice a week?"

"Done." They both laughed at the familiar pattern of haggling. It was an old joke between them. "I'll expect to hear from you when you settle in at Fort Bragg. And you tell Johnny to call me at his earliest opportunity."

"I should be seeing him later today at our first team briefing. I'm sure he'll call you tonight, if he can, with the full report on my fiancé."

"Good Lord, my little girl is engaged." A trace of wonder entered her father's tone. "Is he what you really want, Sarah? Is he a good man?"

"He's the best, Dad. You'll understand when you meet him. I think you'll get along well, once you get used to his Cajun way of speaking. It's deceptively calm, but underneath he's like a coiled spring, ready for anything."

"That's a good quality in a soldier, but what about a husband?" He sounded skeptical.

"Xavier is a man of honor, Dad. Like you and my brothers. You'll see. I would never fall for a clunker."

"Let's hope not." Her father was clearly reserving judgment, but she hadn't expected anything less. "You tell him his first priority is keeping you safe. If he doesn't, he'll answer to me."

That was so typical of the men in her family. She'd bet anything poor Xavier would hear the same thing from every one of her four brothers.

"I'll tell him. But Dad, seriously, he's even more protective of me than you are."

The big difference with Xavier was that he also understood she was a skilled and intelligent woman. He let her do her job, but he was always there to back her up if she got into trouble, like any good partner. He knew she was there for him in the same way. That's what made them so perfect together.

"I'll take that as a good sign."

"I have to go now, Dad."

"All right, sweetie. You stay in touch and watch yourself. Those military boys play a lot rougher than us cops."

"I know, Dad. I love you, too. Talk to you real soon."

She pressed End on the encrypted mobile phone she'd been issued and stowed it in her utility belt as Xavier turned to look at her.

"Did he give you a rough time about me?"

"No rougher than I expected, but you're worth it." She reached for his hand and squeezed his fingers. That was about as far as she'd go with the public displays of affection. She wasn't wearing her police uniform any longer, but Xavier was still in his army togs. They'd have to be discrete.

She liked the black fatigues she'd been issued. They felt good against her skin, and they had a lot more pockets than her old uniform. There were few insignia on the new clothes. Just enough to indicate that she was part of a team being formed at Fort Bragg. Anyone seeing her on base would know she belonged there and was not to be trifled with. That was good enough. They didn't need to know her rank, identity, or exact purpose on base.

It was all top secret, after all.

Nobody knew she and her new fiancé were zombie hunters.

Chapter Two

"I've had just about enough of being a guinea pig, doc," Sam groused when he caught sight of her walking into his hospital room.

"I expected as much." Dr. Sandra McCormick breezed into the room, leaving the wide door open behind her. "Which is why I'm springing you. Before you get too excited, I suggest you talk to Commander Sykes. He has new orders for you."

Lieutenant Sam Archer, U.S. Army Green Beret, had been in the hospital for the past couple of days. He'd been infected with the zombie contagion in action on Long Island. His commanding officer had administered Sandra's experimental serum and it had actually worked. Instead of dying and reanimating as a zombie, Sam was still very much alive, and all indications were that he was now completely immune to the contagion.

Thank goodness, Sandra thought, he'd had the right mix of antigens and immune response to combat the contagion, with Sandra's serum, and to mutate it into something that gave him super fast healing and endurance. He hadn't been born with the natural immunity like Xavier Beauvoir and his girlfriend, Sarah Petit. The serum had given Sam the extra edge that, when combined with his blood chemistry, made him immune.

It was a scientific breakthrough, but Sandra's work hadn't

been perfected yet. The same serum had been tried on another victim, Sandra's former colleague, Dr. Sellars, and it hadn't worked. He'd died, taking his despicable secrets with him.

"So when did you get here? Dr. Daniels has been in to check on me a few times, but she wouldn't tell me where you were."

"You were stable but still unconscious most of the time when they transported you off Long Island. I was confident you were out of the woods, and I had a few loose ends to tie up there before I could leave. It didn't take long. I packed my belongings and drove down here. I got in about an hour ago. I had to get my I.D. card first, but I wanted to check on you as soon as possible."

"Thanks, doc." He grabbed her hand gently when she would have moved away. "I mean it. You and your magic serum saved my life. I can't thank you enough."

She paused to meet his gaze. "I'm just glad it worked." The moment stretched, and she understood from the seriousness of his expression how he felt. She truly was glad he'd been saved by her experimental serum, but it did little to eradicate the guilt she would carry the rest of her days for allowing the contagion to spread in the first place. "So tell me about Dr. Daniels." She made an effort to lighten the mood as he released her arm. "I've spoken to her on the phone, but I've never met her."

"She's great, but she's not you, doc. She's a lot more cavalier about my condition." He put on a hurt puppy face that she wasn't buying. It was clear he was trying to make her laugh, and it worked.

"That's because Dr. Daniels is a researcher. She isn't used to dealing with big crybabies like you." A cool brunette walked through the open door, joining their conversation. "I'm Mariana Daniels. You're Sandra, right? I recognized your voice from our phone conversations."

They shook hands, and Sandra liked the other woman right off. She had a firm handshake and a no-nonsense manner that she respected.

"Thank you for taking such good care of Sam. I was sure he was all right when he left, but it's always helpful to have a skilled person to follow up."

"You just passed me off to the next doctor, like an old, used-up guinea pig." Sam's comically sad face made both women laugh.

"I wouldn't have let them load you on that transport plane if I hadn't been absolutely confident in the care you would receive down here, lieutenant. Dr. Daniels and I were in constant communication when you were first admitted to her care. Give me a little credit."

"Don't let him fool you, Sandra," Mariana said in a conversational tone. "These Special Forces guys are tough as nails. Sam's been trying to con me into letting him out of here since he first woke up."

"Well, I reviewed the test results Mariana sent me by e-mail while I was on the road. Everything looks good. If I didn't know better, I'd assume you were one of the naturally immune people." Sandra liked delivering good news. Doctors didn't always have that pleasure, which is part of the reason she'd opted for research instead of private practice. "Your end results are exactly the same as the few immune samples we have, Sam, so if they're fit for duty, so are you."

"Hallelujah." He flipped the sheet off his legs and sat up on the side of the bed. "So I can get out of here?"

"Not so fast, soldier." She laughed, putting one hand on his solid shoulder to slow him down. "There's the little matter of clothing, and I'm reasonably certain there could be some paperwork involved." She looked over at Mariana for confirmation. The other doctor nodded in agreement.

"I'll take care of all of that," Mariana volunteered. "Pardon me for saying so, but you look awfully tired. I assume your trip down here took its toll on you. Why don't you grab a catnap in your quarters? The commander called a meeting for the entire team tomorrow. You're off duty until then. You might as well take advantage of it. Once the action starts picking up again, you probably won't have time to breathe."

Sandra had been told Mariana had dealt with the fallout of the outbreak at Quantico. The military had taken all the research team members into custody as soon as they realized what had happened. They had been sequestered and only allowed to research ways to stop the creatures. A few days of intense work had created the toxin the soldiers used to destroy the zombies. That was it. That was the only thing they had been allowed to work on after the initial outbreak.

They hadn't been allowed to see any of the victims or study their remains. They hadn't even been told about the single survivor of the SEAL team. Mariana, a doctor at a small base clinic near the edge of the training grounds and forest that surrounded the base, had been the only military doctor to treat a survivor. She probably knew better than anyone how tough things could get when zombies were on the loose.

"I'll take that advice." Sandra pushed her hair back from her face with a weary hand. "I'm beat. I like driving, but this trip was just a little too long for my tastes."

"Why didn't you fly?" Sam asked, clearly curious.

"I wanted to pack up my personal belongings and bring some of them with me. Frankly, I'm not crazy about flying and I really wanted to have my own wheels here." She didn't like to tell people the main reason—that she was afraid because of what had happened to her dad. That was too personal. And it made her feel like a ninny to admit her fear.

"I guess I can understand that. Good thing you have the rest of the day to recover though," Mariana said with a friendly grin. "Things have been quiet around here for the past day or two, but I have a feeling things are going to start to pick up any minute now. Starting with the team meeting Commander Sykes called for tomorrow. I think it's the first time all of us will be in one place together. It'll be interesting to see the full cast of characters that are involved now."

"I guess it's strange for you to have such a large and diversified team. You were one of the first to learn about the problem, weren't you?" Sandra asked conversationally.

"Yeah, I found out the hard way. Damn zombies showed up on my porch with Simon right behind them, darts flying." She shuddered at the memory. "After I saw the first one disintegrate, he had to tell me what was going on. Simon tried to keep my involvement a secret, but when the contagion spread and they asked him to help, I couldn't let him do it alone. It's strange to be part of such a large team though. At Quantico, Simon was the only one actively hunting the zombies."

"Really? I would've thought a lot more men would have been involved. They didn't tell us much, but I know the original six test subjects escaped and made more."

"Oh, yeah. Those six decimated a platoon of Marines and then all of Simon's SEAL team. He was the only survivor."

Sandra felt her heart clench in anguish. "That many?" she whispered.

"Yes, unfortunately." Mariana's tone had grown solemn as well. "He took it hard. He'd worked with some of those guys for years. He lost a lot of friends to the contagion."

"That's awful." The guilt Sandra felt compounded with every word.

"But you're on the team now and I'm glad for it. I've been studying Simon's immunity but it'll be really helpful to pick your brain about how this all started and what you've already tried to neutralize it."

"Yeah, I'm looking forward to working with you, too, Mariana."

"Gee, I'm sorry. I've kept you talking when you're tuckered out from your trip. Tomorrow will be soon enough to start. I'm quartered with Simon in the same building you're in. There's a cafeteria two buildings down on the right. How about we meet you there tomorrow morning for breakfast and then we'll head down to the lab together?"

"Sounds perfect." Sandra scrambled for her pocket and the slip of paper Matt had given her. "I'm supposed to call this number Commander Sykes gave me to get a ride back to my building."

"Oh, don't worry. Simon's down the hall having blood

drawn. I make him give me a sample every week so I can note any changes that might occur. He'll take you back."

"Are you sure?"

"No problem." She made a shooing gesture with one hand. "He can give you the lay of the land, too. This base is confusing until you get your bearings. He'll be glad to help you out."

Sandra was impressed by Simon Blackwell. She would have been scared of him had she not seen him in the company of Mariana. He was different with Mariana around. His steely gaze softened with obvious love and caring for his fiancée.

He was quite helpful showing her around the base. He left her with polite courtesy at the building Matt had taken her to earlier in the day. She could tell he was skeptical about her—or maybe that was just his usual demeanor. She'd seen a similar hardness in many of the soldiers she had treated at Quantico, though she hadn't had much interaction with the Marines. Simon though, he took that toughness to a whole new level.

Of course, he was a retired Navy SEAL. Those Special Forces guys were rumored to be a cut above the regular soldier, and after meeting Simon and Matt, she was inclined to believe it. Sandra speculated on the various people she'd met today as she unpacked her belongings and settled into the rooms she'd been given. It was a small apartment, but clean and nice enough.

She'd had a hell of a day. First the drive, being run off the road and threatened by that slimeball, then her encounter with Matt Sykes and the men on his team. Yeah, all in all, it had been a banner day.

With any luck, tomorrow would be a lot simpler, not to mention calmer. She liked Mariana, as she'd expected. They'd worked together by phone for a little while now and seemed to have developed a good rapport. Sandra actually looked forward to working with her in the lab the next day, which was something new. She hadn't liked any of her coworkers since joining the original quasi-military team all those months ago.

Finishing her unpacking, Sandra was too tired to go looking for the cafeteria. She had a few snacks left over from her drive that made a makeshift dinner. She consumed the half sandwich, bag of chips, and can of pop, then headed straight to bed. It was early, but she was completely worn out from the excitement of the day.

Sandra felt a hundred percent better the next morning. She met Mariana and Simon for breakfast, surprised to find some of the other members of the team already there. Apparently the men woke up at zero-dark-thirty to do what they called PT. She soon learned that acronym translated to physical training. Judging by the rippling muscles all around, every last one of these guys was a fitness nut.

But good Lord, what a view.

Never one to attract hunks like these, Sandra sat quietly next to Mariana, enjoying watching the men interact, kidding each other and comparing prior duty stations. It was a varied group that seemed to have a wealth of experience. Sandra was more than a little intimidated just listening to the men talk among themselves.

Mariana engaged her in medical conversation, but the men really dominated the table. Sandra didn't mind. She was used to being the quiet one. The one people talked over or ignored. It was her lot in life.

Then Matt Sykes walked in and joined their table. The sheer wattage in the smile he turned on her was enough to make her toes curl. Suddenly everyone was looking in her direction as the commander made a beeline for the empty seat next to her.

"You're looking well rested this morning, Dr. McCormick," Matt said by way of greeting as he sat down and arranged his tray in front of him.

"Thanks. I conked out last night and slept for about ten hours straight."

The table had grown quieter as everyone watched their new commander interact with the newest member of the team. Maybe it was just the novelty of her first meal with the group that garnered so much attention. She hoped that was the case, because then it would wear off as soon as they got used to her. She didn't think she could stand this kind of scrutiny all the time.

"Glad to hear you're settling in." Matt smiled again, and she had to catch her breath. The man was potent. In fact, all the men at the table were handsome, but none affected her as strongly as Matt Sykes.

Not good. For all intents and purposes, he was her boss, even if he wasn't a scientist. It wouldn't do to have a crush on her boss. No, not good at all.

She had to nip this in the bud. Matt Sykes—gorgeous Greek god of a man as he was—was not for her. He was just too . . . too handsome, too male . . . too much of everything.

Conversation picked up as the men started to talk again, including their new commander. Sandra went back to her usual role of observer as attention shifted away from her. She liked the way the men deferred to Matt yet seemed to feel a sort of common bond with him. It was clear they respected him.

Matt was a Navy SEAL like Simon, though he was retired from field action now. He rode a desk these days, for whatever reason, but his experience showed in the way he handled himself around these men who were still active participants in Special Operations.

Like herself, he was a little older than the rest of the people at the table. If she had to guess, she'd say Matt was closer to forty while the others were closer to thirty. Heck, Matt might even be older than that, but his physical form was impeccable. He had the body of a twenty-year-old. Only the slight graying at his temples and the smile lines around his stunning eyes betrayed him.

Of course, she was no one to judge. She had a few wrinkles around her eyes herself these days. She didn't think of herself as old by any stretch of the imagination, but she did have a few regrets. Getting her education and gaining prominence in her work had always been more important to her than dating or looking for a life partner.

Seeing Mariana and Simon interact made her realize what she'd let pass her by. She was simply unprepared to start learning the skills most girls mastered in their teens now. She was too old to learn how to attract a man. The depressing truth was that she was too old to attract any but the most desperate of men at this point. And she didn't want desperate. She wouldn't settle for just anyone. Especially not after meeting Matt and his men.

Matt would fuel her fantasies for a long time to come. She was honest enough with herself to admit it in the privacy of her own mind. He was devastatingly handsome and the most powerful, Alpha-type male she'd ever been around. Simply put, he turned her on. Just by breathing, he made her female parts come alive as they never had before for any other man.

Too bad he was totally unattainable. Too bad she had no idea what to do with him even if she could manage to somehow capture his interest. Dreams like that never came true. Better to keep him a fantasy for those lonely hours in the middle of the night when she longed for a lover in her lonely bed.

"You about ready?" Matt's voice broke into her silent reverie.

She blinked, looking at him. "What?"

"Just asking if you were done. I have some electronics for you in my office. I didn't realize you'd be here this early or I'd have brought them with me to breakfast."

"Oh." It took her a moment to register what he was saying. "Mariana and I were going to check out the lab." Mentally, she kicked herself for the rather dull-witted reply.

"My office is on the way. If you don't object to a slight delay, I'd feel better if you were outfitted properly before you got to work today. Everyone on the team has already been issued a sat phone and headset. I'd like for you to keep them with you while on duty so we can stay in contact without having to scramble for a phone in case there's an emergency."

"Sounds reasonable." She looked at Mariana. "Do you mind a small detour?"

"Not at all." Mariana smiled warmly as she waved away the issue. "It's on the way. Won't take but a minute."

They bussed their trays and stepped into the early-morning sunshine. The rest of the men took their leave and went off in other directions while Matt, Sandra, and Mariana headed for his office.

Matt ducked inside, leaving the women to enjoy the fresh air. He returned a minute later with a phone and headset, which he handed to Sandra. He spent a few minutes explaining the basics of how the equipment worked. She asked a few questions, having never seen such technology before, but it wasn't difficult to pick up. Within five minutes, she felt confident that she knew how to operate the electronics.

"Don't forget the meeting this morning. You'll have a couple of hours to check out your workspace in the lab, but don't get too caught up," Matt warned with a friendly smile. "I've called the entire team together so we can all meet each other and talk through our strategy and duty assignments."

"I'm looking forward to it," she responded politely.

In truth, Sandra didn't really care about the meeting either way. She'd sit in the background and observe as usual. Strategy wasn't her strong point, and she already knew what was expected of her work-wise. She was there to work on the tech end of things. That was her only area of expertise. She couldn't fight the monsters. Not physically. No, she'd use her scientific expertise to try to annihilate them.

It was the soldiers who would do the actual physical work and employ the strategies he wanted to talk over at this meeting. But she would attend. It was expected of her and she always tried to live up to her employers' expectations. She didn't like confrontation, and she didn't like to make waves. She'd attend. She just wouldn't contribute much unless asked directly.

John Petit arrived at the meeting room feeling a little out of his element. It was good to be back on a military base, but after what he'd been told about his new assignment, it had a sort of *Twilight Zone* feel. He was still tempted to believe someone was playing a colossal joke on him. After all, zombies didn't really exist, did they?

John was all too afraid this wasn't a joke and some mad scientists really had crossed the line and created the living dead. It would be up to him and the rest of this makeshift team to put an end to it. He'd been given basic information on the other members of the team. Most were either Spec Ops warriors or scientific personnel.

But there was one new member of the team who truly troubled him. She was the whole reason he'd been asked to join the team, in fact, and he just couldn't wrap his head around that whole scenario. Who would have thought his little sister would get mixed up with zombies after all, much less that her involvement would lead to his being taken from his post at the CIA to join the top secret zombie-hunting team?

He was sure stranger things had happened, but he didn't know where or when.

"Johnny!" A petite fireball rocketed across the room and into his arms for a bone-crushing hug.

"Hey, sis." John realized they were causing a bit of a scene, but he didn't care.

He'd learned only recently that Sarah had been savaged by zombies and had turned into some kind of GI Jane, working with the Special Forces to hunt the creatures down. Frankly, he couldn't believe it. He had felt so much better when he'd thought her work as a county cop involved nothing more dangerous than writing speeding tickets. Now, of course, he knew differently.

He hugged her close for a long moment. "Are you okay, punkin?" He eased away to meet her gaze.

"I'm great. I bet you didn't expect to find me here." He never could stay mad at his baby sister when she looked at him with those big puppy-dog eyes.

"You can say that again."

"Punkin?" Another man's voice broke into their reunion.

John looked up to meet the gaze of a soldier standing a few feet behind his sister. The guy had a decidedly amused look on his face as Sarah drew out of John's arms.

She turned and stubbed one pointed finger in the man's chest, a huge grin on her face. "That goes no further, Xavier. I mean it."

The army guy lifted both hands palms outward in a gesture of surrender, a wide smile on his face.

"I see your friend knows when it's wise to retreat." John stuck his hand out to the other man for a shake. "I'm John Petit."

"Xavier Beauvoir." The soldier returned the gesture.

"Xavier, this is my brother, Johnny," Sarah added unnecessarily. She looked uncomfortable and that well-remembered expression immediately set alarms bells ringing internally. Something was up.

"I figured that out, Sarah," the Green Beret answered a little too familiarly. John bristled. They looked just a little too comfortable together.

"John, I spoke to Dad earlier. He wants you to call home tonight if you can. I expect he'll want your report on Xavier." She touched the soldier's arm and laughed up at the other man. He was definitely missing something here.

"Why's that?" John included both of them in his challenge.

Sarah smiled at him in that disarming way she had perfected over the years. "Because he's my fiancé. We're getting married."

That set John back on his heels. His baby sister engaged? To this . . . soldier? What was she thinking? Who was this guy?

"Isn't this kind of sudden?" John didn't know what else to say. He'd been blindsided.

"Jeez. You sound just like Dad. He said the exact same thing." She made a tsking sound but soon relented. "Actually, you're probably the only one in the family who'll understand exactly what drew us together so quickly."

Then it dawned on him where they were and what they

were doing here. A top secret briefing about the zombie problem. Holy shit. His little sister had been roaming around the
woods hunting zombies with her Green Beret friend—scratch
that, fiancé—for the past couple of weeks. No wonder they'd
grown so close. Combat situations often spawned deep and
lasting friendships. You didn't really get to know a person
until you faced death with them.

Realization dawned. His little sister was nobody's fool. If
she felt so strongly about this guy, she had to have good reason. John stepped up and made an effort to give the guy the
benefit of the doubt. They'd be working together now. John
could observe firsthand how the big Green Beret treated his
baby sis. If the army guy put a toe out of place, he'd have John
to answer to.

"God, Sarah. I can't even imagine what you've been
through in the past weeks." Her face paled and he knew it had
to be even worse than he'd thought. His attention turned to
the soldier at her side. "Thank you for taking care of my sister,
Captain. I look forward to getting to know you better."

"Me, too, John. I know it's a shock, but it's the right thing.
She and I were meant to be together."

John wasn't much for sappy talk, but he respected the
straightforward words from this special ops soldier. That and
the look in his sister's eyes led him to believe there was something to this relationship. Something real that had a shot at
lasting a lifetime.

"I got a preliminary briefing when they brought me in on
this. You both survived attacks, right? And now you're immune?" Both Sarah and her fiancé nodded. "So you've been
what—out there hunting zombies for the past couple of weeks?"

"That's right," Sarah answered. "Xavier sprung me from
the hospital after I woke up, and we've been working on the
problem ever since. We've had four . . . or was it five?"—she
looked at Xavier for confirmation—"more encounters with
the creatures since then. We've learned a lot about them and
managed to track back to one of the scientists who was creating them. He's dead now. Attacked by a zombie in my back-

yard while he was trying to abduct me again." Her face hardened in a way John had never seen. Then her words penetrated his spinning mind.

"Again? Shit, Sarah! You were abducted by some mad scientist? Twice?"

"Once. He only got me once. He tried for me once more, but a zombie took him out before he could get me to his car."

John couldn't believe he was having this conversation with his little sister. She was so calm about it and she could have been killed any number of times . . . or worse.

"Xavier rescued me the first time." She patted the big man's arm affectionately. "Second time, too, come to think of it."

"Now chéri, you did your part to get yourself free. I was just backup." The Green Beret looked decidedly miffed by it, too. John took that as a good sign.

He would've asked more questions to get to the bottom of the story, but just then the meeting was called to order and they took their seats around the conference table. A navy commander took the head of the table and began to speak.

John listened with half an ear, trying to process all the surprises he'd had in the last day or two. Zombies, black ops, his sister engaged, and now this top secret briefing. And he'd thought his regular job with the CIA was interesting. It had just morphed into something out of a horror movie. Or a comic book.

Chapter Three

M att had noticed the Petits greeting each other. It had been hard to miss when Sarah launched herself at the man who shared her coloring, if not her height. John Petit was a much larger and more dangerous version of his younger sister. It was clear they were siblings from their angular features to their hair, but John was as big and honed as every man here, and he had a personnel file that consisted mostly of large blocks of black magic marker.

Almost everything recent had been redacted for national security reasons. Ostensibly he was a run-of-the-mill CIA operative. Of course, with the CIA there was seldom anything run-of-the-mill. In reality, Matt suspected John Petit's missions were more on the dark side than the light. Black ops was his specialty if Matt didn't miss his guess. Of course, he would never get confirmation of his suspicions. Not through official channels at least.

He'd seen enough by now to know a spook deserving of the name when he saw one. John Petit wasn't just a spook. He was a phantom.

Matt took his place at the head of the table, and everyone else seemed to take that as their cue to take their seats. This was the first time he'd had everyone all in one place. It was an eclectic mix of skills and specialties, and Matt was in charge of the whole shebang.

"Thank you all for coming." Matt waited while they settled in. He didn't have to wait long. "I thought it would be beneficial to get us all together in one place so we can take stock of what we know, what we need to know, and how we're going to go about learning it. First, let's start with the background of this mission and how we came to this point. We have some new faces here, so I'm going to start at the beginning and then I'll ask each of you in turn to add your piece. In fact, Dr. McCormick, you might start with a brief description of your role on the initial scientific team."

Sandra McCormick squirmed in her seat as all eyes turned to her. Though she'd been on base at Quantico all through the initial outbreak, Matt had never seen her before a few days ago. She looked nothing at all like her personnel file photo. In fact, in person, she was stunning in an elfin sort of way. Because of her photo he'd been expecting a super geek of indeterminate age. What he'd gotten was a siren with auburn hair, green eyes, and the most seductive tilt to her lips he'd ever seen.

It was all irrelevant, of course. It was entirely inappropriate to notice how beautiful she was with anything more than calm detachment. Still, the man inside the commanding officer had sat up and taken notice the moment he'd seen her and was reluctant to be silenced. Matt struggled to remain objective around her and failed miserably.

For all he knew, she could sympathize more than she let on with the rogue scientists who wanted to continue the zombie research. She'd done it herself. She'd gone against orders and continued testing and perfecting her serum to counteract the contagion on her own. That lack of discipline and disrespect for orders from the highest possible authority could be a problem. Matt should view her with suspicion, but anytime he got near her, his objectivity went right out the window. He'd have to be more on guard around her. She could be a danger to his mission, and he had to be wary.

"I was a junior member of the original research team at Quantico," Sandra began in a soft voice that got stronger as she went along. "The goal of our research was to stimulate cell regeneration in living tissue, to promote faster healing and possible invulnerability. The more senior members of the team decided to take the testing to the next step after we'd done all we could in vitro—testing individual cells in Petri dishes. I don't know which doctors voted for using cadavers, but it was a majority, and a week later the Marine Corps shipped us several bodies that had been donated to science. Testing began, and the reagent had an unanticipated effect. The corpses reanimated and walked out of the lab in the middle of the night. The next evening, the so-called zombie attacks started."

"Thank you, doctor." Matt picked up the thread. "At first, the base commander sent out Marines to try to locate the bodies. When the first Marines didn't come back, they sent out more. Eventually, they called on my group of Navy SEALs. We were doing specialized training in the area and were the closest special ops unit that could be spared. That's how I got involved. We lost everyone—all the Marines and all my SEALs, except for Simon." Matt gestured toward the only other navy man in the room.

"I turned out to be immune." Simon took his cue to pick up the retelling. "After that, I went into the woods each night with the toxin the geeks—sorry, doctor—" Simon sent Sandra a rueful grin but she didn't seem to take offense. In fact, she smiled and Matt had to kick himself mentally to refocus on the discussion. Damn, the woman was dangerous when she smiled. "The science team had developed a toxin. I used it to take care of the problem in the woods. All the Marines who'd been infected, as well as my former teammates." Simon's expression grew troubled and sad. Matt well understood, as did most of the men around the table. Mariana reached out and took Simon's hand, visibly confirming what Matt already knew.

"Simon came to the on-base clinic after one particularly bad night and I patched him up," Mariana took up the thread of the story. "I'm a navy doctor, but was totally unaware of the research going on at Quantico until then. I was stationed there and rented a cabin out on the edge of the base, practically in the woods, so it wasn't long before the zombies showed up at my door. My next-door neighbors, an elderly woman and her granddaughter, were attacked, as was my postman before we could put an end to the problem."

"That's when they disbanded the research team," Sandra added. "We'd been kept sequestered until then, only asked to develop a toxin that could reverse the effects and destroy the reanimated cadavers. We did that, but were still held until they'd all been dealt with." Sandra looked guilty, and Matt couldn't help the little bug of suspicion that rode his shoulder where she was concerned. "We thought we were going to be charged with something but in the end they decided to disband the research team and made each of us sign documents stating that we would never follow that avenue of research again on pain of arrest and detention."

"But you *did* continue the research?" Matt prodded. He probably shouldn't have, since it would take them off course in the chronological retelling he was after, but he couldn't help himself.

"Only on a serum to counteract the effects of infection," Sandra said quickly. "I was afraid some of the senior members of the research team wouldn't let their work go that easily. As it turned out, I was right." The challenge in her green eyes made him want to go head to head with her—and not entirely in a combative way. Damn, the woman got under his skin.

"All right. Let's move to the next outbreak." Matt needed to get back to the job at hand. He couldn't let Sandra distract him. "All was quiet for about six months and then a zombie turned up here at Fort Bragg."

"Just one at first," Xavier Beauvoir spoke up. "It was sighted in the woods and reported to the MPs, though nobody realized what it really was, of course. They checked out the report, but couldn't find it. That night they sent out my unit to look for it." Devastation and anger crossed the Green Beret's face. "I woke up to discover I was immune and most of my unit was dead. By that time, you'd been brought in, sir." Xavier nodded toward Matt. "And Simon was here, already at work. I helped him until you ordered me to pick a small team and head to Long Island." Xavier turned to the woman sitting next to him, pretty in her new black fatigues.

"I was sent out on a prowler call to an abandoned building near Stony Brook on Long Island. Up until recently, I was a county cop on Long Island," Sarah Petit informed the group. "There were two of the creatures waiting for me in that abandoned building. They attacked and smashed my head on the concrete floor. I woke up almost a week later in the hospital. Xavier had come in and taken over. I started working with him the next day and we began investigating. We discovered Dr. Sellars, a member of the original research team, had set up shop on Long Island and was actively working on the research again."

"His new, improved zombies seemed to be able to follow rudimentary commands and could even speak a few words. The one I've heard most often is master." Xavier made a disgusted face. "Sellars set himself up as the master of a small army of zombies that were harder to kill and smarter than the previous versions. It takes four darts each to bring one of the new models down, and they're capable of working together to set traps. That's how we met Donna." Xavier gestured toward the youngest person in the room, a fresh-faced young girl seated near the end of the table.

"My boyfriend, Tony, and his entire football team got infected somehow. Tony took me hostage to use as bait, I later realized. While Xavier was trying to save me, the others were herding Sarah toward a van Sellars had set up to kidnap her." The girl's expression reflected the horror she must've felt that night. "Tony bit and scratched me before Xavier could stop him. I woke up a few hours later in the grass and walked back to my dorm. I felt awful, so I checked myself in to the campus clinic where your guys found me a bit later. I'm immune, too."

"So far, that brings us to four naturally immune people,"

Matt reminded everyone. "Simon, Xavier, Sarah, and Donna."
Matt turned again to the youngest and newest member of the
team. "Donna, why don't you tell everyone a little about yourself?"

"Well, I'm not like the rest of you." She seemed embarrassed. "I was supposed to graduate in a couple of weeks with
a master's in chemical engineering. I'm twenty-five and since
I'm immune and have a technical background, I'd be happy to
help in whatever way I can. I saw what this did to Tony and
his friends. We can't let that happen again to anyone else. Not
if we can help it."

Matt liked the way she included herself in the team. He
wasn't sure what she'd be able to contribute besides her immunity, but he was glad to have her in the group. At the very
least, she could work with the science team.

"I'm sorry I left you in that field, Donna," Xavier said with
obvious regret. "They'd snatched Sarah and we had to get her
back."

"I told you before that it was okay." Donna smiled kindly
at Xavier. "I totally understand. I would've done the same
under the circumstances."

"You're a peach, *petite*." Xavier's Cajun charm came to the
forefront. "I got Sarah back, but not before *mon ami* over
there got himself bit." Xavier gestured toward Lt. Sam Archer,
the man who'd been Xavier's XO, or executive officer, on the
mission up north.

"You got me back by sticking a huge needle in my chest,
Captain," Sam answered with audible humor. It was clear
these two were old friends and worked together well. "I woke
up in Sandra's lab feeling like death warmed over."

"Right." Matt took over again. "He gave you the serum
Dr. McCormick has been working on, and it made you immune. So you're the first induced case of immunity we've got.
We're up to a total of five people who can interface with the
creatures without fear of the contagion." The repetition of
facts brought everyone's focus back to the matter at hand.
"While Sarah was being held prisoner, she heard Sellars on the

phone with one of his comrades. Specifically, she heard names. Jennings, Rodriguez, Zhao, and Krychek." He pointed to a whiteboard along one wall where he'd already made some notes. "We believe two of those names—Jennings and Rodriguez—refer to two members of the original science team. The others are more problematic and that's why you've been brought in, John. We need you to check the possible foreign and/or terrorist contacts."

"Roger that," John replied. "Already in process."

"You seemed to be the logical choice because not only are you a former Marine, now a CIA operative, but being Sarah's brother, we figured you'd realize something was up when she quit her county job and took this one. The easiest way to keep a lid on everything was to bring you in since we needed CIA input anyway."

"Never thought my little sis would be instrumental in getting me this kind of gig," John joked, earning a few chuckles from around the table. He seemed basically easygoing, which made him a good fit for the team. Matt thought he'd work out well.

"All right. That brings us up to the present and why we've all gathered here at Fort Bragg. Simon, give us a sitrep about the action on base."

Simon proceeded with the situation report.

"Yes, sir. It's been a trickle of infected individuals. Not the kind of large groups reported on Long Island. It started with one who infected some of our guys. We took care of that situation and since then we've had a few show up every couple of days. Usually one creature that infects a few other innocents along the way before we can track it down and end it. We haven't been able to figure out where they're coming from or why they're trickling in like this."

"Which is where we start." Matt stood, going to the whiteboard. He began diagramming where each person around the table fit into his plan of action. "We're going to attack this on several fronts. First, we use our immune personnel in the field. Simon, Xavier, Sam, you're primary. Sarah, you're with them on cleanup, but I want you to take the lead when it comes to scene investigation. Any clues you turn up, I want you to follow up, interfacing with whoever else you need on the team." Nods all around answered his orders. "Reno and Lew, you're combat team backup. I want you on tactical support for the primaries at all times when they're in the field. Further, Reno will coordinate field operations of the cleanup teams. Which brings us to the next prong of this attack. The science angle. Dr. McCormick, you're to continue your work on your immune response serum. I also want you to work with the cleanup teams on after action reporting."

"In what way?"

Sandra obviously didn't like calling attention to herself, but she spoke up anyway. Matt liked that. He figured she just assumed she'd been brought here for her serum and nothing else. In a way, she'd just passed a little test. She'd proven to him that she would speak up if she needed answers. It boded well for their future working together and for having her as part of the team.

"If the cleanup guys find anything strange, I want you in on it. I also want to step up testing of the remains. We need to know what strain of contagion we're working with. Do you think you can reverse-engineer it from the remains? I want to know if this is the same contagion you worked on originally or if it's Sellars's souped-up version . . . or some other version."

"I'll see what I can do," Sandra replied, jotting notes on her pad.

"So we've covered the combat angle, the scientific angle, and touched on the investigative part. John, you'll be working on the farther reaching aspects of the investigation—the foreign and terrorist possibilities. You'll be working closely with Sarah and the cleanup teams who'll be doing more detailed forensics at each scene from now on. That brings me to you, Donna." He smiled, trying to set the girl at ease. She was eager and had a good head on her shoulders. He could tell she felt uncomfortable in this group. It was his intention to help her find her footing.

"I don't know how I can contribute, but I'm willing to help however I can."

"That's good." Matt praised her, glad to see her responding to his overtures of friendliness. He'd tried to charm Sarah when he'd first met her and failed miserably. Sarah had seen right through him. Donna, though, was less experienced and a little less jaded, perhaps. "You're immune, but you don't have the skills that would make me comfortable asking you to go out in the field with the combat team. Your technical background makes me want to put you under Dr. McCormick's wing, or working with the cleanup teams."

"I can do both," Donna volunteered. "Sandra and I talked a little about this already."

"Dr. McCormick?" Matt raised one eyebrow in Sandra's direction, asking without words for her to elaborate.

"My experiments are small scale and I don't really require a full time lab assistant. I could use Donna's help from time to time, but not every day. And she's immune. She could be of help to the cleanup teams, able to handle certain items, vetting them for potential evidence, without the need to decontaminate them first. It might speed up the process."

Matt considered the idea. "That makes sense. But if you're going to be out in the field at all, I'd like for you to learn some basic self-defense. All the guys on the cleanup teams are armed. They're all military and have been specially selected for the job because of their high security clearance, skills, and technical knowledge. How do you feel about carrying a weapon, Donna?"

"I don't have anything against it, and I already know how to shoot a rifle. My dad goes deer hunting upstate New York every fall and he taught me a little, though I've never hunted or killed anything." She looked uncomfortable again.

"Hopefully you'll never have to." Matt nodded at her. "You're already on the payroll, so we can issue you a sidearm. Sarah, would you be willing to give Donna a little instruction? The other members of the team can help you as well. And John, I see from your file that you were a martial arts instructor at Camp Pendleton while you were in the Corps?" John nodded in answer. "Would you be willing to give Donna instruction? We all need some PT in our schedule, so if we could get up a regular class a few times a week, we could keep this in-house. What do you say?"

"I'd be happy to, sir. It would help me keep my skills sharp as well, since it looks like I'm riding a desk for most of this op."

"Don't worry. This is a fluid situation. Things can change on a dime, but for now, we'll work it as outlined. We need you on that desk, John. The foreign aspects of this could be disastrous for our country and for the world." Matt leveled a serious look at the young man. John wouldn't get any field action on this op. He wasn't immune, and Matt was disinclined to send anyone else to their death against the zombies.

Sandra's research might yield results to make everyone immune. Or not. They'd have to wait and see. Until then, only immune personnel would be sent into possible combat situations.

"Yes, sir." John didn't look completely happy about the desk assignment, but Matt knew he'd follow orders. They all understood what was at stake.

"We'll have the first of our safety briefings this afternoon after lunch." Matt went over the schedule with the group, noticing that the scientific types started to take notes while the combat troops merely nodded, committing everything to memory. It would be a challenge to run a mixed team like this, but Matt was up for it.

The meeting broke up shortly thereafter and everyone scattered to their various assignments. The men of the combat team headed out the door together for some more PT while the women congregated near the door to chat. Only John Petit remained of the men and judging by his expression, he wanted to say something privately to his new commander.

Well, that was to be expected, Matt thought. He understood John's unique position. If Matt were in John's place, he'd be chomping at the bit to be let out in the field. It would be up to Matt to convince John he was exactly where he needed to be.

Matt headed directly for John's position, standing off to one side of the door near the women, but not part of their talkative group. John saw him coming and seemed surprised when Matt held out his hand for a friendly shake.

"Welcome to the team."

"Glad to be here, sir," John replied politely.

"Your sister's been a valued asset since she became involved in this. I have no doubt you'll be the same." Might as well get the family issues out of the way, Matt thought.

"I appreciate the vote of confidence, sir. I only wish I could be out in the field with the other guys—and my sister." He shot a concerned look over at Sarah who stood with the other women, oblivious to Matt and John's conversation.

"I understand, John. But you have to realize the limitations on this mission. We've already lost too many good men to this horror. That's reason enough to keep anyone who's not immune out of the field."

John looked pained but resigned. "I see the logic of it, but it's a hard pill to swallow when my kid sister is being sent out."

"Totally understandable, John." Matt nodded as he followed John's gaze to the petite woman who had already faced zombies and kidnappers and come out on top. "If there's any way we can get you out in the field safely, I promise you we'll do it. Until that time, though, we need your expertise following the foreign connections. Aside from Sarah, you're the only trained investigator we have on this team. Sarah's skills are more in hands-on crime scene work. From everything I've heard and read about you, you're better suited to research and following leads in unconventional ways."

John cracked a smile. "You could say that."

Matt understood the grin. CIA operatives never did anything in conventional ways. In fact, the file he'd been given on John indicated the man was anything *but* conventional when he was running down bad guys. Though the file had been heavily redacted, Matt had learned enough to know that John was a much needed asset on this team.

The women moved out of the room at a sedate pace, and Matt and John followed. Sarah looked back and beckoned to her brother to join her while she walked ahead with Donna Sullivan and Mariana Daniels. John excused himself and left Matt at the back of the pack. He noticed when Sandra hung back from the others, letting them outpace her. She was good at fading into the background.

Matt sped his pace just slightly until he was walking beside her. She gasped when he snuck up on her, and he had to stifle a chuckle. Apparently he hadn't lost the ability to be stealthy when the situation called for it.

"I reserved the gym facilities for sixteen hundred hours," Matt said softly, gaining her attention.

"Yes, I know. I heard you say that during the meeting."

"I'd like especially for you to attend, Sandra. You can use the machines, even if you don't want to participate in the martial arts practice, but I'd like for us all to gather as a group."

"An exercise in team building?" Sandra asked. She was a smart cookie. She'd grasped the reason for his insistence on this group PT session right away.

"It couldn't hurt. We have a diverse group of people here. I want them to feel more comfortable with each other."

"And sweating together will help us work together, right?" She raised one eyebrow, an amused smile tilting one corner of her mouth. "All right, I'll be there."

Sure enough, at 1600 hours, when the team gathered, Sandra was among them, wearing form-fitting sweats. She was so petite he could span her waist with his hands. The soft fabric clinging to her curves made his mouth water. He'd never seen her in something so . . . enticing.

John called the group to order, taking his place at the head of the class. He'd act as sensei and Matt would be his second. They were both highly ranked martial artists. John held a fifth-degree black belt, while Matt's was third-degree. The other guys were all first-degree black belts in various forms of martial arts and would most likely separate from the ladies, who were mostly beginners.

Matt didn't think it would hurt for the women to see just how highly skilled the male team members were. Just as the men would benefit from seeing the women making an effort to learn self-defense. Each of these guys could judge for themselves how well each woman could handle a physical threat. This was as much an exercise in evaluating everyone's level of skill and preparedness as it was a team-building effort.

Matt called the group to order and they formed loosely around him on the matted area. The gym was big enough to accommodate them, with a row of machines off to one side that included treadmills, stationary bikes, and weight equipment. They had the area to themselves for this first workout.

"I expect we'll break into two groups after the warm-up." Matt stood next to John as everyone else arranged themselves in a loose semicircle around them. "I'll take the less experienced folks on that side of the mats, and the rest will form up with John on this side."

"Meaning, you get to work with all us girls," Donna teased. Matt was glad to see she felt comfortable enough with him already to do so.

He grinned at her. "Rank has its privileges." Everyone laughed at his comeback and the easy tone was set for the workout. "John, if you'd lead us in the warm-up." Matt stepped to the back of the class, letting John sort out who would stand where.

He lined them up in rank order as would be in a traditional martial arts *dojo*. Matt should be up at the front of the class, but he decided to hang back. He would observe and nurse the constant pain that went with him everywhere.

Matt's combat career had ended with injury—as many Special Forces careers did. He'd messed up his back so badly that it would never be the same again. He still practiced martial arts. In fact, he'd regained a lot of mobility through exercise, but he would never be able to hold his own again with someone like John Petit or the other guys, for that matter. The spirit was willing, but the flesh was weak.

He still had the skills to be able to teach less experienced students. The women would be easy for him to deal with and it would free up John to work with the front line troops on this mission. All except Sarah.

When they formed two groups, Matt was surprised to see Sarah Petit go with the less experienced group. Another odd thing—Mariana Daniels hadn't shown up at all, though Simon was there.

Before the real work of the class could begin, Matt decided to speak with Simon. They'd finished the warm-up and everyone was milling around, taking a short break before continuing. Matt motioned to Simon and he came over.

"Where's Mariana?" he asked without preamble.

Simon looked decidedly uncomfortable. "She . . . uh . . . well . . . she's been feeling poorly and I told her to sit it out tonight. She could probably participate in kata practice, but I'd really like to keep her away from any actual sparring right now."

"Why?" For the life of him, Matt couldn't understand Simon's reasoning. Mariana had faced the zombies more than once. She should take any opportunity to learn how to defend herself, in case it happened again.

"Well . . . see . . . she's . . ."

"Pregnant!" Donna broke in. "Isn't she?" Donna had been unabashedly listening in to their conversation.

Simon blanched, nodding.

"I knew it!" Donna crowed.

Matt was stunned. He'd never even considered the possibility. He really wasn't used to dealing with women on his combat teams. "How did you know?" he asked Donna, curious.

She laughed again. "I can think of only one thing that could make a Navy SEAL so uncomfortable to discuss. Well, maybe a few more than that. I bet he'd never go buy tampons for his girlfriend, either. Of course, she won't be needing those for a good long while now that she's got a bun in the oven. Congratulations, Simon." She patted his shoulder and sauntered off, already spreading the news to the other women. Simon just looked stunned.

"Is she always like that?" he asked Matt.

Matt shook his head, watching the women react to her news. "I couldn't say, but I guess we'll find out."

Simon grimaced as he turned back to Matt. "So yeah, Mariana's pregnant. That's why I think we should keep any potentially dangerous activity to a minimum, for the time being. She'll want to exercise, but sparring isn't something I think she should be doing."

"I agree one hundred percent, Si." Matt clapped him on the shoulder. "Congratulations. Imagine that. Next year at this time there'll be a little version of you and Mari running around underfoot. I bet you're happy."

"Stunned, to be honest. I didn't really think of it happening so soon. Now that it has, I'm beginning to enjoy the idea. It's kind of awesome and scary all at once."

"I can only imagine." Matt stepped away as John called his group to order. "Please give Mari my best wishes and tell her she's welcome to join us for whatever part of the class she can handle."

Simon thanked him and hustled to take his place on the mats with the other guys. Matt turned to his little group and wondered where to begin.

"Have any of you done any martial arts before?"

Matt expected Sarah to at least have had some training. Until recently, she'd been a county cop. When she raised her hand, Matt wasn't surprised. What did surprise him was Sandra's raised hand.

He turned to Sarah first, since she was closest. "Did you study with your brothers when you were a kid?"

Sarah laughed. "Far from it. Our dad didn't think it was lady-like, so I wasn't allowed to learn. I took a few training courses with the police department. That's all."

Matt was surprised. "Well, you won't face that same attitude here. I think it's important for every member of this team to at least know how to defend themselves if necessary. If nothing else, it's good exercise." Sarah nodded in agreement and he turned to Sandra. "How about you, doctor?"

"I have a green belt in *go ju ryu karate*. I know that's probably quite different from what you'll be teaching us here." She seemed to want to downplay her abilities. Matt wouldn't let her do that. She was a vital member of this team, even if she spent most of her time in a laboratory and not in the field.

"You'll be surprised at the similarities, I'm sure. This is good. You can help me demonstrate the moves." Sandra indicated her agreement as he turned to the last member of his small group.

"I've never done anything like this before," Donna answered without being asked. He was discovering she was a forthright kind of person. He liked that, though he'd have to get used to her lack of military discipline. "But I'm eager to learn."

"Good. We can build on that enthusiasm," Matt replied, standing and facing the three ladies.

Chapter Four

"Wouldn't you rather be working over there with the guys, instead of babysitting us girls?" Sandra asked.

"Not really. I'd hate for one of them to put me back in traction." Matt gestured to the other side of the mats where the guys were sparring full force.

"Traction?" She looked really concerned. Matt was uncomfortable with the subject but willing to be honest with her. He'd learned early on in his command that if you wanted honesty from your troops, you had to give them the same courtesy.

"My combat career ended because of an injury. My back is permanently messed up. This is about as good as it will ever get. I spent a long time in traction, and most of the doctors said I would never walk again, so I'm actually very grateful to have this amount of mobility."

Sandra shook her head. "I'm impressed. I had no idea you were hiding that kind of injury."

"Not hiding, exactly. Just dealing with."

She looked contrite. "I'm sorry. I didn't mean that the way it sounded. I'm actually impressed at how well you manage. I had no idea you'd been injured at all. That kind of thing must cause you a lot of residual pain."

His mouth tightened just thinking about the spasms he sometimes had to deal with. "It's manageable."

Mostly he ignored the pain. Sometimes it got so bad that he couldn't disregard it, though. When that happened, he did the best he could to muscle through the pain until he could get horizontal for a while. A few hours of sleep usually suppressed the spasms and let him continue his work.

"When I was in med school, I spent some time in orthopedics," she said quietly. "I even considered making it my specialty before I was selected for a unique molecular biology program. If you ever need anything, I could probably help."

Matt was touched by the shy offer. "Thanks. I'll keep that in mind. I'm doing much better lately. I only have difficulties once in a while. Luckily, this isn't one of those times." A small white lie there. He did feel a little strain in the area as they practiced, but it was controllable.

They spent the next ten minutes working on the combination. Sandra was a fast learner, and he was able to partner her with Sarah, who had also quickly understood the principle of the movement, so he could give Donna another round of instruction. All three women were doing much better than he had expected, in fact. Donna was by far the least talented of the group, but she was doing well, considering. She had a sort of contagious enthusiasm, which almost made up for her lack of coordination.

The class certainly wasn't dull with her around. She managed to make them laugh more often than not, and the time sped by as they learned several new moves.

Matt moved on to a more complex combination, using Sandra as his practice partner. She moved well and had a natural grace that he found enchanting. He'd noticed the feminine sway of her hips before, but feeling her warm body under the thin cotton of her clothing as he helped break her fall was something even more distracting.

Her fragrance wafted to him like a siren's call, and the heat of her body radiated through his hands, straight to his libido. He had to step back and get a hold of his response before he embarrassed both himself and the good doctor.

"You can let go now."

Sandra's soft voice drifted up to him as he knelt over her on the mat. He still had hold of her shoulder with one hand; his other hand was at her waist. He realized his mistake almost at once and let go as if she'd burned him.

"Sorry. My mind wandered." She looked up at him with those sexy green cat's eyes of hers, studying him as if he confused her. He couldn't blame her.

The poor woman probably had no idea just where his mind had wandered to. A nice girl like her would likely be scandalized by the thoughts that had raced across his fevered imagination.

Images of her sweet, naked body straining under his as he took her in a sweaty, heavenly rush of dominance. He'd imagined for one blissful moment the way he'd possess her soft depths, pounding into her as she welcomed his strong thrusts, her voice crying out, spurring him on as she wrapped her legs around him.

Damn. If she was only half as potent as his imagination, she'd be lethal.

But he couldn't think of her that way. She was part of his team. A woman under his command.

She wasn't strictly military, and that allowed him some leeway he otherwise wouldn't have, but he didn't intend to bend the rules too far. No, it was bad enough he already had two couples in his new command. He couldn't afford the distraction a deeper personal relationship would bring. Mari and Simon were one thing. Both were now civilian contractors. Likewise, Sarah was not, nor had ever been, part of the military. Her fiancé, Xavier, was still in, but he knew how to follow orders.

While Matt didn't doubt the women in their lives came first—above and beyond any order Matt might issue—he still trusted both Simon and Xavier to follow his lead. Their girlfriends, he wasn't as sure of, though both ladies had already proven their ability to fight the common enemy. What Matt really didn't want to do was add to the couple count.

Even thinking about Sandra in an intimate way was dangerous. He couldn't afford the distraction—not for his team and not for himself. He had to be one hundred percent on target here. This command was too important, both to him personally and to the world at large. He couldn't afford to screw it up.

He stood and extended a hand to Sandra, who still lay on the mat. She took his hand, and he fought against the warmth that spread from her much smaller hand to his.

"Are you okay?" she asked in a low, concerned voice as he helped her to her feet. "Is it your back?"

He seized the ready excuse she'd given him, glad to have some explanation for his strange behavior. Even if it wasn't entirely true.

"I'm all right. Just a twinge." He reached around to rub his back with one hand for good measure, but his words backfired.

"I'll take a look later, if you like. Maybe I can give the area a little therapeutic massage. It might help. Just take it easy for now and don't overexert."

Damn. That sounded a little too good. The truth was he'd like to feel her fingers on his body. Anywhere on his body. The idea of that act was making him sweat. Matt had to calm down and get back to business. He had to push thoughts of Sandra's skilled hands on his flesh aside for now.

Much as he'd like to take her up on the offer of a massage then and there, he had to remind himself that they weren't alone. Donna and Sarah were waiting. Watching him and Sandra. A quick glance told him Sarah had one eyebrow raised quizzically in their direction. No doubt she sensed something in the air. She was too good a cop to miss the blatant signals Matt was trying so hard to hide.

"I'll be careful," he replied noncommittally as they resumed their positions. He had to get back on track and teach these newcomers the basic skills they might need to protect themselves. That was his mission here today. That had to be his goal.

He had to put aside his attraction to Sandra McCormick.

She was too tempting and all too beautiful for his sanity. It wasn't going to be easy to ignore that. Then again, as a retired Navy SEAL he wasn't a man used to taking the easy path.

Partnering with Matt Sykes was even harder than Sandra had expected. Oh, he took every precaution not to hurt her as he demonstrated the martial arts moves he was trying to teach. That wasn't the problem. She'd been thrown harder by Donna in practice. Matt guided her down to the mat light as a feather, controlling her descent in a careful and considerate way.

No, the problem was her reaction to him as a man. She'd been attracted to him from the start, but being near him—close to him this way—was kicking up the attraction another notch. His hands were big but gentle on her as he ran her through the combination move that ended with her flat on her back beneath him.

And that position brought on a whole other train of thought that was dangerous in the extreme. She wondered how it would feel if he crawled over her . . . naked. She could feel the heat of him through the worn fabric of their clothing. How much better would it feel skin on skin?

He was a large man. She'd known that theoretically. But having him toss her around as if she weighed no more than a feather brought home to her the real strength of him, the power behind his well-built frame. Even with a career-changing back injury, he moved with all the grace of a jungle cat. Matt was a man in his prime who was intensely attractive to just about anyone with two X chromosomes to rub together.

She fantasized about rubbing up against him, their naked flesh creating a friction that would probably burn her alive. Just the forbidden thought of it was heating her blood to an almost uncomfortable degree. She wanted him to climb over her and claim her. To stalk her like the male animal he was and put his mark on her. She wanted him. Like she wanted her next breath.

It was impossible, of course. He was the commander of this little operation and she was keeping some very dark secrets from him. Aside from that huge obstacle, she sincerely doubted a guy like Matt would even look twice at a lab geek like her. Sandra knew she cleaned up rather well, but she was by no means femme fatale material. Matt, no doubt, could have any woman he wanted. Why would he waste his time with a mousy scientist?

He wouldn't. Which was just as well. She couldn't afford to complicate her life even more by getting involved with anyone, much less the leader of the team that was working to fix some of the mistakes she'd made in the past.

Her thoughts flashed back to that night in the lab. The first night they'd tested the contagion and the first batch of zombies had risen. She'd run into the night, inadvertently letting the creatures out. That one foolish mistake would forever weigh on her conscience. Such a simple thing to have caused so much grief. All she had to do was bar the door and the creatures would probably have been contained.

But she hadn't barred the door. She hadn't even reported the incident. Once the day shift had discovered the lab empty, nobody had thought to ask if anyone had been tasked to watch the experiment overnight. Though they worked for the military, the science team hadn't run a tight ship. Duty schedules varied widely depending on the needs of the experiment, and nobody ever quite knew where everyone on the team was supposed to be at any given time. They operated more or less on the honor system and a task-related basis. You worked until you finished your assigned task, no matter how long that took.

She'd managed to escape blame for letting the monsters out of the cage. She would never forgive herself for her cowardice that night. If anyone ever found out she'd been the one to let them out, it would bring all kinds of suspicion down on her. By hiding her involvement, she'd dug herself into a hole she would never be able to climb out of.

Add that to the fact that she'd naïvely helped Dr. Sellars with what seemed to be a few harmless equations, and it would be easy to suspect her of playing for the wrong team in this game. Which is why nobody could find out. Especially not Matt. He would lock her in the brig and throw away the key. If she was locked up, she wouldn't have a chance to correct the wrong turns she'd made. She wanted, more than anything, to try to make things right.

Sandra had much to atone for, and ridding the world of the zombie contagion had to be her main focus for the rest of her life. However long that was. With Rodriguez after her and the possibility of her secrets being exposed at any moment, she had to concentrate on her goal and pray she had enough time to fix everything before her past caught up with her.

She managed to push lusty thoughts of stripping Matt naked and licking him all over to the back of her mind for the rest of the class. Barely. She grew concerned though, when he became less and less talkative. He seemed preoccupied, and she could think of no other reason than that his back was causing him pain. She'd gone into medicine initially because she'd had idealistic ideas about helping people. It was hard for her to watch anyone in pain—especially those who tried so valiantly to hide it.

She was relieved when the class ended with both groups joining for a final cool-down exercise period and some parting words of advice and encouragement from John. Matt had faded to the back of the room when the beginner and advanced groups reunited, but he was always on Sandra's radar. She knew where he was without looking. She was becoming attuned to him, and she wasn't sure whether that was a good thing or a bad thing.

Either way, she knew just where to find him when John ended the class. Wasting no time, she made a beeline for him. She saw him try to duck away, but she wasn't going to let him suffer alone in silence. Not when she could help him.

"Commander, can I have a word with you?" she called out as he was about to leave. Caught, he turned back toward her. It would look odd if he ducked out now. Too many of the others had heard her request.

"Sure, doctor. Would you mind talking on the way to my office? I have an important call to make and need to get back there." His words were polite, but she saw the slight wrinkles of pain edging his dark blue eyes.

She wouldn't make this harder on him. "Perfect. My lab is on the way."

She grabbed her jacket from the bench along the wall and headed for the door. Matt held it open for her to precede him. She had to squeeze between him and the door frame, invading his personal space and inhaling his masculine scent. Damn. The man was potent and dangerous to her sanity.

He fell into step beside her as they walked away from the gymnasium. She watched his gait carefully. Now that she knew what to look for, she realized he had a slight hitch in his step. She probably wouldn't have noticed it before he'd told her about his back injury, but it was there.

"How's your back?" She decided the direct approach would be best with a no-nonsense man like Matt.

"I'm all right, doctor." His lips thinned and tightened. She took that as a sign he was lying—or at least minimizing the problem.

"It's okay, Commander. I can help, if you'll let me. You don't have to suffer in silence, and I won't report any minor treatment I may give you. I won't get you in trouble with the personnel office if your injury is worse than you want them to believe."

He stopped short on the path and turned to look at her. His expression was hard to read.

"You'd lie for me?"

He seemed to be testing her, and she didn't like it. A shiver ran down her spine.

"I wouldn't lie. But I also am under no obligation to report casual treatment of personnel not directly related to the contagion. If I gave any of the non-immune personnel an aspirin for a headache, I wouldn't have to report it. Same goes here. If you need some therapeutic massage to ease the pain in your spine, I see no reason to have to report it. On the other hand, if I discover you've done serious damage to yourself, I would strongly advise you to seek your orthopedist, which would put you back in proper military channels. No harm, no foul."

He seemed to consider her words, his eyes narrowing and his expression unreadable.

"Neat and tidy." He stared at her for a moment longer before beginning to walk again, this time at a slower pace. "All right. I'll let you examine my back, but that's all. It's been worse than usual of late, and it would be reassuring to know what's going on back there, but you were correct to assume I didn't want to take the chance of being put out of commission because of my injury while all this is going on." He sighed heavily. "If it put the mission in danger, I'd take myself out of the picture in a heartbeat, but I'm riding a desk now. I can't see how a bad back would make a difference in how I perform my current assignment."

"That's reasonable," she allowed. "And for what it's worth, I agree. You're needed here, Commander. You're the glue that makes this whole weird team stick together and work. I can't envision anyone else in charge of this mission."

"Me neither." He smiled for the first time, just a slight hint of a grin at one corner of his mouth as he slanted a look down at her. "So where do you want to do this?"

"My lab? I have diagnostic equipment there we could use if we need it, and nobody gets in without me letting them in. We'll have privacy."

Matt nodded. "Okay, but I'm on a schedule. About how long do you think it'll take?"

"An examination shouldn't take more than fifteen or twenty minutes. Treatment will depend on what I find."

"Fair enough."

He turned with her toward the walk that led directly to her lab rather than staying on the main path. Within minutes they entered her laboratory.

* * *

"There's a cot in back here you can use." She tossed her jacket on the lab bench and motioned for him to follow her toward the back room.

"I wondered why that was there when I inspected the place prior to your arrival."

"Experiments can't tell time. Sometimes an incubation phase will run into the night and someone has to be here to take the samples off the heat, or to add a reagent at a particular time, or whatever else needs to be done. If you miss that window of opportunity, days' worth of work could be ruined. Better to catch forty winks in the lab with multiple timers to wake you than to chance getting snug in your bed somewhere else and sleeping through the critical moments."

"Makes sense." Matt looked around the small room at the back of the lab. There was an even smaller attached bathroom. The bedroom—if it could be called that—had just enough space for a twin-size bed and a small dresser complete with mirror.

"Take off your shirt."

Matt jumped a little at the blunt request but quickly covered his surprise. He shouldn't have taken such simple words as some kind of sexual invitation. She was a doctor. She needed to see his back in order to assess the damage. It was a logical request. Too bad his body had gone into overdrive at the mere idea of getting even partially naked in front of her.

Because thoughts of taking off his clothes inevitably led to thoughts of her doing the same. Man, he had it bad. He wanted to see her creamy skin and learn if that dusting of faint freckles on her cheeks could be found in other interesting places on her luscious body. He wanted to learn the color of her nipples, their shape and taste, and if she was as sensitive to his touch as he hoped. He wanted to feel her softness under his hands and against his body. He wanted to drive into her so that she would never forget the merging of their two bodies into one.

He wanted . . . the impossible.

"Don't be shy, Commander. I'm a doctor." She gave him a teasing smile as she turned away, and he realized he'd been standing there, mute, as she bustled around the room, bringing in basic supplies from just outside the door. "I'm going to get the ultrasound machine. Take off your shirt and lie face down on the bed. I'll be back in a minute."

Left alone, Matt shook his head at his unreasonable reaction. The forced intimacy of working together on the mats must have sent his libido into overdrive. She was the most attractive woman he'd ever met, but he really had to get himself under control.

So deciding, he shrugged out of his shirt and placed it neatly on the dresser next to . . . a bottle of lube?

Damn. There went his mind again, straight into the gutter. He'd better get face down on the bed before she saw the way his erection tented his pants.

He scrambled for the cot as she rolled a boxy piece of equipment into the small room. She squeezed between it and the bed as he watched.

"Scoot over a bit, if you can. I'll have to sit on the side of the bed to make this work. There's not enough room in here. Sorry."

She sounded enticingly apologetic as he moved to the far edge of the bed. He felt the other side dip when she sat beside him, their hips connecting, sharing warmth on the small bed.

"How many surgeries did you have?" Her offhand question was the only warning he got before her fingers landed on his skin.

He had scars. He knew they were there. Enough doctors had looked at them over the years since his injury and subsequent treatment. But he'd never felt anything like this. Sandra's touch sent fire through him. A cleansing, burning flame of desire that went straight to his cock.

"Matt?" Her soft voice called him back. "I can see at least three separate surgical scars here. It must've been bad. Did you have only the three surgeries, or more?"

"Just three," he managed to choke out as her fingers traced

lightly along the edges of scar tissue. He couldn't feel every-thing because of the puckered, damaged flesh, but he certainly felt enough. He did his best not to squirm as she examined his scars.

"How did this happen?" She must have bent closer because he could feel her breath wafting across his skin as she spoke.

"I fell off a building and landed on my ass in the dirt." He didn't go into detail about which particular Middle Eastern hellhole that damned domed building had been in, and luckily she didn't ask. Even after all this time, details about most of his prior missions were still top secret.

"Fractured vertebra or ruptured disk?"

"Both." He grunted as she probed with her fingers in a sensitive place. "Lucky me."

"Sorry." She eased the pressure. "How many guys did it take to carry you out of there?"

"None. The situation was hot. I shuffled out on my own. To be honest, the adrenaline blocked the pain till we were back on the boat."

"Ooh rah," she said quietly, as if distracted by her examination. "Brace yourself. I'm going to squirt some gel on the small of your back for the ultrasound. It will probably feel chilly at first. Sorry."

That was all the warning he got before a line of cold lube was laid down on his flesh. Now the bottle that had sent his mind into the gutter made sense. A moment later, the broad head of the ultrasound wand was pressed into his back, spreading the lube out and around the site of his old surgeries.

"I can't see too much with this tool, but some of the soft tissue damage should be apparent. I'd need an MRI to know more."

"It's just a little residual pain. Nothing I haven't felt before. I don't think I need an MRI." The last thing he wanted to do was get the attention of the docs who'd have to report changes in his condition.

"Let me be the judge of that, okay?" She continued to move the wand around on his back. He looked over his shoulder to see her watching the little screen on the machine next to his bed.

She hit a few of the buttons every few seconds and made some prints of certain areas. He couldn't see much more than a black and gray blur on the screen, but she seemed to find it fascinating. After a few minutes she gave a satisfied sigh and shut down the machine. She took a moment to wipe the residual lube off his skin before sitting back.

He rolled carefully to his side to look up at her, propping his head on one hand. "So what's the verdict?"

"It doesn't look too bad. I don't see any evidence of further rupture in the same area. On a scale of one to ten, what level is the pain you're experiencing?"

"Minimal. Maybe a two or three," he answered at once. She didn't look like she believed him. "Okay, maybe a little higher when I bend the wrong way." She still didn't seem satisfied with his answer, so he rolled and sat up in the bed, bringing himself awfully close to her.

Her eyes widened and zeroed in on his abdomen. She looked panicked, and he realized with a little thrill of masculine ego that she wasn't as unaffected by him as he'd thought. He'd done his best to keep the washboard abs of his youth, and he swore the flush on her pretty cheeks was a sign she'd noticed. Damn.

How was he supposed to resist her if she wasn't as immune to him as he'd believed? What if she welcomed his advances? What if she was as hungry for him as he was for her?

Damn it all to hell and back. He was about to find out.

Leaning in, he watched her reactions closely. Her breathing sped up, the blush on her cheeks increased, and she didn't meet his eyes. She also didn't move. As he invaded her personal space, she remained still as a statue . . . waiting.

"Look at me, doc," he whispered, nudging her chin gently upward with one knuckle.

Her green eyes were mysterious as she raised her gaze to meet his.

"What do you want me to say?"

Confrontation. He hadn't expected that. She took the bull by the horns and faced him head on. He liked her spirit.

"Just tell me the truth, Sandra. Are you feeling this, too?"

She seemed to consider her options. He could see the idea of flight flash through her mind only to be negated by something softer and more daring.

"I feel it," she whispered.

He felt as if they were on a precipice. One false step and they'd both be lost. He wouldn't let that happen. He wanted her to want the same things he did. He wanted her to be lost to the same madness he was feeling. He shouldn't. He knew damn well he shouldn't. But it was already too late. This train was racing down the track. Destination unknown.

"Well then." He moved his hand from under her chin to cup her cheek. "I guess the only question then is, what do we do about it?"

"Who says we have to do anything about it?" She didn't move away, but she didn't move closer, either, much to his frustration.

Her challenging words brought out the warrior in him. He didn't want to let her escape. Not when he was so close to discovering something vital. He didn't know what, but he felt in his bones that whatever it was, it could be key to his very existence. He couldn't let her go now.

"No way, sweetheart. I'm not letting you out of this that easy. Despite all the reasons I thought I had for ignoring this . . . thing . . . between us, I can't. Not now. Not when you've admitted you feel it, too. I don't know exactly what it is or where it will lead, but I can't let it go now."

"Then you've answered your own question." He read acceptance in her eyes. He wasn't thrilled with the lukewarm response, but he'd take it if that was all he could get.

Dammit. She wasn't going to get away with it. Not if he had anything to say about it. He was about to force her hand when she pulled away from him.

*   *   *

Sandra had to make a hard decision. Either go with the incredible feelings Matt stirred in her or reject them and stick to her plan. Such as it was.

It really was a stupid plan. What sort of red-blooded female would pass up the opportunity to be with an incredible guy like Matt, even if only for a short time? A crazy one, that's who. Certifiably insane. There was no doubt about it.

She was going to do it. She was going to reject him. It was probably the most foolish thing she'd ever done, but damn if she wasn't going to do it.

"I'm not comfortable with this, Matt." She stood abruptly.

He backed off. "What exactly are you uncomfortable with? Is it me?"

She was tempted to say yes, but that wasn't right.

"It's not you. It's more who you are." She squirmed under his scrutiny. "You're my boss."

He flopped onto his back, sighing heavily as he stared up at the ceiling.

"I'm almost afraid to ask." He looked from the ceiling to her. "Have you been hassled by men you worked with before? Because in no way do I want to hassle you, Sandra. Ever. That's not what this is about."

"I'm flattered, Matt. Really." She stood, pausing by the door. She couldn't do this anymore. One more minute in his presence and she'd give in—to hell with the consequences. "I need some space."

She stepped through the door, but Matt's hand on her arm made her pause. His touch was gentle, but it stopped her in her tracks.

"I apologize if I misread anything—"

"It would be wrong of me to let you believe that." She cut off his words but couldn't face him. "I am attracted to you, Matt, but I can't let it go any further than that. Not now. Maybe not ever. Please just accept that."

His hand dropped from her arm, and she felt him move away.

"I'll accept it. For now." She heard the bedsprings squeak as he sat down again, but she still couldn't bear to look at his face. "I hope I haven't made things awkward between us. Are you still okay working under my command?"

She nodded. "I'm okay with your leadership. In fact, I wouldn't want to work for anyone else on this mission. Let's just forget this. Forget it all."

"I wish I could, doc. I wish I could."

Chapter Five

Matt was glad Sandra was so confident in his leadership. He wasn't so sure himself. Especially not when he returned to his office to find a small listening device poorly hidden under his desk.

A cautious man, Matt usually looked around for changes in his environment whenever he entered a room. It was part of his SEAL training that had spilled over into all areas of his existence. Observation had become a way of life.

Even distracted by thoughts of the moments spent alone with Sandra, he still noted the slight disarray of the papers on his desk. Normally, that could be explained by the activity of one of his support staff. They frequently came in and left documents for him.

But that, coupled with the misalignment of his desk drawers, alerted him to look deeper. He had one of those old wooden desks. It had been in service for many years and had developed quirks. The drawers didn't like to close all the way unless they were aligned perfectly. It had taken him a few days to get the hang of the stubborn piece of furniture, but he eventually had discovered all its secrets.

The way the drawers sat now—not fully seated in their slots—told him someone had been in them since he'd left his office. That wasn't normal. His staff knew not to mess with the private areas of his desk. There was no reason for anyone to delve inside unless they were looking for something.

Curious, Matt checked the desk minutely, even getting down on the floor to look underneath. There, adhered to the underside, he found a small black speck. A bug.

Someone was spying on him.

Matt debated his next move. He could remove the bug, in which case he would alert the spy that Matt was onto him. Or he could leave it and perhaps use it to his own advantage. It only took a moment to decide. He left it where it was and began the slow and deliberate elimination of all sensitive information from his workplace.

Matt would treat the office and all within it as suspect.

An hour later, Matt admitted John to the secure communications bunker on base. Matt had an important call to make, and John Petit's intelligence background and deep, personal family connection to the success of this team made him the most logical person to trust.

The call was to no less than the admiral who was currently head of USSOCOM. He was the centralized authority over all Special Forces and the ultimate military authority where this mission was concerned, reporting directly to the president.

The call connected, and Matt faced a large screen that showed the secure communications room at MacDill Air Force Base in Tampa, Florida. The admiral was there, alone. Just as there was nobody monitoring Matt's side of the conversation except his invited guest, John. No techs. Nobody who wasn't supposed to hear what was said here.

The techs did their job connecting the call, then left. They also maintained the security of the equipment at all times. Matt had asked John to watch over the technician's shoulder this morning before the call went through as an added layer of protection against eavesdropping and espionage. Matt was satisfied the call was as secure as he could make it.

"Sitrep," the admiral barked without preliminaries.

"Sir, we have an internal security problem, which is why I

requested this secure call. I found a listening device in my office."

"If I may," John interrupted, "I'm not surprised. Agency intel suspected a leak coming from Fort Bragg based on increased chatter from certain foreign intelligence outlets. Specifically among known agents of the Chinese military."

"And they're talking about the contagion specifically?" the admiral cut in.

"Can't be one hundred percent sure, sir, since they're careful to use code words. But there is a big sale being discussed. A sale of some kind of biomedical technology. Certain key names were mentioned in conjunction with the negotiations enough times to raise a few red flags."

"Who else knows about the intel?" the admiral asked sharply.

"No one, sir," John replied. "I set up a computer search of the Internet and what phone conversations we have access to when I was read into this mission with results filtering directly to me. It's standard enough it won't raise any eyebrows and secure at the highest levels. I'm confident the data search is secure on the Agency end."

"Commander, needless to say, this is not good. Either get your house in order or I'll find someone who can. Am I clear?"

Matt felt anger stiffen his spine. "Clear, sir. I'll take care of it. I wanted to be certain you were aware so that sensitive communications don't go through my office. I plan on trapping the mole."

A gleam entered the admiral's eye on the other end of the video monitor. The old man actually cracked a grin.

"Misinformation can be a powerful tool as well."

"Yes, sir," Matt agreed with an answering grin. "I will be working all angles to uncover the extent of the rodent problem."

"Good. Keep me apprised. I'll give you some leash on this, Commander, but wrap it up quickly. We can't afford to let this go on too long. The information is too sensitive."

"Understood, sir."

The call flickered off, leaving Matt and John alone in the darkened room.

"Do you have any workable leads, John?" Matt turned to face the man on his team who was most experienced in the international spy game.

"I've discovered a San Francisco connection I'd like to check out. A lot of the calls went to a particular number. If I can make contact, they might lead me back to the person who's trying to sell the technology."

"Good. Can you take Donna with you on this? I don't want anyone flying solo unless it's absolutely necessary, and she needs some field experience."

John looked pained but eventually agreed to take the young woman under his wing for the quick trip to San Francisco. Matt and John parted company and each set off on their separate tasks. John went to arrange a trip for two to California. Matt went back to his office, thinking about creative ways to catch a mole.

"Dr. McCormick?" A beefy sailor approached Sandra as she bought lunch at the base cafeteria the next day.

She didn't recognize the man and was leery of talking to anyone she hadn't met before. Then again, she was on a military base. The place was about as secure as it got. And they were in a busy public place. This man might've been sent by Matt or another member of the team.

"Yes," she answered cautiously.

"I have a message for you." Her alert level lowered considerably at his words. It was as she'd thought. One of the team must've used this strange sailor as a courier. His next words stopped that thought in its tracks. "It's a message from your old friend, Dr. Rodriguez."

It was a message from the team all right. The *wrong* team. Dr. Rodriguez had made his intentions clear the night he forced Sandra's car off the road.

"I want no part of anything Dr. Rodriguez has to say," she told the man. She looked him over, storing details of his appearance and uniform insignia in case she needed to describe him later.

"That's unfortunate." He gave her a measuring look. The guy gave her the creeps. No doubt his uniform was as false as his smile. She had no doubt he was one of Rodriguez's hired thugs. "Dr. Rodriguez doesn't want to take no for an answer."

"He'll have to. Sellars died doing what he damn well shouldn't have been doing. I'm not going to end the same way."

The creepy guy smiled, showing off perfect white teeth. Had to be caps. "Rodriguez sent a message to Sellars. Guess he got it."

"Are you saying Rodriguez sent the"—she lowered her voice, looking around to be sure she wouldn't be overheard— "creature after Sellars?"

"I delivered him myself," he confirmed. "Very effective, I thought. We got Sellars with his own creation. Nobody could trace it back to us."

"Then why are you telling me this? And why did you want Sellars dead? I thought he was with you one hundred percent." Something strange was going on here. She didn't understand the dynamics of how this was playing out among the bad guys.

"Consider it a warning. The same could happen to you if you don't play along, doctor." His eyes gleamed evilly. "Sellars was causing more harm than good. He had to be cut loose. The asshole brought too much attention to the project. He was a loose cannon."

"So you killed him? Isn't that a little extreme?"

"He needed killing." The man looked excited by the idea. His reaction chilled her to the bone. "Now what's your answer?"

"I already told you. No."

"Are you sure? You wouldn't want us to tell your new friends about your past indiscretions, would you?"

"Do your worst. I refuse to get involved any more than I already have."

"Wrong answer." His eyes turned even colder.

"Look." She steeled herself, gathering her courage. She wouldn't cave to threats. "I refuse to get involved in this. You tell Rodriguez to leave me alone. I won't play his game."

"He's not going to like your answer, doctor. In fact, I don't much like your answer, either. You'd better reconsider." He grabbed her by the arm, and her cafeteria tray almost went flying. That gave her an idea.

"You'd better take your hands off me." Her voice was pitched low. She tried her best to sound menacing, but the gorilla squeezing her arm didn't seem impressed.

"You gonna make me, buttercup?"

Now she was mad. "Did you know the cafeteria was serving goulash today? I hear it's awfully good." She looked down at the heaping plate on her tray, then back up at the fake sailor.

"You wouldn't dare." He wasn't tall, but he was wide. The guy was built like a tank and his grip would definitely leave bruises on her arm.

"Try me."

The man looked around the crowded cafeteria and seemed to think better of threatening her in such a public place. His grip tightened excruciatingly before he released her, finger by painful finger.

"You're going to regret this, doctor. Mark my words."

"They're marked," she responded angrily. "Noted and totally ignored. Go tell Rodriguez to shove it up his ass and leave me alone." She'd never been so rude in her life, but the situation definitely called for it. One didn't cower before a bully. If she showed weakness here, Rodriguez would never let up. "If I ever see you again, I'll sic the MPs on you faster than you can blink."

"If you ever see me again, I'll be the last thing you ever see."

The bottom dropped out of her stomach at the blatant threat and the coldness in his eyes. This man was a killer. She was playing with dynamite here.

Over his shoulder, she spied Matt walking into the cafeteria. He spotted her, and a frown wrinkled his brow as he started toward her. The last thing Sandra wanted was a confrontation between this thug and Matt. Even though Matt was bigger, he was also injured—permanently partially disabled, though he refused to admit it. This guy could probably take him apart piece by piece. Sandra didn't want to be responsible for that.

She also didn't want anyone on the team to know that she had been approached by the bad guys. They were only just beginning to trust her. This kind of contact would make all their doubts resurface.

She realized they could possibly use this thug to track down Rodriguez, but she didn't see how they could capture him without a serious public confrontation. She and Matt would be right in the middle of it, and she had no doubt the fake soldier was armed to the teeth.

Maybe it was cowardly of her, but she made a split-second decision. "Get out of here now unless you want a fight on your hands." The fake sailor looked around and saw Matt heading for them. "Your uniform makes you a chief petty officer." Sandra looked with deliberate disdain at the insignia. "Though I doubt anything about your uniform is genuine. The man heading this way is a full commander. He outranks your disguise to a considerable degree. One word from me and you'll be in the brig."

"Nice play, doctor." He backed away, a sinister smile on his swarthy face. "You win this round. You won't be so lucky next time."

"There won't be a next time. You stay away from me and you deliver that message to Rodriguez, too. I won't have anything to do with him or anyone like him." She had to be firm. The fake sailor was going, but Matt was getting closer. Luckily, the cafeteria was very crowded and large enough that it took him some time to negotiate the people and the tables to reach her.

"You'll regret this, bitch." The man cursed her and left.

Sandra blinked. Nobody had ever called her that to her face

before. Nor had anyone ever spoken to her with such venom in their voice. She had made an enemy. Unfortunately, there was little she could do about it.

She refused to drag Matt into a confrontation that could potentially put him back in a hospital bed. She also refused to allow doubt about her loyalties to become an issue with the team. For now, she'd keep this little encounter to herself.

"Friend of yours?" Matt asked, coming up beside her as the fake sailor faded away into the crowd.

"No. Just a case of mistaken identity." She tried her best to sound casual. Matt seemed to accept her words at face value.

"Have you eaten yet?" He looked down at the tray in her hand, and a flush actually reddened his skin for a minute. "Let me rephrase that. Do you mind if I join you for lunch?"

"Not at all. I'll stake out a table while you get your food."

"Sounds like a plan. I'll be right back."

His smile made her feel guilty, as though she was leading him on. She'd asked for space, but here she was, inviting him to dine as if nothing was going on between them. Or worse—as if she wanted more of what almost had gone on between them.

She still didn't know exactly what she wanted. Or rather, what she could safely allow. It had kept her up most of last night, worrying. She wanted him and wonder of wonders, he seemed to want her, too, but the situation was the next best thing to impossible.

She was in a tight spot, there was no doubt about that. She wanted to be honest with Matt, but there was no way he would understand what was going on in her life, or some of her questionable—or downright bad—decisions up to this point. He would never understand how gullible she'd been or how stupid. For a smart woman, she could really be a dope sometimes.

So much of the current situation was her fault. Matt's job was to fix her mistakes, whether he knew it or not. She feared that if and when he ever found out the full extent of her guilt, he'd hate her. It would be so much worse if they became closer than they already were. She understood that intellectually. Somebody just had to tell her heart. Silly thing, it didn't seem able to resist the man.

Matt came back to her, his tray heaped with a lunch about double the size of hers. Then again, he had to weigh close to twice what she did. The man was pure muscle and built on the large side, well over six feet tall. He sat opposite her with a grin that she returned unconsciously. He had such a great smile. It was hard not to respond to it.

"I'm glad you're still talking to me after yesterday," he said with an attractively innocent lift of his lips. She shouldn't have been surprised. Matt was both a charmer and a take-charge kind of guy. It made sense he would approach their strained situation head on.

"Of course I'm still talking to you. I meant what I said, Commander. Let's just put yesterday behind us and move forward from here." She began eating. She hoped he'd let the topic die there.

"Still, I owe you an apology."

Darnit, he just wouldn't let sleeping dogs lie.

"Not necessary. It's best to just forget it."

He stilled, drawing her attention. When she met his gaze he was as solemn as she'd ever seen him.

"What if I can't forget?"

That knocked the wind from her sails.

"We have to." It was as simple as that. Couldn't he see how hard it would be otherwise?

"Says who?"

Sandra wasn't sure how to respond to that. Looking downward, she toyed with the fork in her hand, stirring her food around on the plate. She could feel Matt staring at her until finally he sighed and sat back.

"Sorry. I'm pushing too hard. I sincerely didn't mean to do that, Sandra, and I hope you'll forgive me yet again." She chanced a look upward to meet his gaze. Frustration was evident in his expression. Good. So she wasn't the only one feeling out of sorts with this entire situation.

"Don't apologize." She wasn't going to let him shoulder all the blame. "This is just a little beyond my experience. I don't know how to deal with it and frankly, I can't spare the energy. Not with so much riding on our shared mission. Fixing that problem has to come first. I'm sorry, but that's the way it has to be."

"You're right." Matt looked away, appearing chastised or perhaps angry with himself. When he turned back to meet her eyes, he looked resolved. "Of course you're right. Again, you have my apologies. You're thinking much more clearly than I am at the moment."

"I sincerely doubt that. My stress level is off the charts lately." She chuckled, allowing at least that much of the truth out. It was a relief to admit it. "I'm not very clearheaded about even the simplest things lately. There's too much riding on our work and too many things that could go wrong. I wasn't built for this kind of pressure. I always thought lab work would be quiet and a nonstressful kind of job. Boy, was I wrong." She made a face and Matt beamed. The man had a killer smile that still managed to turn her insides to molten lava. Damn.

"You're doing a great job, Sandra. Just in case nobody's said it, I want you to know you've already earned the team's respect for creating the serum that saved Sam's life. And I can see you're holding up extraordinarily well under really tough circumstances. Everyone knows that and nobody appreciates your hard work and loyalty more than I do." He reached across the table to place one hand over hers. His sincerity warmed her heart, and his unexpected words made her feel even more like a louse.

"So how's your back?" She made a rather obvious volley to change the topic. Thankfully, he allowed it, removing his hand from hers and returning his attention to his meal.

"It's okay. In fact, I'll be getting more of a workout for the next few days. I sent John and Donna on a fact-finding mission to California. They developed some leads that I want them to follow up. It'll be a good chance for Donna to get some investigative experience, but that also means I'll be leading the PT sessions while he's gone."

"You won't work out with the guys, will you?" She cringed at the way that sounded. "I mean, who will teach us girls?" she amended, but the look he gave her said he knew what she'd really meant.

"I'll still work with you and Sarah. I figured I'd leave the guys to beat each other up during the sparring part of the class. They ought to be good at that. They're all self-starters and most have about the same skill set as me. I don't really need to lead them because I can't show them much that's new. John is the man for that. He was a highly ranked martial artist even before he joined the Corps. They only made him better. He was the guy who taught the instructors that would then go out and teach their men. The teachers' teacher, if you will."

"He seems so quiet. I never would have guessed."

"It's usually the quiet ones you have to be careful of." He winked playfully as he finished the last bite of his lunch.

"Well, just promise me you'll take it easy, even if you're leading the PT classes. You don't want to risk re-injury."

"Yes, Mother." He saluted her with his bottled water before draining the last few swallows.

"I am nobody's mother."

He laughed outright at her disgusted tone.

"You ready? I don't want to rush you but I'm heading back to my office. If you're going back to the lab, I could walk with you."

"I'm done." She stood, grateful for the escort. She didn't want to run into that fake officer again. Matt would be an effective shield for the time being. At least until she got back to her lab.

The phone on Matt's desk rang as soon as he walked in the door. He picked it up, identifying himself as he placed his hat on the desk for the time being.

"Please hold for Admiral Chester, sir."

Well that was a surprise. Chester was Matt's immediate superior in the chain of command. He'd been giving Matt a lot of leeway up till now, allowing him to bypass Chester and report up to the Special Ops Command admiral instead. So it was interesting to hear from him now.

"Sykes? How are things going down there? I heard you had a problem with your office staff."

Now that was interesting.

"There have been some small issues," Matt allowed. He wasn't sure what this phone call—on an unsecured line—was all about, but he'd play along. Cautiously.

"I want you to do a full review of all your staff. I'm going to send someone I trust along to help you. A bright young officer who specializes in personnel issues. She has my highest recommendation. Ensign Bartles will be of great help to you, I'm sure."

Matt didn't like the sound of this at all. Up till this point he'd been able to carefully pick and choose who he wanted on his team. Except for the folks who'd been added to his team by reason of their immunity, he knew all the personnel and had worked with them before. Adding a new person would be difficult.

But he couldn't refuse. Not when the person came highly recommended from his direct superior. Matt had to suck it up and accept the newcomer. He'd also have to keep his eyes wide open. This move was suspect and would alert whoever was spying on him already that they had to be more careful. Altogether not the move Matt would have taken had he been in Admiral Chester's shoes. Then again, Chester had never impressed Matt as being all that bright.

"Thank you, sir." The words nearly choked him, but Matt had to comply with his superior's wishes.

"Bartles should be arriving today and will be in your office tomorrow. I expect you to put the personnel matter in her capable hands. She'll clear the decks for you. Mark my words."

Great, Matt thought. Just great. Another chess piece being thrown into the game. Just what he needed

Sure enough, bright and early the next morning a blond

bombshell of an ensign showed up polished and perfect in his office at the appointed hour. Matt had to hand it to Admiral Chester. This woman was a first-class stunner. If she'd been sent as a distraction or as Chester's personal spy, he was in for a rude awakening.

While Ensign Beverly Bartles would have been enough to turn the head of just about any man, Matt was surprisingly immune. He realized with a nervous pang that the only woman who had the power to distract him lately was a petite and powerful scientist with red hair and green eyes. Damn. When had she gotten to him so completely? Matt didn't know but he suspected it was only moments after he'd seen her in person for the first time. She was just that potent.

"Sir, I've been tasked by Admiral Chester to review your personnel and assist your command in any way possible."

Matt didn't miss the deliberate double entendre in her otherwise circumspect words.

"Thank you, Ensign. You'll find the personnel files in that drawer." He pointed toward a filing cabinet at the back of the room. "You may take the files to your desk, which is out in the main area, past Lieutenant Riley's desk. He'll show you where, if you can't find it. I expect you to return the files to Riley's possession each time you leave your desk. They are not to be left unattended at any time. Understood?"

She agreed and with little room for conversation, she headed over to the filing cabinet and dug in. Her head popped up only a moment later.

"Sir, there seems to be some files missing. I was told there were combat troops assigned to your team as well as support people. These files seem to be all support personnel."

"You're correct, Ensign. I want you to start with those. I'll be reviewing the combat troops myself." His tone brooked no argument though she looked like she dearly wanted to object. "If you have what you need to get started, you're dismissed, Ensign. I have a lot of work to do."

"Aye, aye, sir." She saluted and took a stack of folders with her on her way out the door.

Matt wasn't looking forward to working with her. She'd just raised an internal alarm inside Matt. She was after the identities of the combat troops. Whether for Chester's personal knowledge or some more nefarious purpose, he didn't know, but she'd get that information over his dead body.

What Chester and his spy didn't know was that there were no files on any of the combat personnel. Not here, at any rate. And none that mentioned their special qualification to be on his team. There were no records of who was immune and who wasn't, by Matt's specific command. The only files were in his head, and he was doing his best to keep it that way.

"Hi, Tim." Beverly Bartles nodded to Lieutenant Tim Riley, Matt's personal assistant. She'd known him for years. They'd served together under Admiral Chester's command before.

"Hey, Bev, you're looking good." The appreciative gleam in the man's eyes wasn't unexpected. Beverly had invested a lot of money in plastic surgeons to look this good. Her body was just one of the weapons in her arsenal, and she used it to full advantage.

"Are we secure here?"

"Unless he comes out of his office, we're good." Tim waved negligently to Matt's closed office door.

"Well then, the admiral wants you to know that he's pleased with the information you've been able to give him to date. In fact, he sent me as a replacement. He has a new mission for you since you've done such a good job here."

"Really?" Tim was so gullible. Beverly wondered how he'd ever lasted this long working private missions for Chester.

She handed him a slip of paper with an address neatly typed on it. "You're to report to this address tonight when you get off duty. Don't even go back to your quarters. Go directly here. Understood?"

"Got it. So, after I'm done there, you want to meet up at my place? It's been too long, Bev."

She smiled, knowing he'd never make the rendezvous but

happy to play along. Let the poor sucker believe he was going to get laid. It didn't matter to her.

"I've missed you, too, Tim. I'll look forward to it."

When Tim Riley went AWOL, Beverly Bartles was ready with proof that he was the spy. She'd uncovered suspect information in his past that looked just a little too pat to Matt, but he wasn't in any position to argue. She was the handpicked, trusted confidant of an admiral. The USSOCOM commander was pleased to have the issue resolved so easily and quickly, though a manhunt was on for Tim Riley.

Matt doubted they'd ever find him. It was a shame, really. Matt had liked Riley, though he'd been the number one suspect for bugging his office. He'd been a rather harmless young officer with more hair than sense.

Now that Riley's position was open, Admiral Chester insisted that Beverly stay on to take Riley's place since she'd already been briefed on the mission. Matt had little choice but to keep her. That didn't mean he trusted her. In fact, he trusted her even less than he'd trusted Riley. But he'd keep her around. Better to keep your enemies in plain sight, he always thought.

Chapter Six

Things rolled along well after that for about a week. Twice in the intervening days, Sandra found messages from Rodriguez meant for her. The first was a slip of paper slid under her door in the middle of the night. It was handwritten and contained only a phone number and the stylized letter *R*.

She recognized that initial right away. Doctor Rodriguez had signed off on all his reports just the same way. The pompous ass.

No way would she ever dial that number. She set fire to the paper and washed the ashes down the drain in her lab, the same way she'd disposed of the card he'd given her on the road. She didn't want to leave any evidence lying around that could link her to that bastard.

The second message was more direct. Someone left a disemboweled squirrel in front of her lab door, using the poor beast's blood to write the words "you're next" on the door panel above.

Gagging, she'd disposed of the poor little thing as humanely as possible, burying it after dark under the bushes at the back of her building. It was clear that Rodriguez—the sadistic bastard—was tired of waiting for her to change her mind.

She hoped it would end there. She hoped that Rodriguez would accept that she wouldn't work for him and leave it at that. He'd threatened her, but what good would it do him to send someone to kill her? She obviously wasn't talking, or he'd have heard it by now. He appeared to have easy access to the base. Chances were, he thought he would know if she'd told anyone about his approach.

But she couldn't have been more wrong.

Matt had sent the combat team on night maneuvers in the woods surrounding the base after reports of strange activity out near the perimeter of the base. John and Donna had flown to Tennessee earlier that day in a continuation of their mission. Matt had briefed everyone at the afternoon meeting that lasted until dinner.

The field operatives had moved out before dark and Sandra had eaten a quiet meal by herself in the base cafeteria before returning to her lab.

Opening her laboratory door, she realized almost immediately that something was horribly wrong. Someone had left her a nasty surprise of the undead kind.

The moaning was her first clue. That and the shuffling sound of human feet moving awkwardly along the concrete floor. It was coming from the small bedroom at the rear of the lab.

As she listened in growing horror, that night in the lab turned morgue at Quantico came back to her in full force. The inhuman sounds coming from the creature's mouth made her spine turn to jelly as her knees threatened to buckle. The sound of it drawing closer was the only thing that spurred her to action.

Sandra reached for the cell phone she'd been issued, flipping it open and hitting the speed dial.

"Sykes," came the crisp reply as Matt picked up on the other end.

"Matt, it's Sandra. There's a zombie in my lab." She heard the tremor in her voice as the creature finally showed itself, emerging from the small bedroom into the dim light of the main laboratory. "Oh, my God, it's Dr. Jennings. They killed him."

Jennings was still recognizable. He didn't have the brown stains of old blood on his hands or the face the combat team had described or the grotesque wounds another creature would have inflicted on him as it attacked. No, Dr. Jennings looked whole, though his skin was gray and his eyes were blank. A walking corpse. And that was frightening enough.

Even more daunting was the knowledge that he hadn't been attacked and he apparently hadn't had time to attack anyone else yet. No, Dr. Jennings had most likely been injected with the contagion deliberately and then dumped here in her lab. She was probably supposed to be his first victim.

No doubt Rodriguez was aiming to kill two birds with one stone. He'd murdered Jennings and intended Jennings to take her out in the messiest, scariest, most gruesome way possible.

"Get out of there, Sandra!" Matt's urgent command barked from the tiny speaker on the phone.

"I can't let him escape." Grim flashes of that open doorway through which the original specimens had escaped into the night sped through her mind. She couldn't let that happen again. If Jennings got out and started attacking people on base, this terrible situation could morph into something much worse.

She couldn't have that on her conscience. Not again.

"I'll try to hold him in the lab until you get here."

"Stay on the line, Sandra. I'm on my way." She could hear clicking sounds followed by doors opening and the pounding of feet as Matt made his way to her. "I'm almost there, sweetheart. Tell me what's happening."

"He's coming toward me." Her legs were literally frozen with fear.

"Where are you? Give me exact positions."

"He was in the bedroom. I'm at the doorway that leads to the hall. He's about twenty feet away now, near the sink area."

Jennings let out an inhuman moan that Matt apparently heard over the phone.

"Shit! Get out of there, Sandra. I'm at the stairs. I'll be there in a minute, tops. Clear out and leave me an open shot."

"You'll have a clear shot, Matt," she said quietly. A burst of courage came from somewhere as she clicked the End button and discarded the phone. Talking to Matt now would only distract them both.

Sandra shifted to one side of the room, taking the zombie's attention with her. Matt would have a clear line from the doorway if he only got here in time.

Matt cursed as the call was lost. He slammed the stairwell door open on the basement level of the building. That's where Sandra's lab was located. Below ground. Hidden. Safe. Or so he'd thought.

Somehow, someone had gotten one of those monsters in, right under their noses. Heads would roll when he figured out how this had happened. If he lived through this encounter.

Everyone who was immune was out in the field. Only now did he suspect that the activity near the perimeter of the base was probably some kind of diversion designed to isolate Sandra. It had worked all too well. Matt wouldn't make the same mistake again. He'd spread his small team too thin, assuming the threat would have to come from the woods to get to the main base. How wrong he'd been. The sick bastards who were making the zombies had to have some way of getting on base without raising any red flags. He'd find out how they managed it if it was the last thing he ever did.

Matt barreled down the hall at top speed toward the open door that led to Sandra's laboratory. He was armed with a pistol specially fitted with the toxic darts that would dissolve the creature into its component parts. Given enough time and a few direct hits, the nightmare monster would be reduced to a pile of organic goo and whatever old scraps of clothes it had worn.

The scene that met him when he skidded into the lab was utter chaos. Parts of the lab had been trashed. Glass crunched under his feet as he entered and did a quick sweep, stopping abruptly when he saw Sandra standing a few yards away, her face frozen in horror. She was screaming something, but the adrenaline in his system made his blood pound in his ears, and time slowed.

He saw her motioning franticly behind him and he turned. Not in time.

A handful of razor-sharp claws raked down his arm sending blinding waves of pain through the arm and into his chest. Shit! The zombie had gotten in behind him.

Before he could do anything, the creature had the muscular part of Matt's left forearm in its mouth, pointed teeth raking through flesh. Blood welled as intense pain snapped everything into sharp focus. Time sped to its normal flow as Matt turned on the creature, using its momentum to break the hideous grip of teeth and claws on skin and bone.

Bringing up his right hand and the pistol, Matt let loose with four dart rounds in quick succession, nailing the creature at point-blank range. He jumped backward and placed two more darts—one in the leg and one in the arm—for good measure. If what he'd heard from the combat troops held true, the guy should start dissolving in about forty-five seconds.

Matt just had to keep him away from Sandra for that length of time before he collapsed from the poison already working its fiery way through his system. He could feel it, pounding along with his pulse. The adrenaline only made it spread faster. He was going to die. And the true horror was that he'd likely rise again as one of these disgusting, mindless creatures. He had to leave enough darts to take himself out before that happened.

He danced around the zombie, trying to keep it distracted and well out of reach for just long enough. The broken glassware made his footing uncertain until he hit a patch near the back lab bench that was clear. He was getting too damned close to Sandra. If that fucking corpse didn't start turning to mush soon, Matt didn't know what he was going to do.

"Get out of here, Sandra! Go!" He tried once more to get her to leave.

She scuttled farther away, into the rear of the laboratory, refusing again.

"He'll dissolve soon. Just a few more seconds, I think."

"This is no time for bravery, sweetheart. I want you gone. Now!"

"Sorry, I can't do that."

"Can't? Or won't. You damned stubborn . . . scientist."

"Is that the best you can come up with?" She almost sounded like she was laughing, but he put it up to nerves. No way could she be so calm with certain death walking not ten feet from where she stood.

Finally—finally—the zombie began to disintegrate. One moment it was walking, the next, it slid to the ground, coming apart on a molecular level. Within seconds, only a patch of slime and old clothing was left on the concrete floor.

Matt could rest. After he took care of one last thing.

"I have two darts left in the pistol and another clip in my belt." He took out the spare clip as he spoke and slid it toward Sandra along the cold black surface of the lab table, along with the pistol. "You have to take me out before I rise, sweetheart."

"No way in hell." Her vehemence surprised him even as she scooped up the pistol and spare clip and shoved them in a drawer.

He was starting to fade as he watched her grab a long needle and some glass vials off one of the lab benches that hadn't been damaged. She looked determined as she headed straight for him.

"Stay clear, Sandra. I mean it. Everything's contaminated and I'm infected. I can feel waves of heat coursing through my body and I'm beginning to lose feeling in my hands and feet. I don't want you to die, too."

She ignored his warning and dropped to his side as he slipped to the ground, losing strength fast.

"Don't worry about me. I'm already immune." She tied a tourniquet as she spoke, reaching for things she'd put on the lab table above them. "And if I have anything to say about it, you will be, too. Dammit, Matt." She cursed as she filled a syringe with her latest experimental serum. "I don't want to lose you to this. Especially not after you came to my rescue." She gave him a watery smile as she injected him in the heart with the new, improved formula. "This had better work."

"If it doesn't—" He grasped her hand in an almost bruising grip as he began to fade. "Don't worry. I always wanted to go out in a blaze of glory. My only regret is that I never got to kiss you."

"I beg your pardon?"

He smiled a little drunkenly. "Always so proper. I've been wondering if I could chip away at that cool demeanor. I guess now I'll never know. I'd like to think I could . . ." His voice drifted as his eyes closed.

Sandra cradled his head in her lap as he slid lower on the floor, going almost boneless as he headed toward unconsciousness. She stroked his stubbly cheek, tears forming in her eyes.

"I bet you could have at that, Commander." Giving in to impulse, she leaned down and placed a gentle kiss on his lips.

As she pulled back, his eyes popped open.

"Did you just kiss me?" He looked more amused than surprised as a gentle smile slid over his lips.

"I must not have done it right if you have to ask."

"Maybe you should try it again, just so I can be sure."

She was about to kiss him again when his body went rigid and his eyes rolled back in his head. Sandra sobbed with relief. He wasn't going to die. At least not yet. His body was responding to the serum like Sam's had. If all went well, he'd be immune when he came through to the other side of the convulsions and muscle spasms.

She nursed him through the first round of reaction but knew there would probably be more to come. She needed help, but she didn't want to leave him. Chancing a quick run to the other side of the room, she grabbed the phone from where it had fallen and brought it back to where he lay on the floor. She dialed with shaking hands, calling for help from the other team members.

The hunting parties were still out on patrol, but she might be able to get someone from the tech side of the team to assist. Donna was gone, somewhere in Tennessee with John, but Mari was probably in her quarters at this hour. She scrolled down the list until she got to Mari's listing and hit Send.

"Sandra? What's up?" Mari answered on the third ring.

"There's been an incident in my lab. I had to inject Commander Sykes with the new version of my serum. So far it looks like he's responding well, but I could use your help with him. We'll need a cleanup team here, too, but I can't spare the time to track anyone down. Could you call it in for me?"

"There was a zombie in your lab?" Mari sounded alarmed and Sandra could hear noises in the background as Mari got her keys and opened and closed doors.

"Yeah, it was lying in wait for me when I came in from dinner. I called Matt and he came over with the darts and took care of it, but he got bitten, so I had to inject him. I had no choice. He'd have died otherwise." Sandra's voice shook as nerves set in.

"I'll be right there," Mari assured her.

"Don't come alone. So far I've only seen the one creature, but there could be more." Fear began to surface as she thought through the possibilities. She wasn't a soldier. It had only just occurred to her that there could be more dangerous surprises in the building or anywhere on the base for that matter. "You'd better call the combat team. I think they need to check things out and maybe put the base on lockdown or something if they can. If this thing got in here, someone had to place him here. Who knows what else they did while they were here?"

"Good point. I'll call Simon. He'll know what to do."

"He's going into another round of convulsions. I've got to go." Sandra disconnected the call, discarding the phone on the floor as she ministered to Matt.

It felt like hours, but it was only about fifteen minutes later that she heard a voice call her name from the hallway. It was Simon. She met his gaze as he flipped the switches near the door that flooded the entire lab with light.

"You okay, doc?" She noticed he kept his weapon raised and ready, his eyes never settling anywhere for long as he checked every inch of the lab and connecting rooms.

"I'm fine." She watched Simon move methodically through the room.

When he reached her side, he made some hand signals to men in the hall. Men she hadn't noticed. They looked like a cleanup team, dressed in protective gear as they moved inside on Simon's signal and set to work.

"Can we move him?" Simon asked, looking down at Matt.

Sandra still had his head cradled in her lap. His face was ashen and sweat beaded his brow, but he was quiet for now.

"Yeah. If we make it quick, I think he should be okay. We can take him up to my quarters. It's the closest uncontaminated place. I want to get him settled before any more convulsive episodes can take place."

Simon bent and scooped Matt's unconscious body into his arms. Sandra stood and followed him to the door, discarding her outer layer of clothes and shoes just inside for the cleanup team to take care of. She'd wash thoroughly when she reached her quarters and be careful not to touch anything on the way up. She didn't want to contaminate anything, but she also couldn't leave Matt. They'd have to decontaminate her bed after she treated him, but she didn't care. She'd deal with that—and the inevitable questions—as soon as Matt was in the clear.

Simon carried Matt up the stairs and through the door Sandra unlocked for him, then placed Matt on her bed. A few moments later, another set of convulsions hit and Sandra was beside him in an instant, helping him through the agonizing episode.

"Is that normal, doc?" Simon asked quietly. She looked up at the soldier who stood at Matt's bedside, looking down at his back. Matt had curled onto his side as the last of the convulsions faded.

"What do you mean?"

"His back. You should look at this."

Concerned, she stood and walked around to the other side of the bed, bending to examine Matt's lower back. There was a distinct bulge in the area where he'd been injured. She could see it rippling through his clothing and grew worried.

Quickly, she pulled his shirt up, tugging it forcefully from his waistband until she could see his skin. The area where the scars crisscrossed his flesh was distended and rippling slowly in an unnatural motion. She held her hand out hesitantly to touch his skin and was shocked by the heat that met her fingers. The surrounding skin was cooler to the touch, which calmed her somewhat, but she had no idea what was going on beneath the surface near Matt's spine.

"I'd heard he was injured," Simon said from behind her. "Looks like old scarring there."

"Yes," Sandra confirmed, but didn't go into detail.

"Could be he's healing."

"What?"

"Well, one of the side effects of immunity is that old injuries seem to heal. I had a bad knee—nothing career threatening, but something I had to watch out for—and now it's gone. Not even a twinge."

"Was it soft tissue damage or bone?"

"Little of both."

Sandra thought quickly. "Same for Matt. He had cracked vertebra and disk rupture."

Simon whistled through his teeth. "I had a friend with something similar. He can barely walk with a cane."

"The commander hides his pain well," was Sandra's only observation.

Simon's phone rang and he stepped away to answer it. He came back a minute later.

"Mari's on her way. I asked Sarah to escort her. They stopped by the hospital and gathered some equipment so Mari can help you safely. Why is it you're not worried about cross-contamination, doc?" His voice was soft but his words were significant. He no doubt suspected something wasn't quite right here.

The time had come. Time for truth. Or at least a portion of it.

She didn't care anymore. Not with Matt's life hanging by a thread.

"I'm already immune. It happened in a lab accident that turned out well for me, thank goodness. Nobody knew. Until now."

"Not even the commander?"

She shook her head. "Nobody. It was safer for me to hide it."

He gave her a sidelong look. "I'll bet."

Anything she might've said in reply was interrupted by a knock on the door. Simon was instantly on alert. He checked the peephole before he opened the door to admit Mari.

After that, they spent about a half hour just cleaning Matt up, removing the blood and contaminated clothing from his unconscious body and the dirty sheets from under him. The two women worked together to remake the bed with him in it as he suffered through the biochemical reactions that would leave him immune from the contagion. Matt was also suffering pain as his back spasmed repeatedly.

"Do you think it's healing like Simon suggested?" Sandra asked as they examined the lower back area. It seemed to be getting less swollen as time went on.

"It's possible. Even likely, I'd say, from what I've observed with Simon. After all, the original intent of the research was to create something that would increase the body's healing ability."

"I'd love to try to see what's going on in there. I did some ultrasound images of his lower back a few days ago," Sandra ventured, knowing Mari would pick up on the significance of having a recent baseline for comparison.

But Mari picked up on more than just the medical significance.

"Commander Sykes let you examine him?"

Sandra tried not to squirm under the other woman's scrutiny.

"He was experiencing some pain during our first martial arts class. I convinced him to let me take a look." She tried to sound offhand. "I'd done some work in orthopedics early in my training. Having those images could really help us figure out what's going on. We could try to scan him again now and compare to the earlier images."

"Where's the machine?"

"Down in the lab. I thought maybe we could ask the cleanup team to disinfect it first and bring it up here. It's small enough."

"Let's do it." Mari slapped her hands on her thighs and stood. "I'll call down to the guys cleaning up the lab." She moved off to one side of the room and pulled out her cell phone, placing the call.

Sandra took the time to examine Matt more closely. She brushed his sweaty hair away from his brow. He was still burning up, but the temperature wasn't life threatening. He'd be okay for now, but she would continue to monitor him closely.

The ultrasound machine showed up shortly thereafter, hand-delivered by one of the cleanup team members, newly sanitized. Mari set things up, plugging it in and flipping switches and dials until it was ready. She positioned herself and the machine at the side of Matt's bed. Sandra was on his other side.

"How do you want to do this?" Mari asked.

"I don't want to put him on his belly with the possibility of convulsions. How about I hold him on his side while you do the scan?"

Mari agreed and they set to work. Rolling Matt was relatively easy. Keeping him on his side required Sandra to move in close to support his shoulders and hip. He was heavy and she had to bend close to him in order to get a good grip. His overly warm body was solid and deliciously muscular. As worried as she was about his condition, she couldn't help notice how good he felt under her hands.

Mari ran the scan as quickly as possible and printed out a few images. They rolled Matt onto his back within minutes. Sandra watched him carefully to make sure he was okay. She was concerned he might still be in for more convulsions, but he seemed to be resting peacefully for the moment.

The two women settled in to wait in chairs, one on either side of Matt and the bed. All was quiet while they examined the two sets of ultrasound images.

"I'll be damned." Mari whistled softly as she passed the flimsy paper to Sandra. "It looks like both the tissue and bone are regenerating."

"Yeah." Sandra was preoccupied as she scanned the images.

"See the way the disk tissue that was removed is starting to fill back in?"

"I've never seen anything like it." Sandra was truly amazed at what the machine allowed them to see in grainy black-and-white.

"Me, neither. I have to admit, it's pretty amazing. Simon has some incredible regenerative abilities, but even I didn't expect this. The commander's tissue was surgically removed. His bones were altered by a surgeon and yet they're reconstructing themselves. He's about halfway there right now, if I'm any judge. If this continues, his back could be good as new in an hour or two."

"Wow."

"You can say that again." Mari sat back in her chair as Sandra kept looking at the images. After a few minutes of silence, she, too, sat back. Slowly, she became aware that Mari was staring at her.

"What?" Sandra asked self-consciously.

"Just curious." Mari's expression spoke of suspicion, not simple curiosity. Sandra felt her stomach clench.

"About what?"

"Since I got here you haven't seemed overly concerned about contamination. Is there something you haven't shared with us?"

Sandra sighed heavily. "I guess it's obvious now that I'm immune. I felt it was safer to hide that fact for as long as possible."

"From us?"

"From everyone," Sandra admitted. "You have to understand, before I joined this team, I was on my own. I was working in the private sector, making my own way. I didn't want the information getting out to the wrong people. I could have made a very big target for some very bad guys if it had been known. The alternative was turning myself into a lab rat for the military. Neither idea appealed, so I forged my own path."

"How long have you been immune?"

"From early on." Sandra felt it wisest not to go into too much detail. "I realized pretty quickly that some of the original science team was bonkers. I didn't want to draw attention to myself, so I kept my immunity a secret."

"You can't keep that secret any longer, I'm afraid."

"I realize that," Sandra admitted. "I'm just glad I was able to help Matt."

Mari's eyes narrowed as she grinned. "So you're on a first-name basis with him?"

Sandra realized her mistake and couldn't control the telltale flush of heat in her cheeks. Mari only laughed softly.

"It's okay, you don't have to answer," Mari assured her. "I won't pry. We all have our little secrets. This situation is hard on everyone. You and Matt deserve to have some happiness."

"It's not like that," Sandra protested weakly. She would have said more, but Matt began to twist and turn on the bed. His back spasmed once more, and both women moved to help him.

They watched over him the rest of the evening, but he didn't convulse anymore. His back spasmed from time to time and they took a few more images of the progress his body was making in repairing itself. The data they collected could be very valuable to her research but Sandra didn't really care. She wouldn't rest easy until she was certain Matt would be okay.

Mari was a big help. She coordinated with the rest of the team and at some point had food delivered. She placed cup after cup of hot coffee in Sandra's hands and didn't ask any further embarrassing questions about her relationship with the commander.

Sandra was glad of her presence. She wouldn't leave Matt's side until he was awake and she was sure he'd be all right.

The hours seemed to drag on until finally, just before dawn, Matt's eyes opened.

"Sandra?" His voice was raw but it was music to her ears.

"I'm here, Matt."

His blue gaze searched for and found her. His relief was visible as the tension left his shoulders.

"You're okay?"

"I'm fine. How do you feel?"

He seemed to consider. "Not good, but not bad, either." He sat up slowly, grimacing as he went. "The serum worked?"

Good. He remembered what had led up to this. It was a good sign for his neural activity.

"Like a charm." She gave him a wobbly smile. Her relief was profound. Seeing him sitting up and taking stock of his internal condition was more than she'd hoped for. He seemed to be recovering much faster than Sam had.

"How's the back?" Mari's voice intruded from the other side of the room and Matt's head swiveled to her.

"Why? What did you do?"

"Nothing," Mari assured him, stepping closer. "But one of the benefits of immunity is radically increased healing. Sandra and I monitored some rather startling changes to your lower back as your body processed the contagion and the serum. I'm just wondering how it feels to you."

Matt shifted his hips on the bed, side to side as he took stock of his spine.

"It doesn't hurt. There's some soreness, but not the pain I'm used to." His gaze turned back to Sandra, his eyes widening slightly with a sort of cautious hope. "Is it healed?"

"We think so, yes." She loved being able to deliver such good news. "You'll be the best judge of how you feel, but Mari and I have been looking at the scans all night and it appears your body has regenerated the injured disk tissue. I want to get an MRI to do a finer inspection but it looks good from what little we can see using this machine." She gestured toward the small rolling console they'd been using throughout the night.

He looked around the room. "I'm in your quarters?" he asked Sandra.

Suddenly she felt defensive. "It was the closest uncontaminated place to put you."

Matt nodded, his mind no doubt going over all he could remember of the night before.

"What time is it and where's my phone? I need a sitrep."

"Simon's downstairs with the cleanup team," Mari volunteered. "He stuck around to guard the place and to be here when you woke. I'll call him."

Sandra opened the drawer of the bedside table where she'd placed some of Matt's gear. She handed him his watch and phone.

"Your wallet and other personal items are in here." She pointed to the drawer. "Your clothes were taken away by the cleanup team for disposal except for what you're wearing." They'd left him in his boxers. "Sam brought over a change of clothes for you last night. He figured you'd need a new uniform when you woke up, but frankly, I wasn't expecting you to be up and around today. It took Sam several days to recover."

"But you improved your serum after you saw how it worked for him, didn't you?"

"I did, but the version I gave you last night was untested. I really don't know what to expect. I'd like you to take it easy until we're sure you're not going to have an adverse reaction."

He shot her a look as he levered his feet to the floor over the side of the bed. She jumped up to help him, but he shook her off.

"Where did you say my clothes were?"

"Matt, this is—" Sandra began to object, but Matt waved her to silence.

"I don't have time for a long recovery. Even if I have to crawl there, I've got to get back to the office today. Or do you want me to be replaced?"

There was something going on here. He was too adamant. There had to be a damn good reason he pushed himself so hard.

"Okay," she said in a slow, deliberate manner as she walked toward the dresser where she'd stowed Matt's clothes in an empty drawer.

Her back to Matt, she caught Mari's eye. A silent communication passed between them. Mari realized something odd was going on, too.

A knock at the door interrupted the tense atmosphere. Mari opened the door to admit Simon.

"Good to see you up, Matt."

"Good to be up." Matt sighed as he sat heavily on the side of the bed. "I need a sitrep, Si." Matt was bare chested and wearing only his boxers, but Simon made no comment.

For the next few minutes Simon reported on the activities of the night. Neither man seemed to mind the presence of the women as they discussed everything in military shorthand that Sandra barely followed. When he finished his report, Matt asked a few short questions, all the while struggling to hold himself in an upright position.

At least, that's what it looked like to her. He was putting a brave face on it, but Sandra could detect signs that Matt wasn't as steady as he'd like them all to believe.

"Order the combat team off duty for some downtime in a staggered schedule. I'd like someone near Dr. McCormick at all times." Matt's order took Sandra by surprise. She turned to look at him, his clothing piled in her hands as she stood near the dresser. His gaze pinned her in place as he continued. "You and Mari can go, Si. I know it's been a long night for you both. I appreciate the way you both stepped up to the plate while I was out of commission."

"Anytime, Matt," Simon answered. Sandra could hear the respect Si had for Matt in his voice even though the words were simple enough.

"If you need anything," Mari said to Sandra as she gathered her things and headed toward the door with Simon, "just call."

Sandra merely nodded, realizing she was going to be left alone with Matt. No doubt the significance of that wasn't lost on either Simon or Mari. Matt wasn't doing anything to hide his intent stare, either. A showdown was coming and this little bedroom was going to be Ground Zero.

Chapter Seven

"If you'll just bring me those clothes . . ." Matt let the sentence hang. Sandra was clearly distracted, probably dreading the confrontation to come. He had no such reservations. With consciousness had come memory, followed by anger and an intense feeling of betrayal.

Sandra had lied to him. Oh, she hadn't lied straight to his face, but she'd definitely lied by omission. She hadn't told him she was immune to the contagion. She hadn't trusted him enough. Maybe that was his fault, but he was still irritated by the fact that she hadn't told him the entire truth.

She walked slowly in his direction, his uniform cradled in her arms. When she bent slightly to drop the clothing at his side, he grabbed her forearms, startling her. Her wide green gaze flew upward to meet his accusatory glare.

"Why, Sandra?" She remained mute and he tightened his grip in frustration, shaking her slightly. "Why didn't you tell me?"

"I didn't tell anyone." He saw the fear in her eyes. "It was an accident. At first, I didn't realize what had happened, then after . . . it was clear I'd be in danger from some of the other scientists if they knew I was immune from the contagion."

"How long?"

He could see tears gathering in her eyes, and he realized he was holding her arms too tightly. Was he hurting her? He was angry, but he didn't want to cause her pain. He let go of her arms as if she burned him and she backed away from him slowly.

"Almost from the beginning."

He didn't like the nebulous way she phrased her answer, but he let it go for now. She was still withholding facts from him, but there were more issues on the table. He'd circle back around to the issue of timing eventually.

"Tell me about Jennings."

He noted her sharp intake of breath. She was afraid. Was it leftover fear from being confronted by a zombie in her own workspace? Or was there more to it than that?

"You probably know he was part of the original science team. I haven't seen him since the group split up and we all went our separate ways."

"What else do you know about him?" He'd have to chip away at her to get at the full truth.

Dammit. He didn't like this at all. Of all the people on his new team, he'd thought he could trust her. But he'd been wrong before. There was already one spy on his staff. Maybe there were more.

What did he really know about Sandra McCormick anyway, besides the fact that he found her almost irresistibly attractive? He shouldn't have let his desire for her influence his opinion of her abilities or loyalties, but he realized that's just what had happened. He'd been willfully blind where she was concerned from the beginning.

"He was a competent genetic engineer but kind of a jerk. He always rubbed me the wrong way, and when I began to fear some of the others, he was on the short list of people I wanted to avoid."

"I'm going to need you to write down that list for me." His gut churned, knowing she'd been holding out on him from the beginning.

She nodded tightly. "All right."

"You don't seem too enthusiastic." As a distraction, and

also because he had to get moving, he unfolded his clothes and slowly pulled them on. "I'm going to start thinking you don't want to play on my team."

"Believe me when I say there's no other team I want to be on."

"Why should I believe you? Tell me that." He stood to pull on his pants and felt himself wobble. Sandra checked her own forward motion before she got to his side, but it was telling that her instinctual move had been to help him. Regardless of her other roles, she was first and foremost a compassionate woman.

"I didn't mean to withhold information from you, but by the time I was approached to be part of your operation, I'd already been approached by others with less desirable aims. Secrecy had become a way of life."

"Someone else tried to recruit you?" Matt felt his anger rise once more, and it gave him strength to shove his arms into his shirt.

"You knew Dr. Sellars had approached me before Captain Beauvoir came to me in New York. I didn't deny that."

"Who else?"

"Rodriguez." The name came from her lips grudgingly. Matt recognized the name. There was a Rodriguez on the original research team. He'd been one of the lead scientists.

"When?"

Sandra sighed and sat heavily in the chair Mari had been using. It was set a few feet from the bed, closer to the door than the chair Sandra had been using on the other side. Worry shrouded her face—that beautiful, bewitching face that had snared him so completely. Damn.

"Do you remember the flat tire I got on the way here?" Matt didn't like the sound of this but didn't interrupt. "The tire didn't blow out on its own. It was shot out." He *really* didn't like the sound of that. "Rodriguez and some goon of his ran me off the road. He wanted me to join his team. I refused. He began threatening me around the time the patrol car showed up."

"You called the cops?"

"First thing." She nodded shakily. "As I pulled off the road I dialed nine-one-one. Luckily Rodriguez talked long enough that he couldn't do anything worse than just threaten me before help arrived."

"Dammit, Sandra!" He wanted to hit something but was still weak as a kitten. "What I don't understand is why you didn't tell me about this long before now. He threatened you. Didn't you think it was important to share that fact with me?"

She looked even guiltier as she met his gaze.

"That isn't the only time he threatened me." She took a deep breath before continuing. "Remember the day you met up with me in the base cafeteria? That guy I was talking to? He was a messenger sent by Rodriguez. I think he was the same guy who was driving the car that ran me off the road. He was about to make a scene before I saw you enter."

"Same question." He was fast losing patience. "Why didn't you tell me?"

"I didn't want a cloud hanging over me. I know you had your doubts about me when Xavier and Sarah first asked me to treat Sam. Just by virtue of my being part of the original science team that developed the contagion, I was already under suspicion. I didn't want anyone to know that some of the old team members had been in touch with me."

"But it would have given you *more* legitimacy to have been honest with me from the beginning." He shook his head at her reasoning. It didn't make any sense . . . unless . . .

Shit.

"What did you do, Sandra?"

It was the question she'd been dreading, but the time had come to pay the piper. At least part of the balance. She'd try to hedge her bets if she could. She'd give Matt part of the truth. The part she could bear to reveal.

"Back before I realized what he was up to, Dr. Sellars contacted me. I'd just started my new job on Long Island and I didn't realize what a slimeball Sellars was. Unlike Rodriguez, who'd always rubbed me the wrong way, I got along well with Dr. Sellars. He was at least polite to me when we worked together before."

"We already knew Sellars e-mailed you, but you denied any involvement with him when the team first contacted you." The suspicion in Matt's eyes nearly broke her heart.

"I didn't tell you the whole truth. While it was true I'd turned down Dr. Sellars when he invited me to dinner to discuss joining his research, that wasn't the only communication I'd gotten from him." She took a deep breath before continuing. She hated this. "Several weeks before, Dr. Sellars asked for my help with a chemical equation he was working on. He didn't say what it was for and he only gave me the part he was having trouble with. Like a dope, I solved his puzzle for him and somehow Rodriguez found out. I began to suspect, when I first examined Sam, that the equation I'd solved had to do with the so-called improvements Sellars made to the contagion. I felt like a fool for not realizing it sooner. Rodriguez knew I'd helped Sellars. He was trying to use the information against me. He threatened me with exposure."

"What did you decide?"

"I was at an impasse. I refused outright to help him in any way, but I really didn't want you to know what I'd so foolishly done. I didn't want you to look at me the way you're looking at me right now." Her voice broke, much to her chagrin. She turned her face away, cut deeply by the accusation in Matt's gaze.

"You were going to let him blackmail you?"

"No!" She shot to her feet, her body demanding action when her heart was in turmoil. "I refused him over and over. I wouldn't have willingly helped him."

"Then what were you going to do?" Matt's voice was quieter, closer. She turned her head and found him standing a foot behind her. He'd moved silently, dogging her tracks. He looked stronger now than he had just moments before.

"I didn't know what to do." She turned completely to face him. "I was letting it ride until something forced my hand, I guess." She felt tears gather in her eyes as remorse set in. "But I never expected anything like what happened last night. I didn't want to put anyone else's life in danger and I certainly didn't want you to be attacked by a creature sent to kill me."

She couldn't see through the tears filling her eyes as she sobbed. Strong arms closed around her tentatively at first, then more securely as Matt drew her against him. One big hand rubbed her back as she trembled, her emotions getting the best of her after so many days of keeping everything bottled up inside.

"I'm so sorry, Matt. I never meant for you to be hurt, and now you've been infected. All because of me."

His arms felt so safe, so warm. His voice rumbled against her as he spoke in a low voice.

"I'm also immune to the contagion because of you, sweetheart. You literally saved my life."

Both his words and tone surprised her. She had expected him to be really angry with her. Instead he sounded almost forgiving and somewhat indulgent. She pulled slightly away to look up into his eyes.

"Then we're even because you saved me, too. It was sent to kill me."

"But it wouldn't have killed you. You're immune." His gaze narrowed.

"Nobody knew that. Even so, that thing still could have ripped me limb from limb."

"You could've outrun it. Retreated and called for help from the combat troops. Why didn't you?"

She fought the urge to look away. He was treading too close to the secret she desperately wanted to keep. She'd have to brazen it out.

"I couldn't let it escape the lab. That happened once before and a lot of good men died. I knew I had to keep it in the lab if at all possible."

"Foolish," Matt whispered, his gaze growing more intimate as he held her. "Brave, but foolish."

"You'll get no argument from me." She'd meant her words

to be amusing, but they dropped to a whisper as Matt drew closer.

His mouth hovered over hers so that she could feel the warmth of his breath on her skin. She wanted to taste him, to know his kiss. She wanted it like she wanted her next breath.

Finally, his head dipped that final short distance and his lips took possession. It wasn't a kiss so much as it was the staking of a claim. His arms enveloped her while his mouth plundered hers. This was no exploratory joining of lips. This was a full-body kiss that rocked her world off its axis.

The temperature in the room went from comfortable to steamy in fractions of a second. Sandra pressed against him, reveling in the strong arms that imprisoned her, the warm body that made her feel so womanly, the hard ridge of flesh pressing against her that made her feel so wanted.

He was aroused. Just like that, there was no doubt in her mind that he wanted her. Just as she wanted him. Had wanted him for days now. Weeks. Since the moment she'd first seen him, Matt had fueled her late-night fantasies and made her yearn as no man had before.

His hands slid lower, cupping her butt as he rubbed against her. She strained against him as well, wanting the clothes between them to be gone. She wanted to feel his skin against hers, his body inside hers.

Matt took her lips with a fierceness he'd never used for a first kiss before. Somehow it was appropriate. She'd brought out the barbarian in him and she didn't seem to mind one bit. She answered his demands stroke for stroke, nibble for nibble, and drove him even higher with her innocent response.

He put all his energy into turning the mere acceptance of his desire into flashing hot, eager demand. He wanted her to want him and within moments, he felt the leap of her pulse under his fingers. She grew hungry for his touch, pushing her body into his. He felt the softness of her clothing against his bare chest and longed to feel more.

He was hard for her and they'd barely even begun to explore each other. She was dynamite in his arms, but he was wary of being burned. He didn't want this whole situation to explode in his face. He had to tread lightly, especially now that he knew she'd been keeping secrets from him. If she'd omitted to tell him about her immunity and the continued harassment from Rodriguez, what else had she kept from him?

Her every movement told him she wasn't being completely honest with him. Whether the information she held back was as serious as what she'd already admitted remained to be seen. He hoped it was something simple. He didn't know what he'd do if it turned out she was withholding something even more serious.

The idea of it made him angry, but it was hard to hold on to his anger when Sandra was in his arms. In fact, it was impossible. She fired his blood, as she had from the beginning. From the first moment he'd met her she'd piqued his interest, and now that she was in his arms, responding to his demands, it felt even better than he'd imagined. She made him want more.

He raised one hand, edging toward her breast, wondering if she'd protest his possessive touch. When she moved closer, practically offering herself to him, he grunted in satisfaction. Covering her soft mound with his palm, he squeezed gently, feeling the weight and size of her in his hand. She was perfect. And the little peak that rose under his palm tempted him to do so much more than merely feel.

He wanted to taste, to learn the flavor of her skin, the contours of her under his tongue.

But not yet.

For now he had to content himself with just this. There was too much yet to be resolved between them. Too many questions unanswered and too many feelings he didn't have the time to deal with right now. Damn, this woman was distracting.

Matt had been a loner for years and never worried about what any of his girlfriends might be thinking or feeling. He hadn't been in any truly serious relationships since he was a young soldier and even then, he'd kept himself firmly in check.

At the first sign that his girl was getting too serious, he was gone. Now, it seemed, he wanted nothing more than for Sandra to be serious—to commit fully to this mission and to him.

A startling thought.

Startling enough to make him draw away from her tempting softness, the fire of her desire, the pulsing arousal of her presence.

He had to get out of here. He wasn't sure who he could trust anymore—not even himself, if he couldn't keep his head together when Sandra was in his arms.

He stepped away, seeing the hurt confusion on her face. He steeled himself against it. Matt couldn't be sure of her at this point. She was still hiding *something*. He didn't know what it was, but he'd bet his left nut that she wasn't telling him everything. Until she came totally clean, he had to be wary.

Without another word he stalked out of the room. He had work to do.

Matt was in no mood to deal with Beverly when he arrived at his office. He was early, which was a good thing. He closeted himself in his office and closed the door—a clear signal he didn't want to be disturbed. He needed the time to get his anger under control and to regroup physically from the night before.

He wasn't one hundred percent up to his peak of performance, but he didn't need to be. He only had to convince the spy in his office—and any others who might be watching for any sign of weakness—that everything was as it had always been. He was riding a desk. It shouldn't be too hard to pretend to be operating at full speed. If he'd still been working in the field, that would be another thing, but luckily he didn't have to deal with that challenge.

He just had to tough out a day in the office.

Along about lunchtime, his peace and privacy came to an end. Beverly knocked on his door and Matt made a pretense of being engrossed in paperwork before he allowed her to enter.

"Would you like me to bring lunch back for you, sir?"

The offer was innocent enough, but Matt wouldn't trust a viper like Beverly not to drug his food.

"No thanks. I'll be going out in a bit. I'll get something then."

He hoped Bev would take the hint as he turned back to his paperwork. No such luck. She hovered in the doorway long enough he had to look up.

"I heard there was a bit of a fracas on base last night. Something about Dr. McCormick's laboratory."

Yeah, Bev was definitely on a fishing expedition. Matt had to play it cool. He also recognized an opportunity to misdirect the spy in his midst.

"Yeah, we had a little disturbance over there. Beats me how the creature got into her lab without anyone seeing it, but these things are good at stealth." Matt hoped he wasn't over-playing his bewilderment, but Bev seemed to be buying it. It was time to make his next move. "Do we have any reports of personnel AWOL from base?"

Bev didn't betray her surprise at his question by anything other than a slight widening of her eyes that he wouldn't have noticed if he hadn't been watching her closely. She was good. But Matt had to be better.

"No, sir. I'll double check but I've been keeping a close eye on duty reports from every sector of the base. Nobody's missing. Or at least, nobody's been reported missing as yet."

"We'll have to keep an eye on that." Matt grimaced, hoping she would go that extra step that would expose her and give him an opportunity to mislead both her and the people she worked for.

"Did anyone see its face? I mean, was the zombie recognizable at all?"

Bingo. She'd opened the door. She'd also just incriminated herself.

"Dr. McCormick saw it clearly, but she didn't recognize him. We know it was male, but that's about all as far as identifying characteristics. She said his face was unrecognizable and the combat team didn't waste time. They just finished him off before he could infect the doctor."

"Tough break," Bev said as if she really meant it. All the while, Matt could almost hear the gears turning in her mind.

Matt got the feeling that Bev knew damned well who'd been sent to destroy Sandra. Jennings had been one of Sandy's colleagues. There was no way she wouldn't recognize him. Matt wanted Bev to think that Sandra was playing along—that she wasn't identifying Jennings for her own purposes. Perhaps that she was hedging her bets so she could play both ends against the middle. He wanted to keep them guessing as to Sandy's allegiances if at all possible.

Bev had tipped her hand. She wasn't just spying on him for Chester. She was in league with the ones who had killed Jennings and sent him after Sandra. Bev was definitely wearing a black hat in this gunfight. It was up to Matt to use that knowledge to his best advantage.

Beverly left for lunch and Matt was fairly certain she'd be reporting to her masters on the morning's developments. Matt gave it forty minutes before he stopped shuffling papers, got up from his desk, stretched, and left the office.

Tempted as he was to go check on Sandra, he resisted, opting instead to check in with Simon. A quick call informed him that Simon was having lunch with Mari in the base hospital's cafeteria. Matt decided to drive the short distance because he was still tired as hell from the ordeal of the night before.

He couldn't let it show. Nobody could know what had happened to him in that laboratory. Only the inner circle that now consisted of Sandra, Mari, and Simon knew and he wanted to keep it that way. At least for now—at least until he had rooted out the rats in his kitchen.

Matt arrived just as Simon and Mari were finishing up their lunch. He grabbed a sandwich to go and went with the couple to Mari's private lab.

"Are we clear in here?" Matt asked Simon as soon as the door closed. Simon had already gone to work checking for listening devices.

"I checked before lunch and found nothing. I also recoded the electronic locks. Only Mari can get in. Not even our cleaning crew has access now." Simon did a thorough recheck of the small space while Matt did his own survey of the inner office.

There were no windows, which negated the possibility of someone listening from far away using a parabolic mic. The air system was independent of the rest of the building because this lab had been built to study infectious diseases, so there was also very little chance of anyone listening through ducts or other access points into the room.

"We're clear," Simon reported as he took a seat on one of the lab stools. Mariana had already seated herself on a rolling desk chair. Matt commandeered another stool.

"How are you feeling, Commander?" Mari asked as Matt seated himself.

"Tired," he admitted. "Very tired, but otherwise okay."

"How's your back?" she probed further, concern in her gaze.

"To tell you the truth, I haven't thought much about it. It doesn't hurt if that's what you're asking. Haven't had a twinge all day, which is kind of surprising, really. I've had to get used to blocking the pain, but every once in a while a spasm would still creep up on me. I haven't had any of those today yet."

"If I'm right, you probably won't have spasms at all anymore."

"Now that would be something." Matt didn't want to talk about himself or his injury anymore. He had bigger fish to fry. "There's a leak in my office. I'm ninety-nine percent sure it's Ensign Bartles, but I want to know who she's working for and who else might be involved."

"Think she's reporting back to Admiral Chester?" Simon asked.

Matt knew there was bad blood between Simon and Chester from years ago when Chester had been captain of a ship that had fled an engagement, leaving Simon's SEAL team high and dry. Chester had weaseled his way out of responsibility for that fiasco because he was politically connected even then, but Simon had never been shy about saying why he disliked the admiral and had told Matt the entire story.

"I have no doubt Chester's getting regular updates from her. He positioned her in my office without my being able to object. It was too convenient the way she showed up right before Tim disappeared."

"You think she had something to do with his going AWOL?" Mari asked.

"It *looks* like Tim ran off when Bartles came in to investigate. That's a little too simple an explanation for my tastes. The more likely possibility to my mind is that Beverly sent him away or did away with him."

"You think she's capable of murder?" Mari seemed shocked by the idea.

"I wouldn't put anything past her." Matt backed off a little. "However, if she's simply reporting back to Chester, then Tim might've been the real problem and he took off on his own. If she's working for someone else in addition to Chester, well, that'd be the real problem. Frankly, I never thought Tim was bright enough to be much of a spy. Bev, on the other hand, is a snake."

"Why so adamant?" Simon's eyes narrowed.

"The conversation I just had with her. I'm convinced she knew the zombie waiting for Sandra was Jennings—or at least someone Sandy should have recognized. Bev was too curious. She came right out and asked if Sandra recognized her attacker."

"Not a question that would have occurred to me right away," Mari admitted.

"That's what I thought," Matt agreed.

"You think Chester is working with the rogue scientists?" Simon asked, clearly concerned but skeptical. "The man is an ass, but I doubt he'd try to sell a secret with this kind of destructive power. He's all about covering his own ass and moving up in the chain of command. I don't think he's got the balls to do something like this."

118 / Bianca D'Arc

"Having worked with Chester for a while now, I'd have to agree. He's got delusions of grandeur, but not megalomania. He wants to chair the Joint Chiefs. Power and prestige are more important to him than money. He probably wouldn't sell secrets just to get rich."

"So then who is Bev working for?" Mari looked troubled. "You think she's passing information from your office to someone from the original science team, don't you? A rogue member of the science team is the only one who could've put that poor creature in Sandra's lab last night."

Simon and Matt exchanged grim looks. Mari had put together the scenario that seemed most likely.

"So how do we find out who her contact is and how she's passing the information?" Simon asked.

"I'm not sure yet," Matt admitted. "I didn't let on that Sandra had identified the zombie as Dr. Jennings."

"Why not? You want to use Sandra as bait?" Simon's eyes narrowed. Mari looked appalled.

"I'd rather not, but I also want to preserve the possibility of doing so. No sense tipping our hand. I'd rather keep Bev guessing."

Simon shrugged. "Makes sense."

"You two are the only ones who know about what happened last night, and I want to keep it that way for the time being. You are also the only two who know about Sandy's immunity."

"We're the inner circle?" Simon sent Matt a quick grin.

"By default, but I'm glad it worked out this way. Both of you have been in on this with me since the beginning. I trust you not to let this go any further. Plus, it works out well since Mari and Sandra will be working closely together. If you're up to it, I'd like you to keep an eye on her." Matt knew what he was asking. Mari could possibly be in even more danger by sticking close to Sandra right now, and she was newly pregnant. If he'd had any other choice Matt would have taken it, but they all knew what was at stake here. This mission was too important to humanity.

Mari was up to the challenge. "I'm not much of a spy, but I don't mind keeping my eyes open."

"You know now that she's immune, so don't take any chances, Mariana. If more creatures show up, you get yourself out of there." Matt didn't like telling the other woman to leave Sandra on her own, but it was necessary. He wouldn't be far. If Mari could sound the alarm, he'd be nearby to help Sandra.

"Do you expect more late-night visits from the undead?" Simon asked.

"She's still in danger. She admitted she's been approached twice before. Dr. Rodriguez asked her to join his team. He's apparently the one behind the problems we've been having here at Bragg. He's got a lab somewhere nearby and he's been working to perfect his formula, sending out the resulting creatures one by one to *test* against our defenses."

"He told her that?" Simon's eyebrow rose in question.

"Not in so many words, but I put it together after she finally told me the truth. It makes sense. He's trying to build a zombie soldier formula. It would only be reasonable to test the resulting creatures against real soldiers—especially since we've concentrated the troops here at Fort Bragg that have faced them before. What better place to test his new creations?"

"That's sick," Mari said with disgust. Matt agreed but didn't say it out loud. What was the point? They all knew the depravity of their enemy.

"So Rodriguez is the man we're seeking," Simon mused. "Have you been able to get John Petit's take on this? His CIA contacts may have good intel."

"John and Donna are on their way to Tennessee. I got a call from him this morning."

"I thought they were in California." Simon seemed intrigued.

"They were. The lead they were following led them to Tennessee and another member of the original science team. So we're going to be shorthanded for a little longer. Si, I want you to lead the combat team as you've been doing. I'll be staying close to base in case the ladies have any problems. I want us all to gradually change our hours to more of a night shift, if possible. Perhaps you can come up with some scientific reason to work late?" He looked at Mari.

"I'm sure we can come up with something. Experiments don't know how to tell time."

Matt remembered Sandra saying something similar and was glad Mariana was on the same page.

"I don't want either of you working alone. I'd like there to always be someone with Sandra in case Rodriguez tries something else. It's clear he and his people have access to the base. Until we figure out how they're getting in, we'll have to be on our toes." Matt didn't like how many avenues of threat were in this scenario, but they'd have to deal with the problems as they came. "Si, I want you to watch the woods. Keep some patrols closer to the edges of the trees to keep an eye on our buildings, if at all possible. We've been focusing on the perimeter looking outward for threats. Let's shift that to look at threats coming both ways."

"We'll be ready." Simon nodded, his expression grimly serious.

Chapter Eight

Matt muscled through the rest of the day with difficulty, but he'd be damned if he was going to betray his fatigue to Bev. About an hour before quitting time, he sent her on an errand to the other side of the base and told her to go home from there. He waited only to make sure she was out of sight before he left his office and headed straight for his bunk. He had only a few hours before dark and he desperately needed sleep. His body was demanding it and he knew better than to push past this feeling knowing what he might have to face that night.

He had a bad feeling simmering in the back of his mind. By now, Rodriguez knew the surprise he'd left for Sandra had failed to kill her. Chances were, he'd try again. Matt had to be ready for anything. He spared only a moment to set his alarm to wake him just before sunset, and then collapsed onto his bed fully dressed. He'd change into dark BDUs when he woke. It was his turn—finally—for night work.

Matt's eyes closed and he didn't know anything more until his alarm began to chirp. He woke feeling only marginally better than he had before he'd gone unconscious but it would have to do. He stood and stretched, swapping his regular outfit for a more casual battle dress uniform—darker-colored fatigues.

One part of him couldn't believe after all this time dealing with his career-ending injury, he might actually be fit enough to return to the field. Even if his back wasn't perfect, it felt a hell of a lot better than it had just yesterday. He was in good enough shape to protect Sandra. He had to be.

Matt clipped one of the small tactical radios to his ear. He'd kept tabs on the combat team a few hours each night using the link but hadn't been part of the op, so he'd kept quiet for the most part. Tonight he'd do the same unless there was reason to do more. He hoped like hell there'd be no reason.

But shortly after sunset, as he slipped into the shadows outside his building, the miniature radio crackled to life.

"Multiple tangos in the woods." A list of grid coordinates followed in Simon's clipped tones.

Damn. The itchy feeling at the back of Matt's neck intensified. Rodriguez wasn't waiting. He was striking again before they had time to regroup—or so Rodriguez thought.

The most they'd had was one or two zombies at a time in the woods, but Simon was reporting multiple contacts. The stakes had just been raised.

Matt picked up his pace. He'd had to wait for full dark in order to escape his building without being seen. As a result, he was behind schedule in getting into position to keep an eye on Mari and Sandra. The two women should both be in Sandra's lab, working together.

He hadn't been pleased with the idea of them working in the lab. It had been breached once before, after all. But Sandra's building was the easiest for him to watch without being seen. Mari's lab in the hospital would have been too exposed. This building was near the outskirts of the base and was mostly empty except for a few day-shift projects. The personnel who worked in those offices were long gone by now.

Matt listened intently as the combat troops faced more than a dozen of the creatures. They had their hands full and Matt was tempted to go help them, but the odds that the attack was another diversion kept him silent and on mission. Matt double-timed it to Sandra's building, a shadow among shadows. He felt so alive in the night—active in a way he hadn't been able to enjoy in far too long. He'd almost forgotten the feeling. If the circumstances hadn't been so dire, he would have rejoiced in his returning ability to really make a difference in the field.

As it was, he was just grateful he could be an ace in the hole, should they need it.

Checking his ammo, Matt entered the building through a side door. He was armed with both conventional weapons and ammunition and the special toxic darts and pistol that would deliver the deadly dose to any zombified creatures he might come across. He was as prepared as he could be as he made his way down a side stairwell to the lab area on the lower floor.

He heard raised voices as he headed down the darkened hall. Moving silently and swiftly, Matt checked the hall as he went. The only activity appeared to be in the lab itself. He could see a large man through the open door, standing menacingly over Sandra. She faced the man defiantly, a flask of some kind of colorless liquid brandished toward the man in her outstretched hand.

"Stay back, you creep!" Sandra yelled at the man. The guy's back was to the open doorway and Matt caught Sandra's eye as he stepped through. Thankfully, she didn't give away his presence.

"Put down the acid, doctor. Make this easy on yourself. If you struggle, I'll only hurt you more in the end. Either way, you're coming with me."

"Fat chance." She sneered at the man, but Matt could hear the adrenaline laced fear in her voice.

Matt advanced. He caught sight of Mariana. She was slumped in a corner, blood dripping down her head. She looked unconscious—or worse. It was time to act.

Seeing no other assailants in the room, Matt sprang at the guy's back, knocking him cold in one fell swoop. He was out of the action and down for the count, but Matt took no chances. He secured the man's hands and feet with heavy-duty cable ties he kept in one cargo pocket.

"Were there any more or just this one?" he demanded quietly as Sandra put the beaker back on the lab table.

"Just him," she confirmed. "He bashed Mari on the head." Sandra knelt at the other woman's side, checking her pupils with a penlight as Mari tried groggily to push her hand away. "Bastard snuck up on her like you did to him. Poetic justice, I'd say."

"Can she be moved?" Matt kept watch on the hallway. It was the only way in or out of the lab. He dragged the bound man out of sight of the doorway and deposited him behind a lab bench.

"Yeah. In fact, she's coming around." Matt looked over in time to see Sandra tuck her penlight into her lab coat pocket as Mariana held one hand to her temple. "Easy, Mari. You got bonked on the head."

"By what?"

"Not what. Who." Sandra pointed toward the unconscious man on the floor a few feet away. "Matt bonked him back for you."

Mariana squinted at him. "Thanks, Commander. I owe you one."

"No problem, doctor. How do you feel?"

"Terrible," she replied, trying to push to her feet. Sandra helped support her as she stood while Matt continued to keep watch. "Who the heck is he?"

"He's the goon who works for Dr. Rodriguez," Sandra said grimly. She looked directly at Matt. "He was driving the car that ran me down on the road, and he was the guy you saw in the cafeteria that day."

"What did he want?" Mariana looked from Matt to Sandra and back again.

"He wanted me to go with him," Sandra replied. Matt could hear the anger in her voice.

"Kidnapping? Why?" Mari seemed confused, her motions slowed by the obvious pain in her head.

"To bring me to Rodriguez so he could try to force me to

work with him. He's attempting to improve the contagion. He's approached me before, but I've refused." Sandra sounded grim. "No doubt Rodriguez sent the creature last night and now this guy."

"So he wants you dead? Or does he want you working with him?" Mariana sought Matt's gaze, her confusion evident.

"One or the other, it looks like," Matt confirmed. "Look, all hell is breaking loose in the woods. I can't call anyone in. As long as Mariana's okay, I think we should make our stand here for now. Until Simon can get free."

He had the radio and was listening to the action still taking place in the forest that surrounded the base. He wouldn't inform Simon that Mari had been hurt. Not yet. Matt had the situation under control, and Simon was in the thick of things.

One look at Mariana and Matt knew she understood. "Don't distract him. I'm okay. I'll be fine until he's out of the danger zone."

"I appreciate your courage, doctor. As long as Sandra concurs with your diagnosis, I'm inclined to say we've got this situation under control here for now. I'm monitoring what's going on in the woods." He tapped the small receiver in his ear. "They've got their hands full. I know better than to break Si's concentration right now."

Mari looked relieved as Sandra supported her. Matt met Sandy's eyes, and a moment of silent communication passed between them.

"I'll help her into the other room where she can lay down. I've got some monitors we can hook up to keep an eye on her condition, but she looks good. I don't anticipate any major problems." Sandra smiled at Mari encouragingly and they moved slowly toward the small back room.

Matt cursed the fact that Mariana had been injured. Simon would no doubt have a fit when he heard what had happened, and Matt mentally kicked himself for not arriving sooner. Simon had trusted him to look after the women, and he'd almost been too late. Matt was rusty, but he would never forgive himself if anything happened to Mariana or Sandra while he was around. He'd been sloppy. He wouldn't let it happen again.

After tonight, things were going to change. Drastically.

Matt secured the prisoner in a corner of the room, fastening him to an old metal radiator. He wouldn't be going anywhere soon. The man was still unconscious and Matt wanted to keep him that way until dawn at least.

"You got anything to keep this guy asleep until sunrise?" Matt asked Sandra when she emerged from the back room a few minutes later.

She rubbed her neck as she came toward him, looking skeptically at the guy on the floor. "I shouldn't sedate anyone with a head injury."

"I didn't hit him that hard. Plus, he was trying to kidnap you. Or kill you. I'd lay odds he's the one dropped Jennings here last night."

Her jaw clenched. "You're right. He shot out my tire, too." She turned resolutely toward a lab bench. A few minutes later, she returned with a filled syringe. She examined the man briefly, even going over his eyes with a penlight before efficiently administering the shot to the unconscious man. "That should hold him for a few hours."

"Good. Now come here." He shouldn't give in to the impulse, but he had to put his arms around her and feel her against him. He had to know on some basic, physical level that she was truly safe.

Her head tipped to the side in question as she walked toward him. She seemed perplexed when he pulled her into his arms and tugged her against his chest, but she didn't object or try to pull away.

"What's this about?" She rested her cheek against his beating heart.

"Don't ask. I'm not even sure myself." He held her for a long moment, soaking in the feel of her in his arms. She was safe. She was with him. All was right with the world.

For now.

Damn, she felt good in his arms.

"I'm sorry I was late. Si's gonna have my ass for letting Mari take a hit."

"She's okay. I wouldn't leave her alone if I thought otherwise, even for a minute." Matt liked the way Sandra's hands smoothed over his shirt in an absent caress.

"But she's pregnant." To him that made all the difference.

"True, but she's not disabled by it." She made a scoffing sound. "We females are much more resilient than you men give us credit for."

"Hey, I didn't mean to bring up the whole war of the sexes." Matt did his best not to laugh too hard. "I can only tell you what Simon's going to say. He's going to read me the riot act—commanding officer or not. And I don't blame him. Damn." He was mad at himself for not being there sooner or figuring a way to prevent what had happened to Mariana.

"Don't worry. I'll protect you." She reached up and stroked his cheek with one hand. Their eyes met, and the moment stretched as humor turned to something far more intimate.

He wasn't sure who moved first, but a moment later, their lips met in a kiss fiercer than they'd shared previously. Lips and tongues met and held, dueling and daring, inflaming and heightening the pleasure that burst between them. An explosion of need fired his gut as he held her, drawing her tighter against his body.

Her softness was the perfect foil for his need. She matched him so well, as if she'd been made specifically to fit into his arms. Her ardor matched his, and for a moment he was tempted to forget all about his duty, the danger, and the others who needed him to be on guard. He wanted nothing more than to take her to the floor and claim her as his own.

But sanity prevailed. Matt did his best to tamp down his need, denying the passion that threatened to break free as he tried to rein it in. He pulled back little by little, moment by moment.

Sandra's lips followed his as he tried to end their kiss. For a moment, he gave in to temptation and prolonged the kiss, enjoying her uninhibited response. Would she be as eager when he was inside her, on top of her, riding her to ecstasy? He thought the answer to that question would probably blow his mind.

Now was neither the time nor place. Mariana needed them. Simon was counting on him to keep the women safe. He'd already almost botched the job. He wouldn't let anything else happen. Not on his watch.

Gathering his willpower, Matt drew away from Sandra, holding her by the shoulders.

"Whoa there, doc. We've still got a job to do."

Sandra's eyes looked adorably sleepy when he gazed down into her face. It took her a moment to snap out of it and come to her senses, which only pleased him more. She'd been as affected as him—maybe even more so, if that were possible. Only his deeply embedded sense of duty had awakened him from the fog of desire that had enveloped them the moment he'd taken her into his arms.

"Wow."

The breathy exclamation did a lot to inflate Matt's ego, but her next words cut him right back down to size.

"Dammit, Matt. Don't do that." She wrestled out of his arms and he let her go, confused by her reaction.

"Sorry," he said reflexively. He really didn't know what he had to be sorry about. She'd enjoyed the kiss as much as he had. That much had been evident.

She waved his words away, bustling back toward the room where she'd left Mariana. "We're staying here for now, right?"

Matt nodded in response, watching her confusion with dawning appreciation. He'd knocked her off her axis with that kiss, and she apparently didn't like it. With an inward grin, he thought with some satisfaction that she'd better get used to it. Regardless of what happened with their shared mission, now that he'd had a taste of her, he wasn't going to stop. He'd have her, again and again, God willing, before this situation was resolved.

He'd better hope things rolled in her favor. He wasn't sure

what he'd do if she turned out to be one of the many villains in this piece. He was too attracted to her for his own good, and he feared he wasn't completely in control of his feelings. He could very well fall in love with her, and what happened then would be anyone's guess.

He resolved there and then to hang on for the ride. Where the roller coaster would land them only heaven knew, but he'd joined his fate to hers—whether she realized it or not—and now they both had to live with the consequences.

Just like that, his life had changed. Whether for good or ill remained to be seen.

Matt remained in the lab while Sandra sought the quiet of the back room. Damn, that man could kiss. He'd just confounded her plan to stay away from him and deny the temptation he represented. She'd wanted more. More kisses. More touches. More skin.

She'd wanted him. For keeps.

A scary thought for a woman who had always prided herself on her independence.

"Everything all right out there?" Mariana asked with knowing eyes.

Double damn. She'd probably seen what Sandra and Matt had been up to. The amused gleam in Mariana's eyes was a dead giveaway.

"Matt's securing the lab. He says we'll stay here for now." Sandra pretended not to notice Mari's amusement. "How are you feeling?"

"I'm okay." Mari put one hand to her temple gingerly. "I never really lost consciousness. I was just stunned. I'm sorry, Sandra. The guy totally snuck up on me."

"Don't be sorry. It's not your fault. If anyone is sorry, it's me for putting you in this situation to begin with. That jerk came for me, not you. So I'm the one who should be apologizing. I'm so sorry."

"Let's call it even," Mari said. "What happened to him? The bad guy, I mean?"

"Matt zip-tied him to the radiator and I gave him a sedative. He'll be out until morning at least."

"I know. I know." Sandra held up her hands in surrender when Mari seemed upset. "But I checked his responses thoroughly before I did it. He seemed fine. Matt said some things that made a lot of sense to me at the time." Her conscience was getting the better of her until she remembered why that scumball had been in her lab to begin with. "In fact, they still make sense. That guy would have killed either one of us and never blinked an eye."

"You said something about him leaving zombie Jennings here last night. You really think he did that?"

"It makes sense. The guy seems to be able to come and go as he pleases on base. He's threatened me twice before." Sandra tried to shrug off the memories of violence that surrounded the man who now lay trussed up in her laboratory. She had to focus on Mariana and make sure the other woman didn't suffer anything more than a bruise from this night's adventure. "How's the head? Any vision issues?"

Sandra spent the next half hour giving Mariana a thorough checkup. Thankfully, neither Mariana nor her baby seemed to be any worse for wear, although Mari would have a little bruise on her head for a day or two.

"You think the commander would let us continue working?" Mariana asked a little while later. "I really would like to finish isolating the protein sequence I was working on. The sample won't last much longer and I'd hate to have to start over."

"We can ask." Sandra wanted something to do as well. Sitting around doing nothing wasn't exactly her favorite pastime.

"You go ask him while I freshen up." Mariana headed for the attached bathroom, leaving Sandra no choice but to face Matt alone. She wasn't sure she wanted to see him after the way she'd pretty much lost control the last time they'd been alone.

There was nothing for it. She had to face him at some point. Gathering her courage and putting on her best poker face, Sandra entered the lab, looking for Matt. She finally caught sight of him in the shadows by the door. He had a clear line of sight on the prisoner, who was still unconscious. He also had a good defensible position by the only entrance to the room.

The reinforced steel door was shut tight and locked. It would take a lot of force to get through it. Too bad Sandra and Mariana had been blindsided as they entered. If they'd had time to get into the lab and lock the door behind them, they'd have been relatively safe.

"Mari and I were wondering if we could do some work," she said tentatively. Damn. She had to find her backbone.

"Should be safe enough." Matt shrugged. "Can you keep away from that side of the lab or should I move our guest?" He gestured toward the unconscious man.

"You can leave him. We were going to work on the equipment over there against the other wall."

Matt nodded, silently observing her. She felt like a bug under a microscope and she didn't like it. Sandra straightened her lab coat and turned on her heel. The man was unnerving when he looked at her like that.

Sandra did her best to ignore him for the next few hours while she and Mariana worked. From time to time she'd look up to find him watching her. At other times he seemed to be concentrating on the earpiece through which he kept tabs on the team in the field.

She hadn't meant to spend the entire night in the lab, but after the renewed attack it was clear they weren't going anywhere before sunrise. Mari gave Sandra first dibs on the cot in the back room so she could grab a couple hours of sleep, then they traded off. Matt positioned himself on a stool by the door to the lab and didn't budge. She thought maybe he napped sitting there from time to time, but he was definitely on watch. If anything or anyone tried to get through that door, she had no doubt he'd be awake and sharp within seconds.

She'd heard of the training many soldiers—especially those involved in special operations—underwent. Part of that was the ability to take combat naps whenever and wherever possible in order to keep themselves going for long periods on very little sleep. But Sandra was still worried about him. He'd been through a major physical ordeal the night before. She hadn't seen him all day. She hoped he'd found some time to sleep, but he certainly didn't look much worse for wear.

Keeping her worries about him to herself was hard, but she managed it until just before dawn. Mariana had retreated to the back room again and the prisoner was still unconscious, so it was just Sandra and Matt.

"How are things going?" she ventured.

"The combat team is starting to get a handle on the situation in the woods. Things should be quieting down anyway once the sun starts to rise."

He sounded alert but she still worried.

"That's good. How are you feeling?" She decided to just come out and ask. "Did you get enough rest?"

"I left work early yesterday afternoon and caught a couple hours of deep sleep, which I've supplemented a bit." He shrugged off his skillful use of napping. "I'm good. How are you and Mariana holding up?"

"She's fine. I'm a little tired, but it's not a big deal. I've pulled all-nighters in the lab before."

He eyed her strangely for a moment, but she had no idea how to read his expression. He was closed to her when before he'd always been open. Her deception had done that and she didn't like it at all. She'd give anything to go back to the easy relationship they'd shared before.

"I'd like to have you both out of here shortly after dawn. Simon will come for Mariana as long as you're sure she doesn't need further monitoring."

"She's good to go," Sandra reassured him.

"Get your stuff together. I want everything ready to go when Simon and the others get here."

She didn't like his ominous tone but didn't have time to question him as Mari came out of the back room, yawning. She moved to the lab bench to check the end stages of the protein incubation they'd been working on most of the night and Sandra joined her.

Dawn broke, though they couldn't see it, below ground as they were. A few minutes later Simon and two others from the combat team showed up. She recognized Sam Archer and the younger man she hadn't interacted as much with. His name was Kauffman, she recalled. Matt intercepted Archer and Kauffman and held a low-voiced conversation with them as he led them to the prisoner.

The two soldiers picked the still unconscious man up by the shoulders and feet and took him out of the room quicker than she could blink. She assumed they'd take care of him until he woke and Matt was ready to question him.

Meanwhile, Simon looked as if he'd been running hard all night as he came closer. He folded Mariana in his arms after being certain she was all right. Sandra had to turn away from the raw emotion on the man's face. It was clear he desperately loved his fiancée. The short glimpse she'd gotten of his expression was enough to make her heart break.

He could have lost her last night, and it would have been Sandra's fault. Yet another layer of guilt to pile on her back. At some point Sandra imagined herself collapsing under the weight of the guilt she carried, but she couldn't let that happen yet. Not until she'd righted at least some of the wrongs she'd committed.

When she looked back again, Mari and Simon were on their way out the door without a backward glance. They were too wrapped up in each other. Sandra envied them that.

"Are you ready?" Matt was at her side. He'd snuck up on her.

"Yeah." She switched off the last of the surge suppressors that supplied power to some of the equipment they'd been using. "Let me just take off my lab coat." She did so and hung it on a peg near the door.

"Get your jacket."

"My jacket?" She turned to face him, confused. "It's upstairs in my room."

"All right." He opened the door, checking the hall before he let her step through. She locked the lab door behind her and moved into the corridor. "We'll stop upstairs for a minute so you can get some of your things." He ushered her into the main stairwell after another quick check to make certain it was safe.

"Why? Where am I going?"

"You're coming with me. In fact, you're staying with me until further notice."

The finality and conviction in his deep voice sent a shiver down her spine. A delicious shiver. It was ridiculous. When she should be quaking in fear, instead she was trembling with desire. Here he was going all caveman on her, and she was actually turned on by it. She amazed herself with her own response to Matt. Then again, she knew if any other man on earth had tried something like this, she would've had quite the opposite reaction.

"Where? Do you live on base?"

"I'm renting a small place just outside the west gate. It's defensible and set back from the road. Since I've been here, I've secured the property with some other bells and whistles that will come in handy now to help keep you safe."

"There's not much outside the west gate. Isn't it mostly woods in that direction?"

They'd arrived at the door to her quarters and he took the key from her, checking the place quickly before he'd let her inside.

"Now that we're both immune, I'm not overly concerned about what might be lurking in the woods. In fact, we might be of some help to the combat team logistically." He motioned toward one of her smaller suitcases. "Pack the essentials for tonight. We can come back for more of your stuff later if necessary."

"You know, I'm not really sure about this."

He turned to her, stepping into her personal space. "I am. You're with me for the duration, Sandy. For better or worse."

"That sounds serious."

"I'm dead serious." His voice dipped low as his arms came around her. "Get used to it."

"Uh . . . Matt . . ."

"You confound me, Sandra. I don't want to want you like this. I don't want to need you . . . but I do."

His words stabbed her through the heart, but she understood what he meant. For her own reasons, she didn't want this need, this insatiable desire. Yet she was powerless against it.

She didn't know what she would have said. Matt didn't give her a chance to speak. His mouth claimed hers in a brutal taking that inspired a primitive need of her own. She clawed at his shoulders not to push him away, but to draw him closer. The dark T-shirt under her hands only got in her way. She wanted it gone.

Pulling upward on the stretchy fabric, she got it free of his waistband, but the tactical vest he wore was a problem. He seemed to realize it about the same time she did. The vest, which he'd opened at some point, slid off his shoulders and then the T-shirt was ripped out of her hands and over his head in record time.

His lips recaptured hers before she could even blink. And then his hands went to the buttons on her shirt. Thick male fingers were amazingly agile as they worked their way down her chest, releasing little buttons with expert flicks. The shirt was swept down her shoulders in one slick move that trapped her arms behind her back as he pulled her against him.

The thin barrier of her lacy white bra was too much. She wanted that gone, too, but he seemed to enjoy the sensation of the lace rasping against his bare chest. He pressed against her, rubbing and igniting a fire in her that wouldn't be quenched easily. All the while, he kissed her. The desperate need of the first moments had gentled into a seduction of the senses that threatened to overwhelm her.

She wanted to touch him, but her arms were loosely imprisoned in the sleeves of her cotton shirt. She was at his mercy, and she liked the feeling, much to her surprise.

His big hands pushed the straps of her bra down her shoulders with slow, agonizing intent. Then his fingers went to the rear catch of the garment, unhooking it with deft skill. A moment later, cool air wafted across her sensitive skin as the bra fell away, tangling in the mess of fabric to drape across her abdomen. She barely noticed the way he'd trussed her up, unable to move her hands but naked to his gaze from the waist up.

Damn. She hadn't known she would like being tied up. If anyone had ever propositioned her with such a thing she would have laughed in their face, but here she was, bound and at the mercy of a dangerous man. It was delicious in a forbidden way that set her senses on fire.

Matt broke the kiss but didn't give her time to do more than gasp for air as his lips swept down her neck, placing biting, nibbling kisses over her skin. Pleasurable shivers raced down her spine as he worked his way downward.

When his mouth closed over one nipple she moaned. There was no hesitation in him, no uncertainty. This man knew what he wanted and didn't let anything stand in his way. He was confident in his ability to please her as he pleased himself. Sandra didn't think there was anything sexier than a man who knew what he wanted, and that his partner wanted it, too. He didn't have to ask. He didn't have to test her response with tentative touches. He knew just what she wanted and gave it to her.

His mouth tortured and teased, leaving her wanting more as he drew away, but it was only a tease. He latched on to her other breast, nibbling gently and making her moan as his fingers toyed with the nipple he'd left wet and wanting.

She squirmed in his arms, needing to touch him.

"Matt," she panted his name as he sucked in rhythm.

The sound seemed to stir him to action as he walked her backward toward the small bed on the far side of the room. The backs of her legs hit the bed a moment before she felt the world spin out from under her as Matt lifted her right off her feet and swung her onto the mattress. He came down over her, barely giving her a chance to recover.

"My arms," she whispered, wanting to touch him.

He didn't reply, but rolled her onto her side and freed her of the cloth that bound her loosely.

Finally. She could touch him. She reached out for him, but was denied as his fingers interlaced with hers and pressed her hands to either side of her head, backs against the mattress. She moaned and wiggled under his weight while his lips captured hers once more and his bare chest rubbed tantalizingly against her excited nipples. He was driving her crazy.

His lips left hers for another exploration of her neck, shoulders, and finally, her breasts. This time he moved more slowly, taking his time and lingering over sensitive places.

She gasped as he licked her skin, driving her into a frenzy of need. He let go of her hands and unfastened the button and zipper on her pants, pushing them downward as she wriggled to help. Her hands were free but she barely noticed, so intense were the feelings he drew from her body.

Her white lace panties followed, and Matt wasted no time pushing her thighs apart, settling between them. One big hand covered her mound, insinuating his long fingers between and into her folds. She sighed and squirmed as he did as he pleased—and pleased her at the same time.

When had he learned exactly how to touch her? How did he know what she needed even before she did?

His fingers moved, sliding inward, and she gasped in shocked pleasure. There was nothing hesitant about him, which made her even hotter. No man she'd been with before had been so commanding or sure of himself.

"Matt." She panted as he began a thrusting rhythm with his fingers. "Please."

"Oh, I like the sound of that." His amused tone made her eyes snap open.

Sure enough he was smiling at her, and that grin held all kinds of male satisfaction. She couldn't hold it against him. Not when he was making her body hum so very nicely.

He stroked her into a frenzy, holding her gaze as his fingers pleasured her body.

"You're mine, Sandra." The possessive look in his eyes made her blood boil with passion.

"No." She didn't know why she was arguing. He was clearly in control and she really didn't mind. Her head twisted from side to side as pleasure rose like an unstoppable tide, overwhelming her.

"Yes," he answered calmly, daring her to argue further. All the while, his fingers continued to torment her body, stroking deep and touching that magic spot within that begged for more even as it sent her spinning higher. "Do you want to come, Sandra?"

"Yes!" The answer was torn from her lips as he began a new, harsher rhythm. She loved everything he did and wanted more.

"That's the word I like to hear." He bent low over her body, whispering in her ear as he covered her body with his. "Come, sweetheart. Come for me right now."

She needed no further urging. It was as if she'd only waited for his permission to go off like a rocket, spasming in his arms as his fingers played her body like a fine instrument.

The pleasure was intense, the moment intimate and nearly infinite as passion tore through her straining body. Matt held her through it all, coaxing every last ounce of response out of her with his skilled hands. Her breath came in heaving gasps and her muscles strained against the tension of the moment. She could feel Matt's eyes on her through it all, but she couldn't focus on much other than the power of her climax.

She shook in his arms until the storm passed. Only then did she notice he'd stilled. Her eyes opened and he stared down at her, his expression unreadable. A muscle ticked in his jaw and his eyes narrowed as if he wanted to say something, but the moment passed.

He removed his hands and lifted away from her.

"We have to go. We've already stayed here too long as it is." He got off the bed and retrieved her clothes, dropping them beside her.

"But what about you?" Her mind spun. Was he really going

to just end it there? He was nearly trembling with his own un-fulfilled need.

"Don't worry. I'll get mine later." He sent her a tight, sexy grin that promised even more pleasure. "I've got to go to the office today. Before that, I want to get you settled in my place. You need to sleep late. You're going on night duty tonight. Consider yourself on the graveyard shift from now on. During the day I want you sequestered at my house. If I'm not with you, you don't go out. Understand?"

It sounded extreme to her, but then she'd almost been kid-napped and targeted for a gruesome death. Perhaps he had a point. She certainly felt safe when she was with him, even if he was being a bit high-handed in this instance. After the orgasm he'd just delivered, she'd cut him some slack, but one thing gave her pause.

"When are you going to sleep?"

"Don't worry. I'm going to leave early from the office today. We'll work out the rest later."

He seemed so certain of success, she couldn't work up much energy to wonder about exactly how he'd work his schedule to accommodate the changes. Then again, her lethargy could be caused by the boneless feeling he'd induced in her body.

She dressed mechanically, her energy sapped. A warm glow had settled in the pit of her stomach and spread outward. The extremes of the night were catching up with her. Bed and a soft pillow were sounding really good at the moment, and she didn't want to waste time arguing with him about nitpicky specifics. The sooner they got to his place—and the bed that no doubt would be awaiting her there—the better. They'd sort out all the other details later.

Chapter Nine

Matt's house wasn't what she'd expected. It was a rental, so she supposed she shouldn't put too much emphasis on the neatly manicured lawn and tidy garden outside or the well-maintained furnishings inside. The knickknacks and photos arranged along the mantel were definitely Matt's personal touches so those were fair game, as was the array of magazines and books strewn around the coffee table—the only sign of disorder she'd seen so far.

The kitchen gleamed. The small dining room looked neat and orderly through the open arch as they walked by, heading down a short hall and passing a door he said hid a closet. Then they arrived at the bedroom. He opened the door to what she assumed would be a guest room only to be confronted with what was beyond doubt Matt's personal space. His bedroom.

Clothes spilled out of a hamper in one corner and a stray sock lay on the floor. Other than that little detail, it was basically clean. It was also definitely a man's space.

Hunter green bedding lay neatly folded back on a king-size bed that ate up much of the space in the small room. Matt was a big guy. No doubt he needed the space. Especially if he often had overnight guests.

A surprising jolt of jealousy fired down her spine, firming it as she turned to him just inside the open doorway.

"You expect me to sleep here?"

"What's wrong with it?" His words and posture turned challenging as he shifted his weight to one side and leaned against the door frame, folding his arms over his chest.

"It's your room." Her objection should be obvious, only it didn't feel right after what she'd allowed him to do to her only minutes before in her room on base.

Still, a woman didn't just give in without some concession on the male's part. Did she? Sandra had never been good at these male-female mating games.

"That it is." He straightened, unfolding his arms and ambling toward her in a slow, deliberate stride that made her back up. He looked like a panther stalking its next kill. Sandra's mouth went dry realizing she'd just put herself on the menu for this highly skilled predator.

"Don't you have a guest room?"

"I do but you can't sleep there." He seemed a little too smug for her comfort.

"Why not?"

"I'll show you." He pivoted on his heel and headed into the hall. She followed, curious.

He went to the only other door in the short hall. It had a complicated looking numerical lock on the doorknob. He entered a code, and the reinforced door unlatched audibly. He opened the door and motioned her closer.

"This is the safe room. It's the reason I rented this house in particular. The owner had made a good start on it and let me modify to my personal specifications. The walls are nearly impenetrable and fireproof. No windows. Reinforced steel door." He ticked off the features as he walked into the room. She followed behind, taking a good look around. "There's a trapdoor that leads out under the house if you really need to get out. And as you can see, I've got computer uplinks and monitors on the property that you can watch from here. If they cut power, there are battery backups built in below the bench top." He lifted one hinged lid that doubled as the surface of a table-height bench, revealing a complex system of wiring and big square blocks that had to be some kind of batteries.

"Impressive." She was surprised he had all this. "You were expecting a siege, or do you live like this all the time?"

Matt laughed. "I like to be prepared but I'll admit I normally don't go this far. When I got reassigned here, I figured I'd better prepare for any contingency. This house already had the safe room, I just improved it a bit."

"And put monitors all around the property." She was guessing, but the sparkle in his eyes told her she was right.

"I like electronics."

"I can see that." She gazed appreciatively around the room as they headed for the door.

He spent a few minutes showing her the use and function of a few of the computers and monitors in the room. It looked pretty straightforward, though the setup was truly space age with a satellite uplink he could use if he needed it for some reason.

"I hooked up some additional night vision cameras in the trees at the perimeter of the property and about fifty yards into the woods. Zombies don't really show up on infrared, so night vision is about as good as it gets to spot them if we end up out here at night. Ideally, I'd like to have you working on base at night, but not if we can't secure the place. Which reminds me, I've still got to question the guy who attacked you. I'm going to see if he's awake yet before I go to the office, so I'd better get a move on."

"What about sleep?"

"I'll sleep when I'm dead."

"Matt." She didn't appreciate his grim humor.

He spared her a small grin. "I'll be okay. I'm going to rearrange schedules today and knock off work early to start the new shifts. It'll work. Trust me."

She did trust him but still worried about him. She followed as he walked back to the door.

"I keep this locked when I'm not here. We'll leave it open when you're in the house. If you need to get in and the door is locked, input your social security number and a seven."

"That's your combination?" She was surprised.

"No. It's your combination. I keyed the electronic lock to let you in on that number since I figured it was a sequence you'd already have memorized. This lock allows up to three different combinations to be added. I use a different sequence." He shrugged. "Same result."

He was thorough. She'd give him that.

"I'm going to grab a shower and change. We can scrounge up some breakfast before I go to the office." He talked as he moved down the hall, heading for his bedroom. She followed at a slower pace. She arrived at the door to find him stripping off his shirt and was powerless to do anything but stare at his near perfect physique.

She'd seen him without his shirt before, but never from this distance. Getting a look at the whole picture, so to speak, made her mouth go dry. He was gorgeous. Fit and muscular without being bulky. He was the epitome of what she'd always thought a physically fit man should look like.

"Oh, darlin', looking at me like that could get you in all kinds of trouble." His sexy, low voice sent a shiver down her spine and sent her gaze winging upward to meet his. "Come here."

Her belly clenched at the command and she was powerless to resist. If asked, she would have said she didn't have a submissive bone in her body, but Matt had a way of turning all her previous perceptions upside down. Almost everything he did made her want him more. Especially after their little interlude in her quarters.

She walked toward him and his arms opened. She stepped into them, feeling welcomed by his warmth, her senses awakened by the sensation of his bare skin against her.

His head dipped and his mouth covered hers. This time, his kiss was gentle, almost exploratory. His hands cupped her breasts and squeezed gently, proclaiming a new kind of ownership that made her sizzle with awareness. Matt had a way of eliciting unexpected responses from her that continued to amaze her.

When she'd expected more of the fierce lover he'd shown before, he instead gave her a gentle caress that was equally as stirring. Perhaps even more so. He kept her guessing all the while inflaming her passion as no man ever had before. He was definitely unique in her admittedly limited experience. Matt was one of a kind.

"We don't have time for this." His lips broke away from hers with obvious reluctance. She tried to follow, wanting more kisses, but he gently drew away, his head lifting too high for her to reach easily. "I'm sorry, sweetheart."

"Not even for a quickie?" She couldn't believe she'd blurted out the scandalous thought running through her mind. She blushed, but he wouldn't let her go when she tried to escape the fire that leaped in his gaze.

"When I make love to you, I want to have time to do it right, Sandy." The promise in his eyes made her mouth go dry in anticipation. She'd just bet he knew the exact way to do her right.

"When?" She'd meant to poke fun at his confidence in his ability to claim her. Instead it came out sounding like a plea. Her blush deepened.

"I'm glad to know you're as eager as I am." His wide grin teased her.

"I meant—"

"I know what you meant, darlin'." He cut her off, reassuring at the same time. "I know from your personnel file that you're not the kind of woman to hop in bed with just anyone. Which makes me either very flattered or very stupid, yet I don't get the impression that you're trying to play me." He drew closer as his voice deepened. "Tell me you're as lost to this obsession as I am and I'll believe it, even though I probably shouldn't."

His head dipped once more, daring her to reach up and take what she wanted.

"Damn you, Matt." She stood on tiptoe and matched her lips to his as she wound her arms around his neck.

This kiss was more tempestuous—something neither of them could control or deny. Her temperature rose another notch, but when she was about ready to explode with the need to take things further, faster, he pulled away and put space between them.

She had the satisfaction of seeing that he was breathing as hard as she was. The obvious and tantalizing bulge behind his zipper made it clear he'd been aroused, too. Only he'd had enough sanity left to pull away before they went any further. Damn him.

"Much as I hate to say it, we really don't have the time right now."

"What's so all-fired important at your office?" She plopped down on his bed feeling a little abused and mildly annoyed.

Matt sighed heavily but kept his distance. "There are things going on in that office that you probably aren't aware of—the least of which is that certain elements in the chain of command would happily replace me in a heartbeat."

"Are you serious?" She'd had no idea.

"Unfortunately, yes." He sighed again.

"I find that hard to believe. You're obviously the best man for this job, Matt. Even I can see that."

The unexpected vote of confidence from Sandra made something inside Matt swell with pride. She was either a really good actress or she truly believed what she'd said. He was betting on the latter.

Maybe he was wrong to lead with his heart, Matt wasn't sure. He'd tried like hell to keep his eyes open and his barriers up, but Sandra was a law unto herself, worming her way into his head and his heart in ways he'd never experienced before and knew he never would again. This woman was special.

She might yet turn out to be a traitor, but he'd placed his bets already and prayed to lady luck and whatever other deities who might be listening that she was on the up and up. Her willingness to help him catch the traitors was working in her favor. He only hoped it was genuine and that she didn't play him false.

"I'm glad you think I'm qualified for the task, doc. There are others who'd prefer their own man in my seat. So far they've been outnumbered. I need to keep it that way."

"Yes, you do." Sandra brushed her hands on her thighs as she got up and headed for the door. "Take your shower. I'll see what I can find for breakfast in your cupboards. It'll be ready when you get out though I can't promise much more than cereal, if you have any. I'm not much of a cook."

"Cereal's fine and I've got plenty of it. Top shelf in the second cabinet from the left." He watched her go with a warm sensation in the region of his heart. She was trying to take care of him. He recognized the behavior, though it was new to him. The last person to try had been his mother, before she died.

He'd loved his mom, and when she'd died when he was seventeen he'd done his best to retreat from the world. He'd joined the army a year later and had only been back home for short visits since. The old homestead just wasn't the same without his mother's warm, loving presence.

Matt hadn't had a real home or a woman to take care of his little creature comforts since then. He hadn't wanted it or sought it, but for the first time he was beginning to think in those terms about Sandra.

Could it be? Could he possibly settle down and recreate that atmosphere of home with a wife, and could that wife possibly turn out to be Sandra?

The thought shocked him. It also felt all too comfortable. Perhaps his subconscious had been trekking down that road for a while now and he was only just realizing it. He knew he'd had a different feeling about Sandra from the very beginning, he just didn't realize until now what it was. He'd recognized her as a woman he could love.

That didn't mean he was ready to trust her with his heart just yet. There were still a few questions that had to be answered about her loyalties and intentions. And he didn't know if he *could* settle down.

He'd lived a lot of his life alone with only his brothers in arms for companionship. He wasn't sure he could change or that he'd even be given time to try to change. This mission was too important, too dangerous. He could easily die here at Bragg—or anywhere he ended up fighting this damned contagion. He'd made a vow to stop the zombie problem or die trying.

Matt shrugged off the rest of his clothing and headed for the shower. He wouldn't get any closer to his goal of ending the zombie menace by dicking around in his bedroom while there was plenty of work to be done. He had to get a move on.

Ten minutes later, he was dressed in a fresh uniform and had tidied up a bit in his bedroom, making room for Sandra, should she decide to unpack her little bag and put her clothes away. He'd let her decide, but give her room to do so if she chose to. He wouldn't say anything. He'd wait and see. Her actions would be his guide. If she chose to move in, so to speak, he'd take it as a good sign that she was willing to commit to at least that much.

Baby steps. He'd take what he could get because he didn't know exactly what he was hoping for. Did he want her to fall in love with him and commit to him completely? He wasn't sure. He was in wait-and-see mode, but one thing he wouldn't wait any longer for—*couldn't* wait, if truth be known—was making love to her.

He had big plans for later this afternoon. She'd better be ready because no matter what, he planned to have her before night fell again. All the other questions could wait. His desire for her wouldn't be denied any longer.

They shared a quick breakfast of cereal and canned fruit Sandra had found in one of the kitchen cabinets. Then, with a final round of instructions for Sandra and a warning to stay indoors at all times, Matt left. Sandra was yawning pretty good as they finished eating, so he figured she'd be fast asleep a good portion of the day. That ought to keep her out of trouble, but just in case, he set his own version of a nannycam to record her movements within the public portions of the house during the day. He could monitor her over his encrypted Internet connection and she'd never know.

He felt only a small twinge of guilt over spying on her. He rationalized that it was for her protection as well as to reassure himself that she was telling him the truth about where her loyalties lay.

Matt used his personal phone tuned to the protected Internet site that carried the signal from his house and monitored it periodically over the next few hours. From what he could see, Sandra cleaned the small mess they'd made in the kitchen that morning and then sequestered herself in the bedroom. Since he didn't have a camera in there, he could only assume she'd gone to sleep. He did have audio pickups, which recorded only the rustling of cloth and a couple of cute, feminine yawns.

She didn't emerge from the bedroom until six hours later. Even through the grainy image presented by the hidden cameras, she looked better rested, which pleased him. She'd need her strength for what he had planned later.

She also hadn't left the house or been in contact with anyone. For now at least, she was walking the straight and narrow. He wanted so badly to trust her but knew he couldn't be too careful. The stakes were too high.

For the first time since moving to Fort Bragg at the beginning of this assignment, Matt was eager—make that impatient—to get home to his little place on the edge of the woods. Why? The answer was simple. The woman waiting there for him made all the difference.

Bev seemed upset with the changes he made to the work schedule. He left her on day shift and put himself on discretionary timing that effectively put a monkey wrench into her usual surveillance of him while he was in his office. Good. Let her figure out how to keep spying on him when he wasn't in the office under her nose all day.

Matt was through waiting for things to come to a head. He'd always been a man of action and decided to make things happen instead of waiting for them to occur at their own pace. It was time to act. That was his best shot at controlling the situation and creating the outcome he desired.

That thought firmly in mind, he left Bev holding down the fort in an empty office and headed home.

Matt found Sandra dozing in his bedroom. A more perfect sight he had yet to discover, Matt thought as he unbuttoned his shirt, his gaze fixed on the woman in his bed.

Her beautiful green eyes opened. His movements must have woken her.

"What time is it?" she asked in an unconsciously sultry, sleepy voice.

Matt drew closer, shrugging off his shirt and letting it drop to the floor. She leaned up on her elbows, her eyes widening.

"It's time I made you mine, Sandy. No more waiting."

The bed dipped as he knelt on the edge with one knee. She sat up, meeting him as he descended. Inwardly, he cheered her willingness. This was going to be memorable. Fast, but memorable. He'd waited too long to claim her to go slow.

Their lips met and he drank in her unique, delicious flavor as he lowered her to the bed, coming over her, one knee on either side of her hips. His hands went to work on her clothes, pulling the soft jersey knit top over her head and pushing her matching dark, knit pants down over her curvy hips. Within moments he had her dressed only in her white cotton bra and panties.

Those wouldn't last long, he promised himself, but he was sidetracked as her little hands swept downward over his bare chest to the button of his pants. He let her do as she pleased, enjoying the feel of her nimble fingers against the burgeoning erection that craved her touch. The brush of her knuckles over his length as she fought with the button and zipper made him catch his breath.

Finally, she got the pants undone and began to push at his waistband. He helped her with one impatient hand, swiping both the pants and his briefs away in one fell swoop, leaving him bare to her touch.

She closed her fist around his hard cock and he nearly shot through the roof. Finally.

He broke their kiss, nibbling his way downward to rest his head in the crook of her neck as he played with the soft skin he found there. She squirmed and he felt the rise of gooseflesh under his hands as she shivered in reaction. He took that as a good sign.

"Damn, baby. That feels good."

"For me, too," she murmured, beginning to move her hand in a stroking motion that drove him nearly insane with need.

He nearly gave in, but he wanted to take her with him this first time. He wanted it perfect. Both of them coming together.

Gritting his teeth, he lifted away from her touch.

"Don't go," she protested.

He spared a moment to kiss her forehead. "I'm not going far. Promise."

Matt reached over to his nightstand and stuck his hand into the drawer. Rooting around he finally hit pay dirt. A box of condoms. He wasted little time snagging one from the box and leaving the rest on the bedside table. No doubt, they'd be using them all. Soon. As soon as he could manage.

He fumbled the packet in his haste and Sandra caught it. He looked into her eyes and was lost. An impish grin graced her curving lips.

"Allow me." Her sultry purr made his mouth go dry and his cock jump.

He sat back on his haunches, careful to keep his full weight off her thighs. He didn't want to crush her.

"Do it."

He could barely get the words out. So many thoughts were

racing through his mind. First and foremost, what had he done right in his life to get this amazing woman in his bed? Hot for him. No—*eager* for him. He'd died and gone to heaven, no doubt about it.

She reached out with slightly hesitant hands and covered him, dragging out the process until he thought he'd lose his mind.

She focused on her task to the exclusion of all else, her head in line with his cock as she sat up beneath him. He loved the single-minded determination in her expression, the appreciation in her eyes. She licked her lips and he almost lost it right there.

"Babe, you're killing me." Her lashes fluttered upward until her gaze met his.

That was it. He couldn't wait anymore.

"Are you ready?" He reached backward with one hand, following the line of her leg downward to the inevitable place that waited for him. He had to make sure she was with him.

She moaned as sticky wetness met his questing fingers. He grinned with satisfaction.

Sliding one finger inside, he tested her depths as she writhed under him, their gazes locked. He added another finger, stretching her. Her hand fisted around him as she finished her task, squeezing in time as he pulsed his fingers into her in a few quick thrusts.

"I'll take that as a yes." Fully covered, he shifted position so that he knelt between her stretched thighs.

Damn, she was gorgeous. Wet, willing, and waiting for him. Her skin was so soft and creamy smooth. So different from his own scarred carcass. He wanted to treat her like a fragile princess, but the devil in her eyes tempted him to let the demon inside him out to play.

"How do you want it, baby?" He lowered himself, lining up his entrance.

There wasn't going to be anything exotic about this joining. He had her where he wanted her and he wasn't going to mess around. She'd be on the receiving end this time in a straight missionary position. He'd get creative later, when they had more time. There were things he wanted to do to—and with—her that made him hot, just thinking about them. Later. For right now, all he needed was to be inside her. Fast. Simple. Hot and hard. As hard as she could take it. She was a pounding need in his brain. In his blood. In his heart.

Don't go there, he counseled himself. Time to think this through later. For now, all that mattered was her soft body under his, ready, willing, and waiting for him.

So what was *he* waiting for? The time for thinking was over. Now was the time for action.

"Tell me," he repeated his question, wanting to hear her voice. She'd been uncharacteristically quiet, and he wasn't going to let her hide in silence. He wanted her full participation.

"Hard," she whispered. The look in her eyes was almost his undoing. "Now, Matt. Don't make me wait."

"No more waiting," he growled as he pushed inside.

The slight resistance of her body told him she hadn't done this in a while. Something about the idea satisfied his caveman tendencies as he went deeper. When he was seated fully, he took a moment to savor the feel of her warm body around him, welcoming him, making room for him within.

"Damn, baby. You feel good."

"You, too." Her breaths came in ragged pants of air while he settled deep and adjusted his position. She was in for a hard ride. He only hoped he could keep it together long enough to bring her with him.

Without further discussion, he began to move. Slow at first, his pace increased rapidly. He'd known he'd have a hard time once he got inside her. He watched her response carefully. The last thing he wanted to do was leave her behind. This first time he wanted everything to be perfect.

And perfect to him meant them coming together, sharing their pleasure. At least for tonight.

Matt pushed more heavily into her, speeding his pace. Sandra made adorable little squeaky noises in the back of her throat that were music to his ears. Her eyes were wild, half lidded and filled with passion as he watched her. She was so beautiful, she took his breath away.

"Getting there," he whispered to her as his pace increased once more. "You with me, Sandy?" One of his hands roamed over her body, eventually reaching upward, drawing her gaze to his as he cupped her head.

She nodded weakly in response to his question. He let a grin lift his lips even as he thrust deep into her.

"Do you need more? Tell me what you want." He was going to come and he would do anything to take her with him. "Tell me what you need."

"You," she answered simply, with a breathiness that made him quiver.

"You've got me."

"Harder."

The whispered plea sent him rocketing into her with added force. He gave her what they both wanted, riding her hard and fast toward the inevitable explosion.

When it came, he fell off the edge of the earth with her. Together they flew outward, toward the stars, her body clamping around his as she thrashed beneath him in ecstasy. He grunted as she screamed his name, a gift he hadn't expected and didn't know he'd wanted until he heard it. It sent him even higher.

Inevitably, when they fell back to earth, they did it together.

He rolled off her, collapsing at her side and drawing her into his arms. She snuggled close as he tried to catch his breath. He needed to clean up a bit before he gave into the exhaustion that rode him after the past thirty-six hours. For now, he'd take a few minutes to enjoy the afterglow of the best first time he'd ever had.

He wondered how explosive they'd be once they learned each other's preferences. She'd nearly blown his mind as it was. Give them a little time together and she'd no doubt ruin him for anyone else.

Funny thing about that startling thought—he found that he didn't really mind. For someone who'd always been a confirmed bachelor, Matt was starting to think in more permanent terms about this troubling woman. Would it bite him in the ass in the end? That was a distinct possibility. Only time would tell.

For now, he would enjoy their time together and let events unfold between them while pushing to resolve the mission as quickly and efficiently as possible. Once that was settled, he would see what was left of them as a couple. If she was as innocent as she claimed—which he fervently hoped she was—things would work out. He'd *make* them work out. If she was more involved than she wanted to admit, things could get more complicated.

Either way, he'd do his best to keep her safe and with him for as long as possible. This was too good to leave behind. Too good to waste. Too good to throw away.

That thought in mind, he gave in to momentary exhaustion and drifted into a remarkably peaceful sleep.

Chapter Ten

It was after dark when Matt woke suddenly. The whoop of a low-pitched perimeter alarm he'd installed on the property had dragged him from his satisfied stupor. He'd slept well beyond the time he should have been up and had them both out of the house. A quick glance out the bedroom window told him it was full dark and something was moving around outside. He could see shadows in the trees at the edge of the backyard. Shadows that weren't even making an attempt to hide their movements yet made very little sound.

"Shit."

Matt vaulted from the bed and threw on the dark fatigues he kept close at hand, plus his combat vest. In its webbing, he had plenty of ammo, including the darts he'd need if his suspicions proved to be true. He shook the bed deliberately as he dressed, waking Sandra. She blinked at him with bleary eyes, coming awake more slowly than he had.

"Get dressed. We've got company outside." He kept his voice as low as possible so anyone outside wouldn't be alerted to exactly where they were in the house.

Luckily, Sandra didn't ask any questions. She rolled out of bed and grabbed her clothes, dressing hastily. Matt spared a moment of regret for the fear in her eyes and the abrupt departure from what had been one of the most satisfying sexual experiences of his life. He would have liked to savor waking up with Sandra in his arms, but it wasn't meant to be.

Maybe someday, after they finished cleaning up this zombie mess, they could take some time off and spend a week or two in bed. Maybe a month. If they survived, that is.

She hustled out of the bedroom carrying her shoes as he pointed toward the safe room. The door was unlocked. Matt went in first to be certain everything was as it should be. The room was clear and he went directly to the monitors.

"Let's see what we're up against." He flipped some switches and hit some keys to get different views on the monitors. As they flickered to life he got an idea of what was waiting out there for them. "Now isn't that interesting?"

"What is it?"

"Remember my former aide who went AWOL?"

Sandra's head appeared at his side, peering intently at the monitor as she slid into her shoes. He noticed she'd shut the safe room door securely behind them. Good girl.

"Tim, right? Damn. He's a first-generation infectee."

"How can you tell?"

"No bite marks." Her tone was grim. "Someone injected him."

"Couldn't he have been bitten or scratched somewhere that doesn't show?"

"I guess, but if that had been the case, there would be some evidence—shredded clothing at least. From what we can see, it looks like his clothing is intact."

"Good point." Matt didn't have much time to ponder the implications at the moment, though they were intriguing. "Looks like he's got a small army of his friends out there with him, and they're all heading this way."

Matt donned his headset and tuned into the combat frequency. He quickly relayed the situation to the others. While he talked and listened on the earpiece, he checked his weapons and made certain he had enough darts in easily accessible positions on his person.

"Roger. I'll do what I can till you get here. Over."

Matt signed off the radio and turned to Sandra. "The rest of the team is close, but it'll be a few minutes before they get here. At the rate those things are moving, the house will be overrun well before the cavalry arrives." He headed for the door. "Stay here. Watch the monitors." He stuck another wireless earpiece into his other ear and picked her cell phone off the holder attached to her waistband. "Keep this on speaker and if you see anything I need to know about, tell me. I've got the team on in my other ear so if I start talking to them, disregard. Got it?" He connected the call and set her phone on the desk next to the computer keyboard.

"I can shoot." Her tentative words touched him.

If he'd had time, he would have taken her into his arms right then and there. But he didn't have time. The creatures moved slowly, but steadily. He had to get out there and keep them away from the house as best he could until help arrived.

"Thank you, sweetheart, but no. I want you safe." He couldn't resist laying a quick, smacking kiss on her luscious lips. He couldn't linger. He had to drag himself away. "There's a spare pistol and two clips of darts in the top drawer of the desk. Arm yourself, but whatever you do, don't open this door. Watch the screens. You can help me a lot by watching the monitors and relaying intel, okay?"

"All right." She cringed, clearly unhappy with the situation. "Be careful." She looked like she wanted to say more, but there was no time. He had to go.

"Lock this behind me," he said as he opened the reinforced door. With a last look and so much left unsaid, he headed out, waiting only to hear the door snick shut and the locks engage before he took off down the hall.

Matt left the house in time to see the first zombie leave the tree line and step into the open area of the backyard. Luckily, this old house had a very large backyard. Matt had a good thirty yards between himself and his former aide.

Tim looked like shit. His skin was gray and there were dark brown bloodstains all around his mouth and down the front of his shirt. His eyes were flat and somewhat unfocused. His clothing was filthy. Formerly clean cut hair was hanging in long, limp, matted clumps on either side of his face. He moved at a steady pace toward the house.

Matt didn't hesitate. He fired his weapon, hitting Tim four times in quick succession, placing his shots in different parts of his body, spreading the toxic darts for best effect. It would take a minute or two for the toxin to take effect. Matt had to keep track of Tim while he dealt with the rest of the creatures behind him.

"Matt." Sandra's voice sounded in his ear. "Tim must've made others. There are a bunch of them at the edge of the woods, and one looks more grotesque than the next."

"Define *bunch*. I need numbers, sweetheart, and landmarks."

"Sorry. Two are about ten feet behind by the giant oak tree on the left-hand corner of the yard. Then there's one a little to their right. Two more about midway and a group of three farther out in the woods on the right hand side of the yard. Nine total, including Tim."

That sounded about right based on what he'd seen on the monitors before he'd left the house. They were getting closer, their paths still converging on his house. Matt didn't like that at all. It was as if they'd been sent specifically to attack his home. That would bear further scrutiny later—after this mess was dealt with.

"All right." He spoke in a low tone that could just barely be picked up by the phone earpiece. "Keep track of them on the monitors. Alert me of any changes. I'm going to do my best to keep them away from the house."

"Don't get too close. Those claws can do serious damage even if you're immune."

"Yes, Mother," he teased, even though he knew she was right. The contagion caused otherwise inert cells to grow and harden, giving the creatures strong claws and crazy, long, stringy hair.

He could see others approaching through the woods. These all had the telltale signs of zombie attack. One was missing both an ear and his nose in addition to other chunks of skin and tissue that had been ripped out by teeth—Tim's teeth, most likely.

One by one, they cleared the tree line and headed toward Matt. He concentrated his fire on one creature at a time. The toxin would reduce them to goo, but it took time to work.

Of the eight other creatures that Tim had probably made after being infected, only two were wearing uniforms. Matt would have to check to see who was missing from their duty stations. The others were wearing civvies. Three were female, dressed in skimpy clothing as if they'd been out for a night of clubbing just before they'd been attacked.

Now their short skirts and tight tops were shredded and stained with dried blood. Their once pretty faces were a horrid sight. They'd been wearing lots of makeup that was now augmented by a stomach-turning horror show of serious injury, bite marks, missing flesh, and dried blood.

Poor kids. They'd died too young and in one of the most awful ways Matt could imagine. He took his shots, believing he was performing an act of mercy.

Matt had plugged darts in six of the nine tangos he'd counted and reloaded twice.

"There are more of them coming into sight in the woods," came Sandra's frantic voice over the phone earpiece.

"How many?"

"Too many!" she barked, then seemed to settle down. "I see at least six more in addition to the four that are now on the edge of the trees."

As he scanned the huge backyard, zombie Tim finally disintegrated. He'd been only a few feet away from Matt when he went from menacing death dealer to a gooey mound of refuse on the grass. The other five creatures Matt had darted would be going shortly, but there were more to deal with while he avoided the ones he'd already shot. A tricky situation, to be sure.

Matt tongued the lip mic on the radio that connected him to the team.

"What's your ETA, Si?"

The combat team had been a little too silent in his other ear while he'd been talking on the phone earpiece with Sandra and shooting darts at anything that moaned.

"Almost there. A minute. Minute and a half, tops. We're double timing it."

"Be advised, I've darted five of fourteen tangos. One is down for good and there may be more out of visual range of my equipment. Sandy's spotting for me."

"That's a lot of targets," Simon commented noncommittally. He was, like most of the men on his team, nothing if not cool under pressure.

"You're coming up behind, so I'm only firing once they clear the trees and I can identify them with certainty."

"Thanks. I'd really rather not get a dart in my ass tonight."

Simon's sarcastic reply made Matt grin even as he took more shots in rapid succession at new targets when they emerged from the tree line. The toxin in the darts disintegrated tissue on a cellular level. It was as destructive to live human beings as it was to the zombies, so darting one of his own people meant certain death. This was one case where friendly fire would be one hundred percent lethal. They all had to keep their wits about them.

Matt had to readjust his position in the yard to avoid the creatures he'd already darted who hadn't disintegrated yet, but he had the situation under control for the moment. More creatures emerged from the trees and Matt reloaded again. He was going through his stock of toxic darts quicker than he'd anticipated.

"Matt, three more just showed up on my screen," Sandra said in his other ear.

Matt turned off the mic on the combat radio earpiece and replied to Sandra.

"You should be seeing Simon and the other combat troops showing up on the perimeter shortly. Keep an eye out. They'll be moving normally, so they should be easy to spot."

"Thank God." He could hear the relief in her voice. "I'll let you know when I see them."

True to her word, Sandra let Matt know the moment she saw the cavalry show up on her monitors. She watched in awe as they coordinated their movements and took out the creatures one by one. It was really amazing how they worked together.

She watched the events unfold on the screens like she was watching an action flick. Only this was real and the stakes were high—life and death—you couldn't get much higher than that.

Sandra breathed a heavy sigh of relief when the last of the zombies disintegrated. The men searched the area looking for more, but none were found. After about a half hour, Matt came back to the house after setting up the combat troops in a protective attitude on the perimeter surrounding the entire home.

She met him at the door, finally disconnecting the call that had been her lifeline, her link to him while she was in the safe room and he faced the danger outside. She rushed into his arms for a much needed hug as adrenaline continued to surge through her body. The last hour had been a little too exciting and the night wasn't even half over yet.

Matt gave her a passionate, lingering kiss, but he broke away before she could get too attached. He turned to the monitors and took a quick look before motioning her toward the door.

"Simon's in the kitchen. I want to discuss a few things with the two of you before we decide where to go from here."

Sandra was surprised she was going to be consulted on a safety issue but went with Matt as he walked down the short hall to the kitchen. Simon was at the window, peering out from the darkened room.

"I won't put on the lights, Sandra. Is that okay with you?"

"It's fine."

She figured he didn't want anyone who might be somehow peering at them from the outside to know exactly where they were in the house. Sandra didn't understand how anyone could be spying on them with all the combat troops spread out over the property, but security was Matt's bailiwick. She'd do whatever he believed would keep them all safe.

She leaned against the kitchen table, which was just visible in the ambient light from the small night light left burning in the hallway. Simon leaned against the counter and Matt stood between them.

"Sandra, I don't want to scare you, but by now you have to realize that you're being targeted much more persistently than we expected. Do you have any idea why?" Matt's tone was grim and she hated the idea that he might doubt her loyalty. Especially after last night.

"Other than the fact that Dr. Rodriguez is a complete jerk who can't take no for an answer, I have no idea."

"Matt, do you think this welcoming party being sent to your house tonight is because of her?" Simon asked. Sandra couldn't see his face but thought his tone held suspicion as he nodded toward her.

"I can't think of any other reason for a mass attack on my home, can you?" Matt turned the question back on Simon.

"I can think of a few reasons the bad guys would want you out of the way, Commander, but the most likely scenario given what's come before is that Sandra's being targeted."

"Question is, how did our enemies know she was out here? How'd they get that intel so fast?" Matt wondered.

"The obvious answer is that she's being followed." Simon shrugged. "Maybe they followed your car when you brought her out here."

"Possible, I suppose, but unlikely. I'd like to believe my skills aren't so rusty that I wouldn't have noticed a tail." Matt frowned in the dim light.

"Nobody's perfect," Simon reminded him. "Still, I know your skills, old friend. Even though you've been riding a desk the past few years, I don't think you'd ever let yourself get that rusty. So we're back to the question—how'd they find out Sandra was here so fast?"

"And how do they always seem to know where to target her?" Matt's brows drew together in a frown. "There have been too many attempts on her that were too close for comfort. They always seem to know exactly where she is. Why is that, Sandy?" He turned questioning eyes on her.

"I swear, I don't know." She didn't like the way he was looking at her. Correction: the way they both were looking at her. She could make out their features, even in the dim light, and they both looked at her with clear suspicion.

"Maybe she doesn't." Simon offered the unexpected olive branch.

"How so?" Matt asked quickly.

"I'm not sure but I think we should let Mari have a look at her. I remember her telling me about the original research team and their various specialties. I think one of Rodriguez's previous experiments involved really small subdermal implants. Maybe there's some kind of tracking device under Sandra's skin."

"You got a battery of shots before they'd let you work on the experimental team, right?" Matt looked at her, and she thought maybe she saw a little glimmer of hope in his eyes. Or was she just fooling herself? She wasn't sure.

"Yes," she answered, thinking back. "As a matter of fact, Dr. Rodriguez administered them. Son of a . . . Do you think he implanted some kind of tracking device without my consent?"

"From what Mari told me, it's possible," Simon answered.

Sandra shot to her feet. "Get me to the lab. I want it out!"

"Calm down, Sandy. We'll go when it's safer. In the morning." Matt's tone was gentle and reassuring. "For now, we hunker down here until we're sure the woods are clean." He reached out and took hold of her hand, drawing her to his side. "Si," he looked at the other man but didn't let go of her hand. "Set up a perimeter. We're holding position here for the rest of the night. I doubt, after that display, that there could be many more zombies elsewhere on base. I think they must've sent them all here. Let's make sure there are no stragglers."

"Yes, sir." Simon straightened and headed toward the door. "Should I call Mari and give her a heads up for the morning?"

Matt squeezed her hand and sought her gaze before answering. "Do it."

"Aye, aye, sir." Simon went out the back door and shut it behind him.

The silence stretched as Matt held her gaze.

"You don't trust me, do you?" Sandra had always believed the direct approach was best in most situations. "Do you think I called Rodriguez or something, to tell him where I am? Do you think I'm playing you?"

"I know you didn't call him." The look on his face was inscrutable, but resolution and belief resonated through his tone.

"You believe me?"

"I believe you didn't call him. As for the rest?" He let go of her hand and sighed. "I know you're still hiding something from me, Sandra. Can't you trust me enough to tell me what it is?"

Oh, God. There it was. He wanted a truth that she feared would change his mind about her for all time. Men had died because she'd allowed those first creatures to escape the lab that awful night. Chances are, some of those men had been Matt's friends. She couldn't forgive herself for her cowardly mistake, so how could he?

Matt watched her face carefully. Panic flashed in her eyes and his heart ached. He knew she was telling the truth about not calling Rodriguez because he'd watched her all day. He wouldn't tell her that. He wanted her complete trust first before he gave his.

Perhaps that was a bit selfish, but Matt couldn't be too careful given the dire nature of this mission. He'd given her more leeway than he should have already. He was tempted to give her everything after the sweet way she'd given herself to him. He had to fight against his instincts. He wanted to trust her. He really did. But he needed to know what she was hiding. At the very least, he needed to be certain it wasn't something that could blow up in their faces before this was all over. He needed to be confident that whatever it was that she didn't want to tell him, it wasn't as vital as she was making it out to be.

"I'm not hiding anything." Her answer was too fast to be true.

"Try again."

He held her gaze and dared her to lie to his face a second time.

Two loud thuds sounded on the back door before Simon poked his head in. Spotting Matt, Simon made his report.

"Perimeter's secure, Commander. And I gave Mari the heads up."

Sandra scampered out while Simon talked, and Matt saw her close herself in the bathroom. The lock on the door sounded with a faint click. Matt sighed. She was running from him. Running from the truth. He'd let her run a little longer, but a showdown was coming and they both now knew it.

"Very well."

Matt decided to give Sandra space. He went into the safe room and checked in with the various units of the team. The combat unit was all around the house. The cleanup team was already on alert. They'd have a big job to do after the All Clear had been sounded to clean up the remains of all those creatures Matt and the rest of the combat squad had reduced to steaming piles of goo earlier.

The members of the science team were accounted for. Simon had just checked in with his fiancée and Sandy was currently holed up in his bathroom. Just one more group to check.

Lew Kauffman had been charged with keeping an eye on the prisoner. Matt had left orders for Kauffman to call when the prisoner woke up, which he probably should have by now. Matt dialed Kauffman's number and waited while the call connected and rang. And rang. And rang.

"Shit."

Matt stuck the combat earpiece back in his ear and opened the mic.

"When's the last time anyone heard from Kauffman?" he demanded without preamble.

"Archer here, Commander," came the snappy reply. "I spoke to him just before we got your SOS. All was clear at that time, sir."

"How did you contact him? He's not answering his phone," Matt reported. "It's not even going to voicemail. It's just ringing off the hook."

"That's not good, sir. Kaufman's solid about comms. Something's wrong," Simon added.

"I was afraid of that."

Matt set about contacting the remaining combat-trained members of the team who weren't immune. There were a couple of Special Forces guys in support positions in addition to Kauffman.

The report came back almost immediately. Not only had their prisoner escaped, but Lew Kauffman had been left for dead. They were taking him to the base hospital where Mari would meet him and take charge of his treatment. They'd do everything they could for him, but it was difficult to say at this point if he'd make it.

Matt disconnected the call with a heavy sigh. A slight movement at the doorway alerted him to Sandra's presence.

"You through hiding from me?" He didn't even bother to turn around and look at her. He was too tired of all this crap. Not only was she driving him crazy, but his mission was falling apart before his eyes; he lost a prisoner and possibly one of his Special Forces brothers this night.

"I wasn't hiding." She edged into the room, leaning against the wall by the door, her hands behind her back, looking at him as he swiveled his chair to face her.

"Could have fooled me."

"What's wrong?" Her eyes narrowed and she moved closer to him, concern in her expression.

"We lost the prisoner and Lew Kauffman is in the emergency room at the base hospital." He gave her the news straight up. No sense trying to sugarcoat any of it. "They're not sure he's going to make it."

"Oh, no."

Matt was pissed off. Somehow Rodriguez had known where they'd stashed the prisoner, even though they'd made a strong effort to hide him on the large base. And now one of Matt's team members was fighting for his life.

"Somehow Rodriguez knew where we were keeping his man."

"More evidence that he might've tagged both his employee and me somehow." Sandra sounded worried but she was right.

"The sooner we get you checked out, the better, but I'm not moving from this location until after sunrise. We're the safest here for now. In transit, we'd be sitting ducks."

"I don't want to wait that long." She was rubbing her arm distractedly. "I've been thinking about where and how Rodriguez could've inserted a transmitter. All I'd need is a receiver tuned to the right frequency—or maybe a metal detector would be easier—to find it. If it's there."

Matt stood. This was something he could do. He had all kinds of electronic equipment in the house. Lots of spare parts he could cobble into something useful.

"Give me a few minutes. I'm pretty sure I can come up with something."

"Really?" She looked excited. Her gaze followed his search through a few boxes he'd stowed under the desk. He nodded absently in answer to her question.

He found what he wanted and cleared a small space on one of the tables. It would only take some minor adjustments. He got out his toolkit—a collection of miniatures that worked well on the tiny electronics pieces—and set to work. After a few minutes, Sandra came over and perched at his side, watching with a worried but hopeful expression on her pretty face.

A few minutes later and he'd jury-rigged a small receiver enough to try it out.

"Where did Rodriguez inject you?"

"Here." She pointed to a spot on the back of her hip.

"What's your best guess? If he'd tagged you, would the thing stay in that general area, or would it travel?"

"Depends on its size," she answered as if thinking aloud. "But anything moving around could prove dangerous if allowed to travel the bloodstream. It could easily cause a blockage. Again, it would depend on size. I've heard of nanotechnology, but what we're talking about here is years beyond where the tech is now from my understanding."

"So you're saying it'll most likely still be in the same area if he put a tag under your skin without your knowledge."

She nodded in agreement. "That's the most likely scenario."

"All right then." He patted the table in front of him. "Sit up here and let's try this out. It's a short-range receiver with limited power, so proximity is helpful."

She leaned against the table in front of him and allowed him to pull the stretchy waistband of her leggings down a bit. Matt tried not to let the sight of her soft skin and the feel of her warm, curvy body under his hands distract him. They had work to do. Fun and games could come later. They definitely *would* come later if he had anything to say about it. The taste of her he'd gotten earlier had only whet his appetite for more.

"How does it work?" she wanted to know.

He held up the small box and began turning the knobs. "I'm going to go through a range of frequencies to see if we can pick up any sort of signal. If we get lucky and hit on the frequency, we'll have confirmed there's a transmitter. Once we know that, we can also use this to determine its location. Then we can do our best to get it out of you."

"Sounds like a good plan." She looked downward, watching the receiver with anxious eyes.

"It is—if it works. Keep your fingers crossed."

It took more than a half hour and an agonizing sweep through multiple frequencies until they hit on the signal.

"Son of a bitch," Matt mused when the radio he'd doctored started to ping. He moved away, then back. The signal got louder the closer he was to Sandra.

"I can't believe this. I can't believe that rat did this to me without my knowledge."

Sandra sounded truly pissed off. Matt hadn't seen her really angry yet. She was kind of cute when she was riled. He knew she wouldn't appreciate that observation, so he kept it to himself while he moved the receiver around her body, trying to pinpoint where the tiny transmitter might be hiding.

Just as they'd thought, it was on her hip. Or more accurately, under the skin of her hip.

"It's right in this area." Matt tapped the soft skin of her hip, just a little behind her.

Sandra's fingers went to the area and began a gentle probing motion.

"It can't be too small if they're picking up the transmission from far away, right?" she asked.

"I'm not really sure what size transmitter he'd have access to or what the newest tech has produced. Wouldn't you have noticed something relatively large?"

"Not necessarily. Some of the shots I got were experimental and not administered in the traditional way. See the scar there? That was from a skin patch test Rodriguez insisted on for the entire team. Now that I think back, he probably tagged us all."

The ramifications of that intrigued Matt.

"What?" She must've caught something in his expression.

"It would save us a lot of trouble if I could get a hold of his list of frequencies. If he knows how to locate all the members of the original team . . ."

"Oh, I see what you mean." Understanding dawned on her face as she thought it through. "If we can get this thing out intact, could you reverse engineer from it? Maybe figure out how to pinpoint the rest of them? Assuming there are more, of course. I could be wrong. Maybe he was just singling me out."

"I'd lay odds there are more. Otherwise, how did they find

the guy we caught? I had him hidden pretty well on base." He shook his head, thinking how Kauffman had been a sitting duck and none of them had even realized it. "As for reverse-engineering, that'll be up to someone more expert in electronics than me, but we'll definitely give it a try. The question now is, can we get this thing out of you?"

"I'd love to do it here and now, but I think we'd need an ultrasound to do this easily. Unless . . ." She probed the area some more, a frown marring her delicate brows. "Put your hands here and here." She pointed to either side of her hip area. "Now stretch out the skin. I think I can see . . . Yes, I see a bump."

"I don't see anything."

"Right here." She pointed to a smooth expanse of her pale skin. "From up here, I can see a tiny little bump. You can't really feel it, but I can see something near the surface. It might be worth a try to make a small, shallow incision. If we can get it out now, I'd feel a whole lot better. At least we can try. If I can't get it, we'll get Mariana's help after daylight."

"All right, what do you need? I have a field medical kit in the corner." He pointed to a red nylon knapsack leaning up against one wall.

She stood from her leaning position on the table and snagged the pack. Rifling through it quickly, she took a few items out, clutching them to her chest.

"Where do you want to do this? The bathroom or kitchen would probably be best because of the potential for bleeding."

"How deep will you have to cut?" Suddenly this strategy sounded more dangerous than it had before.

"Hopefully not too deep. If I can't get it easily I'll leave it for Mariana, but I'd at least like to try to get it out now. I don't want this thing inside me anymore."

He could understand that.

"Bathroom." He led the way out of the safe room and into the nearby bathroom. She trailed behind, clutching her supplies to her chest.

When they got inside the small room, she immediately laid out the stuff she'd taken from the kit. He saw antiseptic, gauze, a scalpel, and other things. Because of the position slightly behind her, Matt knew she'd need his help with this, if only to hold her skin taut while she dug out the tiny bump only she seemed to see. He hoped she could get to it easily. It would save them a lot of grief if he could use that transmitter to mislead Rodriguez a little before the bastard realized they were onto his little scheme.

"What do you want me to do?" Matt asked, frowning as he saw the blade she would use to slice into her flesh.

"Wash your hands with that antiseptic soap, then put on the sterile gloves in that package. I'll want you to disinfect the area and then hold the skin taut like you did before."

He could do that. He scrubbed his hands as she finished her preparations, pulling her pants to her knees and pushing her panties down just far enough to clear the area she'd indicated before. Then she scrubbed her own hands and shrugged as she dried them on a clean white towel.

"I don't think I'll have to cut too deep. From what I can see, this little guy is pretty close to the surface."

She opened a couple of antiseptic wipes allowing him to pull the little swabs out of their protective foil wrappers with his sterile gloved hands. He cleaned the area on her skin and then she gave herself a small dose of topical anesthetic. She used another antiseptic wipe to sterilize the blade, a pair of pointy tweezers, and her fingers. She nodded toward Matt as he knelt at her side.

"Now just hold the skin taut and keep it steady." She held the scalpel at an odd angle given her position. She was twisted around to reach slightly behind her. It was awkward, but it would work.

She took a deep breath, held it, and cut into her skin. She went shallow at first, looking for the little bump only she could see from her vantage point at almost ninety degrees from the surface she was working on. Matt faced the cutting area head on, watching carefully for any sign of something electronic that shouldn't be there, inside her skin. She wasn't bleeding much, which was good.

"You see anything?" she asked.

"No." Dammit. He wasn't seeing what they both knew had to be there.

"Wait. I can go a little deeper. I'm right over the bump." She put action to her words, and the blood began dripping down her side. Matt soaked it up with a gauze pad and she made the incision deeper. "Okay, use your fingers to spread the incision and grab the tweezers. Poke around a little and see if you can find it."

Matt didn't like the idea of hurting her, but he knew this had to be done. He did as she instructed, using gauze to soak up the blood that had pooled. When he removed the gauze, he saw it. A telltale sparkle of gold just under the skin.

"I see it."

She sighed heavily. "Thank goodness. Can you get it out?"

"I think so. Hold on." Matt grabbed the tweezers and went after his prize. It took three tries, but he got it out in one piece.

Putting it aside on the bathroom counter for a moment, he grabbed more gauze and put pressure on her wound. She took over the job as they both turned to peer down at the tiny little dot of gold that had been inside her.

"Looks like a teeny tiny circuit board," she observed in a quiet voice, as if talking too loud would shatter it.

"That's exactly what it is, I'd wager." He flipped it over with the tweezers. "We'll know more after we let some of the guys look at this. For now, we'll keep it safe."

He took a small plastic bag from his pocket and placed the tiny chip inside. Closing it securely, he tucked it back into his pocket for safekeeping.

"Now let's get you fixed up." He turned back to her and checked under the gauze to see how she was doing.

The cut wasn't deep or long. It didn't require stitches—just a bandage. Her body was doing the rest at record speed. Since becoming infected with the contagion, she apparently healed as fast as the other immune members of the team.

The contagion had started out as an experiment in boosting immunity and healing. In a rare, precious few, it worked as had been intended, giving them the ability to heal wounds without scarring in record time. Unfortunately only a tiny percent of the population had the right body chemistry. For the vast majority of people, it killed, then reanimated their corpses into something straight out of a horror flick.

Matt covered the wound with a clean, square, white gauze pad and secured it with a length of tape. His hands went to the waistband of her white panties, riding low, under her hip. She jerked when he moved them downward instead of up.

"Matt?"

"Let me touch you, Sandra. Just for a minute."

He'd had about all he could stand of her bare flesh without touching her in a more intimate way. Things were so complicated between them now, but he knew one thing for sure. The tiny transmitter meant she hadn't been communicating her location to the enemy willingly. She hadn't betrayed them—or herself—in that way. She might still be keeping secrets from him, of course. He wasn't stupid. It was enough to know for now that she hadn't been lying when she said she didn't know how Rodriguez's men kept finding her.

His gaze swept upward to meet hers. Astonishment gave way to something much hotter, much more sinful in her eyes. He felt it, too.

"Are you sure you want to?" Her voice dropped low to tease along his senses. Damn, she was sexy without even trying.

"Want?" He had to laugh at himself and the desire that rode him. "It's more like a need, sweetheart."

Her eyes flared with excitement. "I'm glad we're on the same page. I want you, Matt." One hand reached out and her fingers tangled in his short hair, caressing, encouraging.

He slid her panties down her legs and freed her of the tiny

scrap of fabric. Heaven awaited him between her silky thighs, and he wasn't going to deny himself much longer. Only long enough to be certain she was with him.

He knelt before her and helped her settle more comfortably on the edge of the countertop. Positioning her just so, he pushed her thighs apart and enjoyed the view. He couldn't resist touching, tracing the delicate folds of the place he most wanted to be—and would be, soon.

Sandra trembled as Matt positioned her. She'd never had such a powerful lover. Not that there'd been that many men in her life. She'd all but given up on finding someone she could imagine spending a lifetime with. Most men didn't seem to want a woman who was their intellectual equal. Even the scientists she'd worked with had preferred the young, nubile receptionists to the slightly older, more educated women they worked with. It was an old cliché that had proven true in her experience, she was sorry to say.

Then there was Matt. Every bit as intelligent as the scientists she'd come to disdain, he was also a man of action with a drool-worthy physique that reduced her to nearly mindless desire whenever he touched her. Or looked at her.

Like he was looking at her now. His gaze set fire to her most intimate places. His touch brought sparks of excitement that made her squirm. Her hips jutted outward, toward his questing fingers, wanting them to push deep. She was more than ready for him.

And then they did. She gasped as first one long, hard finger slid deep inside, then two. He thrust into her in a gentle, slow rhythm that made fire race along her midsection in a slow, intense burn.

"More," she pleaded, surprised to hear her own voice.

He complied, adding another finger, stretching her for the thick penetration that would follow. Matt's cock was as big as the rest of him, which was to say, huge. She'd never had such a well-endowed lover, and after that first time she'd been a bit sore. Her body's newly ramped-up healing abilities didn't allow her to suffer long, and she certainly wasn't complaining.

The pleasure he'd given her had been truly amazing. Never had a sexual encounter given her such an all-consuming climax. While she knew part of it was due to the devastating equipment Matt possessed, an equal, if not greater, part had to do with the mysterious man himself.

Matt fascinated her in every way. Physically he was daunting. Attracted from the first minute she'd laid eyes on him, there was no doubt she wanted his body. Working with him had been another experience that only made her admire him more. She liked his quick wit and loved the flashes of compassion he tried so hard to hide. He was a man she could love.

He was a man she did love.

The realization came in a blinding flash. She trembled, panicked for a moment. She loved him?

Oh, God. She loved him.

She was in trouble now. Delicious, sinfully sweet, incredibly tempting trouble, but trouble nonetheless.

His fingers found a spot within her that made her scream his name. No time to think. Only feel.

That's it. Just feel what he was doing to her. Making her body dance to his tune.

She gave herself up to the sensation. The future would take care of itself somehow. She didn't want to think about it now. She wanted only to bask in this moment out of time, this incredible pleasure with a man she loved.

Damn. Love. She hadn't expected that.

She'd deal with it later.

Matt stood, his fingers still lodged deep inside her. His gaze sought hers and a devilish grin lifted one corner of his mouth. She wanted to kiss it. To capture that lazy, smugly male amusement.

"You liked that?" His voice rumbled over her senses like another caress while his fingers made shallow, pumping motions, his gaze holding her pinned.

"Yeah." She was reduced to one-word answers. Sandra panted softly as she tried to catch her breath.

"You want more?"

She allowed herself to smile. "You know I do."

"Then what are we waiting for?" He suited action to words and removed his fingers from her body.

He moved swiftly, his lips meeting hers in the sweetest kiss. He was ravenous and demanding as only their mouths touched. Her fingers went to his shirt, tugging and pulling along with him as he quickly shed his clothes, all the while still kissing her.

He broke the kiss as he fished in the medicine cabinet for something. A second later, she saw the foil wrapper in his hands. She would've taken it from him, but he was in too much of a hurry. He covered himself and pulled her close again.

Finesse was gone in the urgency of the moment. He pushed between her thighs, sliding into her with only slight difficulty. She was wet with desire and glad he'd taken time to prepare her. She was more than ready for his possession and knew what awaited her in his arms. Sandra was eager to find that bliss again.

He entered by slow degrees, pulling out a little only to slide deeper on the next gentle wave. When he was seated fully, he stilled and she basked in the feel of him, the complete and utter possession of his big frame wrapped around her, plunging deep within. He owned her in that moment and she didn't mind at all.

Strange that. She'd never experienced such an all-consuming need to give all she had to a man. To let him take control. To be in total charge of her body and her pleasure.

Matt was a special case. He would always be special to her, no matter the outcome of this disastrous affair. He was her lover. Her love. No one else would ever take the piece of her heart she'd surrendered to him. Even though he didn't know it.

The thought made her sad, but it also gave her strength. She wanted to enjoy this stolen time with him. It might be all she ever got. She would take it and run with it, and hold this memory against the future—if she had a future. Times were desperate. More desperate than they'd ever been for her. She would enjoy what she could with Matt, while it lasted.

"Matt," she whispered as he began to move, unable to keep silent while her body lit up like a firecracker on the Fourth of July.

The hard length of him touched her most sensitive places, rubbing her into a frenzy with very little effort. It wouldn't be long before she exploded like a rocket and burst into a million fragments of fire in the sky. How she longed for it, wanted it, yet wanted this incredible feeling to last. She couldn't have it both ways. Eventually, pleasure would be overcome by ecstasy.

Thank God.

Matt began to move. Slow, rocking motions gave way to deeper, harder thrusts until she was whimpering on every pulsing beat. He drove her steadily and swiftly toward the intensity of satisfaction Matt had taught her.

"Are you with me, baby?" His voice was harsh in her ear, his breathing heavy. He was so tall, his body nearly enveloped her. It felt comforting and safe, only a little overwhelming.

"Yeah." She nearly howled as desire overwhelmed her. She was close to exploding. All it would take was a little more . . .

Oh, yeah. She came swift and hard. Matt knew just how to move to make her climax on cue. She felt him follow her over the edge, up to the stars and back again.

They held each other tight, clinging to each other as if they were the only solid things in the universe. They alone existed in a world of sheer bliss where nothing else mattered but the two of them, wrapped in each other.

All too soon, it came to an end.

"Damn, sweetheart, you make me forget everything. We've got work to do, but I'll be damned if I can work up enough energy to care right now."

She laughed. She couldn't help herself. He'd summed up exactly her feelings as well.

"Do you think anyone would notice if we called in sick today?" she mumbled against his chest. She could feel as well as hear the rumble of his laughter against her cheek.

Chapter Eleven

Sandra hid another yawn behind her hand. This was going to be a long day, but she refused to sleep until she understood the ins and outs of the chip that had been implanted into her body without her consent.

Matt had escorted her to the base just after sunrise and summoned a few men to a part of the base she hadn't seen before. It was where the cleanup team was housed—a separate building built back in the forties, and from the looks of it, abandoned several times since then. The thick walls gave it the feeling of a bunker and provided security that many of the base's newer buildings couldn't boast.

The outside of the structure looked awful. The inside, however, was another story. There were lots of open office space and corridors of private bedrooms in a barracks area, along with plenty of storage for the high-tech equipment the cleanup team used.

Only a few specialists had been drafted to man the cleanup team. They were tasked with removing any trace of the destroyed zombies from the field of battle. Each member of the combat team carried a supply of transmitters they would drop on each one of their kills.

If not distinguished from their surroundings somehow, the

possibility of overlooking a bunch of old clothes and organic goo in the woods—which was the most common place to find and fight the creatures—was too high. Standard operating procedure for the combat team was to mark each pile of remains with a transmitter. After daylight, when the coast was clear, the cleanup team would come in and locate each kill by its radio signal and recover the remains. They would also sanitize the area to prevent the spread of any stray contagion that might otherwise occur.

The team tagged evidence and collected samples that Mariana and Sandra used in their ongoing studies of the contagion. All the material that had been recovered to date was kept in this building, which had a secure vault beneath it. It was an old-fashioned bunker with steel and concrete doors that had been added to in recent years. There were now state-of-the-art electronics guarding the highly classified material as well.

Matt had introduced Sandra to the lead electronics tech, a rather serious man named Wolf, of all things. He was tall, golden skinned, with icy blue eyes. From his features and name, she would bet he was some kind of German and Native American mix. His full name was Wolfgang Blackfeather, and he'd been introduced to her as a consultant, though he wore his fatigues with easy familiarity. To her, that meant he'd been—or still was—a soldier like all the other guys on the team. The others certainly seemed to treat him with respect, as if they knew his skills and found them equal to, or even above, their own.

Wolf had taken the little transmitter and stuck it under a microscope. He worked silently for the most part, but had allowed Sandra to take a look at every step of his process, explaining the workings of the minuscule device to her along the way. It was very educational.

The device turned out to be very straightforward. The damned thing had been broadcasting a ping that would provide Sandra's location to anyone who knew the right place to look, every few minutes since it had been implanted.

"As long as we keep this in a pH-neutral saline environment, it will keep transmitting," Wolf said in his quiet way. "It seems to be drawing energy from the ions in the solution."

"It was using my body's natural salinity to power itself?"

"I believe so. It has no independent power source. It's smaller than anything I've seen before, and it makes sense to have it utilize the chemistry of its anticipated environment."

"That's diabolical."

She was appalled by the idea that such a thing was even possible. This technology was way ahead of anything she'd seen before, and she had prided herself on being at the cutting edge of biotech.

"Your friend Rodriguez had access to some amazing stuff," Wolf commented in his calm way.

"He's not my friend. Never was." She wanted to make that perfectly clear.

Wolf bowed his head slightly. "My apologies. I only meant that you'd worked with the man before." He turned back to his instruments. "Other than the power source, this thing is similar to an RFID tag used in many commercial applications."

"What does that stand for?" she asked.

"Radio frequency identification. It's used in a lot of different ways. One way is to label items so when they're brought past a scanner that's tuned to the right frequency, the item is automatically identified and charged to a particular account."

The phone rang and Wolf went to answer it while Sandra stole another glance at the tiny chip under high-powered magnification. It really was the most amazing thing. Scary as hell, too. She'd been easy pickings for their enemies. All Rodriguez had to do was pinpoint her location using this hidden chip and send his goons after her. The bastard.

"We've been summoned." She jumped at the soft words. Wolf had snuck up on her. The man moved as silently as his namesake.

"Where to?"

"Commander Sykes wants to talk to us in the conference room. Come on, I'll show you where it is."

He switched off a few lights and motioned for her to precede him out the door.

The conference room was larger than Sandra had expected. It looked like most, if not all, of the combat team was already there, along with the members of the cleanup crew. Mariana waved hello. She was seated next to Simon. The two looked good together. Comfortable. Like they belonged together and didn't really care who knew it. Sandra envied her colleague just the tiniest bit.

Then Matt caught Sandra's eye and motioned her over. He'd saved her a seat next to him. That was as close to a public statement as anything among this group. He'd just tipped them all off that something was special about their relationship without having to say a word. A warm feeling spread through her body. Maybe she didn't need to be so envious of Mariana and Simon's relationship after all. Sandra took the seat next to Matt, and he called the meeting to order without further ado.

"First off, I want you all to know that I've sent two technicians from the cleanup team to Tennessee. They're going to assist John and Donna, so we're going to be a little short staffed until they can get things under control down there. We have enough of our own problems or I'd send more help to them. As it is, we're stretched too thin. As of today, we're going to get more centralized. We're all moving in to this building. It's the most secure building we have fully at our disposal, and I believe there's truth to the old adage that there's safety in numbers. So I want everyone who's not already bunking here to pack up your gear today and move to one of the empty rooms in the barracks area on the second floor. And we're going to buddy up. Nobody leaves this building alone—day or night. Our adversaries have proven they can get on and off this base with impunity. From here on out, nobody goes anywhere alone."

A few people looked around curiously, but most took the news in stride. These soldiers were used to orders changing on the fly.

"As you all know, we've had a major increase in zombie activity the past couple of nights. Unfortunately, I expect that trend to continue. A change of tactics is in order. I'd like to start taking the fight to the enemy instead of the other way around. We've had a few direct attacks on Dr. McCormick. I don't think they've given up trying to get to her." All eyes were suddenly focused on Sandra, and she did her best not to squirm under their scrutiny.

Matt gave a signal to one of the men near the door and the lights were lowered. A second later, a projector went on and Dr. Rodriguez's face shone against the side wall of the room, which doubled as a screen.

"This is the member of the original science team we now believe is responsible for our problems here at Bragg. Dr. Emilio Rodriguez. He's a biotech expert who apparently has some dangerous friends. The man we captured and lost yesterday is a known associate of his. Allowing the prisoner to escape was a tough break and I blame myself." Matt paused a moment, a pained look on his face. "Lew Kauffman is going to be okay—I got an update right before we began this meeting—but he'll be laid up in the hospital for a while, I'm sorry to say." Hard expressions greeted him at this news. Kauffman was a member of the combat support team and clearly had a lot of good friends in here.

Sandra saw Matt nod at Wolf. He got up and went to the projector. Wolf tapped a few keys, fiddled with something, and a few seconds later a microscopic image of the circuit board they'd dug out of her hip appeared on the screen.

"This is a locator chip that we found implanted under Dr. McCormick's skin." Matt nodded to Sandra, then looked at the tech expert. "Wolf, tell the team what you've discovered, please."

Wolf went into more technical detail than Sandra expected,

showing several views of the chip to give the rest of the team an idea of its minuscule size. Scowls shone on many of the faces around the room as he drew his short presentation to a close. He sat down, returning the floor to Matt.

"I believe the prisoner must've had one of these under his skin, too. That had to be how they knew exactly where to find him. Sandra was tagged without her knowledge, and I believe Rodriguez may have tagged other members of the original science team in the same way. Mission objective has expanded to include the takedown of Dr. Rodriguez and if at all possible, the seizing of his technology, files, and equipment. If we can learn the secrets of his tracking system, and if he's really able to pinpoint the location of the other scientists, we could do the same. First we need to find Rodriguez's base of operations. Wolf's heading up that task. Once we know the location of his headquarters, the combat team will be working on a plan to secure the area."

Sandra read grim determination on many of the faces around her. These guys were goal oriented in a major way, and Matt had just handed them a challenge.

The meeting broke up shortly thereafter, and Matt motioned for her to stay behind while the others filed out of the big room. Mari stayed, too, though Simon took off with the other soldiers.

"Mariana's got an idea I'd like you to examine," Matt said once the three of them were alone.

"I've been working with the formula of your serum and Sarah Petit's blood test results. I believe I've isolated the particular protein sequences in her blood that allowed for her spontaneous immunity." Sandra was intrigued by Mari's words. "I then compared the sequences to those in her brother's blood. Having siblings on the team opened a unique avenue for study considering one had already been proven immune and the other is still in his natural state."

Sandra recognized the scientific importance of testing two people who had such similar genetic makeup. The only way the experiment could be better is if they'd been given identical twins to work with, but that was asking too much. Siblings was what they'd gotten. Siblings would have to do.

"That was a really good idea." Sandra congratulated the other doctor.

It was a smart move from a scientific standpoint. One that Sandra would have thought of if she hadn't been so distracted by all that had gone on in the past few days. Good thing Mariana was on the ball. Sandra's usual focus had been blurred lately, her mind in a state of chaos.

"Thanks. What I've discovered—I believe—is a way to make John Petit immune."

"Are you kidding?" Sandra was shocked by the idea.

"He has almost all the same protein sequences as his sister, except for two that could potentially pose a problem if he's exposed to the contagion. Based on my lab studies, he has a less than fifty percent chance of being spontaneously immune."

"Those are not good odds for him." Sandra frowned. "But you've isolated the problematic proteins?"

"Yes." Mari looked triumphant. "Which is why I think we could coax his body into a much higher probability of achieving immunity."

"Before exposure? The serum I developed is designed to negate exposure after the fact. Changing someone's genetic makeup before they're exposed seems too risky, not to mention the ethical problems. I mean, we don't know the long-term effects."

"I wouldn't even consider this under normal circumstances, but we're in a bind and I don't want John dying if we have a way to prevent it." Matt's expression was troubled as he spoke for the first time during this exchange. "John and Donna are in a volatile situation, and Donna isn't really up to the task, even though she's immune. John needs to be able to fight without risking his own life every time he faces one of those creatures. If he were to become an infected, I hate to think what he could do. From the beginning we've noticed that some of the person's skill and ability survives their death.

John is an elite warrior. We've had a hell of a time tracking soldiers who've been turned. John would be a nightmare to neutralize, and Donna just doesn't have the skills. Nor can I spare anyone from here right now." Matt ran a frustrated hand through his hair. "I think we need to give him the option." He blew out a sigh. "I want you to look at Mariana's work, Sandra. Put your heads together and be as sure as you can that this will work before we go any further."

Sandra was uncomfortable with the idea of testing a theory on a live subject, even if John turned out to be willing. Still, it would advance their research considerably, no matter the outcome. Sooner or later, they'd have to put their theories to the test. If John was willing, Sandra would put all her energy toward being certain the test was as safe as it was possible to make it, under the circumstances.

"Okay," she agreed cautiously. "I'll take a look. Where are we working today?"

"I have some guys moving your lab over here as we speak," Matt replied. "There's a lot of space in this old building. It's not quite as comfortable as where you were, but it's a lot more secure. Now that we know the base isn't safe, I'm kicking myself for not having us all here in the first place. Come on, I'll show you where we're setting you up." Matt headed for the door, and Sarah and Mariana followed him out and down the corridor.

A few flights of stairs and several more hallways later, they arrived at a big space that was fast being converted into a makeshift laboratory. The guys had already made good progress setting up tables, and even as they watched two more groups arrived with equipment from Sandra's lab.

It took an hour or two to get everything set up, but Mariana and Sandra were able to start working almost right away. The guys worked around them, putting everything else in place while the two women put their heads together in one corner of the large room.

It didn't take long for Sandra to verify Mariana's work. She may have come to the team as a general practitioner, but Mariana definitely had a good head for research. They worked well together, and before Sandra knew it more than two hours had passed. The fourth time Sandra yawned, Mariana closed the reference book she'd been holding with a bang that startled Sandra into nearly jumping off her stool.

Mariana laughed. The twinkle in her eye was hard to resist and Sandra chuckled, too.

"Time to get some much needed sleep." Mariana began putting things away. "Doctor's orders."

"Don't worry. I won't argue with the prescription. I'm beat." Sandra got to her feet slowly, suddenly remembering something vital. "Only . . . I don't know where I'm supposed to sleep now."

Mariana's attention shifted over Sandra's shoulder. "I don't think that'll be a problem much longer."

Sandra turned to find Matt coming into the room behind her. He looked as tired as she felt, but his fatigue didn't slow his determined stride. She had to hand it to him. The man had outstanding stamina—as she was coming to know firsthand. She felt her cheeks heat with a blush as the slightly racy thought crossed her mind.

"Looks like the lab is coming along. Anything else you need brought in here?" Matt asked both ladies.

Mariana surveyed the room, her hands on her hips. "No, it looks like they've got just about everything we need for now, thanks."

"So what's the verdict on your research?" He looked at Sandra expectantly.

"My conclusions are the same as Mariana's. Her reasoning is sound and the treatment should work to make John immune to the contagion."

A look of grim satisfaction crossed Matt's features as he nodded. "How soon can you be ready to try it?" This time his question was directed squarely at Mariana.

"The reagents are already prepared. We can do it any time."

"Good." Matt looked at Mariana directly. "I'd like you to leave at first light to rendezvous with John and Donna. I've already talked to John about this in some detail, and he wants to proceed. There will be a small plane waiting to take you to Knoxville and back."

Matt didn't bother looking at Sandra. He knew she'd be concerned by his decision to proceed with testing their scientific theories on John. In a way, it was reassuring that she was so concerned about the idea. It told him she had a heart—unlike the other members of the original science team. Most of those heartless bastards didn't care who they injured or killed in pursuit of their goal.

The way Matt understood it, Mariana would give John a series of injections over a few hours. They'd know within a short amount of time whether the plan worked as intended or not. Worst case, John could die, though Mari had said she thought the odds of that were slim. John might also respond badly to the injections, in which case, he could become unfit for duty. Again, the odds of that happening were low, Mariana had assured him. Matt thought it was worth taking the chance to proceed because if it worked as they thought it would, John would survive the session immune and able to fight the zombies without fear of infection.

Right now, Matt needed all the skilled immune fighters he could get. John had the skills; all that was missing was the immunity. It was Matt's hope that Mariana would take care of that on her little excursion to Knoxville, and they could all get on with their assigned missions.

Matt spotted Simon lurking near the door and motioned him inside.

"Almost done here?" Simon asked with a smile for his fiancée.

"We were just going to call it a day," Mari assured him. "The commander just told me he's sending me to Knoxville to see John and Donna."

Simon's eyebrows shot up and he sent a questioning look in Matt's direction.

"It's only for a few hours. Mari can fill you in on the particulars."

With those few simple words, Matt had given clearance for Mariana to discuss her latest work with her fiancé. He figured she probably already shared a good deal of her work on the project with him, since he was participating in the study rather closely.

For a while they'd been the only two working on the project at all. They'd dated many years ago but broke up over Simon's career. The zombie problem had reunited them after Simon was exposed and became immune. He'd been the first immune soldier. He'd been the one sent in to eradicate the original problem. The only one. He'd done a hell of a job against awful odds, and then he'd tried to fade into the shadows after completing the mission and settle down with the woman he never should have lost in the first place.

He and Mariana had gotten a second chance, and Matt knew if the contagion hadn't resurfaced they'd be living on a farm somewhere by now, happily married and starting their family in peace. As it was, Mari was pregnant and Simon had been drafted to continue the dangerous work of fighting zombies. Only now he was part of a bigger team and he wasn't the only immune man who could combat the creatures.

While their peace had lasted, Mariana had tried to figure out more about how Simon's systems had been affected by the contagion. She'd been researching it on her own, with Simon's cooperation. He'd been her willing guinea pig from the start.

There were few secrets on Mari's side of that relationship. On Simon's side, Matt wasn't so sure. He'd worked with Simon for many years in special operations. They both had very high security clearances and knowledge of things that were meant to be kept top secret. There was a lot about his work that Matt had never been able to discuss with anyone other than his immediate teammates. The same had to be true for Simon, yet he'd managed to form a committed, healthy relationship with Mariana. That was something to think about.

For years, Matt had thought he'd never be able to commit

to a woman because of the nature of his job. Then Sandra had walked into his life—and right into the middle of his mission. For the first time, he could share a mission with a woman he had feelings for. It was a novel experience that still made him feel a little strange.

Somehow, Simon and Mari were making it work. Maybe there was hope for Matt and Sandra, too. Only time would tell.

"If that's all, sir . . ." Simon looked at him questioningly, and Matt realized he'd been silent too long, keeping them all waiting.

"That's all I've got. You should probably both get some rest."

"Aye, aye, Commander. That's just what I was thinking." Simon held out his arm for Mari to take and with not much further ado, he escorted his fiancée from the lab, leaving Sandra alone with Matt.

"You ready for some downtime?" he asked quietly. Matt had a mysterious expression on his face that Sandra could almost interpret as . . . a sort of caring concern. Whatever it was, it touched her. When he stretched out his hand, she took it without hesitation and allowed him to lead her from the room.

"Where am I bunking?" she asked on their way out the door.

"With me."

She shouldn't have been surprised by his calmly resolute tone.

"Won't that raise eyebrows?"

"Probably." He let her precede him through a doorway that led to one of the many staircases in the old building. "But I don't really care. You've been in harm's way more than I like, Sandra. I'll be damned if I let you out of my sight any more than I have to."

That sounded a little more serious than she'd expected. She knew she was having trouble separating her heart from her mind where Matt was concerned. He'd attracted her from the very beginning. Everything she'd learned of him since had only increased her crush on him. She admitted in the darkness of her mind that she was already half in love with the man. It wouldn't take much for her to tumble head over heels, and that would spell disaster.

She was holding out on him. That last secret—her secret shame—would destroy any chances for them. She knew it. She understood the danger of getting more involved with him. This could only lead to heartache for her if and when he found out the truth.

But she was powerless to fight it. She wanted whatever time she could have with him. More than her next breath.

He led her to a narrow corridor with lots of doors. He opened the last door at the end of the hall, and she wasn't surprised to discover it was a bedroom. Old fashioned and painted a rather depressing green color, this section of the building must have been used as a barracks at one time. She'd bet the other members of the team were happily snoring behind those other doors she'd passed on the way to this one.

"It's not a palace, but it'll do." Matt stepped into the room behind her and shut the door.

The bed was a double. Surprising in a barracks setting, but since the room was at the end of the hall, more than likely it had been designed for the commanding officer of the rest of those quartered here. She knew RHIP meant rank has its privileges and often those in charge got a little more room to maneuver than those under them. So the head man got a bigger bed, which suited her fine. If Matt was going to insist on bunking with her, she didn't want either one of them to wind up sleeping on the floor.

Matt was already shrugging out of his shirt, moving around the room, letting his fatigue show. The man had to be beat. As she was. The bed looked too inviting. This was no time to quibble over sleeping arrangements or what the rest of the team might think. Let them think whatever they wanted. Sandra was too tired to worry about it now.

She kicked off her shoes, removed her outer layers, and unhooked her bra under her T-shirt. That would have to be enough. She was too tired to do much more. She pointed her feet toward the bed and collapsed on it, her eyes closing almost immediately.

A soft male chuckle behind her was the only warning she got before a warm body settled onto the mattress beside her. Matt's strong hands lifted her, moving her around on the bed to his satisfaction.

"You can't be comfortable like that," he said.

"Like what?" she mumbled, her face smushed in the pillow.

"In all those clothes."

"Too tired to change into my nightie," she complained.

"No problem." Big hands raised the hem of her T-shirt over her head, lifting her as if she weighed nothing at all while he stripped her bare in a matter of seconds. Her pants were pushed down, along with her panties, and within a minute she was naked. "That's better."

Matt's voice purred with satisfaction near her ear as he settled on the bed with her in his arms. Skin to skin. He was naked, too.

Oh, my.

He spooned her, one hand cupping her breast as his body cocooned her in warmth. Her nipple beaded against his palm as her breathing sped.

"Sleep," he ordered, a chuckle clear in his tone.

"You get me all hot and bothered and then you expect me to sleep?" she groused, but it was halfhearted at best.

"We both know we're too tired to do each other justice right now. I promise I'll make it up to you later."

"I'll hold you to that."

Sandra woke to warmth, Matt's strong arms around her. His hand still clasped her bare breast and his fingers moved back and forth on her skin, arousing the flesh beneath. The louse was awake and had been touching her body, making her hot. It had felt like a dream, but now she realized the dream lover was all too real.

"That's not fair," she complained with a small smile.

"It's only unfair if I don't follow through," he replied smoothly, nipping the flesh of her neck. His mouth was warm, his lips damp against her sensitive skin. "I wouldn't leave you hanging, Sandy. You know that."

"Thank heaven for that." She tried to joke with him, but she was too excited. He'd done a good job of getting her primed even before she woke. The sneak. The delicious, adorable, incredibly skilled sneak.

He rolled, turning her in his arms until she was above him. Not what she'd expected.

"You're letting me be on top?"

His grin said it all. It was full of deviltry and desire, seduction and satisfaction.

"I've fantasized about watching you ride me," he admitted. "Besides, why should I do all the work?" His playful wink dispelled his smart-alecky tone. She chuckled along with him.

"All right, let's rope this little doggie and let the cowgirl ride." She grasped his already hard cock in one hand, aware of his sharp intake of breath, liking what she so obviously did to him when she touched him. She held the power now—while he let her. She liked that.

He flipped a little foil packet up between his fingers. The man had come prepared. She liked that, too.

"You've been planning this rodeo for more than a few minutes, haven't you?" She shot him a suspicious look.

"I had to do something to kill time until you woke up. I thought through a bunch of different ways we could do this and decided on this one. For now." His expression held a promise that sent a shiver down her spine. Her hand tightened fractionally around him.

"We'll have to explore some of those other ideas."

"Oh, I fully intend to. But first . . ." He ripped the wrapper with his teeth.

She reached for the condom and took great pleasure in teasing him while she slipped it over him.

Everything went very fast from there. Fast, but pleasurable.

Sandra wasn't inclined to wait anymore than Matt was. She sheathed him and positioned herself with little fuss, pausing only to draw out the feeling of connection, the long, wet slide into perfection as she seated herself over him.

Damn, that felt good. She stretched like a cat, enjoying the feeling of him inside her before passion took over.

"This is exactly what I dreamed about. You look good up there, and feel even better." Matt's hands roamed up her torso, landing under her breasts, cupping them as the tips of his fingers played with her nipples.

She couldn't help herself. She had to move. She began a gentle jog, lifting herself a little and relishing the slide of him inside her on the way back down. As her pace increased, his hands moved downward to help. His strong grip on her hips assisted as her thighs began to feel the strain.

But strain didn't matter. Nothing mattered but the incredible pleasure of him inside her, stimulating her sensitive channel, making her feel things she'd only ever felt with Matt. He was special. As special as a man could be to a woman. There was no other like him.

She was doomed. This man was so deep inside her mind and heart, she doubted she'd ever be able to be with another man like this. He'd ruined her for anyone else.

Then one of Matt's hands moved downward, teasing the apex of her thighs. His talented fingers rubbed over her clit in a circular motion, shooting electric currents through her body and sending her into orbit.

She cried out his name as she came. He didn't give her a moment to think before he rolled her under him, still joined. He began a thrusting, grinding rhythm that stole her breath and pushed her beyond what she'd thought was her limit.

"Come with me, Sandy. Do it again for me, babe." Sweat beaded his brow, and the fierce desire on his face spoke to her own spiraling desire.

Shocked by her own response, a muffled scream tore from her throat as a second orgasm rocked her. She realized only dimly that Matt joined her this time, slamming hard into her and his muscles going taut as he came hard. Her eyes opened and she saw the strain on his face, the utter bliss he found in her was a gift she hadn't expected. It made her feel like a queen. She'd done this to him. This strong man let down his guard for her and let her in—if only for this.

She'd take whatever she could get from him. She cared for him too much. So much, it nearly broke her heart. And filled it again.

Later, when the afterglow began to fade, Matt left the bed and headed for the attached bathroom. Sandra lounged, boneless after an amazing climax that had gone on and on. Had that really just happened?

And how soon before they could do it again? She smiled as he came out of the bathroom, a towel around his hips and water sticking to the spiky ends of his short hair. He smelled of soap and glistened with water droplets she wanted to lick off his skin.

"Stop looking at me like that or there's going to be trouble." His slow, sexy grin said it was the most delicious kind of trouble imaginable.

"Is that a threat or a promise?" She rolled on the bed, stretching.

He flicked his towel at her playfully, pausing as he dried himself off. Man, was he gorgeous. But he was also . . . dressing?

"We don't have time now. Consider it a promise for later." He pulled on his shorts and threw the damp towel at her. "Get up, sweetheart. We have work to do."

The work that night turned out to be blessedly routine. Matt escorted Sandra to the new lab space where she spent her time deep in study and research. He went to the office he was using inside their new headquarters and did a little paperwork before the combat teams went out after dark. Then he went to the tactical support area and supervised as the reports came in. All was quiet in the woods around the base that night.

By morning there had been no zombie sightings and no suspicious activity of any kind. They'd had a quiet night, thank goodness, but Matt knew it couldn't last for long. Rodriguez was out there, still plotting and planning . . . and making more creatures as he tested and perfected his technology.

Matt and Sandra rendezvoused just after dawn at the room they shared. They didn't speak, but their shared goal was clear. Sandra stepped into his arms with a soft smile, a look of yearning on her beautiful face that mirrored his own.

Without words, he took her to bed. They undressed each other, and their lovemaking this time was slow and deliberate. It had all the passion of their previous encounters with none of the urgency. Matt lay her beneath him and claimed his space between her soft thighs, stroking slowly within. He sat back, lifting her hips to rest over his thighs so he could watch each joining and parting, each thrust and retreat. He loved it when she moaned his name and he loved watching her come around his cock as he stroked her into orgasm after orgasm.

He tested his stamina, glad to find he could bring her pleasure three times before he took his own. They collapsed together, tangled in a mess of arms and legs. Sleep claimed them both and he roused only to make love to her again, this time from behind. He slid into her, spooning her luscious body with his, loving the feel of her delicate skin next to his rougher body.

Soon that wasn't enough. He lifted her by the hips, positioning her to his satisfaction on all fours. He slid within her again, thrusting in increasingly hard strokes from behind while she whimpered little sounds of need. Reaching around with one hand, he stroked the tiny nub that brought her such pleasure, knowing he needed her with him this time. He couldn't hold out. He wanted to come fast and hard, and he wanted her with him.

She cried out his name when she climaxed, taking him with her. The strong sheath of her inner muscles contracted on his cock, coaxing him into a pulsing release that made his head spin and his breath come in ragged gasps. She was amazing.

He collapsed with her after cleaning up the protective

sheath he'd worn, and they slept again in a sated stupor. Only
the persistent ringing of Matt's cell phone roused him later in
the day. He rolled over in the rumpled bed to find his phone
tucked in the pocket of his scattered clothes. He checked the
number and got out of bed, moving to the bathroom to take
the call so he wouldn't disturb Sandra, who was still fast
asleep.

"Sykes," he answered.

"Sir, we have a few police reports filtering through our
search matrix. Seems like more than a few civilians are being
reported as missing today." Sam Archer was on the other end
of the line. Matt recognized both his voice and the number
that had come up on his screen.

The news was not good. Not good at all.

"How many?"

"My latest count is fifteen civilians."

Damn. "Male or female?"

"That's the odd thing, sir. They're mostly female. And
young. Most in their twenties and single. They're being reported by friends and family that expected them to be somewhere they aren't. The common factor is that they went out
for drinks with friends last night. Now they're missing and the
friends are missing, too."

"They're snatching girls out of bars now?"

"Sounds like it. You have to admit, they'd be easy pickings
for the right people."

The thought made Matt wince. It was bad enough when
zombies attacked hardened soldiers—or even young soldiers
who at least had some training in how to defend themselves.
The thought of the creatures attacking young women out for a
night on the town was difficult to comprehend.

"What else?" Matt knew there had to be more for Sam to
have woken him.

"There's activity on the base perimeter in three locations."

"What kind of activity?"

"Tripped sensors in two remote areas. From the speed, size,

and heat signature, we're assuming animals—probably deer—walked into our coverage area."

"But we're not taking any chances," Matt reminded him. "Have you sent anyone out yet?"

"Just about to do so, sir."

"Good. Send 'em," he confirmed the standing order. "And the third location? What was the activity there?"

"Cut fence in an area we'd already wired."

The team was slowly stringing wire that carried a low-voltage current around the perimeter of the base but the work was proceeding slowly. The base perimeter was enormous and densely wooded in areas.

"When?" Matt asked.

"About seven minutes ago."

"Make that location the priority."

"Already done, sir, but we're stretched pretty thin." Sam had done the right thing in waking Matt. This was a delicate situation, and Matt had to be the one to make the tough decisions about troop placement.

"We have time before sunset. Is the cut fence accessible by road?" Matt knew the areas they'd been able to wire quickly were the most accessible. It was the rougher areas deep in the woods the soldiers were having a hard time covering.

"Yes, sir. It's about ten meters from the east side access road near gate fourteen."

"All right then," Matt thought about the layout of that area. The cut wire should be out in the open if he remembered correctly. "Send out two members of the cleanup team in a jeep. Give them a long lens and feed their video signal to tac ops." He used the abbreviated name for the tactical operations area they'd set up inside their new headquarters. "Instruct the men not to leave the vehicle. I want them to see if they can identify the break in the line and feed us video. We'll determine how to proceed depending on what they can show us."

"Aye, aye, sir."

Matt ended the call and went back out into the bedroom. Sandra was stretching, starting to come awake.

"What time is it?" she asked in a voice raspy with sleep.

"Time to get up." He swatted Sandra's luscious bare ass, wishing he had time for more. She was sweet. The most delicious lover he'd ever had, and he was quickly becoming addicted to her.

He thought maybe she felt the same. Every once in a while he'd catch her looking at him with such a strange expression on her face . . .

There was no time to puzzle over it now. They had work to do.

"Where's the fire?" She sat up in bed looking adorably rumpled. He watched her head for the attached bathroom, determined not to let her distract him. At least not too much.

The door closed and he heard the shower turn on. Only a few minutes later, it shut off again and she came out. He'd dressed and checked his messages and e-mail in the time it took her to shower.

"John called from Tennessee. Things should be wrapping up down there soon. That's the good news. The bad news is, we have activity in the woods and missing persons reports to sort out. I expect there's going to be some action tonight. Our quiet time is over. We're due in the conference room for a planning meeting before the night shift starts. As I said before, we need to bring the fight to the enemy, not wait for them to come to us."

"Sounds dangerous." She looked worried.

"Dangerous for our enemies, Sandra."

"I'm glad you're so confident." She reached for her clothes.

"It's the only way to succeed." That was a truism he'd learned in his years in the Special Forces.

She only shook her head as she began to get dressed and he watched with great pleasure. She was beautifully built beneath her conservative attire.

"Stop staring." She laughed. "You're making me nervous."

"You're beautiful, Sandra. Surely you know that." Her

pretty blush made him realize she wasn't aware of her own al-
lure. He'd fix that. He'd make her believe. Too bad they didn't
have time now or he'd show her again how attractive he found
her.

"I thought you said we were in a hurry." He realized he'd
been staring and shook himself.

"You're right." He gave her a smacking kiss before opening
the door and ushering her out. They walked down the hall and
made their way through the old building toward the conference room.

Once there, Sandra sat beside him again. He didn't particularly care what the others thought about their relationship.
Simon and Mari were engaged, as were Sarah and Xavier. It
didn't impede their ability to do their jobs and everyone knew
it. No sense trying to hide the fact that he had something going
on with Sandra. These guys were too observant—it would be
almost impossible to keep them in the dark on something like
this.

He called the meeting to order and began handing out assignments for the evening. The cleanup crew was on the day
shift, so they'd be going off shift shortly. He'd built in some
overlap to the schedule deliberately. He went over the reports
from the day shift and reviewed new developments. They reviewed the video the two-man team in the jeep had sent. It
turned out to be nothing. The wire had been cut by a con-
struction crew that was doing routine maintenance on the
gate. The animal readings were just that. A herd of deer had
been spotted near one of the tripped sensor locations, and it
was likely the same story on the other one, though nothing
had been seen by the men sent to check the area.

Mariana was back from her short trip to Knoxville. For the
moment, Matt was keeping the news that John had successfully been made immune to himself. Only Mariana, Simon,
Sandra, and Donna knew besides himself. Not exactly a secret, but not common knowledge, either.

The most important thing on the agenda for this get-
together was the action plan for that night. Matt wanted de-

tailed input from the combat team, since they'd be heavily involved. They spent the majority of the meeting working out
ideas with the fighting personnel. The final plan they arrived at
was relatively simple. They would use the tracking device
they'd taken out of Sandra to lure the bad guys and their zombie friends into an ambush.

"Won't Rodriguez realize we've discovered the tracker?"
one of the men asked.

"Not necessarily. Not if we take them all out."

"Okay, so we neutralize the zombies. That's a given. But
what if they have a spotter? I mean, there's got to be someone
herding them to us. They don't think for themselves, that I've
seen," Simon pointed out.

"Exactly," Matt agreed. "And before now, we've never had
the opportunity to pick the battleground. If we do this right,
we control the circumstances. We can set up the ambush to
handle not only the creatures, but we can put a team in place
to spot the spotter. A spotter of our own, if you will."

The men didn't waste time after that, planning a strategy
that would net them a big win—if they could pull it off.

Chapter Twelve

Sandra was nervous, but Matt's steady presence calmed her somewhat.

"Just act naturally. We're going to eat a nice dinner inside and then after the sun goes down, the guys will get you to safety while the rest of us deal with the attack we hope will come."

"Only someone as crazy as you would *want* to be attacked by zombies." She tried to make light of the situation, but they both knew it scared the heck out of her.

"The location is perfect. This satellite dining facility is small and near the woods. There won't be many people here at this hour, and if we time it right, we can keep the action in the wooded area."

"What if your timing is off?"

"Then we'll go with Plan B." He shrugged nonchalantly but she knew he wasn't as cavalier about that option as he seemed.

"What's Plan B?"

"We lock down the mess hall and keep everyone inside. There aren't many windows, so they won't see much. Then we take care of the problem outside."

"This whole thing sounds risky to me." She was uneasy with the whole setup.

"I won't lie. It is risky. I don't want more civilian casualties and I certainly don't want anyone seeing the zombies as we engage them, but on such short notice this is the best place we could come up with that was believable. Rodriguez has to know that I'm keeping you close now that so many attempts have been made to get you. It makes sense that I would bring you to this remote mess hall rather than someplace farther from our new headquarters. If he's as connected to the news on base as I think, he'll already know all about our move to the new building."

She looked around the mess hall. The building was of older vintage, like the rest of this outlying area of the enormous base. It served a smaller contingent of older, less populated buildings. At this hour, there were few personnel inside. Most went home for dinner or to one of the larger, more modern facilities elsewhere.

Sandra supposed Matt was right. He was, after all, the commander of this very special team. Even now, he had the tracking chip in a sealed plastic vial of saline in his pocket. When they left the mess hall, Sandra was supposed to peel off from Matt under cover of night and head for safety with Sam Archer acting as escort until she was safely back inside the new headquarters building. Then Sam would rejoin the combat team who would probably already be engaging the enemy in the woods behind the mess hall.

At least that was the plan.

She hoped it worked. Frankly, she didn't have the greatest confidence. Not that she doubted Matt and his men. Her real concerns were about the bad guys and whether they would behave as rationally as Matt's plan envisioned. For all she knew, the zombies would attack the mess hall directly and not wait for her outside.

As the meal drew to a close, she found herself growing more nervous. She had a part to play in this little drama and had to get it right. Any minute now, they'd get up from the table and the plan would be set in motion.

Matt's hand landed over hers as she reached for her water.

Damn, he had good hands. Strong and manly with calluses from what had to be years of weapons training.

"Calm down. You're shaking like a leaf."

Damn. She didn't realize she'd been that obvious.

"Sorry." She made a conscious effort to calm herself. "I'm worried. I just can't help thinking something's going to go wrong."

"Let us worry about that. All you have to do is your part. We've got the rest covered."

Just in case, she'd brought a vial of her experimental serum. If anyone who wasn't already immune got bitten or scratched, she might be able to help them survive—if their body chemistry reacted well to the serum. That was a big if.

She'd improved on the serum a bit already, but there was still a ways to go to get it so that it would work on everyone, regardless of their particular chemistry. Still, it was worth a try. The contagion brought almost certain death. The serum had at least a slim chance of saving someone who'd been exposed.

"I hope it all goes as expected. I'm just worried it won't. These guys haven't really played by our rules to this point, and I fear they won't do it this time, either."

"My guys are all experienced improvisers. If the plan goes south, we'll compensate. Don't worry. We've got every base covered." Matt stood, picking up both trays. "It's time to get this show on the road."

She followed him to the door, aware when he pulled the tactical radio earpiece from his pocket. He placed it in his ear so fast she almost missed it. He was connected to the team outside, able to hear their reports.

"Everything's good to go," he told her. "I want you to walk with me to the switch point. We'll meet up with Sam at the end of the walkway, and you go with him as quickly as possible. Got it?"

She nodded. "Be safe, Matt." She wanted to say so much more, but the words stuck in her throat.

She wanted him to know she loved him, but fear kept her

silent. Fear of rejection. Fear he wouldn't feel the same. She was afraid of so much. The plan seemed to be full of holes. She was worried about him and his men. Even immunity to the contagion wouldn't save them from being ripped limb from limb or eaten alive if they got surrounded by the creatures.

Sandra tamped down her fear and put on a brave face.

"Ready?" Matt asked, his hand on the door handle.

"Ready as I'll ever be." She sent him a grim smile. Impulsively, she placed one hand on his arm. "Promise me you'll be careful."

He covered her hand with his and squeezed lightly.

"I will if you will. When Sam meets us I want you to go with him without delay. I want you safely away before the battle begins. I need to know you're safe."

She nodded. "I promise."

"Then I do, too." The corner of his lips rose in the barest hint of a smile.

The slight gesture warmed her heart beyond all expectation. Matt pushed open the door and they headed out together.

They left the mess hall together, but if all went as planned, Matt would be ditching her at the end of the path nestled between the old brick building and the tree line. Sam would take his place and escort her to safety. The ambush was set a little farther on, in a more secluded area that the team had all agreed would be the most likely attack point.

The woods were denser, the lighting less intrusive, and the area was sparsely inhabited. The zombies would have a clear shot at whoever they caught in that area. The reverse was also true. The combat team had plenty of cover to set their trap. Now all they had to do was spring it.

Only a short way down the path, a man stepped out of the trees directly to their left, catching their attention. Half his face was missing. Torn away by the zombie who had killed him.

"Ah, hell," Matt cursed low, opening the channel between himself and the rest of the combat team. "They jumped the gun. It's going down on the walkway. Get over here. Move now."

Matt pushed her behind him, simultaneously digging out the dart pistol he'd concealed under his jacket. It was already loaded and an expert flick of his finger dismissed the safety. He took aim and began firing without hesitation. Four darts in succession hit various parts of the zombie's body, spreading the dose for maximum effect.

Sandra looked around, gasping when she saw another bloodstained body with a half-eaten face clear the tree line about ten feet from where she was standing.

"Matt, there's another one!" She pointed to her right, where the creature advanced. She backed away, but there wasn't much space. The path was bordered on one side by a short hedge with a strip of grass behind it that led right up to the foundation of the building. On the other side was more grass that led up to a small copse of trees that ran the length of the building.

Matt fired four more shots and then paused to reload. It appeared he had spare clips in his pockets. She wondered how many he had on him, when two more creatures stepped out from the tree line. She could see more working their way through the tree trunks at their steady, unrelenting pace.

"Where are you, guys?" Matt talked into the small radio clipped to his ear.

She didn't hear the answer, but the curse he bit off under his breath spoke volumes.

"What's going on?"

"Equipment malfunction." He turned to fire more darts as he pushed her over the short hedge and into the grass strip between the building and the paved walkway. "They'll be here in five. We just have to hold these guys off until the cavalry arrives."

"I hope we can last that long," she muttered under her breath.

"Son of a—" Matt cursed as a full half dozen zombies converged on them. One had a broken arm that dangled at a nauseating angle as it walked. All sported the obvious signs of zombie attack. At least three had missing fingers that looked, even from this distance, as if they'd been gnawed off. Two had parts of their noses missing in different configurations that turned Sandra's stomach when she chanced a look. Then she noticed that more than a few ears had gone missing as well, and all had dried bloodstains down their mouths and over their clawed hands.

There wasn't much room to maneuver in the area between the building and the path. For all their plodding, the creatures actually moved pretty fast. The steady pace was deceptive. They covered a lot of ground in their rhythmic way. A brick wall at her back and a semicircle of zombies in front, only Matt stood between Sandra and a painful death at the hands—make that claws—of the undead platoon heading their way.

"To the right, Sandy," Matt urged as he kept firing at the advancing enemy.

There was one bit of good news. The first one had finally disintegrated. The bad news was that the others were all still standing and heading in their direction—even the ones with darts sticking out of their bodies. The toxin in the darts hadn't done its job yet, but it would. Given enough time. It was up to Matt and Sandra to stick it out and keep themselves out of range long enough to let the toxin do its thing.

Sandy felt along the brick wall behind her, edging to the right as instructed. Her hands scratched along the old, worn brick until they encountered something smooth and cold.

Glass.

There was a big window in the side of the building. Hallelujah.

She shrugged out of her jacket, moving quickly, and wrapped it around her hand a few times before punching through the glass with all her might. It hurt her knuckles, but the fabric did a good job of protecting her skin from the broken glass. Thankfully this was an old building and it had regular old glass panes, not tempered glass or Plexiglas or safety glass of any kind. It broke easily into jagged spears that tinkled and crunched as they fell to the floor below. She used her cloth-wrapped hand to break away the bigger shards that stuck out, making a big enough hole for them to step through.

"We're in," she told Matt.

Looking over her shoulder toward him, she realized they had nowhere to run except into the building. The creatures had effectively cut them off. On the bright side, two more zombies had disintegrated into piles of slimy goo. Still, the toxin wasn't working fast enough. They had to buy more time.

"Go," Matt ordered.

Sandra didn't waste any time jumping through the hole she'd made in the window, into an empty room. High ceilinged and bare of furnishings, her footsteps echoed around the room, bouncing off the brick walls and concrete flooring. The room was large with a chalkboard along one wall, like a classroom or some kind of old-fashioned conference room.

Matt followed her in, two of the zombies fast on his heels. They bottlenecked outside the window for a few seconds while they jockeyed for position, each seeming to want to go in first and neither giving way to the other. Mostly mindless as they were, they didn't seem to grasp the idea of cooperation or courtesy.

Sandra would have laughed if the situation wasn't so critical.

"Try the door." Matt pushed her toward the room's only door while the duo at the window finally figured out how to get in.

They did it without regard for the jagged edges of glass sticking out all around the neat hole Sandra had made. They didn't bleed much, she noticed absently, though the glass made long, deep gouges into their skin. It looked like the majority of blood they'd possessed when living had already drained out of their previous grievous injuries.

Sandra made it to the door and turned the handle. The hardware was a little loose in its mooring, but it wasn't locked. The knob turned and the door opened into a darkened hall. She looked both ways, surprised to see the shadowed hall looked like it ran most of the length of the building, with doors opening off it at regular intervals.

Matt backed toward her and the open door, keeping himself between the advancing creatures and Sandra. She was appalled to see even more zombies finding their way in through the window. They were multiplying faster than she'd have believed if she wasn't there experiencing it.

"The team is on its way. They'll come in from behind. As long as we can stay ahead of these guys, we should be okay."

"The hallway is clear," she reported.

"Good. Go!" He shooed her toward the open door and she went without further comment. Matt followed, closing the door and looking around—probably for something to block it with. "We have to contain them." His tone was grim.

"Can't we just stay here in the hall and pick them off as they try to follow us?"

"The toxin takes too long to take them down, but it's as good an idea as any. We'll retreat only when we have to. Go up to the end of the hall and make sure our exit is clear. The last thing I want to do is get boxed in here."

Sandra ran up to the end of the dark hall and pushed open the door.

Only to come face to face with the business end of a gun barrel.

"Not so fast, doctor."

She knew that voice. Far from being the rescue she'd hoped for, this was something much worse. It was the guy who'd attacked her in the lab. The man who worked for Rodriguez.

She squeaked. It was embarrassing, really. She couldn't get a word out for the fear that rose to choke her.

"I was going to let the monsters finish you off, but now I'm not so sure." The goon motioned with his gun, shooing her back the way she'd come.

A quick glance told her Matt was still at the other end of the hall, trying his best to contain the zombies in the classroom. But even as she glanced toward him a second time,

Matt backed away from the opening and a zombie stepped through the door and into the hall. He was followed by another and another until Matt was in full retreat up the hall, directly toward her and the man with the gun.

Of course, Matt had a pistol in his hand, but it contained lethal toxic darts.

Matt turned to face her and took in the situation with one bright-eyed glance. The hallway was dark, but she could see his face as he moved closer. He walked right up to her, ignoring the slow but steady advance of the zombies behind him in the hall.

"You don't want to do this," Matt said to the man behind her.

"Why's that? All I have to do is keep you both here long enough for my little friends to get close enough to infect you. Then my troubles with you both will be over at last. Of course, I could shoot you both now, but that would feel sort of anticlimactic. I really want you to join the rest of the creepy crawlies and turn you back on your friends. There's a kind of poetry in that, I think. And I want you to suffer."

"Why?" Sandra asked, feeling the butt of the gun prodding her forward to meet Matt.

"Because you've both managed to piss me off."

The man stopped walking. Sandra followed suit. Matt continued to advance until he stood only a few feet from her.

"This could've been so much easier if you'd just accepted Rodriguez's offer, doctor. You could've had it all. But no. You're a stubborn bitch." He pulled her hair and she gasped at the sudden pain as her head snapped back.

"There's no need for that." Matt's tone was both placating and disapproving.

"Drop the weapon," the man instructed Matt.

Pausing only a second, Matt lifted his hands in a placating motion, pointing the pistol toward the ceiling before he dropped it to the floor. It made a clattering sound that echoed down the hall.

"Now back up. I want you to be the first to get bit." He

sneered his words, clearly relishing the idea of watching Matt die a horrible death.

But this guy was sorely mistaken if he thought a scratch or even a bite would kill Matt. Obviously their attacker didn't realize Matt was immune. Or that Sandra had been immune longer than anyone.

Sure, they were still in danger from physical attack by the creatures, but the contagion wouldn't kill them. Really, the only person at risk from the contagion here was their attacker. He was behind the eight ball and didn't even know it.

"Let her go." Matt's tone was unequivocal.

"Sure. Why not?" The man pushed her toward Matt, using her hair as a handle.

She crashed into Matt's chest, free of her attacker. He'd let her go, but not before pulling out more than a few hanks of her hair. Damn, that hurt.

Matt clutched her close for just a minute before putting her to the side. He didn't push her behind him, she noted. The zombies were moving steadily closer, and their assailant continued to threaten them both with his handgun. They were definitely stuck between the proverbial rock and hard place.

Something had to give, but she didn't know what. She had to trust that Matt had an ace up his sleeve. He carried himself with enough confidence that she assumed he knew something she didn't.

"What's in this for you?" Matt asked. "You think Rodriguez is going to keep you around once you've lost your usefulness? He already offed Tim."

"Tim was a wimp. He deserved what he got for lousing up his job."

"You're not far behind. How many times have you failed in your attempts to get to Dr. McCormick?" Matt taunted the man.

The goon shot Sandra a look filled with both hatred and disgust. "You've been a royal pain in the ass, doctor. The commander has that right. But I have the last laugh. This time, you're going down."

"Not quite."

A new voice spoke from the side of the hall, from one of the numerous doorways. It had opened silently in the darkness, and only the gleam of his eyes and the dark metal in his hands gave away the presence of Sam Archer.

"It's about time, lieutenant."

"Sorry, sir. This one tried to delay us, and I'm sad to say it worked. To a point." The dark line of his assault rifle was leveled at the intruder. "Drop your weapon."

It was standoff time. Until hands grabbed their attacker from behind. Pale hands pushing down on his shoulders with great force. The face exposed as the man sank downward in surprise was ashen gray, disfigured, and bloodstained.

Before they could do anything, the sharp yellow claws drew blood and the gaping maw dropped open, the head bending to allow teeth to sink into the man's neck. He screamed like a little girl. A little girl in agony.

After that, everything seemed to happen at once. The man's weapon discharged wildly toward the ceiling, and Matt pushed Sandra to the floor. Sam and Matt were on top of the guy in a split second, prying the zombie loose and drawing him away. Sam shot the creature point blank several times as more of the combat team began pouring into the corridor from other doorways along the hall.

Around that time, the zombies Matt had shot began disintegrating one by one as they closed in from behind. Sandra realized Matt had darted them all and was just waiting for them to implode while he'd tried to protect her from the more imminent threat of the man with the gun.

Chaos ensued. One of the guys tried to push her into an empty room, but she wasn't going. Everyone here was immune except for the guy who'd orchestrated this entire debacle. He'd escaped answering their questions once already. She wasn't going to let him die if she could help it. He could lead them to Rodriguez and end this whole mess, but she had to keep him alive to do so. She had to at least try.

First, though, they had to finish with the zombies. None of

the men would let her back into the hall while the zombies still stood. One by one, she watched them collapse in on themselves. Matt had taken care of all the creatures that had followed them in through the window. Sam took out the one that had attacked Rodriguez's man, and the rest of the team checked all the other rooms, calling the all clear within about five minutes.

All in all, it went faster than she'd anticipated. Fast enough that she still had time to try to save their attacker's life.

"Let me through." Sandra pushed past the big guys who stood watching over Matt and their former prisoner.

"Better not to see this, ma'am," Sam said in a somber tone. "It ain't pretty."

"I might be able to save him."

Matt pinned her with his gaze. "You've got the serum on you?"

"I brought it with me. Just in case." She brandished the small vial in one hand, a disposable syringe in the other. She'd had both in her purse.

"Give it a try." Matt backed off to give her room to work.

Sandra moved fast. She knew if this was going to work, timing was critical. She dropped to her knees at the man's side and prepared the syringe, estimating dosage based on her visual assessment of his size.

Positioning the syringe carefully, Sandra stabbed the victim with the long needle, injecting the experimental serum directly into his heart for maximum effect. He screamed at the pain of it, but there was no time for anesthetic or other niceties.

"You trying to torture me, bitch?" he spat out, breathing hard when she removed the needle.

"I'm trying to save your life."

"Don't bother. I'd rather go all zombie on your ass and take you out that way." He looked just ornery enough to do it, too.

"Won't work. I'm immune."

"Dammit, I *told* Rodriguez . . ." Whatever he was going to say was cut off as his body went into convulsions. This reaction was a good sign, but it would be a while before they knew if the new serum would work with this man's body chemistry.

"Where is he?" Matt demanded as the man came out of the episode a minute later. Sandra looked up to find Matt kneeling by her side and Simon standing guard over them. "Where's Rodriguez hiding? Where's his lab?"

"Lab?" The man's eyes narrowed as he focused on Matt. "Wouldn't you like to know?" He gave the ghost of a laugh. This man was as bitter as they came, she thought. "Your pet bitch knows all about labs, doesn't she? And the zombie Marines she freed that night so many months ago. She started all this. All she had to do was close a door." His gaze pinned her as her body froze in shock. "Isn't that right, *doctor*?" He spat the last word like a curse.

"I did not—" she tried to protest, but the words died in her throat as she felt Matt stiffen beside her.

"Come off it, bitch," the man swore. "You were the one left to watch the experiment that night. You're the one who ran out of the building and let them loose. You're the one responsible for all the men those original few killed and all those who came after. You're killing me right now. How does that make you feel?"

As far as attacks went, this one cut to the bone—and beyond. It sliced into her soul.

She didn't need to look up to know that Matt and Simon had heard every word. The cat was out of the bag. They finally knew the secret she'd been so desperately hiding.

The man on the floor went into another convulsion, preventing her from saying anything. This was worse than before. Violent and scary. He seized so hard she thought she could hear his bones creak. Then he collapsed.

Sandra administered CPR, trying desperately to revive him, but after a few minutes, she had to give up. He was dead.

"He's gone." She stood and stepped away from the man's body. "There's nothing more I can do for him."

"That's it then." Matt pointed his weapon and fired.

It was only a few minutes before the man disintegrated before their eyes.

Sandra stood back, unable to meet Matt's eyes. She feared what she would see there, now that he knew she'd let those original zombies out into an unprepared world. She'd caused so much havoc—when something as simple as remembering to close the door to the lab might have prevented much of the devastation that followed.

It was all so pointless. The guilt she'd carried so long threatened to overwhelm her, but she had to face it. The time for hiding had abruptly drawn to an end.

She looked up not to find Matt standing before her, but a red-faced and scowling Simon.

"Is it true? Did you let those original zombies out?"

Mutely, she nodded. Her misery was complete.

"I hope you realize you're responsible for the deaths of a lot of good men. Good men who were my friends." Simon choked up and his eyes went flint hard.

"That's enough, Si." Matt stepped between them, pushing Simon back physically.

That he would stand up for her—especially knowing what he knew now—gave Sandra some glimmer of hope. She couldn't see Simon past Matt's bulk, but she felt the tension in the air as the men faced each other down.

Because of her. She'd done this. She'd set friends against each other. And so much more.

She had so much to regret. So much guilt to carry around.

"Enough."

She didn't realize she'd spoken aloud until Matt turned slightly to face her. The look on his face was one of incredulity. He was no longer the indulgent lover or the stern commander. A stranger's face looked back at her. Cold eyes that she couldn't read.

That stare struck her like an arrow through the heart. She stumbled one step backward but stopped before she could show any more weakness.

"Simon's right and for that I apologize. I know it's not

enough." She stepped backward, wanting to escape before she started bawling. "It'll never be enough."

That was it. She couldn't say more without sobbing and she wouldn't show these predators her soft underbelly. They'd rip her to shreds.

She turned and walked away as calmly as possible, not letting her shoulders shake even as tears flowed freely down her cheeks. She wouldn't let them see her vulnerability. The team would only think she was putting on some kind of dramatic show. They didn't trust her anymore. Perhaps they never had fully trusted her.

She regretted that, too. She'd really liked Simon and especially Mariana. They could have been friends, given half a chance, but not now. Not after the truth had come out in such a bad way. Any glimmer of hope for a friendship after this was all over was gone now. Simon would never forgive her, and she didn't blame him.

Worse though was Matt's coldness. Her love folded in on itself, rejected. It made her chest ache with a pain unlike any she'd ever known.

"Good to have you back." Matt greeted John and Donna as they reported to his temporary office in the old building for a debriefing. They'd returned to base only minutes before and reported directly to the new team headquarters. "Please be seated."

Matt sensed something in the air between the two newly returned team members. Donna kept glancing at John with uncertain motions. John was a much cooler customer. Matt couldn't tell what was going on from John's poker face, but Donna was much less adept at hiding her nervousness.

They sat side by side in front of his desk. Donna looked worried. John's spine was rigid though he looked otherwise nonchalant to the casual observer. Something was definitely up here. Matt looked from one to the other, allowing the silence to lengthen.

Donna shifted in her seat, but John remained cool. He wouldn't crack. Matt sighed.

"Okay. Spill. What's going on?"

John shrugged and reached a hand out to the side. Donna put her much smaller hand in his all too familiarly, and Matt suddenly understood.

"Donna and I are a couple now, sir," John said simply, almost defiantly. "If that disqualifies either of us from the team, then so be it."

Matt had to laugh. "Well, why not? We seem to be running some kind of matchmaking service around here lately. What's one more couple?"

"Scuttlebutt has it that you're involved with Dr. Mc-Cormick," John said in an accusatory tone. Matt figured John mistook his sarcasm for disgust, so he let the disrespect slide—to a point.

"Don't believe everything you hear." Matt grimaced. Simon had kept his mouth shut about Sandra's costly mistake for now. Matt wasn't sure how long it could remain hidden. Everyone on the combat team had lost friends to the monsters. They all had a personal feeling about how this contagion had gotten out. They wouldn't welcome the news of what Sandra had done—or failed to do. They wouldn't welcome her if they knew. "For the record, I won't answer any questions about myself and Sandra. Not for you. Not for anyone."

"Then you know how we feel."

"Understood." Matt nodded, glad to put this situation behind them for now. "Now that's out of the way, we can get back to business."

John and Donna proceeded with their report on the action in Tennessee. They'd taken out one of the original science team—a mentally unstable female scientist who'd moved into her ex-husband's mansion on the lake. She'd wreaked havoc on the local fishermen as well as her ex-husband and his new trophy wife. They'd been the first she'd killed, and the carnage had spread from there. The evildoer had built her own little private zombie regiment that hid at the bottom of the lake during daytime.

"I can't believe they were sheltering in the lake during the day." Matt shook his head at the bizarreness of it all. He'd thought he'd seen everything, but this mission just got weirder and weirder.

"She'd told her husband to go jump in the lake . . . and he did," Donna confirmed. "It was a good place to stash them. They were dead. They didn't need to breathe, and the lake had deep parts murky enough to keep them well hidden and out of sunlight."

"What about the fish?" Matt asked. It would be a nightmare if there was now a lake full of zombie fish. "You'd reported you believed there was no cross-contamination. I assume that still holds, right?"

"Yes, sir," John answered. "Donna took lots of samples and I checked over the lake visually as well as talking to a bunch of the fishermen. Nothing strange going on with the fishing, according to them." He looked to Donna, who continued.

"The preliminary results of testing on the remains show the strain of contagion the scientist was using was carefully tailored to affect humans only. Also, the initial samples from the lake itself show no signs of cross-contamination. There are a few more tests to run, but so far, everything looks clean."

"Donna, I want you to assist in the lab. Your chemical engineering background could prove helpful," Matt ordered.

"She's good in the field, Commander," John surprised him by saying.

Donna looked over at her newfound boyfriend. "Thanks for the vote of confidence. I thought you'd be happy to have me out of the action."

"I would, but I also like keeping an eye on you." The smile he sent her was intimate. "And the commander needs an accurate assessment of your abilities so he knows where to use your talents best."

"For now, the lab is the best place. I'd like her to be armed, though. We've had security problems, which is why we all moved into this building. Sandra's been targeted and attacked in her lab, in an off-base home that I knew had been secure previously. She was even approached by one of Rodriguez's men in the base cafeteria a while back. So being stuck in the lab may not necessarily be the safest place in the world. You're immune, Donna, and now you have some valuable experience in battle against these things. You'll be issued a pistol and multiple dart clips. Are you okay with that?"

"Absolutely." Both Donna and John had grown very serious as Matt laid out the problems the rest of the team had been facing on base while the pair had been on their little road trip.

"Good." Matt was more than pleased with her quick answer.

He liked the idea of having Donna's skills available inside the lab where Sandra would be working, just in case there was trouble with the security of their new building. He didn't think there would be, but then he'd been wrong about the issue before—to their detriment.

And it would be good to have another pair of eyes on Sandra. He wasn't sure how he felt about her anymore. He was conflicted. His heart was saying one thing while his mind said another. Through it all, he couldn't quite understand why she'd felt the need to lie to him.

Matt put the confusing thoughts from his mind to deal with later. He had to focus on the here and now. Having John and Donna back—albeit as yet another couple on the team—was more than helpful. Right now, they needed every person they could get. Especially those immune to the contagion.

From all accounts, Mariana's treatment of John had worked like a charm. He'd been exposed to the contagion after the treatment, during the action in Tennessee, and lived to tell the tale. He also had the same regenerative healing powers as the others who were immune. It would be good to have a man of his skills able to participate fully in the action.

"John, you're with the combat team. All hell has been breaking loose in the woods and we could use the help."

John grinned almost evilly. "Glad to be of service, sir."

Chapter Thirteen

"Hey, you're back." Sandra was surprised to see Donna enter the new lab.

"Just got in a little while ago. We had to talk to Commander Sykes for a bit, and then he sent me to you." She lifted a knapsack in her hand. "And I come bearing gifts." She placed the bag on the lab bench and opened it carefully. "Samples that need testing as soon as possible."

"Samples?" Sandra moved closer, intrigued.

"Didn't you hear we'd run into a pocket of zombies in Tennessee?"

"Yes, I'd heard. I assume it's all taken care of, since you're back."

"Yup. They're all gone, so we came home." Donna looked really pleased with herself.

"Then what are the samples? The remains are tested by the tech guys normally."

"Oh, yeah. I know that. These are samples from the lake. The zombies were hiding in there during the day. We didn't find any evidence of cross-contamination and the few tests I was able to perform on site were negative, but we have to be sure."

"Hiding *in* the lake?" Sandra was intrigued by the idea—and sickened. Cross-species contamination could be disastrous on so many levels. "I can see why we need to push your samples to the top of the testing queue. Hand them over." Sandra made space on the bench and brought over a few empty test tube racks. "When do you want the results?"

"Oh, Commander Sykes assigned me to you for the time being, so I can help with the testing."

Now that was interesting news, but not totally unexpected. Despite the fact that Donna was immune, she probably still wasn't much of a fighter.

"Great. I could use the help. Mariana is getting follow-up blood samples from some of the guys. She'll be back in an hour or so. We can get a good start on these in the meantime."

The two women worked together until Mariana returned to the shared lab space with a rack full of tubes of her own. Mariana greeted Donna warmly when she saw her, giving her a slyly amused smile.

"So I hear you and John are involved." Mariana certainly didn't pull any punches, putting Donna on the spot almost immediately.

Sandra figured Simon hadn't told Mariana yet about how Sandra had let the zombies out, way back when. If he had, she suspected Mariana would have already asked her point blank about it. Mariana was a no-nonsense person, and Sandra respected her for that. Still, she really didn't look forward to the interrogation she might be subject to when Simon finally spilled her secret. It wouldn't be a comfortable conversation, that was for sure.

Donna's chin dropped as she ducked her head, grinning from ear to ear. She was shy, which was kind of cute on the younger woman. Sometimes Donna made Sandra feel so old by comparison. This was definitely one of those times.

"Yeah," she confirmed, then seemed to regain her confidence as she lifted her head to face them. "He's pretty amazing."

"He's pretty spooky, if you ask me," Mariana kidded. "Of course, some folks say the same thing about Simon, so don't take it to heart. I mean it in a good way."

They shared a laugh as Donna talked shyly about her budding relationship with John and how it had come about. Apparently, facing death together had accelerated their courtship considerably. Sandra was happy for them, but worry was her constant companion these days and she was concerned about their future. The long-term effects of exposure and immunity to the contagion were still unknown.

"What about you?" Donna turned the attention on Sandra. "I hear you and the commander are a couple now. Good for you."

Sandra groaned inwardly. "Don't believe everything you hear. Matt moved me in with him because I'm being targeted by Rodriguez and his men. I think he figured the only way he could be sure of my safety was if he watched me himself."

"Don't tell me there's nothing romantic going on," Donna insisted.

"Okay. I won't tell you." Sandra turned resolutely toward her workbench.

"Oh, no, you don't." Donna grabbed her elbow and coaxed her to turn around again. "Spill."

"There's nothing to spill." Sandra sighed and ran a weary hand through her hair. "Matt and I almost had something, but I doubt it will go anywhere now."

"Why not?" Donna really didn't know when to stop.

"We've had a falling out." Sandra didn't see any way out of this conversation. If she had, she would have taken it gladly.

"Over what?" Great. Now Mariana was getting involved.

Sandra wasn't sure what to do. Here was a chance to tell her side of the story. A chance to set the record straight. But telling the secret that wasn't so secret anymore might also turn these women against her for all time. Really, what choice did she have? They'd find out sooner or later, she was certain. Better to have at least some control over how the information was presented to them, right?

Sandra took a deep breath for courage. She could tell both Donna and Mariana were growing more concerned the longer she deliberated over her answer. Both knew now that something more than a simple lover's spat was dividing Sandra and Matt.

"I was keeping a secret from him, and it came out in a rather unpleasant way." She searched for words. For a way to make this sound better than it was. "The night the zombies were unleashed on the world—the very first night—I was there. I was the person left on duty overnight in the morgue. I was the one the zombies attacked first. That's how I got infected and how I became immune. I was also the fool who ran into the night to get away from them . . . leaving the door open behind me. I let them out of the lab. My foolish, headlong flight allowed them to escape into the woods, only to infect and kill so many more men who were sent after them."

Dead silence greeted her confession. Sandra imagined she could hear the clock on the wall ticking away the beginnings of friendship she'd started with these women.

"Oh, honey, don't blame yourself." It was Donna who spoke first. "You didn't know what would happen. Nobody did. I think you were damn lucky you turned out to be spontaneously immune, and I know from whence I speak. The same thing happened to me. I was attacked and left for dead, toyed with by those monsters who had been people I once knew. I've never been more frightened in my life. I tried like hell to get away from my attackers. We were outside, but if it had been indoors, I doubt I would've had the presence of mind to shut the door behind me if I'd managed to escape."

Sandra was grateful for Donna's eager willingness to forgive her blunder, but Mariana's steady gaze made her nervous. Mariana was older and perhaps wiser than the younger woman. She also had seen the effects of that first infestation firsthand and knew the pain her fiancé experienced, having lost his best friends to the initial attacks. Simon, too, had been one of the first to face the creatures. He'd prevailed, proven to be immune to the contagion, but he'd come close to death more than a few times.

All because of Sandra's biggest mistake to date.

"Such a simple thing to cause so much havoc," Mariana

said in a contemplative tone. "I'd wondered what had Simon so upset."

"He had every right to be upset with me." Sandra spoke when the silence had dragged on too long for her stretched nerves.

Mariana regarded her with a steady, no-nonsense gaze. "I can understand why you hold yourself responsible to some extent. If you'd barred that door and alerted someone on the military side, a lot of pain and death might have been avoided. On the other hand, I doubt I would have done any better under the same circumstances."

Sandra's breath eased out, and only then did she realize she'd been holding it. Mariana's understanding wasn't something she would take for granted—if that's really what her well-considered words were leading up to.

"What really happened that night, Sandra?" Mariana asked, eyeing her sharply. "I've often wondered how the situation developed. How it got so out of control, so fast."

Mariana was giving her a chance to tell it like it was. The other woman's expression clearly said she was reserving judgment, willing to listen. That was way more than Sandra had gotten from either Simon or, especially, Matt.

"I was alone on overnight duty in the lab that had been converted to a morgue. They'd brought in cadavers for the next phase of testing. The experiments had started late that afternoon and nobody expected much to happen. Especially not as fast as it did. I was only supposed to monitor the progress overnight." She shivered remembering the cold chill that had permeated the darkened room. "I heard a noise. I'd turned off most of the lights in the lab so I got up to investigate. It turned out to be the first one rising. As I passed a table, one of them grabbed my arm. I got infected by him, though I didn't realize it until much later. I fought him off and ran for my life. The others were rising by that time and I only barely escaped."

"That's like something out of a horror movie," Donna whispered, moving closer. "Nobody knew what the contagion would do at that point, right? You were the first to see it. Damn. That must've been really scary."

"I've never been a fan of horror movies. What happened in that lab scared me beyond anything I can even describe."

"I bet." Donna, bless her, was as sympathetic as Sandra could have hoped.

It was Mariana who still seemed to be reserving judgment, and that worried Sandra. She would have liked to have Mariana's understanding—one colleague to another.

Finally, Mariana seemed to thaw. She held out her hand and Sandra took it. Mariana pulled her close for a quick hug.

"That can't have been easy for you. Like I said, I doubt I would've done anything differently than you did under the circumstances." Mariana released her and stood back. "It's obvious you've been carrying this guilt for a long time. You need to let it go. Simon may come around in time. If not, it's not your problem. You did the best you could. As have we all."

"I wouldn't blame Simon if he never forgave me," Sandra said honestly. Of course, it wasn't really Simon's forgiveness that was upmost in her mind.

"He lost a lot of friends to the contagion. So did Matt. The spec ops community is a small one, all things considered."

And there it was. Matt was what really mattered. His opinion was the most important one to her. Everybody else could want to burn her at the stake, but if Matt believed in her, it would be enough.

Too bad she doubted he'd ever speak civilly to her again. She'd betrayed his trust by not telling him sooner. She'd had her chances, but she'd let them all pass by. Too afraid to trust him with her heart.

Yet, here she was, heartbroken over him. She hadn't been able to protect herself from the pain of loving him.

And now she'd lost him.

"Don't look so sad." Mariana clasped her shoulder. "He'll come around."

"I'm not so sure."

"So there *is* something going on between you and the commander," Donna said from her side. "I'm so sorry. I didn't mean to pry before." The younger woman looked anxious.

"It's okay. I guess we're the talk of the team since Matt moved me in with him." She laughed brokenly. "I don't even know where I'm supposed to sleep anymore."

Donna put an arm around her shoulders. "Don't worry. We'll take care of you if needed, but I think our fearless leader has a strong possessive streak when it comes to you. He had some hard words for John when he mentioned your relationship."

That was news to her. Sandra was surprised, and a little ray of hope sprang up out of nowhere. She tried not to let that little ray shine too brightly, just in case. It wouldn't do to get her hopes up only to have them crushed. She had to be cautious with her heart. It couldn't take much more damage.

The women worked together companionably until they were summoned to an impromptu meeting with the rest of the team. Everyone gathered in the conference room. Matt was the last to appear. When he walked in, the room quieted and all eyes focused on him.

"The techs found some things in the remains." Matt slapped a file folder on the table in front of him. "My former assistant, Tim, had one of the same trackers in him that Dr. McCormick had implanted without her knowledge in her hip. So did our escaped prisoner. He also had a wallet on him with a number of false I.D.s under a couple of different aliases. With the help of our investigative contacts," he nodded toward John, "we've traced them back to his real identity."

Matt signaled for the lights to be lowered as he turned on the projector. The former prisoner's face illuminated against the screen much larger than life.

"Meet Leroy James Mertle. He's a native of this area. His grandfather owned a farm just outside of town, which he inherited. I'd lay odds that's where Rodriguez is hiding out. John requested satellite time, and we have initial surveillance reports that indicate activity inconsistent with typical farming activity. We may have caught a break."

"Were the eyes in the sky able to spot anyone we know?" Sarah asked from the end of the table as a series of enhanced satellite photos circulated on the screen.

It was her brother who answered. "We haven't had a whole lot of time to watch the place yet. CIA is streaming images to us whenever the satellite is overhead." John checked his watch. "The next pass should be in another two minutes." He fiddled with the laptop he'd set up on the table in front of him, rechecking the wire that led to it from the data projector at the center of the table, facing the screen against the far wall.

"I want us all to watch that next surveillance feed. Combat team, I want you to get the lay of the land and formulate an infiltration plan. Everybody else, keep an eye out for anyone who might look familiar. Rodriguez and his people seem to have an easy time getting on and off this base. Any of you may have seen someone that works for him at one time or another. Sandra, I want you to tell us if you see Rodriguez. You've seen him recently and know what he looks like better than any of us."

She nodded, surprise in her gaze as she met his. He wondered what that meant. Had she thought he wouldn't talk to her? Was she regretting at all the fact that she'd lied by omission to him? Did she regret keeping her secret—or simply that it was out?

He had so many questions for her and no time to ask them.

That time would come, he promised himself. Later. He'd make time. He didn't want to let her walk out of his life without knowing the answers to those questions. Those, and a slew of others.

The most important of which was, had any of their time together been real? Had her heart been engaged as completely as his? And could they somehow salvage something between them?

He wasn't sure he really wanted to know the answer to that last question. On the one hand, his life would be a lot easier without her to complicate it any further. On the other, he wasn't sure he could live without her now that he'd glimpsed what it could have been like.

He wanted her love. And her trust. He'd thought he'd had the first, but the revelation of the secret she'd been hiding had shattered any illusion that she'd trusted him.

Matt had suspected she was keeping some kind of secret from him, but he hadn't expected it to be something so important—something directly related to their shared mission. He could have understood if the secret had been of a more personal nature. He would have tried to understand if she'd tried to hide a former lover or some foolish personal problem. But the details of the creation of the contagion and how it spread to the outside world were vital pieces of information that should have been revealed to him long before now. She should have told him from the start.

He'd thought they'd gotten beyond that kind of thing. Way beyond. But apparently not. He'd been wrong about her. Wrong about the trust he'd thought had been building between them. Wrong about the love that had blossomed in his heart, only to be shot down.

"Satellite is streaming in ten, Commander." John's voice broke into his silent reverie.

Matt gave the nod to dim the lights so they would be able to see the projection more clearly. He pushed aside the awkward minute of silence that had fallen in the room and allowed the darkness to engulf him. All eyes turned to the screen, watching intently as the video feed came to life.

The images were grainy at first, then clarified. Even Matt was impressed with the quality of the image. The CIA had access to some truly nifty toys in orbit.

"The structure at the top right of the screen is the farmhouse," Matt informed those gathered, using a laser pointer to highlight the area on the screen. "This is a small utility shed and this larger building here is the barn, according to the county assessor's report. The last onsite visit was in May of last year, so keep in mind that things may have changed since then."

"Activity in the southwest quadrant," John pointed out.

"I see him. Anybody recognize him?" Matt solicited the room at large.

The man was a little too indistinct.

"I can zoom in," John volunteered.

"Do it," Matt ordered, watching intently.

The man was leaving a small outbuilding that wasn't on the assessor's plans. The individual was heading for the farmhouse at a brisk pace. If they didn't identify him now, they could lose their chance of doing so later. The satellite stayed overhead for only a few minutes at a time.

John punched keys on his laptop and the image zoomed. It grew grainier for a second, then resolved. Matt heard a familiar feminine gasp. His gaze swept down the table to Sandra. She sat rigid in her chair, her eyes glued to the screen.

"That's Rodriguez," she whispered. Turning toward Matt and meeting his gaze in the gloomy room, she spoke in a firmer voice. "That's definitely Dr. Rodriguez."

Satisfaction flowed through him. They'd just caught a big break.

"All right then." He nodded his thanks to Sandra for speaking up and confirming what he'd already surmised. The man hadn't changed too much from his file photo. His hair was a little longer, but other than that, Dr. Rodriguez hadn't altered his appearance much, the overconfident bastard. Matt forced himself to look around the table at the rest of the team. "You all know what to do. I want to have our team in place tonight before dark. We're going to take him down."

Matt motioned for Sandra to stay after the meeting. He had a few things he wanted to say to her before the action started again.

"Sandra, you're on lockdown. I don't want you leaving this building until further notice."

"You can't be serious. The guy who was after me is gone. I doubt I'm in much danger now."

"You're in danger every minute until Rodriguez is apprehended. Don't doubt it. If Leroy Mertle," he stumbled over the name, "could come on and off base with impunity, what makes you think someone else in Rodriguez's employ can't do the same?" He paused a beat before continuing. "No, you're still in danger until the threat has been completely neutralized. To me, that means until Rodriguez is in my brig."

"If this is some kind of revenge for my not telling you about . . ." She trailed off, seemingly unable to finish.

"About what?" He couldn't resist taunting her. "You know what? Forget it."

"It's obvious you haven't forgotten anything," she muttered.

"Damn straight I haven't forgotten. How could I? You lied to me, Sandy. That's not something I can forget."

"I never lied." Her tone was adamant.

"By omission, you certainly did. I knew you were keeping something from me and I should've trusted my gut instincts, but I rationalized my concerns away. I didn't think you would keep something that could have been vital to our mission from me. I trusted you to be straight with me on that at least. Turns out I was wrong."

"Tell me how knowing I'd forgotten to close a *door*"—her voice broke on the word—"could have made a difference to our mission!"

She had a point, but he wasn't about to give in.

"I didn't want to get into this with you now." He ran one hand through his hair. It was shaking slightly and that small loss of control annoyed him even more. "In fact, I'm done. You have your orders. Follow them. And don't let the door hit you in the ass on the way out." He purposely looked down at the papers that littered the table in front of him, dismissing her.

"I'm not one of your soldiers. I don't have to follow *orders*." She nearly spat out the words and her body trembled in anger. "In fact, I'm done. With this mission. With this team. And especially with you."

She stormed out of the room and he followed but stopped short upon finding Simon just outside the door, waiting for him. He had his arms crossed before his chest and stepped in front of Matt when he would have pursued the fleeing woman.

"Let her go."

Matt thought about his options. He didn't seriously think Sandra would do anything risky or foolish. She probably just needed a chance to calm down.

He slammed his hand against the door frame. "All right. Gather the men. I want to go over the battle plan."

"You gonna be okay, skipper?" Simon's voice was pitched low.

"No," he answered honestly. "But I'll survive."

Sandra was so angry she thought maybe steam might be coming out of her ears. She was also hurt. She felt like her heart was breaking all over again. Tears blinded her as she reached the door to the stairwell. She didn't really know where she was going. She just had to get away. Away from Matt. Away from the accusation in his eyes. Away from her guilt.

Of course, she knew there was no getting away from the guilt that followed wherever she went. In a way, it was a relief to have the truth out in the open. Sure, Simon despised her and Matt wasn't far behind. All in all, it turned out about the way she'd expected.

The only consolation was Mariana's understanding and Donna's compassion. Remembering that, she headed for the lab. She was about to enter when she heard voices from within the room.

"I wouldn't want to be in her shoes right now. The commander looked really ticked off," Donna said. She didn't know the half of it.

"It'll blow over in time," Mariana assured her. "But for now, I think they're in for a rocky road. Matt Sykes doesn't seem the type to forgive or forget easily."

Yeah, Mariana had that right. Matt wasn't ever going to forgive her, Sandra thought.

"Are you concerned about Simon going out with the combat team tonight?"

"I worry whenever he goes out on a mission," Mariana admitted. "This has all got to come to a head. The sooner the better, as far as I'm concerned."

"I feel a bit safer knowing the guy who kept infiltrating the base has been taken care of. I bet Dr. McCormick is breathing a lot easier on that score, too."

Come to think of it, she was, Sandra realized. While there were still enemies out there, the only one she'd seen on base was this Leroy character. He was gone, so the most immediate threat had been removed. That didn't mean she was totally safe yet, but it did give her cause to feel some relief.

She stepped away from the doorway and headed in the opposite direction. She didn't want to see anyone yet. She needed some air.

Matt met with the combat team and finalized plans for the assault. They would go as soon as everything was set. The plan was to attack in what was left of the daylight so they could secure the living bad guys first, then wait till after dark to get any undead inhabitants who might be on the property.

The combat team would approach through the woods that bordered the farmhouse. That scrap of woodland meshed neatly with the base perimeter, which explained how the zombies were getting on and off base so easily. His men would use the same method to get to the farmhouse without being detected. Only, they weren't going alone this time.

"Sir, I have to suggest once more that you are too important to this mission to be stomping around in the bush with us. You should stay here." Simon, his oldest friend on the team, repeated his objection to Matt's plan to go with them on the raid.

"Noted. But there's no way I'm staying home this time." He flashed Simon a bloodthirsty grimace.

After the day he'd already had, Matt wanted to get back in the action. His injury had sidelined him too long. The zombies he'd taken out after dinner last night had given him a fresh taste of real combat, and he missed it. If there was more action to be had, he wanted in on it, regardless of the fact that he was *management* and should rightfully be overseeing things from the sidelines. One more immune warrior on the mission was another few percent chance they would succeed. Matt was through sitting on the sidelines.

He also wanted something to do, other than sit around and think about how annoyed he was by Sandra's actions. He'd thought they could have something special, and she turned out to have betrayed his trust. He wouldn't get over that soon, even if his heart demanded some kind of resolution.

He was leaning toward forgiving her and asking her back in his life, which didn't sit well in his mind at all. But his heart was dangerously close to taking control. It wanted her, no matter the cost in pride or self-control. It loved her. Scratch that. *He* loved her.

Damn. He'd been avoiding that word but it kept popping up. Regardless of what she'd done—what she'd told him, or hadn't told him. He was still in love with her.

"Look, Matt," Simon spoke quietly so that only Matt could hear. The other men were bustling around the room, readying their gear. "If you insist on doing this, at least stay to the rear. You haven't operated as part of a team in the field in a long time. I don't mean to insult your skills, but you know the guys have worked on group maneuvers more than you in recent weeks. They've established a rhythm. You know better than to mess with that, right?"

Matt sighed. "I do. And I understand your concern, Si. I'll hang in the back, but I *am* going on this mission. I've sat on my hands too long, and I won't be held back anymore when we're finally drawing this thing to a conclusion."

"I can understand that," Simon allowed. "It'll be good to have you along, skipper."

"As long as I don't get in the way, right?" Matt was able to laugh at himself and bring a grin to Simon's face as well.

They were old warhorses. They'd been going on ops to-gether since they were young SEALs. Matt's injury had side-lined him too soon, and it had been some time since he'd been in the field. Simon knew that better than anyone, and Matt understood Simon's warnings came out of friendly concern. He could respect that. As long as Simon could respect the fact that Matt would not be sidelined ever again. He was back in action now and would be for as long as his newly healed body allowed.

Matt checked his gear, loading the pockets of his combat vest with extra clips of darts. They'd need them after dark, he was certain. For the more ordinary foes, he made sure he had enough traditional ammunition for his favorite assault rifle. He'd missed going on missions with the big hunk of metal he kept well oiled and in peak condition. He'd put in a lot of quality time on the range and knew his skills were still sharp with his weapon of choice. He just hadn't been allowed out to play in the real world with the big boys in far too long.

Simon was right to warn him off. He wasn't in battle-ready condition to lead the team and he knew it. But he did have the skills to keep up and assist the rear guard. He'd plant himself in back and let Simon do the leading, as he'd been doing since this team formed.

"It's your show, Si," Matt reassured his old comrade. "I'll hang in the back and be ready to follow your lead."

Simon grinned as he finished loading his own vest. "It's about time the roles were reversed."

"I won't let you down."

The old friends shared a grin. Together the two had gone through a lot over the years and both knew they could depend on each other to be there when needed. The bond between brothers in arms was strong and even stronger between Spe-cial Forces brethren.

Chapter Fourteen

Matt ducked behind a tree and blended into the shadows, following Simon's lead. They were through the convenient hole in the perimeter fence the zombies had no doubt been using and now entered the farm property. Simon led the team of ghosts through the woods toward the outbuildings where they'd begin their silent assault.

The soldiers were going to sweep from the outside in toward the farmhouse. There were a couple of small outbuildings hidden under the tree canopy. The first structure turned out to be a regular barn that held a rusty tractor and other farming implements that had seen better days. The team cleared it and moved on.

The second hidden outbuilding turned out to be a zombie safe house of sorts. Simon and the rest of the team began firing darts from every entry point. The door, windows, and even cracks in the old wood became portals for firing the nearly silent darts at the half dozen creatures that were hunkered inside the dim interior, hiding from the dappled sunlight that shone through the leaves.

The team waited a few minutes to be sure all the zombies disintegrated before moving on to the next part of the plan. The main barn waited, as did another small shed and the farmhouse itself.

Simon went ahead with the majority of the team, as planned. Sam and Matt acted as rear guard while the team cleared the main barn and the outbuilding.

"The shed is the lab. Couple of gurneys and some lab equipment. Nobody here right now," Simon reported over the tactical frequency they all used. "The shed's clear. Moving on to the farmhouse."

After that, it was all rather anti-climactic. Simon and the team advanced through the house, finding it mostly empty. They encountered only minor resistance in the kitchen where two gunmen were posted, probably as security. The combatants put up a fight, so it was no surprise they both ended up dead, though Matt would have preferred to take them alive.

"Sir, you'd better get down here." Simon's tone hit Matt in the gut. He knew Simon was in the basement.

"What is it?"

"Rodriguez. We've got him cornered, but he has a hostage. He wants to talk to the man in charge."

"Who does he have?" Matt asked as he double-timed it down the stairs, leaving Sam and most of the rest of the team on guard above ground.

Matt skidded to a halt at the bottom of the stairs. The area was open except for a few support beams and two people. One was Rodriguez. The other . . .

"Sandy."

"Come no closer or the girl dies."

What the hell was she doing here? Matt felt dismay fill him, and anger began to seep upward into his heart. That wouldn't do. He had to keep his head. He had to stay cool. Emotions could only get in the way in a situation like this.

Rodriguez looked panicked. His hair was in disarray and his clothes were rumpled like he'd been caught napping. He had Sandra around the waist with one beefy arm and held a loaded syringe to her neck with the other.

"The contagion?" That had to be what he had in the needle. "You want to turn her into a zombie? Kill her like all the others you've murdered with your so-called research?"

Thank God the man didn't seem to have a gun, knife, or other conventional weapon. Still, Matt would approach with caution until he was certain Rodriguez didn't have anything more dangerous to Sandra on him than the syringe.

"She should have died long ago," Rodriguez spat. "The minute she refused to aid my research, she signed her own death warrant."

The relief that coursed through Matt at Rodriguez's words was all out of proportion to the situation. Sandra had refused to help Rodriguez, as she had claimed. She had been telling him the truth about that at least. With all that had happened, he had doubted her claims of innocence. But here was the man himself, clearing her of any collusion. A heavy weight lifted off of Matt's heart. She'd been telling the truth when she said she'd rather die than help their enemies.

No matter what this looked like, he made a decision to trust her. He didn't know how Sandra had ended up here, in Rodriguez's hideout. He was sure that story would be a good one. It was time for him to take a leap of faith. He had to give her a chance. He only hoped it didn't blow up in his face.

Matt edged closer.

"Stay back or I'll kill her!" Rodriguez was wild eyed with fear and anger.

"You don't want to do that. She's your ticket out of here, right? Come on. Tell me what you want in exchange for the doctor."

"I want a plane. A small plane with no transponder."

Matt pretended to think. "Gee, planes are hard to come by, and it wouldn't have anywhere to land close by around here. How about a helicopter. I can have one of those here in ten minutes."

"Okay." Rodriguez seemed to consider the offer. "Helicopter to an airfield. Then I want a plane and pilot."

"Where would you go? You have to know you wouldn't be able to land anywhere without us knowing."

"I have my resources. I have allies you couldn't even begin to imagine."

"Admiral Chester? Ensign Bartles. I know you killed my previous assistant, Tim. I also know he was working for you and your so-called allies, spying on me. Did you seriously think I was so dull I wouldn't notice a fox in my own hen-house? Give me some credit."

"We knew you knew about Tim. That's why I took him out." Rodriguez backed away a step, dragging Sandra with him. Her eyes widened, but she seemed calm. "Now get on the phone and order that chopper and the plane."

"No." Matt sighed. "I'm afraid I can't do that."

"I'll kill her! I'm not messing around."

"I know you aren't, and I know you are fully capable of killing."

"You would stand by and watch? I thought you cared for her." Rodriguez's eyebrows rose and shock took over his expression.

"That I do," Matt admitted. It wasn't as hard to say that out loud as he thought it would be, in public. He didn't want to hide his feelings anymore. "I care for her a great deal. Which is why I want you to put down the needle and surrender."

Rodriguez gave a nervous laugh. "You've got to be kidding."

"I'm afraid not. Put it down, doctor, and I'll take it easy on you."

"This guy is nuts." Rodriguez seemed almost to be talking to himself. "It is you who should be dropping your weapon and calling for my transportation. There is a phone right over there." He nodded toward a desk along the wall. "Pick it up and make the call."

Matt glanced at the phone, then back at Rodriguez.

"Tell you what. Move the needle away from her neck and I'll pick up the phone."

Rodriguez seemed to consider. "I guess it doesn't matter where I stick her. One scratch with this and she's dead anyway."

That's what he thought.

Rodriguez moved the hand holding the needle away from

Sandra's vulnerable neck and settled it down near her arm. The point stuck into her clothing a millimeter or two, no doubt very close to the surface of her skin. It didn't matter, of course, but Matt counted the potential for tangling in the fabric of her shirt as an extra pad on the split second timing he'd need if he was going to jump Rodriguez.

Of course, he still wasn't really sure if he would *have* to jump Rodriguez. He had time to play with this scenario, and he still needed to know if the man had any conventional weapons on his person.

Then Matt would solve the puzzle of just how in the hell Sandra had wound up here. To someone else, this could look really bad. It might look like she'd left the safety of their new headquarters, despite all orders to the contrary. Like she did it on purpose. Like she was in collusion with Rodriguez after all.

And Matt might have believed that. He had no doubt some of his men were thinking along those lines even now. But Matt trusted her. Foolish as that may sound in this situation, he trusted that she wouldn't betray him. She may have lied in the past by omission, but that was before. This was now. And now—after all they'd been through together—he trusted her.

Hell, he loved her. As far as he was concerned, you couldn't have love without trust. What he felt was a deep, all-consuming love that filled his heart near to bursting. He wanted a future with Sandra and he'd do anything he had to in order to get that future. Anything.

Including humoring a bastard that threatened to kill her when all Matt really wanted to do was rip Rodriguez's head off. With his bare hands. Slowly, and as painfully as possible. Matt wanted Rodriguez to suffer for all the horror and death he'd caused, and especially for the way he'd been terrorizing Sandra.

So Matt played along, stalling for time. While he kept Rodriguez distracted with talk, Matt was aware of the other members of his team positioning themselves around the basement. There was a window high above and behind where Rodriguez stood with Sandra. This old house was built into the side of a hill, and half of it stuck up above the soil line so much that they'd put in a window to let in light.

It would also let in Sam Archer and a righteous boatload of hell and damnation all over Rodriguez's pansy ass. Matt could hear the team's terse reports over his earpiece as they slid into position.

"Now you pick up the phone," Rodriguez prodded him. Matt didn't move except to tense his muscles in preparation for action.

"If you say so."

Matt kept his tone steady and his eyes on Rodriguez. He wanted to be ready for whatever the unpredictable scientist might do next. One thing was for sure, Rodriguez would never be ready for what was about to be unleashed on him.

When it went down, it did so at lightning speed.

Sam smashed into the room through the window and grabbed Rodriguez from behind, glass and wood splinters flying every which way. The little bits of glass tinkled as they crashed to the tile floor of the basement. Sam and Rodriguez ignored the glittering, sharp rain as they wrestled for the syringe. Matt saw the needle flash as he grabbed for Sandra and pulled her toward him, out of harm's way.

Rodriguez, to his credit, tried to put up a fight. Admittedly, it wasn't much of a struggle, and Sam subdued him with little trouble. It was only moments before it was all over.

"Do you have the syringe?" Sandra asked in an urgent voice.

Sam tossed it through the air and Matt caught it without managing to stab himself. He saw Sandra flinch in his peripheral vision. He noticed her cringing, too, and her worry was sort of endearing. He offered the filled syringe to her, and she took it gingerly into her hands.

"What's going on?"

"This is the latest version of the contagion. With this we may be able to come up with a better way to stop the creatures or improve my design for the serum. We've had to reverse-engineer from remains up till this point—and not very successfully. This is a big break, scientifically speaking. We need to get this to the lab for study."

"Are you kidding me?" Matt was filled with frustrated anger.

Did she not realize she'd almost gotten herself killed? Was her research the only thing she cared about? Matt stalked off to cool down before he throttled her. He looked around the large basement area to take stock of the situation, and almost simultaneously Simon called the all clear.

Sandra heard the pride and satisfaction in Simon's voice as he announced they were in the clear. It went through her, radiating down her bones. They'd captured Emilio Rodriguez, the man who'd threatened her for the past few months. They'd also secured a sample of his latest contagion for study, which was quite a coup.

With Rodriguez in custody, she was finally safe. She could hardly believe it. He couldn't threaten her anymore. Her secrets had been revealed, Rodriguez had been captured, and somehow she was still standing after all that. Sandra let the idea sink in while the men took care of business. She really hadn't expected to survive this deadly game, yet here she was.

The men put zip-tie cuffs around Rodriguez's hands and marched him up the stairs. He was out of sight faster than she could have imagined. She watched Matt confer with the members of the combat team a few yards away.

His mood was angry. She could tell from the sharp movements of his hands and the set of his broad shoulders. No doubt he was suspicious of her again. Finding her in Rodriguez's lair didn't look good. Even she knew that.

Would he believe her when she told him how she'd gotten here? She wasn't sure. She hoped he would. She hoped he'd give her a chance. Give her the benefit of the doubt. But even she had to admit her track record for telling him the truth wasn't the best. She wouldn't blame him if he didn't believe her. Trust was something you earned, and she'd done precious little to earn his.

She watched Matt issue orders to secure the rest of the

property and search the house and grounds. The men scurried into motion, and Matt turned, his gaze searching the area until it landed on her.

She could tell by the way his muscles tensed that he was working himself up a good head of steam as he stalked the length of the basement to stand in front of her. He faced her, just looking at her until she started to fidget under his scrutiny. Those blue eyes pinned her, making her feel like a bug under a microscope.

"Now would you like to explain how in hell you came to be here?"

She cringed, knowing he wouldn't like what she had to say. Especially not in his current mood.

"I was tricked into leaving the building," she admitted. Boy, did she feel stupid admitting to how easy it had been to dupe her. "I got a call on my cell phone telling me that Mariana had been captured and was being held hostage by Rodriguez's men. I asked for proof they really had her and was instructed to look out the window on the northeast corner. The one by the secondary door on that side."

"You didn't think this was important enough to tell somebody?"

Oh, yeah, he was really angry, and she couldn't blame him. She just had to muscle through her explanation and hope he would understand.

"I was near the door already, so I went to the window and looked out. I saw someone in the distance, wearing a white lab coat. The person was about her size and struggling against the man holding her. I thought it was Mari. I really did. The man on the phone was pressuring me, telling me he'd kill her if I didn't come out right that minute. I was all alone on that side of the building. There was no one to tell and no time to waste."

"What the hell were you thinking?" He took her shoulders in his hands and shook her just once.

"I thought I should trade myself for Mari. They would only kill her and her baby. I couldn't let that happen when it was me they wanted."

"Noble, but stupid, Sandra. God!" He shook her again and let go, visibly trying to control his frustrated anger.

"I realized the minute I opened the door that I'd been duped," she admitted. "In my own defense, I wasn't thinking too clearly. Not after . . ." She didn't want to admit she'd been so affected by their argument.

Sandra didn't know what to say to make this situation any better. Her rescuer had turned into an angry tyrant, and she didn't know how to avoid his ire.

"That is it!" Matt sounded furious. "I am through watching you put yourself in danger. What the hell were you thinking, leaving the building alone? You were supposed to stay put. To stay safe."

He grabbed her around the waist and planted a kiss on her lips that shocked the breath right out of her. It was all out in the open now. All his fear for her safety. All his caring. All his love.

Dare she believe it?

"Oh, Matt." She gasped for air when he broke the kiss and hugged her close, nearly lifting her off her feet. His irritation seemed to have dissipated somewhat—or morphed into passion.

"I love you, dammit. How could you take such a risk? If they'd killed you . . ." His voice trailed off as he buried his face in her neck.

Oh, yeah, she believed him. Miracle of miracles—he loved her. The admission was too raw, too pure. He wasn't censoring himself. He meant exactly what he said.

"You don't sound too happy about it." She found the energy to joke.

"On the contrary." He rubbed his stubbly cheek gently against the side of her face, holding her close. "But this isn't the time or place." He lifted his head and eased his hold fractionally. "I have a lot I want to say to you, Sandy, but it'll have to wait until we tie up some of these loose ends." He looked around the basement at the men standing there, watching them.

Nothing showed on their faces—they were too well trained to betray their thoughts so easily—but Sandra knew they had to be speculating about her presence, and their commander's involvement with her. It made her uncomfortable to think they might disapprove.

Matt kissed her once more, and she put away any coherent thoughts for later.

"Uh, Commander," a throat cleared from the bottom of the steps.

Matt sighed as he dragged his lips away from hers. He didn't let her go, resting his forehead against hers. It felt so good to have her in his arms again.

"What is it, Sam?" He didn't even look in the other man's direction.

"Sir, Rodriguez is ready to go and the house is secure. We found an office chock full of documents pertaining to Rodriguez's research."

Now that was good news.

"Any sign of the list of frequencies for those little transmitters he's so fond of?"

He gazed into her eyes and stroked her hair with one hand, unwilling to let her go just yet. He didn't care who saw him holding her. She was his, dammit, and he wanted the world to know it. Such thoughts might have scared him before but not any longer. He was on the verge of something momentous here. Too bad they were in the middle of an op. Otherwise, he would have already carried her off to his cave and claimed her like the primitive man he was.

"Not yet, sir," Sam's voice broke into his thoughts, refocusing him. "John is interrogating the prisoner, but he's not being very cooperative right now."

"That'll change. Put Sarah on the task of searching the office and get Donna over here to assist. Bring her in through the woods along with the decon team. Once they clear the place we can call in the rest of the techs to help with the search. Is that all?"

"Almost, sir. Simon wants to know how you want to take Rodriguez back to base—loud or quiet?"

"Quiet," Matt answered at once. "Definitely quiet. We'll walk him back through the woods the way we came in. If he still has allies out there, I don't want them to know the doctor's been shut down until the last possible moment. We'll keep him under wraps as long as we can."

"Yes, sir." Sam headed back up the stairs.

"The ones who took you off base. How many were there?" Matt asked Sandy. He let her go and stood facing her. It was time to get back to work, despite how much he wanted to go on holding her in his arms.

"There were two of them. Both male. The smaller man wore the lab coat, and after they had me they weren't concerned about letting me see their faces. That worried me until they said Rodriguez wanted me alive. They couldn't kill me. He wanted to do it himself."

"They still could've hurt you." His gaze met hers, and he knew she understood what could have happened. "They could've hurt you real bad, Sandra. It was foolish to leave the building, no matter how pissed off you were at me."

"I know that. Heck, I knew it as I pushed open the door, but I thought I was trading myself for Mari. I didn't want anyone else to pay for my mistakes. I'm sorry, Matt. I shouldn't have kept secrets from you, but I was so afraid you'd never forgive me."

"A wise man once said, never say never."

"You're quoting James Bond at me?"

"Why not? Everything about this mission has a surreal quality to it." He shrugged. "But not the part about finding the love of my life."

"You really mean that?"

"With all my heart."

"I do, too," she said. "Love you, I mean. More than anything." Her voice dropped as his mouth lowered to capture her lips again in a kiss of longing, desire, and promise. There was no time to explore further, they both knew, but the kiss spoke of commitment and the future.

When he let her go, they were both smiling. And trembling.

"We'd better get out of here. There are a multitude of things to do before we can call this part of the mission complete." He held out one hand to her and she took it. It was symbolic. They were partners now. They'd face what came, together.

The team set out through the woods about twenty minutes later. Matt had decided he and Sandra would go with the group that would take their prisoner back to base. They all knew there still might be some zombies hiding out in the forest. Sandra would be going back to base after her ordeal, and he wanted to be certain she and the rest of the team, along with Rodriguez, got there safely.

Sandra had identified the casualties from the first floor of the house as the two men who had kidnapped her from the base. Both seemed to be hired guns, much like Leroy had been. Preliminary identification made by a quick and secure phone call back to the tech team on base confirmed they both had long criminal histories. Rodriguez was probably using their underworld contacts to do things in a less than legal manner.

Rodriguez had argued and fumed at being marched out of the house and through the yard until Simon had slapped a wad of duct tape over his mouth. Even so, he struggled as he was led along into the trees. Once he realized they were walking into the forest, Rodriguez seemed to give in. His sudden cooperation set the hairs at the back of Matt's neck on edge. Rodriguez knew something—or was planning something. Matt sent a quick hand signal to the rest of the team. Almost imperceptible nods answered his warning. The men had picked up on it, too. They were on guard.

Matt dropped to the back of the group, taking Sandra with him. His hand on her elbow tightened until she looked at him.

"Take this." He handed her his secondary dart gun. Her

eyes widened and she barely suppressed a gasp of surprise. "Use it if you have to."

"Do you think there'll be trouble?" Her gaze darted around the gloomy forest, and she kept her voice blessedly low so that only he could hear her.

"Maybe. Best to be prepared." He tried to reassure her but knew he'd missed the mark. Oh, well. Better she be on edge than lulled into a false sense of security. "Just be sure whoever you aim at with those darts is already dead."

"I won't shoot anyone I shouldn't." She grimaced.

"Hopefully, you won't have to shoot anyone at all." He began walking faster in order to catch up with the team that had gone on ahead. It wouldn't do to become separated.

"Amen to that," she muttered, following his lead.

As it was, he was almost too late. He saw the movement behind the rest of the party before the rear guard did. Matt raised the alarm.

"Sam, behind you! Three tangos at five o'clock." Matt began firing even as the rest of the team sprang into action. Three ragtag, bloodstained, and disfigured beings moved steadily onward, their only goal to make more like themselves. To kill and maim and infect.

No more. They'd meet their end this night, and all the living people here—except Rodriguez—were immune. No more zombies would be made. Not if Matt had anything to say about it.

But the three creatures were followed by three more. Then even more came streaming steadily out of the brush. Everyone was firing now, even Sandra. Matt noticed that she placed her shots carefully, backing away as the zombies advanced on them.

"Where are they coming from?" Matt wanted to know. He asked the question aloud, inviting Sandra's input.

"Looks like a break in the kudzu vines over there. There's got to be something behind it. Maybe a structure of some kind where they hide out during the day?"

"Or maybe a cave. There are a few in this area." Matt kept aiming and firing even as he sorted through the puzzle.

He paused only to reload. Sandra took one carefully placed shot for every three or four of his. That was good. She was making her shots count. She hit what she aimed at. She just did it at a much slower pace than he and the rest of his men. Matt had plenty of spare ammunition in his combat vest. When Sandra finally finished the clip that had been in the pistol, he tossed her a few spares.

She was in retreat from the suspected cave entrance, as were they all. It took some time for the darts to work, and the creatures kept advancing until they disintegrated midstep. But someone had to get closer, to be certain none escaped the suspected cave.

Matt signaled for most of the team to move forward in a flanking maneuver. They'd take the fight to the zombies instead of waiting to be overrun. If they could overtake them at the bottleneck, they stood a better chance of controlling the battle and getting them all with little fuss.

"Sandra, stay back here with Sam and Rodriguez. Keep count of the zombie kills as best you can and try to make sure none of them slip away, but don't move away from Sam. Stay safe."

"Where are you going?" Panic flared in her eyes.

"We're going to try to stem the flow. Once they're out of wherever they've been hiding, it gets too far out of control. If we can get them at the entrance, we can control the action." He saw understanding dawn in her eyes.

"Be careful, Matt."

"You too, sweetheart. Stay with Sam and retreat with him if necessary." He kissed her quick before he left with the rest of the combat team.

Simon was across from Matt as they approached the point where the zombies were coming from simultaneously. They'd sent some of the men down the center as decoys, to lead the creatures away from the real angle of attack—either side of the exit point. It was an orchestrated play to gain time and a little distance from the zombies who'd been darted and needed time to fall. It also brought Matt and Simon closer to the fresh reinforcements that kept coming through the curtain of vines.

"We've got to get to the source and make sure we have them all," Matt said over the radio that connected him with the combat team.

"Where'd they get so many? Intel never reported these kinds of numbers," Simon groused.

"Look at them. They're newly made. Civilians, most of them. From the way they're dressed, it looks like Rodriguez was trolling a bar for new recruits."

Indeed, the women matched the descriptions of the missing persons reports—they were young and wearing jeans or short skirts. Their high heels were mostly gone, and their little colorful shirts were torn and bloodstained. Makeup was long melted and smeared, and jewelry sparkled from what was left of ears and fingers in a drunken, disturbing display.

The men were wearing civilian clothing but many looked like off-duty soldiers. A few others had biker tattoos and clothing that was now tattered and stained. Their hands were bloody and scratched, their faces gnawed away in some cases. It looked like many of the men had put up a good fight, but the contagion had taken them in the end.

"There's a popular road house not far away. It has a large, dark parking lot," Simon mused. "It'd be easy pickings to get the customers as they stumble out on their way home."

"Especially if someone was able to control the zombies they sent out to do the deed. Rodriguez's so-called improvement on the contagion allowed him to give simple orders."

"Like, 'don't let anyone out of the parking lot alive'?" Simon asked in a grim tone.

"Or like, 'build me an army,' " Matt agreed as they moved into position. "Rodriguez was gearing up for war. He probably made most of this little army last night. There ought to be a lot of missing persons reports today and for the next few days as people don't show up where they're supposed to be. You can't kill this many folks without someone noticing."

The team was almost ready to begin the next phase of the maneuver. By waiting to fire until Simon and Matt were in perfect position, they'd avoided drawing the zombies' attention. The plan was to let the rest of the team handle the zombies already out in the forest while Matt and Simon took positions to get them as they emerged from the vines. Eventually, the soldiers could contain the monsters in the bottleneck—or so they hoped.

However it worked out, all these poor creatures had to be dealt with. A speedy end was preferable, but the team would end it however it had to. None of this zombie army could be allowed to escape.

The soldiers set up the flanking maneuver and Matt gave the signal when they were in position. He and Simon opened fire at the same time, the rest of the team closing the gap in a pincer maneuver that cut off the fresh zombies from the ones they'd already darted, leading the doomed creatures away so they could disintegrate away from the new field of battle. They'd essentially cleared the deck to begin the battle again—this time on their own terms.

The men who herded the darted creatures away would keep them occupied until the last was a pile of goo on the forest floor. Meanwhile, Matt and Simon would be the first line of defense, sending already darted zombies on their way to the herders. Like shooting fish in a barrel.

After several minutes and a few clips of darts, Sam Archer approached Matt from the side.

"Where's Sandra?" Sam was supposed to be watching over her and Rodriguez.

"John showed up and took over so I could bring you fresh supplies," Sam explained.

Matt didn't spare the time to look at Sam, but he could hear the telltale metal tinkle of ammunition clips.

"Just in time, lieutenant. I'm nearly out of ammo," Matt reported, never taking his eyes off the creatures that kept pouring out of the small opening in the dense vines.

"I've got it covered, sir." He refilled one of the side pockets on Matt's vest with fresh clips even as Matt continued to fire.

"Trade places?" Matt nodded and dropped back so Sam could take his place.

So far, the plan was working pretty well. None of the zombies were getting past the choke point without being darted. From there it took some creative running by the other members of the team to lead the zombies away to where they could fall apart minutes later.

The vines were getting trampled the more creatures that came out of the small opening in the dense leaves. As the tenacious kudzu collapsed under the weight of so many shuffling feet, Matt could see the mouth of a cave clearly. It wasn't a large opening, thankfully, and allowed only one creature out at a time. But the cave beyond must be pretty large if the sheer number of zombies emerging was any indication.

The place didn't smell great. The air wafting from the cave entrance reeked strongly of both bat guano and death. The zombies didn't smell too good as their flesh aged. These were of relatively new vintage, but so many of them in one place didn't make for pleasantly scented air. The presence of what had to be a few hundred bats only added to the lovely aroma.

"Smells like shit down here," Sam observed as they tightened the noose.

"No kidding." Matt had fallen back to a support position and was observing their progress.

The plan was working well. Now if they could just run out of zombies before they completely ran out of ammunition.

Suddenly static came over his earpiece as if someone was trying to report in but was stopped mid-transmission. Over the partially open mic he could hear some faint grunting noises. Sounds of a struggle. Matt's head swiveled as he accounted for all the members of his team. And Sandra. Where was she?

Shit.

"Hold this position. I'm going to see what's going on. Don't let any of them get past you."

"Aye, aye, sir." Sam didn't even nod as he continued to fire in rapid sequence at the emerging zombies. He knew his job.

Matt headed through the dense woods at a fast, silent pace. Not only was Sandra not where he expected her to be. Neither was Rodriguez.

Matt stumbled over something soft. A leg. John Petit lay on the ground, the back of his head covered in blood. A bloody tree branch lay nearby. Someone had hit him pretty good, but Matt had no time to check how bad at the moment.

"Man down," he reported over the headset. "John is down. Rodriguez and Sandra are missing. In pursuit."

Not even a second later, the blast of a conventional gunshot echoed through the night.

"Sandra!" Matt took off at a run toward the denser forest from where the shot had come.

Chapter Fifteen

Matt broke into a small clearing and skidded to a halt. There was Sandra—his beautiful Sandra—standing over Rodriguez, a smoking gun in her hand. John's SIG Sauer, if Matt wasn't mistaken.

Rodriguez rolled around on the forest floor at her feet, clutching his arm to his chest and spouting profanities in Sandra's general direction. She had shot the bastard. Rodriguez wasn't going anywhere.

"Damn, you're beautiful." The words slipped out as Matt noted the determined grimace on her gorgeous face.

She looked up at his words, meeting his gaze with clear relief.

"He jumped John and tried to get away."

"So I surmised." Matt fingered the mic and reported back to the rest of the team. "Rodriguez is down. Sandra shot him in the arm."

"Way to go, doc," Sam replied over the radio. Matt could hear the pinging whiz of darts being fired in the background before the connection closed. His team had his back. His and Sandra's, too.

The cave emptied out shortly thereafter, and the last of the zombies turned to goo a few minutes later. Leaving Simon behind to watch for more possible activity, Sam, Matt, and Sandra helped Rodriguez and John limp back to base through the woods. John was a little worse for wear, but luckily Rodriguez hadn't managed to hit him that hard.

Of course the accelerated healing that was a by-product of John's immunity helped considerably. By the time they were back inside their secure building, John was almost good as new, though nothing would ease the embarrassment of being bested by a fat scientist. Matt had no doubt that John was going to take some ribbing from the guys when this was all over. For now, he took charge of the prisoner, marching Rodriguez to the secure area they'd set up for just that purpose.

"Now, doctor, we'll continue our little discussion, shall we?" Matt heard John say to Rodriguez as they went down the hall.

Matt trusted John to get the job done right. He was CIA, after all. He'd probably forgotten more about interrogation than Matt had ever known. Matt would join them . . . later. He would give John a chance to wear the man down first, then Matt would come in when Rodriguez was ready to talk.

Judging by his obstinacy to this point, Matt figured he had a couple hours to kill. At least. Which meshed nicely with his plans.

"Don't you want to question him?" Sandra looked after the men disappearing down the hall.

"I do," Matt smiled at her. "But not now." He moved closer to her. "Right now I have something much more important on my mind." His arm stole around her waist, drawing her closer.

"But don't we have to move fast on this?"

"Oh, I intend to move very fast." He almost laughed but managed to contain his amusement.

The simple fact was that something momentous happened out there in the woods, and he found it impossible to let the most incredible moment of his life go by uncommemorated. If he had more time, he'd spend a few days locked in a hotel suite with the love of his life. As it was, they had only a few minutes—an hour at most—before he had to act on their shared mission. It was late at night. He could steal a few minutes, but not many. Still, some was better than none. The team had their orders and knew how to carry on in his absence.

He turned her toward his new office. He had to lead her through a large, open office area in which many of the noncombat members of the team had desks. Only a few were occupied at this time of night, and he didn't do more than nod in the direction of the workers as they watched him pass. His office was in sight. It had an old-fashioned, padded leather wing chair, no windows, and most important, a working lock on the heavy oak door.

Matt opened the door and hastily did a quick check of the room. Empty. He shut the door and backed her up against it. One hand reached down and flipped the lock with a satisfying click.

"Why did we come here, Matt?" Her pretty green eyes searched around the small room, puzzled but excited.

"It was the closest place I knew we could be alone."

Her gaze shot back to his. "What have you got in mind?"

"Something we're both going to remember for a long time." He kept his voice pitched low, mindful of the people working just beyond his office door. The fact that there was a slight chance the outsiders might hear something through the thick walls only added to the thrill of the moment.

"Really?" Her expression said so much more than her words. She seemed both amused and turned on. A good combination, as far as he was concerned.

"Oh, yeah. You're going to make me a very happy man in a few minutes." He couldn't resist injecting humor into the experience. He felt sort of giddy, which wasn't something he experienced often in his life. In fact, he couldn't ever remember feeling this way before.

"Very sure of yourself, aren't you?" she teased.

"That I am, ma'am," he agreed, smiling down at her. "And happier than I've been in a long time. Because of you." He felt his heart melt at the soft expression that overtook her beautiful face. "The only thing that would make me happier is if you agree to be my wife."

"What?"

"Marry me, Sandy. I want you in my life—permanently."

"Are you sure? I mean, I know I wasn't quite truthful with you before. I want you to know I'll never lie to you again, even by omission." She looked pained at the memory of what had gone before. "Are you really sure, Matt?"

"As sure as I am about anything nowadays. I love you and I want you to be my wife and my partner, for as long as we have left."

"I want that, too." Happiness filled him at her soft answer. "I love you, Matt."

She jumped upward a few inches, stretching to kiss him. He helped, bending his neck to meet her halfway. This was a kiss of honesty and pure, unadulterated love. A kiss of commitment and a kiss for the future.

When he pulled back, he was breathing hard. A kiss that had started as a sweet declaration of love had turned to steamy passion. He wanted to claim her in the most basic way, to make her his own.

"Matt?" Her eyes were deliciously dazed. Oh, yeah, this woman matched him in every possible way. She was as eager as he was, if that look on her face was any indication.

"I thought we needed a moment to savor." He stroked her cheek. "It's not every day I ask a woman to marry me, you know. In fact, I've never done it before."

"Never?" The fog over her senses seemed to lift a little. "I'm flattered." Her teasing tone was countered by the enchantment in her eyes.

"And I'm grateful. Grateful I found you." He placed a kiss on her cheek. "Grateful you're the amazing woman you are." Another kiss just grazed her mouth. "And grateful you said yes when I asked you to be mine forever."

He kissed her more deeply this time, prolonging the contact as he rid her of her clothes. She helped, her smaller fingers making short work of buttons and zippers. Her clothing dropped around her in a circular pile of fabric pooling at her feet. She didn't seem to mind. Her nimble fingers then helped him out of his outer gear and stripped off his shirt.

Before she could go any further, he lifted his head away from her ravenous kiss. She was delightfully bare, standing facing him. Her delicate skin was flushed a delightful shade of pink and her eyes were dazed.

"You're so beautiful." He stroked her hair back from her face.

She rolled her eyes. "I'm glad you're nearsighted."

He laughed at her unexpected humor. "There's nothing wrong with my eyes. My vision is twenty-twenty, and you're the most attractive woman I've ever beheld." He could tell she was uncomfortable with the compliment. "Why don't you believe me?"

"I have a mirror, Matt." She ducked her head, still blushing despite her grin. He'd work on that. She didn't believe in her own beauty, which was something he'd have the pleasure of convincing her about for the rest of their lives.

"I don't know what you see when you look in that mirror of yours, but to me, you're the most beautiful woman in the world. You always have been. From the first moment I saw you, you took my breath away, Sandra, and I've been in a tailspin ever since."

The expression on his face when he said those words made her heart clench. She really was what he wanted. She could tell. She felt the same way about him. Only she'd never expected to be so blessed to have his love in return.

"Is this real, Matt?" She stroked his chest with one hand, wanting to feel his skin, to know he was really there and that this wasn't just some kind of dream.

"If it isn't, I don't want to wake up." His smile filled her world.

He bent and picked her up, one muscular arm under her knees, the other around her back. He was so strong. She'd never been carried like this before, and it was incredibly romantic. He sat in the massive, leather wing chair, with her on his lap. Her bare bottom came in contact with the worn canvas of his pants, and the tactile sensation made a little thrill race up her spine.

It felt incredibly naughty to be sitting here, in his office, on his lap, entirely nude while he still wore his pants. There were people working just on the other side of that wall. At any moment, someone could knock on the door or call on the phone. Team members knew where they were. Some probably speculated about what they were doing, but none knew for sure.

Or at least they wouldn't if she could manage to keep her voice down. The door was heavy wood, and the walls in this old building were solid, but there was still the distinct possibility of being overheard if things got too loud. And things could get loud. Matt had a way of bringing out the screamer in her she'd never known existed.

Of course, it looked like he had a quickie in mind. Maybe she could keep her vocal expressions in check for a little while. Then again, that little edge of danger in his chosen location for this rendezvous was more exciting than she would have believed.

"I didn't realize you were into kink, Matt."

"Kink? You think making love in my office chair is kinky? Oh, sweetheart." He chuckled. "I can see we're going to have a fun time broadening your horizons."

She was tempted to ask him what he meant, but the sparkle of deviltry in his eyes promised more than she could probably handle at the moment. What mattered was that they'd have time to explore all sorts of things together once their mission was completed. For now, they'd have to make do with these stolen moments out of time.

"Aren't you going to take these off?" She tugged at the waistband of his pants.

"Why don't you help me?" The smile he turned on her was pure daring.

Her hands lowered to his waistband and she let her fingers do the walking over the hard ridge pushing against his zipper.

"Like that?" She held his gaze as she repeated the caress.

"You know I do. But why don't we take this to the next level?"

He lifted her by the hips, repositioning her over his legs so that she straddled him, her thighs spread wide on either side of his. Open. Vulnerable. Willing.

"You're keeping these on?" She tugged on the fabric of his pants.

"Oh, yeah." His voice was gravelly with passion. "We don't have a lot of time, remember? And someone might be looking for us." His eyes flared at the hint of danger.

"In which case they'd find me naked as the day I was born and you still clothed." She ran her fingers over his deeply muscled chest. "At least partially." Her fingers trailed downward again.

"Unzip me," he ordered in a low, sexy tone.

Licking her lips, she did as he asked, freeing his thick erection. He pulled a foil packet from one of his cargo pockets and handed it to her. She knew what he wanted. Without a word, she opened the packet and covered him.

The way he looked at her made her heart glow and her blood sizzle. Love sparked desire in his eyes and turned it to a simmering hot flame that stood ready to engulf her.

She wanted it all. She wanted him. Forever.

"Take me in, sweetheart," he encouraged her, lifting her hips in his strong hands and guiding her even closer until they were chest to chest.

She lifted her thighs over the armrests of the chair while he helped her raise her hips just enough to get him into optimal position. Lowering over him, she took his hard length inside in one long slide of intense pleasure. Nothing had ever felt so good.

When he was fully seated within her, they sat facing each other, her thighs over his in the big chair, entwined like pretzels. She loved the sensation of him filling her, stretching her, claiming her. It was the most basic expression of the love she felt in her heart. Her body accepting his, joining, connecting on a primal level. It was beautiful and profound.

And sexy as hell.

The leather of the chair was smooth against the backs of her legs. The worn canvas of his pants touched her here and there, slightly abrading her skin. The rough texture only heightened the pleasurable sensations.

"Much as I'm enjoying this, we need to move, sweetheart," Matt ground out between his teeth. She could see he was on edge. Truth be told, she wasn't far behind.

"Help me," she pleaded, unsure of her own strength in such a position.

"Here." He repositioned her hands and moved her legs slightly. "Hold on to the back of the chair and use it for leverage."

It worked. She could move on him using the new placement of her thighs, and the solidity of the old chair helped her pull herself upward. She began a slow rhythm as his hands went to her hips, guiding and assisting. His strength helped, lifting when she rose and allowing for a long, slow slide back down.

Before long she was breathing hard, and a glow of exertion lightly sheened her skin. His too. The faint, musky scent of him drove her wild and made her speed up, even as her muscles began to protest.

"Yeah, baby. Almost there," Matt coaxed, his mouth against the sensitive skin of her neck.

Someone knocked on the door.

Sandra gasped in shock, but Matt never slowed the pace.

"Sir?" A man's voice floated through the closed door to them.

"Whatever it is will have to wait," Matt shouted back.

"Yes, sir," the voice replied smartly, then said nothing more.

"Do you think he's gone?" Sandra asked.

"Do you want him to be gone?" Matt countered, raising one eyebrow in challenge as he met her gaze.

Shocked, her eyes widened. "Don't you?"

Matt shrugged. "I don't really care either way." His mouth descended to nibble on her skin once more. "Let them listen to how much I love you. Let them envy me—the luckiest son of a bitch in the world." He nipped the cords of her neck as she squirmed on top of him.

The fever in her blood rekindled; she would not be denied. She began to move on him even more forcefully, driving to the inevitable end she wanted so desperately, the need increasing with every passing second. Even the thought of someone listening at the door didn't deter her. In fact, it only heightened her need.

"Matt!" she cried his name, trying to keep her voice low. It came out on a whimper of need, a small gasp of hunger.

"I love you, Sandy. Come for me now," he ordered, straining with her as they approached the precipice together.

That was all it took for her to crash over the side, riding the wave of passion. He followed behind, his body clenching beneath her as pleasure swamped them both, drowning them, surrounding them, engulfing them in ecstasy.

She couldn't speak for long moments. Couldn't think. Couldn't process anything other than the feel of him beneath her, within her, and the sweeping satisfaction they'd found together. Nothing could mar the perfection of this moment. She collapsed against him, lowering her arms from the chair back to wrap around his shoulders.

"I love you so much," she whispered as the afterglow settled over her body, warming it from the inside out.

They sat like that for some time, enjoying the moment and basking in the perfection of their love.

Before the beautiful haze faded completely, Matt moved them both to the leather couch along one wall to rest for a few minutes. They were stealing time and would have to get up sooner rather than later, but just for a minute or two, it was good to lie down, cradling the woman he loved more than life in his arms. He'd remember these stolen moments for the rest of his life.

Matt didn't allow himself to doze long. After only a quarter of an hour or so, he gently roused Sandra. She'd fallen asleep against his heart. Though he hated to wake her, he knew they had work to do this night. More than just their lives and happiness were on the line.

Her sleepy eyes blinked open, and the hazy pleasure he read there touched his heart. He steeled himself against the lethargy that urged him to stay just a little longer in this idyllic cocoon of bliss. Resolving himself, Matt sat up, taking her with him.

"Much as I'd love to lie around here all night and make love to you, we still have work to do." He frowned. "I used to live for my work, but right now, I'll admit, it's a drag. I finally have someone in my life who is more important to me than my job." He tilted his head, considering. "I never quite thought it would happen to me."

"But you're happy about it, right?" Uncertainty crept into her tone.

He pulled her close. "Damn right I'm happy about it. Ecstatic, in fact. And once we tie up the loose ends of this mission, I'll be glad to show you just how ecstatic. Repeatedly. Right now, though, duty calls." He let her go and stood, looking around for their clothes.

Her outfit was still on the floor arranged in the loose ring of fabric she'd stepped out of only moments before. His shirt was a few feet away. He gathered the pieces and shrugged into his shirt before handing her clothes to her. Watching her dress, he knew he'd never get tired of the sight. She was utterly gorgeous and still so innocent, which was odd for a woman her age in this society. Then again, she was highly educated and almost as driven as he was, if not more. It was likely she hadn't had a lot of time for relationships. Matt had led a similar life in the past few years. Until now. Meeting the love of his life had changed everything.

"What are you going to do?" she asked him.

Matt had to refocus on the mission. He had a plan, but he still had to put it into action. That was the only reason he'd found the strength to let Sandra go. Otherwise, he'd have made love to her again, over and over, all night long and then some.

"I'm going to roust Beverly Bartles out of bed and arrest her ass, for one thing. Rodriguez implicated her. That's enough for me to detain her. Just what I needed, in fact. Then we'll see if we can't get her to flip on her boss. She's been spying on me for Admiral Chester. She's also been working for Rodriguez. The big question is whether Chester is in league with the rogue scientists, too, or is Bev double-timing him?"

"Considering his rank and position, I sincerely hope it's the latter," Sandra said. "I'd hate to think an admiral was willing to sell out to the highest bidder. Especially on something as detrimental as this. If he's willing to sell this technology—which has the potential for killing so many—what else has he been willing to sell?"

"Exactly the question that sends chills down my spine." Matt's mouth firmed into a grim line.

Beverly reached for her mobile phone in the darkness. The insistent, shrill ring had awoken her.

"This better be good." She really didn't like being awakened in the middle of the night.

"You should be nicer to me, Bev. I'm about to save your miserable skin."

She sat upright, recognizing the voice immediately. It had to be serious for him to call her directly.

"What's going on?"

"Rodriguez has gone off the grid."

Oh, no.

"He disabled his beacon?"

"Not before transmitting the capture signal."

"Shit. I bet Sykes has him. They moved their HQ and

there's no way I can help get him out. The new location is too secure."

"There's only one thing to do." She understood that tone and the cryptic words.

"I'll do it."

"Good. I'll set up your transport. Check for coordinates by text message in fifteen minutes. That should give you enough time."

Beverly was already out of bed, dressing for the work ahead. They'd devised a contingency plan in case something like this happened. She'd thought it a waste of time when he'd made her go through it with him, describing every last detail about the base, but she was glad for the preparation now. She knew exactly what to do and how long it would take.

"Roger that." She disconnected the call and stowed the phone in its secure holder at her waist.

There was little in the small room that she wanted or needed. All would be provided for her when she reached her destination, and nothing here had been hers for very long. She lived a disposable life now, never putting down roots in any one spot. It was safer that way.

She had no time to waste. She had a lot of work to do and only a short time to do it. This would have to be fast, but she was prepared. Bev found the emergency documents she'd prepared and hidden in her living quarters. Leaving them where they would be found, she systematically destroyed certain other items that she'd had secreted around the room.

She would leave only enough to be certain to lead Matt Sykes and his team to a much bigger fish than she appeared to be. With any luck, that would distract the hunters long enough for her to make a clean getaway.

Satisfied by her quick work, Bev felt the vibration at her waist that alerted her to an incoming text message. Checking the screen quickly, she smiled in grim satisfaction. Her contact had come through again. She picked up the bag of things she'd take with her and headed out the door. She was never coming back here again, but she felt no remorse or sadness. She had done her job and would be richly rewarded, no matter the colossal screwup Rodriguez had committed. He'd always been a little unhinged in her opinion. All the parties involved knew he'd been a weak link, so there was no surprise that he'd gotten himself captured.

They'd prepared for exactly that contingency, which was one of the main reasons Beverly had been put in place. Now it was time to activate the plan. It was also time for her to go. She wouldn't miss the base or the people. She had bigger fish to fry—and a plane to catch.

A small team prepared to storm Bev's bedroom. She was bunking in the BOQ—the bachelor officers' quarters—on base, so all she had was one room to call her own. Sarah and Xavier were to accompany Matt inside the room. Sam was watching outside the room's only window. Matt had recalled Sarah from the farmhouse for just this purpose. Her skills as a former cop would be more useful here for the time being. When they were all in position, Matt counted them down.

"On three," he whispered, following through with the rest of the countdown before springing into action.

Matt went first, kicking in the door. Xavier followed with Sarah hot on his heels. After checking the closet and under the bed, Matt crossed the empty room to the window. Sam was outside in the bushes, out of sight.

"She's not here," Matt told Sam over the radio. They were using a separate frequency for this small-scale op. "Stand watch."

"Aye, aye, sir." Sam melted back into the predawn shadows to watch and guard.

Sarah and Xavier were already busy methodically searching the small room. This wouldn't take long.

"What do you think?" Matt asked them both.

"She's not coming back," Sarah said with disgust lacing her tone.

"What makes you say that?" Xavier challenged. "Her

clothes and toiletries are still here. Doesn't look like she took much. If she'd planned to leave for good, wouldn't she have taken more of her stuff with her?"

"None of this stuff is expensive or irreplaceable. Common, cheap brands of makeup and personal care items. Uniform clothing. Even the few sets of civilian clothes are cheap and easily replaceable. Nothing personal—no family photos, trinkets, letters." She ticked off the points of evidence on her fingers, then gestured to the room in general. "Nothing personal was left behind. If she had any of those things to begin with, they were most likely in her purse, which is missing. She traveled light. At most she has maybe one bag with her. Probably a change of clothes and whatever important trinkets and papers she might've had with her. We probably won't find any clues in what's left here. Except for her fingerprints, which we already have and aren't much use anyway; the place looks to me like it's been sanitized. I'd lay odds Bev is gone for good."

Matt glanced at Xavier with one eyebrow raised in question. Xavier shrugged in apparent agreement.

"Sounds reasonable."

"All right." Matt was not just disappointed. He was pissed. "I want to know how she knew to get out of Dodge. You two stay here and do a thorough search. Maybe she missed something when she vacated. I'm going to my old office to search there. I'll take Sam with me. I still don't want anyone on the team going anywhere outside our secure building alone, so you two need to stick together and check in with the comm officer every fifteen minutes."

"Yes, sir. We're happy to oblige," Xavier drawled, his words thickly accented.

Xavier's smile was aimed at Sarah, and for the first time Matt didn't envy the couple. He had his own fiancée now. He was no longer on the outside looking in.

Matt left the two lovers to their search of the room. Sam met him outside, and together they walked rapidly toward his old office. He hadn't used the place in a while. Not since mov-

ing into the older, more secure building. It had only been a day
or two, but it felt like years. So much had happened since he'd
made the decision to pull the plug on Beverly's spying and
move the team into one central location. He'd left Bev behind,
ostensibly to hold down the fort, but he'd really devised the
plan as a neat way to push her out of the loop and away from
his daily activities.

It had worked, neat as a pin. Even better, she couldn't com-
plain because he'd left her *in charge* of the office. An empty office. Matt had the last laugh on that one, at least, even if it
looked like Bev had gotten him back by skipping town in the
dead of night without a trace.

He entered the office cautiously, using his key. The place
was deserted, as he'd expected.

What he didn't expect was the neatly typed letter waiting
for him on top of a stack of folders on Bev's desk. He took a
quick survey of the office before returning to the intriguing letter. Cautiously, he picked it up.

Congratulations, commander, the note read. *You win.*

"Cryptic," Matt commented, handing the slip of paper to
Sam.

"Short and sweet, too. From Bev?" Sam asked.

"It looks like her handwriting," Matt confirmed.

"What did she leave for you?" Sam pointed to the desk.

Matt paused to glance at the files that had been stacked
under the note. Opening them one by one, he scanned the contents. They contained some of his preliminary research on the
zombie attacks at Fort Bragg and elsewhere. He hadn't seen
these files in a while, and it looked to him like Bev had done
some work on them. She'd highlighted certain passages and
drawn a maze of arrows and circles in bright colors on a few
of the pages in each file.

She'd also added annotations, drawing seemingly unrelated
events together in a way Matt hadn't anticipated. She'd laid
out patterns in the data he hadn't seen before and would not
have known to look for. They were too subtle. Perhaps in time

he would've made the connections, but he admitted he hadn't had enough of the common factors previously to connect these particular dots.

"Looks like she drew you a map," Sam commented, nodding at one of the folders Matt had left open on the desk as he looked at the one beneath it.

"More than you know, Sam," Matt said absently as he continued to read.

One exchange in particular drew his attention. Admiral Chester had issued orders for the personnel change that inserted Bev into Matt's office, and shortly thereafter Tim had died, turned into a zombie.

Bev had circled the date and time stamp on the orders. Either accidentally or deliberately—and Matt now believed it was the latter considering the way she had left and the evidence she'd left behind—the orders were dated *after* Bev's arrival on base. Add to that her personal cell phone records, which she must have added to the file . . . now they were interesting. The records indicated Beverly had called Admiral Chester at home shortly before the orders were faxed through to Matt's office from Chester's home fax machine. Voilà. Just like that, a conspiracy was born.

Bev had given him probable cause to investigate Admiral Chester. All wrapped up in shiny fax paper and tied with a bow.

Beverly Bartles didn't look back as she boarded the small charter plane in the early hours before dawn. The flight crew consisted of only one pilot. Nobody else. He didn't even glance at her as she boarded. He simply closed the cabin door behind her and then shut himself inside the cockpit.

A moment later, she heard the engines rev in preparation for departure. The small jet rolled away from the hangar and onto the tarmac. Minutes later, it was airborne.

Beverly felt her fear of capture slough away with each mile, each moment that passed. She'd made her getaway. Her secrets were safe. She'd given Matt Sykes enough to keep him busy and his attention focused elsewhere. An admiral was a much bigger fish than a mere ensign, after all. Too bad Sykes didn't realize the admiral was only a small player in a much bigger game.

She smiled with smug satisfaction as she poured herself a finger of expensive bourbon and settled back into the luxurious leather seat. These private jets were comfy. When she got her cut of the money, maybe she would buy one of her own. She would be able to afford all sorts of luxuries once she had her share.

Beverly settled into a light doze, dreaming of the easy life she would lead once this was all over. She felt safe enough for the moment to grab a little shut-eye.

Twenty minutes later, she was fast asleep when the Praxis Air charter jet burst into a ball of flame. Tiny bits of debris rained down over a farmer's field for a good five minutes. Very little was left of the jet, or its occupants.

"Is it done?" the voice on the phone asked.

"It's over." The man in the office answered. "I've got to tell you, I don't like this at all. You're ruining my father's company. This is the second jet I've destroyed for you. I'm going to have the NTSB crawling all over my ass in an hour. I won't do it again. This is the last time."

"There's no record of Bartles being on the jet, right?"

"Of course not. Just the pilot. I made it look like he was returning the jet to our home base for repairs. Just a ferry flight to get the jet back here. I'm going to blame the crash on his poor judgment in thinking the jet was fit to fly. Pilot error."

"Tidy." Satisfaction sounded in that voice.

"That's what you pay me for. But this is the last of my dad's jets I'm losing. Understood?"

"It would bring too much suspicion were we to destroy another one of your father's toys, so you needn't worry. I will, however, still require his planes to fly my potential buyers around. The sooner we cut the final deal, the sooner we both strike it rich."

"Charter flights are the bread and butter of this company. It won't be a problem to fly your buyers around. You know that."

"Very well. I'll leave you to your NTSB visit. I'll be in touch in a few days. As soon as the furor dies down a bit."

The man in the office hung up the phone with a muffled curse. This was getting much more complicated than he'd bargained for. Sometimes he wished he'd never become involved with this whole mess, but the money was too tempting to turn down. He never thought he'd have to kill people or destroy two of his father's prized jets, not to mention having to deal with the National Transportation Safety Board.

If the old man would just loosen up on the reins and give him access to more cash, he never would have been put in this position. It was all the old man's fault, really. Served him right he'd lost two jets over the deal. His stinginess with his own son had caused all this.

The man, standing alone in the office, cursed again. Even if he'd wanted to get out now, he was in too deep. He'd killed. He'd falsified too many documents to recall. The only way out now was success. They'd sell the technology to the highest bidder, and his cut would set him for life. He could buy the island he had his eye on and retire there with any number of beautiful women who liked expensive living. He didn't have to limit himself to just one female companion. He could have as many as he liked whenever he wanted them. However he wanted them.

The old man's disapproving gaze would never land on him again. He'd finally be free, with his own money. He'd never again face the threat of being cut off without a cent. He'd be his own man. Finally. And for good.

It was a heady thought. A smile graced his lips as he dreamed of the freedom all that cash would buy him. That was what made all this worthwhile. Freedom from his overbearing, judgmental, stingy father was the goal that would help him put up with all the questions and investigations. All the disapproval he'd face from the old man and the suspicions of the NTSB.

He just had to keep his eyes on the prize—an island of his own with a bevy of beauties at his beck and call. Yeah, that's what kept him going. That, and all the money he could ever hope to spend.

John circled Dr. Rodriguez. He was sitting behind a table in an empty conference room. A video camera taped the entire interrogation for future reference. Matt sat across the table, watching Rodriguez squirm under John's masterful interrogation.

"We know Ensign Bartles was feeding you information," John informed him.

Rodriguez refused to speak. He merely drew invisible circles on the tabletop with his finger. Matt watched the man while John tried to elicit a response. So far, John hadn't gotten him to say anything else. Since the failed attempt to escape in the woods, Rodriguez had clammed up.

"We know about Admiral Chester. He's already in custody."

Was that a flicker of response?

"Chester isn't talking yet," John went on. "But he will. You know he will. He hasn't got the balls to hold out very long. Especially if they offer him a deal for cooperating. He'll sing like a choir boy and sell you down the river. You know it's true."

"You're lying. You haven't got him." Rodriguez's hand fisted on the table.

There. Now that was the kind of response they were aiming for. They were getting to him at last. Rodriguez was clearly angry.

John *was* lying, of course. Chester was missing, too.

"Sorry. It's true."

John pulled out his smart phone and flashed a photo of Admiral Chester looking a lot worse for wear, sitting behind bars. Wolf was pretty good with Photoshop and had whipped up the image at John's request.

"How long do you think it'll be before he tells us everything?" John holstered his phone and glanced at Matt. "We've got a bet going around the team. I've got him spilling what he knows around lunchtime." John glanced at the clock. "Doesn't give you a lot of time to get in on the deal before him. If you talk to us, they may go easier on you."

Matt noted the lack of anyone from the legal side of things. They hadn't called anyone from the judge advocate general office—JAG. They wouldn't let a civilian lawyer anywhere near this. Not yet. Maybe not ever. Knowledge of the contagion was something that had to be kept limited. It was beyond top secret. It fell into the world of the blackest of black ops. There would be no showy trial. No mixing with a general prison population for this man.

No, Rodriguez was most likely going so deep in a hole that no one would ever see or hear from him again. He didn't seem to realize it, and that gave them some leverage. For such a book-smart man, Rodriguez was sadly inept when it came to real-world living.

Even now, the scientist was eyeing John as if he was on the verge of talking. Matt watched the telltale hand on the table. It remained clenched.

A loud thump sounded as that beefy fist came down hard on the table. Frustrated anger showed on Rodriguez's face. He'd cracked. Finally.

"Chester was supposed to be on a charter flight out of Dulles Airport. I was to be on another from Fayetteville."

"Destination?" John prompted.

"I don't know. We were just supposed to board the planes, and the rest would be taken care of. We were to rendezvous all together to plan our next step."

"So there's somebody else pulling your strings," John mused aloud. "Who?"

"Oh, no. I won't give that up until I'm certain I have a deal. I want to talk to a lawyer." Rodriguez's hand unclenched, and he sat back in his chair, apparently at ease. He knew he's just pulled the ace from his sleeve. He'd given up Chester, but there was an even bigger fish he could give them.

Maybe the man wasn't as inept as Matt had thought.

"No lawyer, but I'll arrange for you to speak to someone with the authority to give you the guarantees you're looking for." Matt spoke for the first time during this interrogation. John stepped back as Rodriguez's attention was redirected to Matt. "First though, I want details about the flight. Airline. Flight number. Everything you know about it."

Rodriguez seemed to consider his options, then sat forward in his chair again, resting both forearms on the table.

"Praxis Air. Charter from Fayetteville airport. All I had to do was make a call when I felt the operation was in trouble and they'd pick me up anytime, day or night. It was all pre-arranged." Rodriguez's passive expression turned to one of disgust. "I called last night and was in the process of gathering my things when you showed up. I should've left earlier."

"Yes, you should have," Matt agreed. He stood and nodded to John.

John would handle the rest of the interrogation from here. Matt had to act on the information they'd just gotten. It was probably already too late, but they had to at least try to capture Admiral Chester at the airport. Matt would need help on this one. He flipped open his phone as he left the room and strode down the hall.

Once the call was made and MPs from the Washington, D.C., area were on their way to arrest Admiral Chester at Dulles Airport—if he was still there—Matt made another call. This time, he needed Sarah. She was a former cop. Her skills would be needed in dealing with the Fayetteville airport.

She would head the small team tasked with grounding the plane that had been arranged for Rodriguez. He wanted her to question the pilot. Unless that's how Bev had gotten away. In which case, they had to find that plane ASAP.

They also had to trace the arrangements that had been made to keep that charter flight open at Rodriguez's beck and call. There had to be a paper trail on that somewhere. It was a lead that had to be acted on at once.

Matt set the wheels in motion, utilizing the members of his team to the best of their abilities. It had been a long night filled with danger and combat. It looked like it would be an even longer day spent tracking down tangos and paper trails. Thank goodness he had a strong team that could handle all facets of this mission. They'd just gotten a lot closer to their goal of shutting down the bastards who were attempting to sell the zombie contagion technology to the highest bidder.

It would be a good day—no matter how exhausted he was.

"Admiral Chester was apprehended on the tarmac as he attempted to board a charter flight out of Dulles," Sandra reported. She'd taken over on comms that morning to interface with the MPs that had been ordered to catch Chester if at all possible.

Damn, it was good to see her. It had only been a few hours, but he needed his Sandra fix in the worst possible way. Even with everything that was going on, he needed a minute just to touch her hand and smile.

"How are you doing, sweetheart?"

"I'm tired, but otherwise okay. There's too much going on to sleep now." Her bright eyes filled with enthusiasm, reminding him of why he'd come down here. "I figure when this is all over, I might hibernate for a month or two to catch up on all the sleep I'm losing, but it's a small price to pay."

The communications console was set up in what Matt had come to think of as the War Room in their new building. It was the large, open office area that led to his new private office. He had assigned positions around the big, open space to every member of the noncombat portions of the team and had state-of-the-art equipment installed.

The communications console had been the first thing up and running. The monitoring station for all the sensors they'd installed around the base perimeter was located here, too. All information needed by the team filtered through this room, and the boards were always manned, which made it one of the safest places in the new headquarters. A good place for Sandra while he went out to take care of business.

She was probably out of danger now that Rodriguez had been captured, but he wasn't taking any more chances with her safety. She was his now. She'd agreed to be his wife. That was something special. He wouldn't let her come to harm, not while he lived. She would just have to get used to his overprotective nature. He figured they had the next forty years or so to work on that. Thank God.

"So where is Chester now?" he asked, trying to focus on the task at hand.

"The MPs in Washington put him on a plane bound for Fort Bragg. He'll be arriving shortly. Some of our guys are going out to meet the plane and escort him back here."

"Perfect." Matt felt an immense sense of satisfaction. At least they'd managed to get Chester. That was a coup in Matt's book. Now they had to build the case that would sink him for good. Chester couldn't be allowed to wriggle out of this one.

"You haven't heard the best part yet." Sandra's eyes shone with excitement.

"Tell me," Matt smiled; her mood was contagious. Or maybe he just felt this happy sensation anytime he was near her. He'd heard love could do that kind of thing, though he'd never experienced it himself before.

"He had a briefcase full of incriminating documents and a change of clothes in his overnight bag . . . alongside about a hundred thousand in cash and forged identity papers."

Oh, Matt liked the sound of that. Apparently, Chester had made a big part of their case for them. The admiral wouldn't be going free anytime soon. Not if Matt had anything to say about it.

Their mission at Fort Bragg was nearing completion. With the capture of Rodriguez, there was a good chance they'd effectively ended the zombie problem that had plagued the base for so long. Of course, the threat still existed of the technology being sold to a foreign power. If Rodriguez was to be believed, there was someone else pulling the strings, orchestrating the show from afar.

Matt knew he'd have to track that person down and end this once and for all before his mission was complete. They had a lot of investigative work ahead of them to pick up the trail and find the puppeteer who was running this farce, whoever he or she turned out to be. The immediate danger of zombies at Bragg was probably over, which meant they could, and most likely would, relocate to wherever the clues led.

Matt's mood was one of immense satisfaction, tinged with renewed conviction. He would track down everyone involved in this sinister plot. He'd taken on this mission and had every intention of seeing it through to the end. Only now, he'd be doing so with Sandra by his side.

Something he couldn't have foreseen when he'd first taken on the job, Sandra had become a beautiful complication in his life. One he wouldn't trade for the world. She completed him in the most basic of ways.

He grabbed her and hugged her close, laying a kiss on her that held all his joy and triumph. She returned it with love.

His heart melted all over again. Would he never get enough of this beautiful, sensitive, adventurous woman? She was his match in every way. The perfect mate to his independent spirit. He knew they didn't have time for more and backed away, letting her go by slow degrees.

"Have I told you how much I love you today, Sandy?"

"I believe you just did." She grinned up at him, her eyes still a little dazed from their kiss.

He loved that look. He'd keep it on her face at all times, if he had to spend the rest of his life perfecting the skill.

"Let's blow this popcorn stand. I want to be alone with you."

"Can we do that?" She looked around the room in surprise. "I mean, there's a lot to do."

"Don't I know it. But I think we can steal a few minutes for ourselves. We deserve it. And hell, I'm the boss. RHIP, sweetheart. Rank, most definitely, has its privileges."

He tugged her by the waist, moving her toward the door at the end of the open office area. It led to his new private office. The one with that memorable leather wing chair and the over-stuffed couch.

She gasped when she realized where he was leading her, but didn't protest too loudly.

"Tell me something, doc. Do you make house calls?" He tilted his head and looked speculatively toward the open door to his private domain. "Or in this case, office calls?"

The grin on her face was all the answer he needed, but she leaned in and kissed him for good measure. She then stepped out of his arms to precede him into the room with a slight sway in her hips that was clear invitation.

"You know I do, Commander." The saucy wink she sent him over her shoulder made his heart race in anticipation.

He followed her into the office and kicked the door closed.

They had a lot to do, but it could wait. Loving his woman would come first, last, always . . . and forever.

Be a little IMPULSIVE with HelenKay Dimon's latest novel,
in stores now . . .

"Hello?"

Katie froze at the sound of the familiar male voice. Then her head whipped around. The main door was open, but the metal security screen was closed and locked. It would be hard for people to see inside and impossible for anyone to break it down, but, oh boy, could she see out.

It couldn't be. It couldn't be. It couldn't be.

She repeated the refrain as she stared at the outline on the other side of the steel screen. Dark hair, broad shoulders, and relaxed stance. She'd know that body anywhere.

That would teach her to want fresh air. If the stifling heat hadn't bothered her, she'd be hiding in the storage closet and ignoring him right about now.

"Can you hear me?" He looked right at her as he said it. Clearly he knew she was there. Could see her, despite the promises in the sales brochure about the door providing protection and privacy. It didn't seem to be doing either at the moment.

With wet hands dripping on the floor beside her sneakers, she stood there. "Uh . . ."

"Not sure if you can see me." He waved his hand. "We met at the Armstrong-Windsor wedding."

Met? Now there was an interesting word for what they did. "Oh, I know who you are."

"Yeah, I guess so." Eric chuckled in a rich open tone that vibrated down to her feet.

She could hear the amusement in his voice. Figuring out how to take it was the bigger issue. She rubbed her hands on the towel hanging out of the waistband of her khaki shorts and adjusted her white tee to make sure everything that should be covered was. "What are you doing here?"

"I can explain if you'll let me come inside."

Talk about a stupid option. "No."

After a beat of silence, he spoke up. "Really?"

He sounded stunned at the idea of being turned down. Apparently the big, important man didn't like it when people disagreed with him.

That realization was enough to make her brain reboot. While running held some appeal, it wasn't very practical. They lived on an island, after all. And she needed to know how he'd tracked her down. "I mean, why do you want to come in?"

She could see his broad shoulders through the thick safety mesh and the way he balanced his hands on his lean hips. He was a man in control of his surroundings, even though this part of town didn't fit him at all. He wore tailored suits and walked into a fancy high-rise office every day.

Many of the folks in the Kalihi neighborhood never ventured near the expensive restaurants and exclusive communities around the island. This was a working-class area with an increasing crime rate, older and lined with warehouses, a little rough. A place where words like "redevelopment" were thrown around but never brought to fruition. In other words, not the place where one would expect to find Eric Kimura.

"I wanted to talk with you," he explained.

She'd been afraid he would say that. "Okay."

He pressed his face close to the screen. "And people are starting to wonder why I'm screaming into a door, so could we take this inside?"

Last thing she needed was for him to be mugged. She tried

to imagine explaining that bit of news to the cops . . . and to Cara.

"I'm coming." Katie rushed over, jangling the keys in her hand as she tried to find the one for the top deadbolt. "Here we go."

Eric didn't hesitate. The second she opened the screen, he pushed his way in and closed the solid door behind him. The controlling move should have made her nervous. Instead, she was strangely intrigued. Hunting her down took some work. Stepping into this neighborhood at five o'clock, which probably qualified as the middle of his workday, created a bit of mystery. Clearly he wanted to find her. Now he had.

He held out his hand. "Eric Kimura."

She stared at his long fingers before sliding her palm inside his. "Oh."

The corner of his mouth kicked up. "But you knew that, right?"

"Pretty much." The feel of that smooth skin against hers brought a rush of heat to her cheeks. She looked down at their joined hands, wondering at what point long turned to *too long* and she had to let go. "I watch the news now and then."

"Ah, yes. Not always the most flattering place to pick up information about me, but not a surprise." He frowned as if the notoriety didn't sit all that well with him. "So, do you have a name?"

"I figured you knew it since you tracked me here and all."

"I have my sources but the exact name was tougher."

Yeah, he had something all right. "Katie Long."

"The caterer."

Looked like he didn't quite know everything. She dropped his hand and backed up a step. No need for them to be this close, sucking up all the air in the room, when there was a big No-Eric zone right behind her. "Her assistant and sister. I'm surprised you went to the trouble to find me."

His head tilted to the side. The wide-eyed look made him look younger, less imposing, if only for a few seconds. "Why?"

This qualified as the strangest morning-after type conversation she'd ever had. "I guess this is the part where I say I've never done that at a wedding before."

He nodded. "For the record, me either."

"And where I insist I'm not the kind of woman who engages in thirty-minute sex romps with strangers." She actually wasn't but there was no way to sell that as a convincing story after the way they'd met.

"I'm not judging."

Of course he was. Hell, she was. When she'd vowed to turn her life around, she'd promised the days of putting herself at risk were over. She wouldn't do dumb things or get involved with the wrong guys. Eric didn't appear to be a loser, but he was most definitely wrong. He was her assignment. She was supposed to keep a safe distance and being under him didn't cut it.

"Maybe just a little judging?" She held up two fingers and squeezed them together.

"Any name I call you would apply to me."

"Very logical."

"You weren't alone in that room."

She tried very hard not to conjure up a visual image of his hands up her skirt. "Oh, I know."

"I admit, that sort of thing isn't a weekly occurrence for me."

She laughed. The contrast between the serious way his brows came together and the humor in his tone did her in. He might be good at sex, but he wasn't all that comfortable with the way they'd met.

That made two of them.

Try Karen Kelley's THE WOLF PRINCE, available now . . .

Her mind was a blank. What had she been dreaming about? Her face suddenly flooded with heat when she remembered. She'd been dreaming of a sexy, very naked, male god, worshipping at his feet like a horny woman who hadn't been laid in over a year. That wasn't true. She'd actually had sex eleven and a half months ago.

Except the man she'd drooled about in her dreams might very well be a corpse right now. Her heart began to pound.

Had Ms. Abernathy buried the body? Did the housekeeper know that would make her an accessory? Darcy grimaced when she thought about sharing a cell with her. Not that she disliked the housekeeper. She'd been almost as much of a mother to Darcy as her adoptive mother. Hmm, and bossy, now that she thought about it. But still, she didn't want Ms. Abernathy to go to prison because she was being overprotective.

Darcy flung the cover aside and jumped out of bed, glancing at the clock. It was barely six. She rushed toward the closet, but stopped at the French doors that led to her balcony. Her room was directly across from the guest house. If something had happened to Surlock during the night, she would be able to tell from her room—maybe.

She opened the double doors and rushed out onto the balcony, then stumbled to a stop. The swimming pool was between her room and the guest house. Surlock stood on the diving board, his arms raised. The sun peeked over the horizon, casting everything in a hazy early morning light. There was enough light that she could see him, though.

She swallowed past the lump in her throat. The man was truly magnificent, and very naked. Right now, she didn't really mind that he disliked clothes. Boy, did she not mind!

His muscles weren't so big that he looked deformed. No, they were just right. His chest was broad with just a sprinkling of dark hair. Her gaze dropped lower. Nice. Very nice.

A burning need grew inside her. For just a moment, she wondered what it would feel like to lie naked in his arms, to have his body pressed against hers. The ache inside her grew until she trembled with need. Her last few dates had been losers. She had a feeling Surlock would be good in bed. He would know how to please a woman.

Her hands curled into fists, nails biting into her palms as she stifled the groan that threatened to explode from her. She needed good sex. Maybe Surlock was a gift from the sex gods and she was meant to have him. It could happen. Before she could get too far into her fantasy, he dove into the water, causing barely a ripple.

She leaned over the balcony. Nice ass. Firm. Hmm, with a tattoo on the upper right cheek. Or a birthmark. Odd, she had a birthmark in the same place. She squinted her eyes, but he was too far away for her to tell exactly what it was. What were the odds it would be the same as her birthmark? She quickly dismissed the thought as she lost herself watching him swim the length of the pool.

The muscles in his back tightened and relaxed as he reached forward in the water. He swam to the end of the pool, then turned and swam back. His movements were those of a professional.

Maybe that was what he was—a swimmer.

Yeah, right, he'd been running around naked in the woods looking for a pool. With a wolf at his side.

What if he'd been raised by wolves? He'd growled at Dr.

Wilson. Surlock did come across as a little wild, untamed. A fantasy formed in her mind. Surlock was Tarzan of the wolves, and he was looking for a woman he could steal away and take back to his den.

She shook her head. Ridiculous. Besides, since she had hit him over the head, Darcy kind of doubted she would be in the running as someone he would whisk away. The thought of spending time lying in his arms was nice, though.

Surlock popped out of the water, levering himself to the side of the pool, slinging his wet hair out of his face. He sat there for a moment, catching his breath, before getting to his feet. Rather than go immediately back to the guest house, he looked up, their gazes locking, as though he'd known she watched him the whole time. He seemed quite unconcerned he was naked.

He didn't smile or wave. Not even a nod. He only stared at her for a long moment, his gaze slipping down her body, caressing her with his eyes, causing goose bumps to pop up on her arms. For a brief moment, something passed between them. He wanted her just as much as she wanted him.

Don't miss Elizabeth Essex's Brava debut,
THE PURSUIT OF PLEASURE,
coming next month!

"I couldn't help overhearing your conversation." He wanted to steer their chat to his purpose, but the back of her neck was white and long. He'd never noticed that long slide of skin before, so pale against the vivid color of her locks. He'd gone away before she'd been old enough to put up her hair. And nowadays the fashion seemed to be for masses of loose ringlets covering the neck. Trust Lizzie to still sail against the tide.

"Yes, you could." Her breezy voice broke into his thoughts.

"I beg your pardon?"

"Help it. You *could* have helped it, as any polite gentleman *should*, but you obviously chose not to." She didn't even bother to look back at him as she spoke and walked on but he heard the teasing smile in her voice. Such intriguing confidence. He could use it to his purpose. She had always been up for a lark.

He caught her elbow and steered her into an unused parlor. She came easily, without resisting the intimacy or the presumption of the brief contact of hiis hand against the soft, vulnerable skin of her inner arm, but once through the door she just seemed to disolve away, out of his grasp. His empty fingers prickled from his sudden loss. He let her move away and closed the door.

No lamp or candle branch illuminated the room, only the moonlight streaming through the tall casement windows. Lizzie looked like a pale ghost, weightless and hovering in the strange light. He took a step nearer. He needed her to be real, not an illusion. Over the years she'd become a distant but recurring dream, a combination of memory and boyish lust, haunting his sleep.

He had thought of her, or at least the *idea* of her, almost constantly over the years. She had always been there, in his brain, swimming just below the surface. And he had come tonight in search of her. To banish his ghosts.

She took a sliding step back to lean nonchalantly against the arm of a chair, all sinuous, bored indifference.

"So what are you doing in Dartmouth? Aren't you meant to be messing about with your boats?"

"Ships," he corrected automatically and then smiled at his foolishness for trying to tell Lizzie anything. "The big ones are ships."

"And they let *you* have one of the *big* ones? Aren't you a bit young for that?" She tucked her chin down to subdue her smile and looked up at him from under her gingery brows. Very mischievous. And very challenging.

If it was worldliness she wanted, he could readily supply it. He mirrored her smile.

"Hard to imagine isn't it, Lizzie." He opened his arms wide, presenting himself for her inspection.

Only she didn't inspect him. Her eyes slid away to inventory the scant furniture in the darkened room. "No one else calls me that anymore."

"Lizzie? Well, I do. I can't imagine you as anything else. And I like it. I like saying it. Lizzie." The name hummed through his mouth like a honeybee dusted with nectar. Like a kiss. He moved closer so he could see the emerald color of her eyes, dimmed by the half light, but still brilliant against the white of her skin. He leaned a fraction too close and whispered, "Lizzie. It always sounds somehow . . . naughty."

She turned quickly. Wariness flickered across her mobile face, as if she were suddenly unsure of both herself and him, before it was just as quickly masked.

And yet, she continued to study him surreptitiously, so he held himself still for her perusal. To see if she would finally notice him as a *man*. He met her eyes and he felt a kick low in his gut. In that moment plans and strategies became unimportant. The only thing important was for Lizzie to *see* him. It was *essential*.

But she kept all expression from her face. He was jolted to realize she didn't want him to read her thoughts or mood, that she was trying hard to keep *him* from seeing *her*.

It was an unexpected change. The Lizzie he had known as a child had been so wholly passionate about life, she had thrown herself body and soul into each and every moment, each action and adventure. She had not been covered with this veneer of poised nonchalance.

And yet it was only a veneer. He was sure of it. And he was equally sure he could make his way past it. He drew in a measured breath and sent her a slow, melting smile to show, in the course of the past few minutes, he'd most definitely noticed she was a woman.

She gave no outward reaction, so it took Marlowe a long moment to recognize her response: she looked *careful*. It was a quality he'd never seen in her before.

Finally, after what felt like an infinity, she broke the moment. "You didn't answer. Why are you here? After all these years?"

Her quiet surprised the truth out of him. "A funeral. Two weeks ago." A bleak, rain-soaked funeral that couldn't be forgotten.

"Oh. I am sorry." Her voice lost its languid bite.

He looked back and met her eyes. Such sincerity had never been one of Lizzie's strong suits. No, that was wrong. She'd always been sincere, or at least truthful—painfully so as he recalled—but she rarely let her true feelings show.

"Thank you, Lizzie. But I didn't lure you into a temptingly darkened room to bore you with dreary news."

"No, you came to proposition me." The mischievous little smile crept back. Lizzie was never the sort to be intimidated for long. She had always loved to be doing things she ought not.

A heated image of her white body temptingly entwined in another man's arms rose unbidden in his brain. Good God, what other things had Lizzie been doing over the past few years that she ought not? And with whom?

Marlowe quickly jettisoned the irrational spurt of jealousy. Her more recent past hardly mattered. In fact, some experience on her part might better suit his plans.

"Yes, my proposition. I can give you what you want. A marriage without the man."

For the longest moment she went unaturally still, then she slid off the chair arm and glided closer. So close, he almost backed up. So close, her rose petal of a mouth came but a hairsbreadth from his own. Then she lifted her inquisitive nose and took a bold, suspicious whiff of his breath.

"You've been drinking."

"I have," he admitted without a qualm.

"How much?"

"More than enough for the purpose. And you?"

"Clearly not enough. Not that they'd let me." She turned and walked away. Sauntered really. She was very definitely a saunterer, all loose joints and limbs, as if she'd never paid the least attention to deportment and carriage. Very provocative, although he doubted she meant to be. An image of a bright, agile otter, frolicking unconcerned in the calm green of the river Dart, twisting and rolling in the sunlit water, came to mind.

"Drink or no, I meant what I said."

"Are you proposing? Marriage? To me?" She laughed as if it were a joke. She didn't believe him.

"I am."

She eyed him more closely, her gaze narrowing even as one marmalade eyebrow rose in assessment. "Do you have a fatal disease?"

"No."

"Are you engaged to fight a duel?"

"Again, no."

"Condemned to death?" She straightened with a fluid undulation, her spine lifting her head up in surprise as the thought entered her head, all worldliness temporarily obliterated. "Planning a suicide?"

"No and no." It was so hard not to smile. Such an arch, charming combination of concern and cheek. The cheek won out: she gave him that feral, slightly suspicious smile.

"Then how do you plan to arrange it, the 'without the man' portion of the proceedings? I'll want some sort of guarantee. You can't imagine I'm gullible enough to leave your fate, or my own for that matter, to chance."

A low heat flared within him. By God, she really was considering it.

"And yet, Lizzie, I think you may. I am an officer of His Majesty's Royal Navy and am engaged to captain a convoy of prison ships to the Antipodes. I leave only days from now. The last time I was home, in England, was four and a half years ago and then only for a few months to recoup from a near fatal wound. This trip is slated to take at least eight. Years."

Her face cleared of all traces of impudence. Oh yes, even Lizzie could be led.

"Storms, accidents and disease provide most of the risk. Don't forget we're still at war with France and Spain. And the Americans don't think too highly of us either. One stray cannon ball could do the job quite nicely."

"Is that what did it last time?"

"Last time? I've never been dead before."

The ends of her ripe mouth nipped up. The heat in his gut sailed higher.

"You said you had recovered from a near fatal wound."

"Ah, yes. Grapeshot, actually. In my chest. Didn't go deep enough to kill me, though afterwards, the fever nearly did."

Her gaze skimmed over his coat, curious and maybe a little hungry. The heat spread lower, kindling into a flame.

"Do you want to see?" He was being rash, he knew, but he'd done this for her once before, taken off his shirt on a dare. And he wanted to remind her.